Hugo was on her heels as she flung open the door and sprang inside.

The wild chase had fanned the flames of Hugo's shocked fury. His breath came swift and ragged. "By God, you stand in sore need of a sharp lesson, miss," he declared. "Come here!"

"Catch me!" She laughed at him, bright-eyed, and jumped backward onto the bed.

Hugo lunged for her as she danced across the bed, and this time he caught her ankle and hung on. He jerked hard. Chloe shrieked as she tumbled facedown on the bed.

He seized the other ankle and hauled her toward him across the wide expanse of coverlet, her skirt rucking up as he dragged her.

Even as he struggled with his suddenly reeling senses that had driven all clarity of purpose from his mind, Chloe twisted on her back. Her eyes were dark liquid pools of sensuality, her lips were slightly parted, her cheeks flushed, golden wisps of hair escaping from her braids in a lustrous mist around her exquisite countenance. The sweet swell of her bosom rose and fell with her swift breath. His eye ran over the flat stomach, the sharp points of her hipbones pressing against the linen undergarment, the long creamy length of exposed thigh.

"Sweet heaven," he whispered in the despairing recognition of imminent surrender. He opened his hands. . . .

VIXEN

ALSO BY JANE FEATHER

VIXEN

Jane Feather

BANTAM BOOKS
NEW YORK • TORONTO • LONDON
SYDNEY • AUCKLAND

VIXEN

A Bantam Book / February 1994

ISBN 0-553-56055-7

Published simultaneously in the United States and Canada

Bantam Books are published by Bantam Books, a division of Bantam
Doubleday Dell Publishing Group, Inc. Its trademark, consisting of the words
"Bantam Books" and the portrayal of a rooster, is Registered in U.S. Patent
and Trademark Office and in other countries. Marca Registrada. Bantam
Books, 1540 Broadway, New York, New York 10036.

PRINTED IN THE UNITED STATES OF AMERICA

RAD   0 9 8 7 6 5 4 3 2 1

VIXEN

Prologue

T HE SHADOWS OF the two duelists, thrown by the massive altar candles, danced long and eerie on the stone walls of the crypt. The only sounds were the soft padding of their stocking feet on the granite tombstone slabs, the singing of steel on steel, and their swift yet measured breathing.

Ten men and one woman watched the deadly ballet. They stood motionless around the walls, barely breathing, only their eyes moving as they followed the dance. The woman's hands were clenched so tightly against her skirt that her fingers were bloodless. Her waxen pallor had a greenish tinge to it, and her eyes, usually the vivid blue of a field of cornflowers, were so pale as to be almost opaque—as pale as her lips.

The duelists were both tall, powerful men, evenly matched except in age. One of them seemed barely more than a stripling, the other a man in midlife, with graying hair and a solid, muscled body that moved with a surprising speed and lightness to combat the youthful athleticism of his opponent. There was a moment when the older man's foot slipped in a trail of blood that dripped from a cut in his opponent's arm. There was an almost imperceptible stirring of the air around the watchers, but he recovered smoothly and only he knew that his adversary had drawn back for the split second necessary for him to regain balance and pace.

1

The knowledge of this courtesy gave Stephen Gresham no pleasure. He neither wanted nor expected such favors in a combat that could have only one end. He pressed the attack with a new ferocity, employing the skills learned and practiced over thirty years, relying on the relative inexperience of his opponent to offer him an opening. But Hugo Lattimer's guard never dropped. He seemed content to let Stephen make the running, parrying with deft economy, turning aside the opposing blade at every thrust.

Stephen could feel that he was tiring and he knew that if greater experience couldn't prevail, then youth would. Hugo was still breathing easily, although sweat gathered on his forehead despite the damp chill of the crypt. Stephen's heart raced and his sword arm was a bodily extension of pure pain. The light flickered in front of his eyes and he blinked to clear his vision. Hugo danced and whirled in front of him, and now it seemed that he had lost the momentum, that control had passed to the younger man. He was being beaten back to the wall. It may have been a trick of the light and his own fatigue, but Hugo seemed to come closer until his vivid green eyes, filled with loathing and deadly purpose, pierced Stephen's body as surely as his sword soon would.

And then it came. A lunge in high carte. He couldn't summon the strength to bring his sword up in order to deflect it and he felt the smooth steel enter his body.

Hugo Lattimer withdrew his blade from the crumpled body of Stephen Gresham. Blood dripped to the floor. He stared, dazed and unseeing, at the faces around the wall. Elizabeth swayed in front of him. He wanted to go to her, to support her, but he couldn't. It was not his right. He had just killed her husband. He watched, helpless, as she slipped unconscious to the floor. And the men who half an hour before would have drunkenly participated in her dishonor averted suddenly sober eyes from the still figure.

Jasper Gresham moved suddenly, a vicious oath on his lips. He knelt beside his father's body, ripping the shirt away from his chest, where the blood pumped forth. It had been a neat thrust to the heart. Stephen would have died instantly. For a second, Jasper's finger traced the strange design pricked into his father's skin above the heart—a tiny coiled serpent. He looked up at Hugo and their eyes locked. It was a silent message, but nonetheless lucid. Somehow, somewhere, Jasper Gresham would be revenged for his father's death.

It didn't matter that it had been a clean death in a duel fought according to the rites and ceremonies of the practice. It didn't matter that in his fifty-two years, Stephen Gresham had fought ten such battles—all to the death. All that mattered to Jasper Gresham was that twenty-year-old Hugo Lattimer had defeated his father and he would avenge that humiliation.

Hugo turned aside. Elizabeth stirred and moaned. No longer able to stand back, he bent to lift her and she shrank from him, putting out an arm to hold him away. Her cheek still bore the shadowy bruise of her husband's hand. Her eyes were blank, and it seemed to Hugo as if the frail body had lost some essential core. She had always been fragile, an ethereal creature of the air and the water. Now, at twenty-two, she seemed to have lost all substance. Whatever will she had once possessed to withstand the blows her destiny had dealt her had abandoned her. She was boneless, weightless, as he gently raised her, despite her rejection. His fingertips lightly brushed her eyelids in farewell. Unless she summoned him, he would never see her again.

He left the dank crypt with its stench of corruption and blood and death, climbing the steps into the frozen winter air of the bleak Lancashire moorland. The stark ruins of Shipton Abbey stood out against a January sky as sharp and clear as glass. The air bit deep into his lungs, but he took it in in great gasps. For two years he had played in that dark and vicious world below. He carried its mark—the mark of Eden—on his skin and its curse in his soul.

Chapter 1

August 1819

IT WAS MID-MORNING when the weary horse finally scented home and turned through the crumbling stone gates into the rutted driveway leading to Denholm Manor. He blew through his nostrils and raised his drooping head, breaking into a trot as the black and white half-timbered house came into view. The hot sun caught the latticed windows and set the red tiles of the pitched roof aglow. The house had an air of neglect, exemplified in the mud-ridged, weed-choked driveway, the tangled bushes, the straggly remnants of what had once been neat, sculptured box hedges.

Hugo Lattimer sat his horse and noticed none of this. He was aware only of his throbbing head, parched mouth, and frying eyeballs. He couldn't remember how he'd passed the hours since he'd left his home the evening before—in some alehouse in the Manchester stews, probably, drinking gut-rot brandy and dallying with whores until he passed out. It was his usual method of getting through the night hours.

The horse, without instruction, trotted through the arched gateway at the side of the house and into the cobbled courtyard. Here it became apparent to Hugo that something out of the ordinary had occurred in his absence.

He blinked and shook his head, staring bemusedly at the post-chaise standing at the foot of the steps leading up to the house. Visitors . . . he never had visitors. The side door stood open, again most unusual. What the hell was Samuel thinking of?

He opened his mouth to bellow for Samuel, when a huge brindled mongrel bounded out of the doorway, barking its head off, and hurtled down the steps, teeth bared, hackles up, and yet, most incongruously, its long feathery tail wagging in fervent welcome.

The horse whinnied in alarm and skittered on the cobbles. Hugo swore and reined him in. The unknown dog pranced, barking and wagging, around the horse and rider as if welcoming long-lost friends.

"Samuel!" Hugo yelled, flinging himself from his mount, wincing as the violent movement sent exquisite pain shooting through his head. Bending low, he brought his head close to the raucous dog and snapped "Quiet!" with a low ferocity that sent the animal backward, his tail now wagging uncertainly, a long, dripping tongue lolling out of his mouth.

Samuel failed to appear, and with a muttered curse Hugo knotted the reins, slapped the horse on the rump, sending him stableward, and took the steps to the side door two at a time, the mongrel on his heels for the moment mercifully silent. In the great hall he stopped, having the eerie sensation of entering a house that was not his own.

A road of sunlight ran from the open door across the muddied stone flags; dust motes danced in the rays from the latticed windows; the dust lay thick on the oak settle against the wall and the massive Tudor oak table. All this was as it always was. But the center of the space was filled with trunks, bandboxes, and assorted items that Hugo at first couldn't identify. Under his incredulous stare, one of these items revealed itself to be a parrot in a large cage. Closer inspection indicated that the bird had only one leg. It cocked its head and offered one of the fouler oaths Hugo had learned during ten years service in His Majesty's Navy.

Bemused, he turned slowly. The dog yipped as he accidentally trod on its tail, now spread out in a feathery fan on the flagstones behind it. "Out!" he demanded without too much hope of being obeyed. The dog grinned, panting hopefully, and stayed where it was.

Hugo's eye next fell on a hat box, or, rather, the bottom half of a hat box. Its lid lay rolled to one side. There were no hats in the box. Instead, he was staring in disbelief at a tortoiseshell cat, her distended sides rhythmically heaving and contracting. As he watched, she delivered a tiny, shiny parcel that she immediately attended to with practiced efficiency. The kitten blindly sought and found its mother's belly and the swollen teat, and the tortoiseshell returned to the business of delivery.

"Ah, you're back, Sir 'Ugo. An' right glad I am to see you. Such goin's-on, as I've never seen." A stout, grizzled man in leather britches, boots, and waistcoat, sporting two large gold earrings, broke into Hugo's fascinated observation of the laboring cat.

"What the hell is going on, Samuel?" he demanded. *"What is this?"* He jabbed a finger at the hat box.

"Looks like she's started," Samuel observed somewhat redundantly, peering at the contents of the hat box. "She picked the 'at box and since it was so close to 'er time, like, Miss said as 'ow we'd best leave 'er to it."

"I appear to be losing my mind," Hugo declared in a tone of mild interest. "Either that, or I'm still in a drunken stupor in a whorehouse and this is some hideous nightmare. *What the hell are you talking about, Samuel. What 'miss'?"*

"Oh, you're back, I'm so glad. Miss Anstey can go on her way now."

The voice was low and musical, with a most appealing catch in it. Slowly, Hugo raised his head and looked across the chaos in the hall toward the refectory door. The apparent owner of the attractive voice stood smiling with an air of total unconcern.

The years fell away and the room seemed to spin. It was Elizabeth, as she had been sixteen years before, on the day he'd first laid eyes on her. It was Elizabeth . . . and yet it wasn't. He closed his eyes, massaged his temples, then opened them again. The vision was still standing in the doorway, still trustfully smiling.

"And just who are *you*?" he demanded, his voice sounding rough and cracked.

"Chloe." The information was imparted as if it were self-evident.

Hugo shook his head in total confusion. "Forgive me, but I remain unenlightened."

A frown crossed the girl's eyes and tiny lines appeared on her brow. "Chloe Gresham," she said, tilting her head to one side as if better to judge his reaction to this further information.

"Jesus, Mary, and Joseph," Hugo whispered. She must be Elizabeth's daughter. He didn't know whether he'd ever known her name. She had been three years old on the night of the duel.

"They sent you a letter to expect me," she said, a hint of uncertainty now in her voice. "You did get it?"

"Who's they?" He cleared his throat, struggling to marshal his scattered thoughts.

"Oh, the Misses Trent, Sir Hugo," a second voice chimed in, and he saw that another figure stood just behind the vision that was and was not Elizabeth. A little lady timidly stepped forward. "From the Trent Seminary for Young Ladies, Sir Hugo, in Bolton. They wrote last month to tell you to expect Chloe."

Her head was nodding almost convulsively, her mittened hands twisting, and despite his bemusement and splitting head, Hugo tried to bridle his growing irascibility. "You have the advantage of me, ma'am. We appear not to have been introduced."

"This is Miss Anstey," Chloe put in. "She's going to a situation in London and the Misses Trent thought she should accompany me here on her way. And now that she's seen you and knows that you're not a figment—"

"A what?"

"A figment of the imagination," she said cheerfully. "We were afraid when we arrived and there was no one here that perhaps you were. But since you're not, Miss Anstey can continue her journey, which I know she's anxious to do since she's expected to take up her duties in a week and it's a very long way from Manchester to London."

Hugo listened to this rushed yet somehow lucid speech, wondering rather desperately if the girl always talked so much and so fast, even though he thought he could listen to that delightful voice indefinitely.

"Now, Chloe, you know I can't leave until I know everything is all right with Sir Hugo," Miss Anstey ventured, her head nodding even more violently. "Oh, dear me, no. The Misses Trent would never forgive me."

"Oh, stuff," declared the confident Miss Gresham. "You can see he's here, in the flesh, so you can leave with a good conscience."

Hugo had the feeling that in a minute she would put those small hands on the governess's shoulders and propel her out to the post-chaise. It was certainly clear who was in charge in this twosome.

"Might I ask why you are to be left?" he inquired. "An honor, I'm sure, but rather puzzling nevertheless."

"You're funning," Chloe said, but the uncertainty was back in her voice. "You're my guardian and the Misses

Trent sent me to you when they decided I—" She paused, nibbling her bottom lip. "Well, I don't know what they told you in the letter, but I'm sure it was a tissue of lies."

"Oh, Chloe dear, you really mustn't," fluttered Miss Anstey. "So impolite, child."

Hugo ran his hands through his hair; the sense of inhabiting some anarchic dream intensified. "I don't know what the devil you're talking about," he said finally. "The last time I knew anything about you, you were three years old."

"But the lawyers must have told you about Mama's will—that she made you my guardian—"

"Elizabeth is dead?" he interrupted sharply. His heart jolted.

The girl nodded. "Three months ago. I only saw her once or twice a year, so it's hard to miss her as I should."

Hugo turned away, the wrenching sadness filling him. He realized now that he'd always carried a tiny flame of hope that she would let him back into her life.

He walked to the front door, staring through unfocused eyes at the brightness of the morning, trying to organize his thoughts. Was this extraordinary visitation the explanation for that strange note he'd received last year? Hand-delivered from the dower house at Shipton, across the valley, where Elizabeth had lived since her husband's death. The barely legible scrawl had said only that she knew he would honor his long-ago promise to be of service to her however and whenever and wherever she should need it. There was no explanation, no words of friendship, no sense that this was the opening he'd been waiting for all these years. He'd had the impression that even the faint signature had been an afterthought, disappearing off the edge of the page.

The note had filled him with such a resurgence of

rage and longing that he'd torn it up and tried to put it out of his mind. Since the war had ended and he'd left the navy, they'd lived seven miles from each other. She had made no attempt to contact him and he'd been honor bound to respect her wishes, even after all this time. And then just a scrawled note . . . a demand. And now this.

He turned back to the hall. The dog had gone to Chloe and sat at her feet, gazing up at her adoringly.

"Letters'll be in the library, I shouldn't wonder," Samuel observed, examining his fingernails. "Wi' t'others ye've not opened. I always said one day there'd be summat important in there."

Hugo glared at the man who'd been his companion and servant since he'd first gone to sea as a lad of twenty. As usual, Samuel was right. The pounding in his head became fierce, and he knew he couldn't deal with this another minute. "Get that dog out of the house," he commanded, striding to the staircase. "And put that damn cat and her litter in the stables, where they belong . . . and put a cover on that parrot," he added savagely as the bird tossed out another example of its dubious vocabulary.

"Oh, no!" Chloe exclaimed. "Dante lives inside—"

Hugo swung his head carefully in her direction. "Dante?" he demanded incredulously. "That dog is called Dante?"

"Yes, because he came out of an inferno," she informed him. "I rescued him from a bonfire when he was just a puppy. Some louts had tied him up and were setting a fire around him. I did think of calling him Joan of Arc," she added reflectively, "until I realized he was the wrong sex."

"I don't think I want to hear any more," Hugo said. "In fact, I *know* I don't want to hear any more." He enunciated his words with great care. "I have not yet been to bed, so I am going upstairs, where I shall probably say my prayers for the first time since I left the nursery. And when I wake up, I devoutly trust that my prayers will have been answered, and I shall find that this . . ." He waved his hand in an expansive movement across the scene in the great hall. "That all this will prove to have been no more than the hideous figments of a disordered imagination."

The parrot cackled in an uncanny imitation of a hysterical drunk. "Get this menagerie out of here!" On which hopefully decisive note Sir Hugo Lattimer took himself to the sanity of his own bedchamber, hearing the fluttering whimpers of Miss Anstey behind him.

He was a chronic insomniac but proficient at catnaps. Ten years of night watches at sea had turned a tendency into immutable habit, one he welcomed since the nightmares haunted his night sleep but visited less often in the short bouts of daytime unconsciousness.

He dropped his clothes in an untidy heap on the floor, crawled into bed, and closed his eyes with relief. The throbbing at his temples lessened with the absence of light. He couldn't begin to think about Elizabeth and the child who looked so like her and yet so unlike her. Some vast mistake had been made. She belonged at Shipton with the Greshams.

The brutal face of Jasper Gresham swam abruptly into his internal vision and he was wide awake again. Jasper was his father's son . . . Stephen's son. No fit man to have charge of a young girl. Was that what Elizabeth had been trying to avoid? But in what kind of madness could her father's killer be considered a fit guardian? A recluse who sought relief from the past in drink and the city stews.

He groaned and turned over. The sound of wheels on the courtyard cobbles came from below the open window. Hope flickered that the post-chaise with two passengers and a menagerie was leaving, and when he awoke this craziness would be over. But he had a prickling premonition that his life was about to undergo a profound change.

Chapter 2

DOWNSTAIRS, CHLOE STOOD on the steps and waved the chaise and Miss Anstey out of the courtyard. The poor lady had been torn between her perceived duty to Chloe and her unquestionable duty to her new employers. But her perceived duty had not been proof against Chloe's brisk dismissal of her fears, and she had finally been persuaded into the chaise, dabbing at her eyes and pouring forth a stream of benedictions on the dear child she was leaving. She bemoaned the disreputable state of the house, the strangeness of Sir Hugo and his servant, and the significant absence of either housekeeper or a Lady Lattimer. The last words Chloe heard were: "Oh, dear, perhaps I shouldn't leave you like this . . . what will the Misses Trent say . . . but then what will Lady Colshot say . . . such a bad impression to arrive late . . . oh, dear . . ."

Chloe firmly shut the door of the chaise, putting a period to the vacillation, and called good-bye. The coachman cracked his whip and the vehicle and its still indecisively bewailing passenger disappeared from Denholm Manor.

Thoughtfully, Chloe turned back to the house. It did seem that there was no Lady Lattimer, although it had been assumed at the seminary that there would be. Chloe had never heard of Sir Hugo Lattimer until her mother's will had been read. She had no idea why her mother had chosen him, but then, she knew almost nothing about her mother, having spent no more than a few days a year with Elizabeth since she was six. The only thing she knew at the moment was that this change in her circumstances could only be for the better.

She knelt down by the hat box. The cat's labors seemed to be over and Chloe counted six damp kittens squirming at her belly. They were curiously repellent, she thought, absently stroking the cat's head, more like baby rats than the entrancing creatures they would soon become.

"Best get that lot out to the stable before Sir 'Ugo comes down." Samuel's gruff voice came from behind her and she stood up, brushing the dust off her skirt.

"I don't think we should move her outside just yet. She'll feel threatened and she might abandon them."

Samuel shrugged. "Not an animal lover, Sir 'Ugo . . . except horses, of course."

"Doesn't he like dogs?" Chloe caressed Dante's massive head, pushing against her knee.

"Not indoors," Samuel informed her. "Gun dogs is fine, but their place is in the kennels."

"Dante sleeps with me," Chloe stated. "Even the Misses Trent accepted that. He howls all night otherwise."

Samuel shrugged again. "I'd best get back to me kitchen. Sir 'Ugo'll be wantin' his breakfast when he wakes."

"Don't you have a cook?" Chloe followed him out of the hall, down a long corridor to the kitchen at the rear of the house.

"Who needs one? Wi' just the two of us?"

Chloe looked around the room with its huge fireplace and spit, the massive table, the array of copper pots. "Only you and Sir Hugo live in this house?" It seemed very odd, but one could become used to anything.

"Tha's right." Samuel broke eggs into a bowl.

"Oh." Chloe frowned, nibbling her lip. "Well, perhaps

you could direct me to my bedchamber. I could move some of my things out of the hall, then."

Samuel paused in his beating of the eggs and gave her a searching look. "You reckon on stayin'?"

"Of course," Chloe said with an assumption of confidence. "I have nowhere else to go."

Samuel grunted. "There's sixteen bedrooms. Take your pick."

"Sixteen!"

He nodded and dropped a pinch of salt into the eggs.

Chloe stood uncertainly for a minute, but when it seemed that the man had nothing further to say, she left the kitchen. The events in her life so far had not encouraged her to expect warm welcomes or particularly friendly exchanges, so she was not unduly troubled by the oddities of her present situation. She was a pragmatic soul and accepted that now, as always, it was up to her to make the best of things and improve on them as and how she could. Anything . . . anything . . . was an improvement on the Trent Seminary for Young Ladies in Bolton, where she'd been immured for the past ten years.

The most important thing was to ensure she was not returned there. To that end, she went in search of the library, where Samuel had suggested her credentials might be found.

The library was as unkempt and dusty as the rest of the house. Dante went snuffling into the corners, his tail wagging furiously as he dug and scrabbled at the skirting board. Mice, presumably, Chloe decided, approaching a table where lay a pile of letters. It was dark in the room despite the brilliance of the morning. The daylight was filtered through grimy diamond-paned windows, and the massive oak beams and dark, paneled walls added to the gloom. She looked for flint and tinder to light one of the tallow candles on the table but couldn't find any, so she picked up the pile of papers and took them to the window.

What kind of a man wouldn't open his letters? Some of these were six months old, she realized, shuffling through them. Perhaps he read his mail only on New Year's Day, or maybe that's when he threw away the previous year's unread.

She found an envelope that bore the seal of the Manchester lawyers who had written to her and told her of the conditions of her mother's will—the conditions that had brought her here. She tucked the letter into her pocket and continued to sift through the remainder. She recognized the thin, spidery writing of Miss Anne Trent, and abstracted this envelope also. She had a fair idea of the contents. They would not be flattering and she'd decide later whether or not to pass on this document to her new guardian.

With the letters in her pocket she set off to explore the remainder of the house. Dante reluctantly left his mousing and followed her up the great carved staircase. A series of passages ran off the landing at the head of the stairs. The house was a rabbit warren of gloomy corridors, faded tapestries hanging on the paneled walls, piles of dust in the corners, and a closed-in musty smell that Chloe was convinced was mice. Judging by Dante's eager lunges and scampering pursuits, the dog also thought so.

She opened doors onto deserted bedrooms with heavy carved furniture and poster beds, the testers and canopies threadbare and in some cases torn and hanging from the frame. She couldn't imagine sleeping in any of them until she came upon a corner room with three windows and a big fireplace. The bed had dimity hangings, rather grubby and faded, certainly, but intact and much lighter and more pleasing than the tapestries and heavy brocades in the other rooms. An embroidered

Elizabethan rug covered the dusty wooden floor. The views from the three windows were lovely—across the moor from one side and over the valley on the other.

She flung open the windows, letting light and air into the room. Dante flopped down in front of the empty hearth with an exaggerated sigh, giving his seal of approval to the choice. The first thing to do, Chloe decided, was to install the cat and her litter away from any further threat of the stables. If they weren't visible, the master of the house would perhaps forget about them. The parrot too.

It took fifteen minutes to put the parrot's cage on the broad windowsill and the hat box with cat and kittens into a cool, dark cupboard. Then Chloe left the room, firmly closing the door on Dante, who yelped frantically for a few minutes as she walked away.

At the end of another corridor she found double doors. The brass handles were not as tarnished as the others she'd noticed, and she had the sudden conviction that the room beyond was inhabited. It must be Sir Hugo's apartments. Inveterately curious, she didn't stop to consider but gently lifted the latch, pushing open the doors, praying they wouldn't squeak.

She stood on the threshold and absorbed the room in silence. It was the largest she'd seen, furnished as heavily as the others. The bed was enormous, the pillars carved with strange animallike shapes, the tester and hangings of gold-embroidered brocade. But it was all now shabby, a shadow of its former glory. The curtains around the bed had been left open and the sleeping man didn't stir as she took a tentative step into the room. The windows were open and she could hear someone whistling from the courtyard below. Presumably, there was a groom or stablehand even if there were no servants in the house.

She glanced at the bed again. Thick chestnut-brown

hair flopped over a turned cheek on the pillow; one shoulder and arm were flung over the sheet across his body. Chloe stared, fascinated, at the bare, muscled flesh. The skin was deeply tanned, the hair on his arms sun-bleached. She had the impression of a powerful mass of body beneath the thin sheet. In the hall, she'd been aware of his height and breadth only peripherally, there'd been too many other things to deal with. But the man whose responsibility she would be for the next four years now struck her as a force of some magnitude, even lying inert in his sleep.

The force was a lodestone, drawing her into the room. She stepped closer to the bed. And then the world turned upside down.

One minute she was upright, the next spread-eagle across the bed, her face buried in the coverlet, one arm painfully caught up behind her back, the ridged muscles of his thighs hard beneath her stomach. Her legs flailed and her arm was jerked upward, bringing tears to her eyes. In reflex, she lay still, and the pressure was slightly relieved.

"You prying little sneak," the furious voice hissed above her. "What the hell do you think you're doing, poking and prying in my room? What were you looking for?" Another jerk on her arm punctuated the livid question, and she bit back a cry of pain.

"I wasn't looking *for* anything." She tried to turn her head out of the muffling confines of the bedding. "Please . . . you're hurting me." Again, there was a minute easing of the pressure. "I wasn't looking *for* anything," she repeated, tears of shock in her voice. "I was just looking—looking *at*, not *for.*"

There was a short silence, during which her position remained the same. Hugo kept his grip on her wrist and became aware of the feel of her body across his thighs.

She was very light . . . as her mother had been. Sorrow flashed, short but bitter, across his mind.

"An interesting distinction," he said after a minute. "And just what were you looking *at*?"

The delicate frame shifted against him and with an unpleasant start he realized her proximity was having an unlooked-for effect. He tightened his grip on her wrist. "Well?"

"Things . . . everything . . . the house . . . I wanted to explore, to learn where things are. And I found the letters from the lawyer and the Misses Trent." Too late, she remembered that she'd not made up her mind about the latter document. "I was going to give them to you. . . . *Please* let me up."

"I hardly think they had to be given to me in my sleep," he observed, wondering why the artless explanation should have sounded so convincing. He released her wrist. "You may stand up."

She pushed backward and he was left without the slight weight, the scent of her hair and body. It was only as the delicate fragrance departed that he realized he'd been aware of it—rose petals and lavender, he thought, with just a hint of clover honey.

"Stand back and let me look at you."

Chloe did so, regarding him warily, massaging her aching arm. She was accustomed to cool greetings, but that had been a decidedly unpleasant experience.

Hugo hitched himself farther up the pillows, noticing absently that his headache had gone and he felt as well as he usually did once the hangover had been pushed aside . . . until the next morning-after. Glancing at the clock, he saw that he'd slept for an hour and a half. Hardly a long night, but it would have to do. He returned his attention to the girl, seeing her clearly for the first time, assessing where she resembled her mother.

He realized with a shock that Chloe Gresham was

stunningly beautiful. He had always thought Elizabeth had been, and her daughter had all the elements of that beauty, but wherever Elizabeth's had been slightly marred, the daughter's was perfection. Elizabeth's mouth had been a fraction too small, her eyes perhaps a scrap too close together, her nose a little too long. Not the kind of flaws one would ordinarily notice, except when faced with perfection.

The girl's fair hair was scraped tightly back from her forehead, hanging in two thick plaits down her back. The effect was to dim the luster of her hair while throwing the planes and shadows of her face into harsh relief. Yet it did nothing to impair the overall impression of a stellar beauty.

Her body was clad in a dull, round gown of drab schoolgirlish brown serge that squashed where it shouldn't and hung loose where it shouldn't. A cleverly designed costume, he thought, if the intention was to conceal womanhood. But still not clever enough to mask the dainty, fragile perfection of Chloe's small-boned, well-proportioned body. His own stirred again, and he tried to ignore it.

"Let down your hair."

The abrupt command startled her, but obediently she untied the ribbons of her braids and unplaited the thick ropes, combing her fingers through her hair as she did so.

The final effect was astonishing. Guinea-gold radiance tumbled thick and straight down her back, framed her face, setting off the brilliant blue of her eyes, the peach-bloom glow of her complexion.

"Dear God," he whispered to himself before remarking, "That is the most hideous gown."

"Oh, I know," she replied cheerfully. "And I have at least a dozen just like it. I think they're supposed to be bushels."

"What?"

"Or is it bushes?" she mused. "Anyway, it's in the Bible . . . thou shalt not hide your light under them." Her eyebrows quirked. "Bushes would make better sense, wouldn't it?"

Hugo rubbed his temples, wondering if his headache was about to return. "I'm sure I'm being very obtuse, lass, but I'm afraid you've lost me."

"They're supposed to hide my light," she explained. "From the curate and Miss Trent's nephew and the butcher's boy."

"Ah," he said. "I begin to see." He leaned back against the pillows, regarding her through half-closed eyes. There would be few callow youths impervious to that radiance. A prudent guardian would certainly attempt to dim it in the wrong company.

Chloe continued to stand by the bed, returning his scrutiny with one of her own. The sheet had fallen to his waist and her fascinated eye fastened on a tiny design pricked into the deeply tanned skin above his heart. It looked like a coiled snake. She had never seen a man without his shirt before and made no attempt to hide her interest. There wasn't an ounce of spare flesh on his upper body, his neck was a powerful column supporting a leonine head with a jutting chin. The chestnut hair was long and flopped over a broad forehead. Tiny lines radiated from his vivid green eyes under bushy brown eyebrows. His mouth was full and generous in repose, but at the moment was tight, presumably reflecting his thoughts. They couldn't be very pleasant thoughts, Chloe decided uneasily.

She put her hand in her pocket and the letters crackled against her fingers. "Would you like to read the letter from the lawyers?" she asked hesitantly.

"I suppose I'd better," he said, sighing. "Where has your timid chaperone gone?"

"To London."

"Leaving you here." He stated the obvious with heavy resignation. Somehow, he would have to untangle this mess, and it would require a deal more energy than in general he cared to expend.

Lawyer Scranton's letter enclosed a copy of the will. Lady Elizabeth Gresham had left the sole guardianship of her daughter Chloe to Sir Hugo Lattimer. He was to assume the management of her fortune, estimated at some eighty thousand pounds, until she married.

Eighty thousand pounds. He whistled soundlessly. Stephen had married Elizabeth for her fortune, that had been no secret. Presumably, on his death it had reverted to her. Four years of marriage hadn't been long enough for him to run through it, and after his death the Greshams hadn't laid hands on it. That was very interesting—he would have laid any odds on Jasper's finagling his way into his young and vulnerable stepmother's affairs.

He frowned, remembering something the girl had said earlier, about not grieving for her mother. "What did you mean when you said you only saw your mother for a few days a year?"

"She didn't like to see people," she said. "I went to the Misses Trent when I was six. I'd go back at Christmas for a week. Mama never liked to leave her room." She chewed her lip. "I think she was ill. The doctor gave her something that she drank and it made her want to sleep. She often couldn't remember things . . . people . . . I don't know what it was."

Suddenly she turned aside, seeing her mother as she had been just before her death, in the room that smelled of strange and unpleasant things, where the windows were never opened and the fire kept burning throughout the hottest days of the year. A woman with thin white unkempt hair and faded eyes that sometimes carried a fearful wildness in them. She would swallow the doctor's medicine and the terror would fade, to be replaced by a blankness. She had never talked to her daughter. Oh, they had said things occasionally, exchanged odds and ends of information, but they had never really talked. They had never known each other.

Hugo looked at the girl's averted back, saw the stiffening of her shoulders, heard the note in the voice that had so far been determinedly bright and cheerful, and compassion stirred. "Why did she send you away so young?" he asked gently.

"I don't know." Chloe shrugged and turned back to the room. "Because she was ill, I expect. The seminary was rather like an orphanage. There were other girls there, whose parents were abroad, or dead." She shrugged again.

And where had Jasper been throughout all this? Had he made no attempt to involve himself in his baby half sister's future?

"What about your brother?"

"Jasper? Do you know him? I suppose you must, since you knew Mama." She frowned. "He never came to the dower house. I remember going up to the big house to play with Crispin, but that all stopped when I went to school. I haven't seen them for a long time. They weren't at Mama's funeral."

Jasper's stepson, Crispin, was four years older than Chloe, Hugo remembered. He could understand, after what Jasper and his father had done to Elizabeth, why she would strive to keep her daughter away from the Gresham family. But he still wondered how she had managed it. What power had Elizabeth, a broken recluse, discovered? Could he have helped her? If he hadn't accepted her edict, could he have weaned her from the laudanum dependency that had been fairly well established at Stephen's death? Stephen had used the opiate to control his wife, and Elizabeth's hold on reality had been tenuous at best.

The violent memories, the old questions, the eternal self-disgust, rose again, bitter and invincible. He closed his eyes, the smell of the crypt in his nostrils; a parade of disheveled women, wild-eyed with drink and excitement, crossed his internal vision. He felt again his own excitement, saw it again reflected in the eyes of his fellow players. It had been his life—this single-minded pursuit of the ultimate sensual pleasure. His life and that of the others, joined by blood and oath in a dissolute quest that destroyed all decency. Until Stephen Gresham and his son had entered a realm of pure evil . . .

Chloe, watching his face, instinctively stepped backward toward the door. His face was a mask of anger, carved and immobile. He opened his eyes and she shuddered at their expression. They were the haunted eyes of a man who looked into hell.

And then abruptly it was gone. He rubbed his eyes with the heels of his hands, then ran his hands through his hair, pushing it off his forehead. "So, why have you left the Misses Trent?"

"They didn't want me there anymore."

"Oh?" He raised his eyebrows in interrogation. She seemed to find the question uncomfortable, judging by her suddenly shifting feet.

Chloe dug the other letter out of her pocket. "It was all because of Miss Anne's nephew," she said. "On top of the curate. I don't think it was my fault, but they seemed to think I'd *led them on.*" This last was pronounced in accents that he assumed were an imitation of the Miss Trent in question. "Although I don't know how they could think such a thing," she said, aggrieved. "Anyway, I expect it's all in here." She thrust the letter at him.

He was aware of her anxious scrutiny as he scanned the closely penned sheet. When he'd finished, he scrunched it up into a ball and tossed it toward the fireplace. "What a pretty picture. Reading between the lines of that poison, lass, one can only assume you're a Jezebel of the first water. A deceitful, designing, lying little flirt from whom no innocent young man is safe."

Chloe flushed. "That's so unfair. I couldn't help it if the curate made moon eyes at me and dropped his cake on the floor and forgot his sermon in church."

"No," Hugo agreed. "I'm sure you couldn't. However, again reading between the lines, I suspect the real mischief lies with Miss Anne's nephew."

Chloe's expression changed to one of deep disgust. "That smarmy toad," she declared. "His hands were always wet and he had these horrible loose lips, and he tried to kiss me, as if I were a kitchen maid. He wanted to *marry* me! Can you imagine?"

"Quite easily," Hugo murmured. "And how did Miss Anne view his suit."

"She favored it," Chloe declared.

Hardly surprising, Hugo thought. What aunt wouldn't want a fortune of eighty thousand pounds for her nephew?

"But when I told her what I thought of Mr. Cedric Trent," Chloe continued, "she . . . well . . . she was horrid. Then she and Miss Emily said I was a bad influence on the other girls and they really couldn't keep me any longer, although, of course, they were very sorry to send me away, as I'd only just been made an orphan, but I had to go *for the good of the seminary*. So they wrote to you, and since Miss Anstey was traveling in a post-chaise that Lady Colshot had paid for, it seemed convenient that she should bring me on her way to London."

"I see." Poor brat. It was a story that revealed much

more than the girl realized—a dark stretch of a lonely and unloved existence. Would it have been different if her father had not died in that crypt . . . ?

He thrust the thought from him and flung off the sheet, swinging his legs to the floor with an unusual surge of energy.

The girl's eyes widened; with a violent oath, he grabbed the sheet again. *"Get out!"*

Chloe fled.

Hauling the sheet around his waist, Hugo strode out of the room, bellowing for Samuel, who appeared at the end of the corridor.

"Get that idiot Scranton out here. Send the boy with the message. I want him here by dinnertime."

"Right you are, Sir 'Ugo." Samuel, imperturbable, disappeared.

Hugo stalked back to his room and flung on his clothes. The girl couldn't stay here—not even for a night. A bachelor household was a completely inappropriate environment, as that lunatic piece of carelessness had just demonstrated. However heedless of convention he might be, there were limits.

Chapter 3

C HLOE RECOVERED HER composure in the unde-
manding, accepting company of her animals. The
one-legged parrot swore softly at her from the
windowsill, where he preened himself in the sun, and
Dante lay with his head in her lap as she sat on the floor
beside the hat box, watching the nursing mother.

Animals had always been her chief companions. She
had a sure touch with the sick, wounded, or abandoned
and an unfailing nose for finding them. Her acquisitions
had not been popular with the Misses Trent any more
than had her frequent embarrassing confrontations with
neglectful or abusive owners. However, Chloe was not
easily turned from a course of action, and when her
anger and pity were aroused, it would have taken much
more than the combined efforts of Miss Anne and Miss
Emily to dissuade her.

Now she stroked Dante's head with a soothing
rhythm until her flush died down and she could imagine
facing her guardian again. Until he'd thrown aside the
bedclothes, she hadn't thought twice about his nakedness beneath the sheet. She hadn't thought twice about
being in a man's bedroom—a virtual stranger's bedroom
—conducting such a long and relatively intimate conversation. She had little experience to go on, but it did
not seem as if that had been a most unusual circumstance. In fact, everything about this business was unusual. Here she was, orphaned and alone, thrust into
the clearly unwelcoming arms of a stranger who lived in
a decaying Tudor manor house on the Lancashire moors

with only a servant for company. And not an ordinary servant either.

Dante stood up and went to the door, whining. He needed to go out, and presumably the cat would need to as well. And they had to be fed. The thought of food made her realize that she was starving, and the need to do something practical for her menagerie chased away any lingering embarrassment about the morning's interview.

She picked up the cat, who mewed at her sleeping kittens but was not reluctant to be carried away. Dante pranced ahead of her as she hurried down the corridor, hoping she wouldn't meet Sir Hugo with her arms full of feline. She dashed across the hall and out into the sunny courtyard, where the cat dug herself a tidy hole under a bush and Dante went off, tail flying, to investigate the stables.

She was halfway across the hall, returning mother to babes, when chaos broke out in the courtyard. The air was split with the frenzied barking of what sounded like half a dozen maddened dogs. The cat leapt from her arms with a high-pitched yowl and belted for the stairs.

"What the devil's going on?" Hugo emerged from the kitchen, wiping his mouth on a checkered table napkin. The cat streaked past him and the cacophony from outside grew to new proportions.

"Beatrice . . . Beatrice, come here. For heaven's sake, it's only Dante." Chloe ran after the frantic cat, now racing up the stairs.

"Beatrice!" Hugo exclaimed. "What sort of a name is that?" Then he shook his head impatiently. "Stupid question. What else would you call her?" He grabbed Chloe's arm, halting her pursuit. "Leave the cat. If that damn dog of yours is causing trouble out there, lass, *you* will sort it out."

"Oh, dear . . . yes, I suppose so," Chloe said, staring

distractedly after the cat. "I suppose Beatrice will find her way back to her kittens . . . mother's instinct. Don't you think?"

"I don't know the first thing about cats and I don't give a tinker's damn. But I want that noise stopped *now.*"

Chloe flung up her hands in defeat and ran back outside. It was hard to distinguish one dog from another in the whirling ball of fur in the courtyard. "Dante!" she yelled, running down the steps.

"Don't get in the middle of them!" Hugo called in sudden panic as she raced to the snapping, growling, barking ball of fur.

Chloe stopped dead. "I'm not a fool! What do you take me for?" Her tone was considerably less than polite. Without waiting for an answer, she ran to the pump in the corner of the courtyard, filled two leather buckets, and lugged them toward the fray.

Hugo watched the diminutive figure struggle with the heavy buckets, but he was still smarting from that flash of insolent impatience and made no attempt to help her.

She heaved the contents of the first bucket over the snarling animals, who immediately sprang away from one another. The second bucketful sent Dante's two opponents whimpering toward the stables. Dante, in apparent indifference, shook himself heartily and trotted over to his mistress.

Chloe bent down to the dog. Hugo couldn't hear what she said, but Dante's head hung, his tail drooped, and he slunk off into the far corner of the courtyard.

Chloe straightened, throwing her hair back over her shoulders. She hadn't replaited it, and its radiance seemed to throw back the sunlight like a halo. She looked at Hugo, her expression uncertain, and he returned the look grimly. With a visible stiffening of her shoulders she crossed the yard toward him.

"I'm sorry if I was rude," she said abruptly. "But I know perfectly well how to deal with a dogfight."

"I assume you've had plenty of experience with that ill-bred, ill-disciplined beast," he stated. "He's to be tied up in the stables. I'll not have him causing trouble with my hounds."

"But that's so unjust!" she exclaimed in vigorous defense. "How can you possibly know that Dante started it? It was two against one, I'll have you know." She glared at him, all apologetic conciliation vanished. "And he's not ill-disciplined. Look how downcast he is because I scolded him."

Hugo had an urge to laugh at this passionate defense of her maligned pet. She reminded him of a Lilliputian. He relented slightly. "If there's any more trouble, he's to be tied up." He turned back to the house and his neglected breakfast. "And I will not have him in the house."

Chloe knew that keeping Dante permanently out of the house would be beyond even such a hardened dog-disliker as Hugo Lattimer, so she was not unduly perturbed by the prohibition. Everyone yielded to Dante in the end. For the moment, though, she left him in disgrace and went in search of Beatrice, who had found her brood without the least difficulty and was once again ensconced in the hat box.

"And now I'll have to find you some food," Chloe murmured, frowning. Her stomach growled, asserting its own claims.

Sir Hugo had clearly been eating his breakfast in the kitchen—another odd circumstance. But with any luck, he would have finished by now and be out of the way. Samuel would be easier to manage.

Unfortunately, her guardian was still very much in evidence when she entered the kitchen. He was leaning back in a chair at the table, one booted leg negligently swinging over the arm, a tankard of ale in his hand. Samuel was clearing away dirty plates. They both turned to the door as she came in.

"I'm rather hungry," she said, feeling awkward.

"Then Samuel will find you some breakfast," Hugo responded, looking at her over his shoulder.

"I had breakfast in Bolton at five o'clock this morning," Chloe pointed out, casting a rapid glance toward the open pantry door. She could see a milk churn, which would be a start for Beatrice, but not much comfort to Dante.

"Then he will find you a nuncheon," Hugo said, still observing her. "Now, what are you looking for? Or is it *at* again?"

Chloe's cheeks warmed. "Nothing."

Hugo regarded her thoughtfully. He didn't think Chloe Gresham was a very proficient prevaricator. "Don't fib," he advised. "It makes you go very pink." Not that that delicate blush did anything more than enhance her beauty.

Dear God, what was he thinking of? Quite apart from whose child she was, she was indecently young for a man in his thirty-fifth year to slaver over.

He thumped his tankard on the table and said crisply, "If you want something, lass, I suggest you come right out and ask."

"Well, I do usually," she replied, wandering toward the pantry in a rather roundabout fashion, as if to disguise her destination. "It usually saves a deal of time, but I don't think you're going to be sympathetic."

"Imagine you're lookin' for summat to give that cat of your'n," Samuel remarked as Chloe peered into the pantry.

"And just where is the cat?" demanded Hugo.

"In my room."

"*Your* room?" His eyebrows vanished into his scalp.

"Samuel told me to choose which I liked," she said, turning back to the kitchen. "I hope that was all right. It's a corner room, but there aren't any sheets on the bed. I was going to ask Samuel where I could find some."

Hugo closed his eyes. Things seemed to be getting out of hand. "You aren't staying here, Chloe."

"But where else am I to go?" The deep blue eyes took on a purplish hue, and he didn't like what he read in them. She was expecting something hurtful.

"I have to discuss it with Scranton," he said.

"Why does no one ever want me?" she said so softly he barely caught the words.

He swung his leg off the chair arm, stirred despite himself. "Don't be silly," he said, going over to her. "That's not it at all. You can't stay here because I don't have an appropriate household . . . you must see that, lass." He caught her chin, lifting it. Her eyes still had that purplish hue, but the soft mouth was set.

"I don't see why," she said. "I could keep house for you. Someone needs to."

"Not an heiress with a fortune of eighty thousand pounds," he said, smiling at this absurdity. "And Samuel keeps house for me."

"Not very well," she stated. "It's so dirty everywhere."

"Got enough to do, wi'out worryin' over a peck o' dust," Samuel grumbled. "If you want to eat, miss, ye'd best come to the table. I can't spend all day in the kitchen."

"I have to feed Beatrice first," Chloe demurred. "She's suckling all those kittens."

Hugo seized the change of subject with relief. He had little to lose by accommodating her in this area. By this evening Chloe Gresham and her dependents would be respectably installed elsewhere. Scranton was bound to have some further information that would provide a solution. "I suppose she can stay upstairs for the time being. But the dog is not to come inside."

"I don't see why it should matter. The house is already so dirty, Dante isn't going to make it worse."

"Has nobody ever told you that it's extremely impolite to criticize one's hospitality?" Hugo demanded, good resolutions forgotten in the face of this intransigent refusal to accept the compromise. "Particularly when one is an uninvited guest."

"That's not my fault. If you bothered to read your letters—" she fired back. "Anyway, why don't you?"

"Because there is never anything of the slightest interest in them . . . if it's any of your business, miss," he snapped, stalking to the door. "I suggest you stop making a nuisance of yourself and eat your nuncheon." The door banged on his departure.

Why didn't he bother to open his mail? Hugo pondered the question as he went into the library, wondering also why he'd allowed himself to be drawn into a pointless squabble with an argumentative and irritating schoolgirl. No wonder the Misses Trent had been so ready to see the back of her. Ten years of that would try the patience of Job.

He picked up the pile of letters and glanced through them. The truth, of course, was that he didn't want any reminders of the past. He didn't want to hear news of the people he had once known so well. He didn't want anything to do with the world he had once inhabited. The memories of the past were so hideous, and he couldn't summon a spark of interest for the future. He hadn't been able to since the war ended, and he'd returned to his sadly deteriorated family home and the recognition that apart from Denholm Manor and an equally dilapidated house in London, he was without financial resources. What fortune he'd had he'd run through in those two years with the Congregation of

Eden before the duel. It hadn't been more than a competency, anyway, but with careful management he could have kept a wife, set up his nursery, maintained the estate, and even taken his wife to London for the Season. But one is not wise at eighteen, and his trustees had exerted no control over the willful, dissolute youth in their charge.

After the duel, in a frenzy of guilt and misery, he had ridden to Liverpool and taken the king's shilling aboard the frigate *Hotspur*. One year before the mast had stripped all vestige of privilege, of youthful excess, from him. It had honed and hardened him. At twenty-one he was promoted from the ranks to midshipman and, as the war took its toll, he moved rapidly upward. Within three years he was commanding his own ship of the line.

During those years he was able to forget . . . except at night, when the nightmares came a-visiting. They were relentless and as far as possible he chose not to sleep during the hours of darkness.

But with Napoleon's defeat at Waterloo had come peace. He'd taken his congé of the king's service and here he was, whiling away his days on the Lancashire moors and his nights in the Manchester stews.

And he was not interested in his mail.

He flung the letters down on the table and picked up a bottle from the sideboard. Its dusty coating indicated vintage rather than poor housekeeping. He glanced at the clock. Half past noon. A bit early for the first brandy of the day, but what did it matter? What did anything matter?

"Why doesn't Sir Hugo open his mail?" Chloe asked Samuel as she spread butter lavishly on a crust of bread.

"None of your business, like 'e said" was the uncompromising response. Samuel dumped dishes in a bucket of water.

Chloe cut a wedge of cheese and chewed in silence for a minute. "Why are you the only servant?"

"Inquisitive, aren't you?"

"Perhaps . . . but why?"

"No need for anyone else. Do right enough on our own." Samuel walked to the door. "There's a chicken wing in the pantry. Reckon it'll do for that cat."

"And Dante?" Chloe said hastily, as he seemed about to disappear.

"'E'll get what the hounds get. Ask young Billy in the stables." He opened the back door.

"And sheets," Chloe said. "Where will I find sheets for my bed?"

Samuel turned slowly. "Still reckon on stayin'?"

"Oh, yes," Chloe said with conviction. "I am going nowhere, Samuel."

He snorted, whether with derision or amusement, she couldn't tell. "There's prob'ly summat that'll do in the cupboard on the upstairs landing. 'Elp yourself."

Lawyer Scranton was a short, fat man with bristling white whiskers and a bald head. He rode into the courtyard on a round cob at the end of the afternoon and dismounted, huffing and puffing as he looked around.

Chloe observed him from her perch on top of an up-turned rain barrel in the corner of the yard, then stood up and came over to him, Dante at her heels. "There's a lad called Billy who'll take your horse," she offered.

Scranton smoothed the skirts of his brown coat and adjusted his cravat, peering myopically at her. "Do I have the honor of addressing Miss Gresham?"

Chloe nodded solemnly, swallowing the bubble of

laughter at this pomposity. "My guardian is in the house somewhere."

"I should hope so!" The lawyer huffed again. He was not accustomed to receiving brusque summonses, and Sir Hugo's had been imperious in its curt urgency. He cast a critical glance around the disheveled courtyard, littered with straw and manure. One of the stable doors hung crooked on its hinges.

A youth emerged from the tack room, sucking on a piece of straw. He kicked an iron bucket, sending it clattering across the cobbles, and sauntered over.

"This is Billy," Chloe said. "Will you take Mr. Scranton's horse, Billy?"

"Reckon so," the youth said, lethargically lifting the reins. He clicked his tongue against his teeth and the fat cob ambled off beside him to the stables.

"Shall we go in?" Chloe offered a hostess's smile even as she wondered which of the dust-laden gloomy rooms would be appropriate for entertaining the guest.

She preceded Lawyer Scranton up the steps. At the door she instructed a disconsolate Dante to stay, and went into the cool of the great hall. The heavier items of her luggage were still lying around, since she couldn't manage to carry them upstairs herself and had seen no one but Billy since her nuncheon in the kitchen.

She took a step toward the library, when the door opened and Hugo stood on the threshold, holding a glass and a bottle by its neck in one hand.

"Oh, there you are, Scranton," he said shortly. "Come into the kitchen. We have to sort this mess out. I hope to God you've got some answers."

The kitchen was certainly the most welcoming room in the house, Chloe reflected. The lawyer didn't seem taken aback at the invitation, and she followed the two men.

Hugo, his shoulder holding the door open for his visitor, seemed to notice her for the first time. He frowned, then said, "Oh, well, I suppose it's as much your business as anyone's. Come on in."

"You weren't going to leave me out?" she demanded in some indignation, wondering why his eyes had become rather clouded.

"To tell you the truth, I hadn't thought about it one way or the other." He put his free hand between her shoulder blades and propelled her into the kitchen ahead of him.

Chloe was not surprised to see that Samuel was to be present at this discussion. He was dividing his attentions between a sirloin of beef turning on the spit in the fireplace and a basket of mushrooms he was picking through on the table.

The lawyer sat at the table and accepted a glass of port. Hugo refilled his own glass from the brandy bottle he held, and sat down. Chloe, who was feeling ignored, sat down and filled a glass of port for herself. She'd never drunk anything stronger than claret hitherto, and took a cautious sip. Hugo gave her a cursory glance, then turned back to Scranton, taking the copy of the will out of his pocket.

"What can be done about this, Scranton?" He slapped the document on the table. "There must be some way to have it overset."

Chloe sipped her port, deciding that the taste improved on acquaintance.

The lawyer shook his head. "As legal as any will I've seen, Sir Hugo. Drew it up myself at Lady Gresham's dictation. Her ladyship was in sound mind and it was witnessed by my clerk and the housekeeper."

Hugo looked at the date of the will. It was October 1818. Had he received Elizabeth's note by then? But he couldn't remember. It was another of those facts lost in brandy fumes.

"Of course, you're not the only one who'd like to see it overset." The lawyer waxed expansive over his second glass of port. "Sir Jasper's been creating such a ruckus. Storming around my office, swearing it couldn't stand in a court of law. But I told him it would stand up to anything. As legal as any will I've seen, I told him."

Hugo's chair scraped on the flagstones as he suddenly pushed back from the table, but he didn't say anything, his eyes were fixed with intensity on the lawyer.

"You should have heard him." The lawyer shook his head. "Such a pother. On and on he went about how he was Miss Gresham's brother—the only fit person to assume guardianship—and it wasn't fitting for a complete stranger with no ties to the family to have her in charge."

"He has a point," Hugo said dryly. And even more of a point if the truth of his dealings with the Greshams were ever to be revealed.

The lawyer seemed not to have heard him. "I told him that the law respects the wishes of the dead above all other claims in these matters, and as far as I could see, there was nothing more to be said."

Hugo sighed. The last thing he wanted was to find himself at daggers drawn with Jasper Gresham. A river of enmity ran between them already. But he knew that Elizabeth had chosen him because he would stand up to Jasper as no one else would. Chloe and her fortune would need protection from the Greshams, and he'd been designated to provide it. But there had to be a way to distance himself from his charge.

He glanced sideways at the girl, whose stillness and silence had been almost palpable during the lawyer's peroration. She reached for the port decanter again and he flung his hand out, catching her wrist.

"That's enough, lass. Samuel, fetch some . . . some lemonade, or something."

"But I'm enjoying the port," Chloe protested.

"Don't have any lemonade anyways," Samuel declared, chopping mushrooms with a blinding speed.

"Water, then," Hugo said. "She's too young for port in the middle of the afternoon."

"But you didn't object before," Chloe pointed out.

"That was before," he said with a vague gesture.

"Before what?"

Hugo sighed. "Before it was made irrevocably clear to me that I have no choice but to assume responsibility for you."

Imps of mischief danced suddenly in her deep blue eyes. "I can't believe you're going to be a prim and stuffy guardian, Sir Hugo. How could you be, living the way you do?"

Hugo was momentarily distracted by those enchanting eyes. He shook his head in an effort to dispel the confusing tangle of emotions and turned back to the lawyer, forgetting the issue of the port.

Chloe, with a tiny smile of triumph, filled her glass.

"I understand Miss Gresham was a pupil at a seminary in Bolton," Scranton was saying.

"Unfortunately, there was a lovelorn curate, a butcher's boy, and Miss Anne Trent's nephew," Hugo said with a wry grin. "The estimable Misses Trent found the lass too hot to hold. However, there must be another such establishment—"

"No!" Chloe broke in with a cry. "No, I will not go to another seminary. I absolutely will not." Her voice shook at the thought of being packed off yet again like some unwanted animal, banished again to a confinement that had become unendurable in its loneliness. "If you attempt such a thing, I shall simply run away."

Hugo swung his head toward her and the green eyes were no longer clouded. They held her gaze steadily, and she almost fancied little spurts of flame in their vivid depths.

"Are you challenging me, Miss Gresham?" he asked very softly.

She wanted to say yes, but those little spurts of flame were too intimidating and the short word wouldn't get past her lips.

"It would be inadvisable to challenge me, you should understand," he continued in the same soft voice that had caused many a midshipman to shiver in his shoes.

Chloe recognized the side of her guardian that she had encountered that morning in the bedroom. It was a side with which she had no particular wish to become reacquainted.

There was total silence in the kitchen. Samuel scraped chopped mushrooms into a pan as if oblivious of the tension. Lawyer Scranton stared up at the smoke-blackened timber of the ceiling.

"*You* don't understand," Chloe said finally in a much more moderate tone. "I couldn't bear it anymore." Then she turned her head away abruptly, biting her lip, desperately blinking away the tears crowding her eyes.

Hugo wondered if she realized how much more persuasive he found appeals to his sympathy than challenges to his authority. If she didn't understand it now, she soon would, if she spent much time under his roof. He remembered her desolate question earlier: Why does no one want me? The urge to scoop her up and cuddle her was as ridiculous as it was inappropriate, but he felt it nevertheless.

"What would *you* like to do?" he asked with a briskness that disguised his sudden compassion. "Where would you like to go?"

"To London." Chloe looked up, the tears miraculously dried. "I want to be presented at court and have my come-out. And then once I'm married and have my fortune, I want to establish an animal hospital. It shouldn't be too difficult to find a suitable husband," she added reflectively, "one who won't interfere too much. Eighty thousand pounds should count for something, and I'm quite pretty, I think."

Elizabeth's daughter had a talent for understatement, Hugo thought. "It shouldn't prove too difficult to find a husband," he agreed. "But whether you can find one willing to support your philanthropy, lass, I don't know. Husbands can be an unaccommodating breed, or so I've been told."

Chloe frowned. "Of course, Mama said Jasper intended me to marry Crispin. And that I certainly shouldn't care to do."

So that was it! Hugo drained his glass and reached again for the bottle. Simplicity itself. Jasper's stepson from his wife's former marriage would thus control Chloe's fortune. There was no bar to such a union—not a drop of consanguinity. Presumably, Elizabeth had intended him to forestall such a plan. "Why don't you care to?"

Her response was sharp and definite. "Crispin's a brute . . . just like Jasper. He rode his hunter into the ground once and brought him home foundered and bleeding from his spurs. Oh, and he used to pull the wings off butterflies. I'm sure he hasn't changed."

No, not a suitable mate for someone with a mission to succor needy members of the animal kingdom. "Why has that foul-mouthed parrot only got one leg?" he asked involuntarily.

"I don't know. I found him in Bolton. He'd been left in the gutter and it was raining."

"Beef's ready." Samuel made the laconic declaration as he turned the spit. "Lawyer stayin'?"

Scranton looked anxiously to his host and received a calm "If you care to."

"Well, I daresay it'll be way past dinner when I get home," he said, rubbing his hands at the succulent aromas arising from the fireplace. "So I'll thank ye kindly."

"I'm starving," Chloe declared.

"Had enough bread and cheese for nuncheon to feed a regiment," Samuel commented, bringing the meat to the table.

"But that was hours ago. Shall I fetch knives and forks?"

"In the dresser."

That hideous dress did nothing to mask the grace of her movements, Hugo thought, watching her dance around his kitchen with an assumption of familiarity that filled him with foreboding. He went down to the cellar to bring up wine.

Chloe pushed her glass forward expectantly when he drew the cork.

"I've no objection to your drinking burgundy, but this is a particularly fine wine, so don't gulp it like orgeat," he cautioned, filling her glass.

Lawyer Scranton sipped and purred. Eating in the kitchen of a decaying manor house in the company of a man and his servant might be unusual, but there was no fault to be found with the fare.

Chloe seemed to agree. She consumed a quantity of rare beef, mushrooms, and potatoes that astounded Hugo, who wondered where in that tiny frame it could all be stored. Elizabeth, as he recalled, had had the appetite of a sparrow. He shook his head in a bemused gesture that was becoming all too familiar and returned to the issue of first importance.

"Scranton, you know both sides of Miss Gresham's family. Are there any female relatives she could go to?"

"Oh, you can't send me to stay with some elderly aunt who'll expect me to walk an overfed pug and polish the silver," Chloe said.

"I thought you liked animals."

"I do, but I prefer the ones that other people don't like."

Revealing, he thought, but said only, "Do you have such an aunt?"

"Not that I know of," Chloe said. "But there was a girl at the seminary who had one."

Someone else's aunt was not helpful. "Scranton?" Hugo appealed to the lawyer, who wiped his mouth with some deliberation and took another sip of his wine.

"Lady Gresham had no living relatives, Sir Hugo. Hence the size of Miss Gresham's fortune. I don't know about Sir Stephen's side of the family. But perhaps Sir Jasper would be of assistance there."

That was a dead end if he was to honor Elizabeth's unspoken wishes. "I suppose I could employ a governess—no don't interrupt again," he said sharply as Chloe's now-familiar expostulation began. "The lass could be established somewhere in the charge of a respectable female."

"And do what?" Chloe demanded.

It was not an unreasonable question, he was obliged to admit. However . . .

"I don't see any other solution. Your education isn't yet complete—"

"It's perfectly complete," she interrupted, forgetting the earlier stricture. "I can do everything any schoolroom miss can do, and a great deal else besides."

"Like what?"

"I can mend a bird's broken wing, and deliver a lamb. I know how to treat a sprained fetlock and foot rot—"

"I don't doubt it," he interrupted in his turn. "But it doesn't alter the facts."

"Why can't I stay here?" She asked the simple question almost without emphasis.

"And do what?" Hugo gave her her own again. "Lancashire is a long way from a come-out in London."

"Maybe not," she said quietly.

Now, what the hell did that mean? Hugo gave up. There was clearly nothing to be done tonight. "It seems there's little choice for the moment. You'll have to stay here tonight."

"I told you so," Chloe said to Samuel with a sweet smile, gathering up the dirty plates.

"Reckon you did," Samuel said.

Chapter 4

THE DOG'S DESOLATE howling was a perfect background to crowding memories. Hugo sat at the pianoforte in the library, a single tallow candle throwing a pool of yellow light over the keyboard as his hands strived to pick out a melody from the past. It was a piece he'd composed for Elizabeth, but part of the refrain was missing from his memory.

Impatiently, he swung away from the instrument, picking up his glass. He didn't think he'd ever played it for her anyway. He drained the contents of the glass and refilled it.

His love for Stephen's wife had been a secret he'd kept from everyone but Elizabeth . . . a secret that the infatuated stripling both nurtured and fed upon during the two years he'd known her. They had never consummated their love. It would have been unthinkable for Elizabeth to have done so, and, despite the gnawing need he had suffered, he had enjoyed the purity of his feelings for her. It was such a contrast to the sewage in which he'd been wallowing.

He remembered the first time he'd met her as if it were yesterday. She had said almost nothing the entire weekend, but he'd been haunted by her beauty; by the shadows in her blue eyes, by the sense of her fragility—and the longing to be of service to her, to rescue her from whatever was causing her such unhappiness, had become an obsession.

It was just after his induction into the Congregation of Eden, as they called themselves, and a meeting was being held at Gresham Hall in Shipton. The society had been founded by Stephen and two of his cronies, and through his son, Jasper, its membership had quickly spread to the younger segment of London's aristocracy, bored with the endless round of pointless pleasures, seeking experiences that would take them beyond the boundaries of the commonplace world.

Hugo had just lost his father when he fell under the spell of the Greshams. Only seven miles separated Denholm and Shipton, and he'd known them slightly all his life. A motherless only child, lonely and directionless, he had eagerly accepted Jasper's overtures after his father's death, and came to see him almost as an older brother, and Stephen . . . not as a father, certainly, but the attention of such a worldly sophisticate, such a prominent member of Society, had flattered his youth and inexperience and compensated in some fashion for the loss of his father.

Under Stephen Gresham's leadership, nothing was forbidden the members of the Congregation; there were no risks that couldn't be taken; there were substances that altered the mind . . . that could as easily create a wondrous world as one so terrifying, it drove a man crazy; there was gaming for stakes that rapidly exhausted a moderate fortune; and there were the women.

He had assumed the women who participated in the orgies in the crypt were willing. Some of them were Society women whom he'd believed to be as eager for the sensual thrills as any of the men. He knew now that not all of them fell into that category; Stephen was not averse to blackmail. The other women were whores, paid more for their participation in one evening than they would make in a month on the streets. Drink and the strange herbal substances that were always in ample supply soon banished any inhibitions.

Until the night Stephen had brought Elizabeth to the crypt . . .

The tall clock in the library struck two. The dog's howling filled the night. Hugo swore and drank deeply from his recharged glass. For some reason, the brandy wasn't taking effect. He was as far from oblivion as ever, and his thoughts were as raw. But perhaps it wasn't surprising, with Elizabeth's daughter asleep under his roof. And that damned mournful mongrel didn't help either.

He went back to the pianoforte, trying to drown out the desolate sound by concentrating on his music. Abruptly, he stopped, listening, wondering what he'd heard. Some tiny sound from the hall. He shrugged. He hadn't heard anything. How could he have over that racket?

And then miraculously the howling ceased. The silence filled his head and he could hear the sounds of the slumbering house, the creaks and shifts of the oak floors, the slight rattle of the casement in the night breeze.

He went into the hall. The door to the courtyard was unlatched. He could think of only one explanation. Presumably, Chloe was intending to smuggle the dog upstairs.

He opened the door. The sky was cloudless and the summer night was bright with stars shining down onto the deserted courtyard. He decided to wait in the hall for her. If he gave her a fright, she had only herself to blame. However, after fifteen minutes there was no sign of either his ward or the dog. And there was no sound from the stables either.

Curious now, he lit a lantern and went out into the courtyard, crossing to the stables where the miserable Dante had been confined. His footsteps were muffled by the littering straw and he lifted the latch on the stable door with exaggerated care. At first he could see nothing and held the lantern high. A puddle of golden light fell on a corner of an open stall. A small, white-clad figure was curled against the dog in the straw, her arm around his neck, her head resting on his flank.

"Hell and the devil," Hugo muttered with a surge of irritation. She was sleeping like the dead. Dante cocked a benign eye at the intruder and his tail thumped in greeting. Obviously, he didn't know at whose orders he was being made miserable.

Hugo set down the lantern and bent over Chloe. "Wake up," he said, shaking her shoulder. "What the devil do you think you're doing?"

Chloe woke, blinking and bemused. "What . . . where . . . oh, I remember." She sat up. "Since you won't let Dante into the house, I had to come to him. I couldn't let him go on howling like that."

"I have never heard such nonsense," he said. "Go up to bed at once."

"Not without Dante," she said flatly. "I haven't slept a wink, it's impossible with him howling. I can't imagine anyone sleeping through it. And now I'm so tired, I'd as soon sleep here as anywhere."

"You are not sleeping in a stable," he stated, standing over her, rocking lightly on the balls of his feet, his hands on his hips.

Chloe regarded him steadily, assessing the strength of his determination, testing it against her own. He'd warned her against challenging him, but this time she had a master card up her sleeve. "Good night," she said with a sweet smile, and lay down again.

"You stubborn little brat!" Furious now, he bent, caught her around the waist, and lifted her into the air. Two things happened very quickly. The feel of her skin beneath the thin cambric of her nightgown, the fragrance of her hair, the burning imprint of her body in his hands, set his head spinning in a way that brandy never did, and as he struggled to control his reeling senses, Dante rose, snarling in a flurry of fur and straw, and sank his teeth into Hugo's calf.

Hugo yelled, kicking backward as Chloe slipped from his slackened grasp to the floor.

"Drop."

Chloe's quiet one-word command had an immediate effect. Dante released his grip, but his snarls continued as he watched Hugo with bared teeth.

"Goddammit!" Hugo swore, bending to examine his bleeding leg.

"Oh, dear, I didn't think he would bite you." Chloe knelt down. "I knew he would protect me but . . ." She bent over the wound. "It's deep."

"I know it's deep! Protect you from what, may I ask?"

Sitting back on her heels, she looked up at him and said simply, "From you forcing me to do something I didn't want to do."

"If you think for one minute that I am going to be intimidated by that damn mongrel in my dealings with you, Miss Gresham, you had better think again," he stated, glaring down at her.

It seemed sensible to back away from further confrontation at this point. Rubbing in her guardian's present disadvantage wouldn't be tactful. "I can't imagine your being intimidated by anything," she said truthfully, standing up. "We'd better go to the kitchen and I'll dress the wound. It probably should be cauterized." She picked up the lantern. "Can you walk? Shall I find you a stick?"

"I can walk," he said curtly, hobbling to the stable door.

Dante bounded ahead of them across the courtyard, up the stairs to the open door, where he paused expectantly, waiting for his companions, whose progress was considerably slower. His tail wagged furiously and one would be hard pressed to recognize the ferocious animal of a few minutes earlier.

Chloe put a small hand under Hugo's elbow as he limped up the steps. It was an absurd gesture, given their relative sizes. "I can manage without support," Hugo snapped, hiding his inner amusement.

Dante lifted one paw, placing it on Chloe's knee as they reached him. Hugo paused, but before he could say anything, Chloe whispered, *"Please.* I promise he won't be a nuisance. He doesn't have fleas or anything, and he's very housebroken."

Hugo looked defeat squarely in the face. He had no affinity whatsoever with domestic animals. Their hair made him sneeze, and he disliked the smell of them even when they were clean. But his diminutive ward had roundly outmaneuvered him. "He can come in tonight," he said with a resigned sigh. "But I don't want him under my feet in the daytime."

"Oh, thank you." Standing on tiptoe, she kissed his cheek, her eyes shining in the moonlight.

Hugo struggled with his reeling senses again. "Don't assume any precedents," he said gruffly. "You may have won this round, but I don't take kindly to having my hand forced."

"Oh, I won't," she said earnestly. "Anyway, there isn't anything else at the moment that we're at odds about, is there?" On which blithe statement she marched ahead of him into the kitchen.

He followed more slowly and stood leaning against the doorjamb for a minute. She had set the lantern on the table and was poking the embers of the fire. Her body in the thin shift was clearly outlined against the light, and the entrancing curve of her hips as she bent to her task took his breath away. A flame spurted and she straightened, turning to face him. Her breasts peaked softly against the material, the nipples a darker smudge.

"There's enough fire, I think, to heat a knife to cauterize. . . . Is something the matter?" Her eyes widened anxiously as she saw his expression.

He ran his hands through his hair. "I can manage on my own. Go on up to bed."

"But you can't," she said, coming toward him. "It has to be properly cleaned, and I know just what to do."

He put out a hand as if to hold her away from him. "Samuel can do it. Go to bed."

"But it's silly to wake him when I'm here."

She had no idea of what she looked like . . . of what she was offering. How could she be such an innocent at seventeen? But then he thought of her life . . . ten years in a seminary, except for a few days at Christmas at her reclusive mother's bedside. How could she know anything?

And there was no one to instruct her but himself. He spoke with studied dispassion. "I want you to go up to your room and put on a robe. And I don't want to see you ever again wandering around this house so scantily dressed."

Puzzlement, followed by chagrin, flashed through her eyes, darkening the blue. She glanced down at her body, saw the soft swell of her breasts, the darker shadow at the apex of her thighs. Her cheeks were pink as she looked up at him, saying awkwardly, "But it wasn't cold and I wasn't expecting to see anyone."

"I understand that. Don't do it again." He went to the table and sat down, lifting his injured leg onto a chair opposite. "Hurry up. I'm bleeding all over the floor, and it hurts like the devil."

Chloe glanced around the room. Hanging from a peg by the back door was a long overcoat muddied at the hem. She thrust her arms into the sleeves, wrapping the quantity of material around her body. "Will this satisfy you, sir?"

He glanced up, and despite the preceding taut exchange couldn't help smiling. "You look like an abandoned waif, lass."

"Not provocative, then?"

For all her innocence, she'd put two and two together quickly enough. "Not in the least," he agreed. Not provocative but enormously appealing. "Could we get this over with?"

She took a knife from the dresser and went to the fire. There was silence in the kitchen. Hugo endured as Chloe opened the puncture wounds with the searing knife tip. He'd suffered worse. He distracted himself with contemplating her surprising competence. Her touch was sure, her knowledge unfaltering, and while she clearly tried to cause him as little pain as possible, she didn't flinch at doing what had to be done.

"Do you have any brandy I could splash on before I bandage it?" she asked, raising her head, a frown of concentration between her brows.

"What a waste." He leaned back with a sigh of relief, the ordeal over. "It'll do more good inside me than out."

"Do you drink too much brandy?" she asked seriously.

"Probably. You'll find a bottle in the library."

Dante trotted after her as she left the kitchen, and Hugo closed his eyes, trying to forget both his throbbing leg and that disquieting arousal. A governess in a discreet, ladylike house in Oldham or Bolton would be the answer. There would be other families in town with young girls about to be launched into Lancashire society, such as it was, and it was inevitable Chloe would be introduced. It wouldn't be London, but it would keep her out of trouble, and with luck she'd meet some ideal suitor and he could be rid of the disturbing responsibility Elizabeth had laid upon him.

Chloe was awakened the next morning by Beatrice's insistent miaows as she stood on her hind legs, futilely tapping at the latch on the door.

"You are clever," Chloe said, sliding out of bed. "Can you find your way outside by yourself?" She opened the door.

Beatrice didn't deign to reply but ran off down the corridor, Dante scampering behind her. The parrot offered a coarse greeting from the windowsill and fluffed his feathers. She scratched his poll and he whistled at her.

Chloe scrambled into her petticoat and stockings and the hideous serge dress. If she wanted water to wash with, she'd presumably have to fetch it from the kitchen. She brushed her hair, began automatically to plait it, then stopped. Sir Hugo had wanted her to take it down yesterday; perhaps he liked it that way. And she had already decided that whatever her guardian liked, she would endeavor to supply, since her plans depended on his cooperation.

Samuel was alone in the kitchen when she went in. "I'm starving," she announced.

"Tell me summat new." Samuel didn't look up from the fireplace, where he was raking the embers. "Reckon you'll find summat in the pantry."

Chloe brought ham, a loaf of bread, a crock of butter, and a jug of milk to the table. "Has Sir Hugo had breakfast?"

"Not as far as I know. There were visitors and 'e went outside. What 'appened to 'is leg?"

"Dante bit him." Chloe sliced thickly into the ham.

Samuel turned around at that and stared at her for a

minute with an arrested expression. "Now, why would
'e go an' do a thing like that?" he asked slowly.

Chloe shrugged and layered thick slices of ham on
the buttered bread. "Just a mistake." She filled a beaker
with milk and took a large bite of her sandwich.

"Strange sorta mistake," Samuel muttered, turning
back to the grate.

Chloe hesitated, wondering whether to expand. Samuel had clearly drawn his own conclusions, and they
were probably close to the mark; he knew how attached
Dante was to his mistress.

Leave well alone, she decided, burying her nose in
the beaker of milk.

"I'm going outside," she volunteered as she put the
empty beaker on the table.

Samuel merely grunted.

Taking the remnants of her sandwich, she left the
kitchen, intending to check on Beatrice and Dante, but
Beatrice streaked past her as she crossed the great hall
on the way to the door. "I'll bring you some breakfast in
a minute," Chloe called after the cat, heading up the
stairs back to her litter. Beatrice paused on the stairs,
cocked an ear, then continued on her way.

Chloe stopped at the open door, staring down into
the courtyard. Hugo stood talking to two men on horseback. She recognized the elder of the two immediately,
and it wasn't difficult to guess the identity of his companion, although she hadn't seen either of them for
seven years.

Still holding her bread and ham, she came slowly
down the steps. Dante ran across the yard to greet her,
tail flying.

Jasper Gresham was facing the steps and saw her first.
He was a handsome man, as his father had been, although there was a certain heaviness to his features, a
florid tinge to his complexion that indicated a life of

dissipation. But his eyes were frightening. They were curiously light and shallow and never seemed to hold an expression for long enough to identify it. They slid and darted, never engaging, yet somehow all-seeing.

"Ah," he said pleasantly. "We're about to be joined by the subject of this discussion."

Hugo spun around, scowling. "What are you doing here?"

Chloe's step faltered at this puzzlingly harsh reception. Then she put her chin up. "I beg your pardon, Sir Hugo, but I didn't know the courtyard was forbidden."

Before he could respond, Jasper said, "Well, little sister, look at you—all grown-up. And how do you go on?" He swung off his horse, took her shoulders, and kissed her cheek.

Dante suddenly growled. Hugo took an involuntary step forward. He knew Jasper Gresham. He knew how Jasper sullied women. Then he took hold of himself. Nothing was going to happen on this sunny morning in the courtyard of his own home, particularly with that mongrel in the vicinity.

"Very well, thank you, Jasper," Chloe responded politely, placing a reassuring hand on Dante's head. "Good morning, Crispin." She greeted the younger man, who had also dismounted.

He, too, bent to kiss her, and Hugo saw her stiffen, although she endured the salute. "Chloe, it's been a long time," Crispin said with a smile that didn't warm his flat brown eyes or do much to enliven his rather stolid features.

"Yes," she agreed, stepping back. She took another bite of her bread and ham and seemed content to leave the visitors to make the running.

Hugo stifled a smile, his concern and annoyance abruptly vanished. Chloe didn't care for her half brother or for Crispin, and she was making that most insolently clear, even while she smiled vaguely at them as she chewed.

"I trust you'll pay us a visit at Gresham Hall," Jasper said, his voice suddenly clipped. "Your nearest relatives, now that your dear mother . . ."

Chloe swallowed her mouthful. "You weren't at the funeral."

"No . . . I was in London."

"Oh." A skeptical lift of her eyebrows accompanied the bland monosyllable.

Jasper suddenly turned to Hugo. "This will is an absurdity," he said. "Can we discuss it in private?"

"There's nothing to discuss," Hugo replied. "Scranton has made that abundantly clear . . . to both of us, as I understand it."

A flush darkened Jasper's cheek. "It's outrageous, and you know it, Lattimer. For God's sake, let's go inside."

Hugo shook his head and said deliberately, "No, I don't think so, Jasper. You are not welcome in my house."

The air crackled. Chloe was astounded. She looked at the two men and felt the hatred coursing between them. Crispin had flushed as deeply as his stepfather and moved forward so that the two stood shoulder to shoulder.

Hugo continued to regard them calmly. Chloe noticed for the first time how disheveled he was. His chin was stubbly, his eyes heavy, the lines of his face biting deep in the harsh light of the morning sun. His shirt was unbuttoned at the neck, the sleeves rolled to his elbows. He wore no cravat, and his leather britches and boots were those of a farmer.

Jasper and Crispin, in contrast, were dressed impeccably in buckskin riding britches, gleaming top boots, snug-fitting coats of superfine, curly-brimmed beaver hats tucked beneath their arms.

"You are insulting," Jasper said.

Hugo offered a mock bow and said nothing. He knew he had the upper hand. He hadn't seen Jasper since that fateful night, and his loathing for the man was as strong now as it had ever been. Allowing it full rein was a heady emotional release.

"I demand that *my* sister come back with me. She needs the care of a woman, and who better than my wife, her own sister-in-law, to provide it. Look at her." He flung his hand out in a dismissive gesture. "Is that any way for a young woman to appear in public?"

"What's the matter with me?" Chloe asked, all wide-eyed innocence.

Hugo could hear the mockery in the question even if the others couldn't. He couldn't restrain his grin. "You've a milky mustache for a start," he said.

"I haven't!" she exclaimed, wiping her mouth with the back of her hand.

"And you have little crusts of sleep in the corners of your eyes," he continued relentlessly. "And mud and straw on the bottom of your skirt. However, nothing that requires a sister-in-law to remedy. We can manage perfectly well ourselves."

"You throw down the gauntlet, Lattimer," Jasper declared softly.

A chill seemed to invade the courtyard. Hugo offered another mock bow of agreement. Chloe realized that the laughing banter about her own disarray had been merely a cover for whatever issue stood between her half-brother and her guardian. And it wasn't just a matter of her mother's will.

"Come, Crispin." Jasper remounted, his face black. Crispin did the same. "This isn't the end of it, Lattimer."

"No, Jasper, I don't imagine it is," Hugo said.

"Somehow, I don't believe I'll meet my match in a drunken sot," the other man said viciously.

Hugo whitened, but he said only, "I give you good day, Jasper . . . Crispin."

The two men rode out of the courtyard without a backward glance.

Chloe looked up at Hugo. "What was that about?"

He didn't seem to have heard her. His mouth was a taut line, the green eyes distant. Absently, he passed a hand over his unshaven chin. "What did you say?"

"Nothing," she said, sensing that the mystery of what lay between her guardian and her brother would not be solved this morning.

He looked down at her and shook his head. "You really are a disreputable sight, lass. No credit to my guardianship at all."

"Well, you're not particularly smart yourself," Chloe retorted. "Did you sleep in your clothes?"

"I didn't sleep," he replied.

"Oh, was your leg hurting?"

"Not excessively." He wasn't going to explain about the tormenting effects of unfulfilled arousal. "I sleep little at the best of times."

"Why?"

He frowned, quoting almost to himself, " 'The innocent sleep.' "

" 'Sleep that knits up the ravell'd sleeve of care,' " Chloe continued promptly. "But Macbeth was guilty of mass murder . . . it's not surprising he couldn't sleep. What could you be guilty of?"

I killed your father. But it wasn't just that. It was all the other things. How many of those women hadn't been willing partners in their violation? It was the one question that haunted him. Stephen had been capable of blackmail. He had abused his wife, coerced her with brutality. He'd have given little consideration to the defenseless women of the streets. . . . There'd been a virgin. . . . *No!* He wouldn't think about it.

Chloe touched his arm, alarmed by the bleakness of his expression. "What is it?"

"Painted devils," he said with an effort. That's what he called them—those hideous images dancing on the walls of his mind. "I need my breakfast. I see you've already had yours."

Chloe wondered whether to press the matter, but decided she didn't have the right. She barely knew him. "Only bread and ham," she said cheerfully. "If Samuel's going to cook eggs for you, I'd like some too."

There was something about the girl that banished the devils, Hugo realized, suddenly lighthearted. "Where do you put it all, lass?"

"I don't know, but I'm always hungry," she confided, accompanying him to the kitchen, Dante at her heels. "I wonder if Jasper will come back?"

"He'll get short shrift if he does." Hugo glanced down at the dog, then gave a mental shrug. He seemed to have been routed in that battle. "Hot water, Samuel, I'm going to shave." He pulled his shirt out of his britches, unbuttoned it, and tossed it over a chair.

Samuel placed a bowl of hot water on the table and propped a small mirror against an empty wine bottle. "Soap's in the pantry."

Chloe perched on the edge of the table, watching as Hugo sharpened the long razor on a leather strop and lathered his face. His hands fascinated her. They were beautiful, elegant, and slender with long, sensitive fingers. For some reason, they produced a strange flutter in the pit of her stomach.

"What's that on your chest?" she asked suddenly. She'd seen the strange little design yesterday, when he'd been in bed. "Is it a snake?"

Hugo's movements stilled, and then he said carelessly, "Yes, it's a snake."

"Why do you have it?"

"Didn't they teach you in that seminary about vulgar curiosity?" he demanded. "Or about the impropriety of making personal remarks?"

"I'm sorry." She looked crestfallen. "I was just interested because I've never seen anything like it before."

"But then, I don't imagine you've seen a man without his shirt before," he said with some asperity, drawing a long swath through the soap.

"No," she agreed. "Did you get it in the navy?"

Hugo sighed and seized the easy way out. "Tattoos are common in the navy. Now, do you have a riding habit?"

To his relief, she accepted the close of the uncomfortable topic without demur. "Of course, but it's another bushel." She licked her finger and picked up crumbs from the tabletop.

"Well, I think it's time to do something about that. We'll ride into Manchester and see if we can't improve your wardrobe." He wiped the soap off his face with a towel and passed a checking hand over his chin. "That's better."

He subjected Chloe, still perched on the table, to a frowning inspection. "But you certainly won't do. Samuel, give the lass a jug of hot water to take upstairs. She needs a good wash."

Samuel filled a copper jug from the kettle on the fire. He surveyed Chloe appraisingly. "I'd best take it up for ye. A puff of wind w'd blow ye away, seems to me."

"I'm a lot stronger than I look," Chloe said, holding out her hand for the jug. "I can dig canker out of a horse's hoof, and they're very heavy to hold."

"Good God," Hugo muttered. "How the hell did you become a veterinarian?"

"The head groom in the livery stables in Bolton taught me a lot. I used to sneak out of the seminary on Sundays and spend the day with him. It wasn't very popular," she added.

"No, I don't suppose it was."

"But there wasn't anything they could do to stop me," she continued blithely. "And then there's a poacher who lives in the village at Shipton. He taught me how to handle birds and small animals."

"I'm amazed the long-suffering Misses Trent kept you as long as they did," Hugo observed.

"I'm sure they were well paid," Chloe said, an edge to her voice. "I spent most of the year there, after all." She hefted the jug and went to the door. "Are we going to Manchester this morning?"

"Unless you have other plans," he said.

"No, I don't believe I do," Chloe responded with his own mock solemnity.

Hugo chuckled, wondering where she'd acquired her sense of humor. Elizabeth had been painfully serious, and Stephen had derived amusement only in extremity. "I have to talk to your bankers. How much allowance do you have at the moment?"

"Allowance?" Chloe blinked at this novel concept. "I've never had any money. If I wanted pin money, Miss Emily would give it to me. But they supplied the bushels . . . and there wasn't much else to spend money on."

Hugo scratched his head. "I haven't the faintest idea what would be appropriate for you." It would depend, of course, on where she lived. After the morning's visit, he no longer considered the possibility of setting her up in a private establishment with a respectable female companion. At least, not within striking distance of Shipton. She'd find it impossible to avoid her half-brother and Crispin in such circumstances.

She was still standing by the door, carrying the jug of water, and he waved her away. "Go and change your dress, lass. I'll sort something out."

"So, what're ye plannin' on doin' with 'er?" Samuel asked as the door closed behind her.

"God knows." Hugo sighed. "You read my thoughts."

"Ye reckon on keepin' 'er here?"

"For the moment, I don't see much choice." But there must be *some* family she could live with other than the Greshams, he thought. It wasn't possible at such a tender age to have no one who cared for her.

It *shouldn't* be possible. But he suspected it was the case. Her life had been shaped so far by a debauched and bloodstained past in which he'd played a defining part. And now it seemed his chickens had come home to roost with a vengeance.

Chapter 5

"How fine you look," Chloe said admiringly, coming into the courtyard half an hour later.

Her guardian had changed his farmer's garb for cravat, buckskins, and top boots.

Hugo regarded her riding habit of brown serge with a grimace. "I wish I could say the same for you, lass. Are all your clothes that ghastly color?"

"Yes," she said casually, examining with a somewhat critical frown the dapple-gray pony Billy was holding. "Am I to ride the pony?"

"I'm not putting you on one of my hunters," he said. "And Dapple's the only alternative."

"Oh." Chloe walked all around the small, fat pony. "The mare I rode at the livery stable was fourteen hands."

"The smallest hunter I have stands at seventeen hands," Hugo said. "This is what you're riding." He caught her around the waist and lifted her into the saddle. "Once you're established somewhere, we'll buy you a decent horse."

"Ah," Chloe said, gathering up the reins. "Well, on that subject, let me tell you my plan."

Hugo swung astride a rawboned gelding, casting her a sideways glance. She offered him a sunny smile. Her hair was back in its plaits, but not scraped away from her forehead as before and a few guinea-gold tendrils wisped beneath a hideous felt hat. Hugo began to wonder if he was losing his mind as a host of completely improper images filled his head.

64

He pressed his heels into his mount's flanks with abrupt speed and rode ahead of her through the arched gateway to the drive outside.

Chloe's pony followed with a rolling gait that promised a slow ride. Dante, securely held back by Billy, raised his head in a mournful howl as his mistress disappeared from view.

"My plan," Chloe said from behind Hugo. "Don't you want to hear it?"

He slackened speed so that she could catch up with him. Her plans so far hadn't impressed him with their practicality. "Not particularly, if it's anything like your previous suggestions," he said. "But I'm sure I'm going to hear it whether I want to or not."

Chloe was undaunted by this less-than-enthusiastic response. "Do you have a house in London?"

"An uninhabitable one," he replied.

"But money would make it habitable, wouldn't it?"

"What the devil are you getting at?" He turned to look at her again. The sunny smile was still in place.

"Well, it's simple," she said. "You need to have a wife—"

"I need *what?*" he exclaimed. His horse skittered on the gravel.

"I've decided that that's what you need," she said. "You need someone to take care of you properly. I always know when people need looking after," she added seriously.

Vaguely, he wondered if she distinguished between people and animals.

When his dumbfounded silence continued, she went on. "If you had a wife, perhaps you'd be able to sleep properly again, and you'd have someone to manage your household, and make sure you were comfortable. And if she had a fortune, of course, it would be perfect . . . since you don't seem to have much money." She regarded him, her head on one side, assessing his reaction to her diagnosis and prescription.

"And just where am I going to find this paragon?" He didn't know whether to laugh or scold her for impertinence.

"In London," Chloe said as if it were self-evident. "Where I shall find a husband, so that I can have my freedom. I've decided that I'm going to keep control of my fortune myself when I marry. Can that be done?"

The sudden switch of topic was so confusing, Hugo found himself responding as if the question were a sensible one, which it most certainly was not. "Under the law, your husband has control of your fortune," he said. "But exceptions are made."

"And as my guardian, you could make sure that happened?"

Where did she get these quaint notions from? He replied with some amusement, "Yes, I could. Always assuming this putative husband was still willing to marry you."

"Oh, I expect he will be," she said airily. "I'll share my fortune with him. And if he's anything like the curate or the butcher's boy or Miss Anne's nephew, nothing will put him off."

Hugo's lip quivered at this matter-of-fact statement. If her previous swains had lost their heads over her when she was camouflaged in ill-fitting brown serge, it required little imagination to guess the effect she would have when properly presented. It seemed that Miss Gresham was not quite as naive as he'd thought her . . . or as she had chosen to present herself hitherto.

Now, that was an interesting thought.

"Anyway, my plan is that we shall both go to London, and I can have my come-out, and you shall find a wife and I shall find a convenient husband," she finished.

"Leaving aside any plans *I* might have for my life," he

said, still humorously, "just how do you intend we should establish ourselves in London?"

"In your house, of course. We can use my fortune to make it habitable and to pay for my come-out, which I believe is excessively expensive, what with a court dress and a come-out ball and everything."

Hugo took a deep breath. "My child, there is an extremely unpleasant word for a man who helps himself to his ward's fortune."

"But that's not what would be happening at all!" she exclaimed. "We would be using my money to benefit me. I have to have somewhere to live and a come-out. This is the simplest way of doing it, and if it benefits you, too, then all the better."

Hugo's patience ran out with his sense of humor. "I have never heard such arrant nonsense," he stated. "I have absolutely no intention of going to London, and if you wish to do so, then you will have to find yourself a suitable chaperone."

"But you are a suitable chaperone."

"I am not. Even if I wanted to be, it's absurd. You need a respectable lady with entrees into the first circles."

"Don't you have entrees?"

"Not anymore," he said shortly. "And if I hear another word of this idiocy, you'll spend the rest of your wardship in brown serge."

Chloe closed her lips tightly. She had planted the seed, and maybe that was as far as she could expect to go in one day.

Back in the courtyard, Dante continued to howl. He'd been tied to the pump to keep him from following his mistress and strained desperately at the leash, nearly choking himself.

A man in laborer's smock sauntered into the court-yard. "What's the matter with 'im?"

"Oh, 'e can't abide being wi'out Miss," Billy said. "You want summat?"

"Casual work," the man said, continuing to look at the dog with interest. "What'd 'appen if you let 'im go?"

"Reckon 'e'd be off afta 'er, like as not. Should've 'eard him 'owling last night, when Master wouldn't let 'im in the 'ouse."

"Powerful attachment that'd be," the laborer mused. " 'Appens like that sometimes, though."

"Aye," agreed Billy. "If'n you want work, ye'd best talk to Samuel. 'E'll be in the kitchen, I reckon. Back door's thataway." He gestured with his chin toward the back of the house.

"Thankee, lad." The man followed the directions.

When they entered the city of Manchester, Hugo led his ward to the George and Dragon, where they left their horses.

"We'll go to the bankers first," Hugo said as their horses were led off to the stables.

"Immediately?" Chloe looked wistfully toward the open door of the inn, from whence emanated the most enticing aromas.

"Yes . . . why, what's the matter?"

"I'm hungry," she said. "And something smells wonderful."

Hugo sighed. "Of course, you didn't have your eggs, did you? We'll find you a meat pie or something in a minute." He chivvied her ahead of him out of the inn yard and into the street.

A troop of men in the jerkin and britches of the laborer were gathered in the town square, marching and wheeling to the orders of a drill sergeant. A crowd had gathered to watch, shouting encouragement and good-humored jeers as the marchers stepped on one another's feet, lost tempo and straggled out of line, or skipped to catch up with their neighbors.

Chloe jumped on her toes, looking over the heads of the spectators. "What's it for?"

A man wearing an unusual white top hat turned toward her. "They're preparing for Orator Hunt, miss," he said in cultured accents. "The reformers have invited him to address a meeting on manhood suffrage next month. They're expecting a big crowd and the organizers reckon it'll be more orderly if they drill groups of participants in advance."

"Such militancy is more likely to alarm the magistrates," Hugo said somberly, taking a hip flask from his coat pocket. "It looks more as if the men are being drilled to offer armed resistance than anything else." He took a swig of his emergency supply of brandy.

The man's clear gray eyes sharpened. "It's to be hoped there'll be nothing to resist, sir. If the magistrates are sensible, it'll go off as peaceably as a Christmas mass."

"I have little faith in the common sense of magistrates when it comes to fear of a radical mob," Hugo said, thrusting the flask back into his pocket. "Come along, Chloe." Taking her arm, he led her away from the crowd.

"Who's Orator Hunt?"

"Henry Hunt—a fire-breathing radical," Hugo told her. "He's a professional political agitator and as far as civil authorities are concerned, every meeting he addresses brings the country one step closer to revolution and the guillotine."

"Oh, I see." Chloe frowned. "Maybe they should listen, then, and do something about it."

Hugo laughed. "Sweet child, that's a utopian viewpoint if ever I heard one."

There was nothing unkind about his laughter, and Chloe couldn't be offended. Instead, she smiled at him, tucking her hand into his arm.

Hugo glanced down at her upturned face and felt as if something had punched into his solar plexus. It was absurd. How could she possibly have such an effect on him? She was just a pretty child hovering on the verge of womanhood. *And wouldn't it be wonderful to take her over that verge?* Dear God, he was heading for Bedlam!

"Is that boy selling pies?"

The prosaic question returned him to reality. Thankfully, he dragged his eyes away from her and looked around.

A boy pushing a wheelbarrow was calling out his wares in an indistinct singsong. However, the smells were enough to identify his produce, warming on a rack over a bed of hot coals.

Hugo bought a steaming meat pie, and then, all thoughts of seduction banished, watched with some amusement as Chloe, standing on the street corner, bit into it. "Good?"

"Delicious. I was about to faint away with hunger."

"Well, perhaps you can eat it while we resume our walk."

Chloe nodded amenably, her mouth full.

Mr. Childe of Childe's Bank welcomed Hugo with a low bow, gesturing toward his inner sanctum. "If Miss Gresham would like to wait in the anteroom, I'll have the clerk bring her some tea," he said with an avuncular smile at the girl in her hideous schoolgirl's serge.

"Oh, no," Chloe said. "I wish to understand about my fortune. And I don't need tea . . . thank you," she added in belated afterthought.

Mr. Childe looked astounded. "But . . . but you can

have no interest in funds and percentages, my dear. Young ladies find such things most boring. I'm sure we can find a periodical for you to look at while you're waiting. . . ." He nodded encouragingly. "The latest fashions, I'm sure, will hold your attention much more than our tedious discussion."

"No, I don't think so," Chloe replied with a sweet smile. "I'm not in the least interested in fashion, but I am most interested in understanding about my fortune. You see," she explained kindly, "I intend to have the management of it myself when I'm married, so I must learn all about it."

Mr. Childe's jaw dropped. He turned in appeal to Sir Hugo, who was looking out of the window, apparently unconcerned by his ward's heretical statement. "Surely not, Sir Hugo?"

"That would rather depend on the husband in question," Hugo responded. "It seems a little premature to speculate, since there's no gentleman on the horizon. However, if the lass wants to sit in, then I see no objection. If she's bored, she'll have only herself to blame, and if she learns something, then that's no bad thing." With a hand between her shoulder blades, he ushered her ahead of him into the banker's sanctum.

It occurred to Chloe that she was becoming accustomed to being moved along in this fashion. She wondered why it didn't irritate her.

She listened intently while the two men discussed financial intricacies. Hugo was patient with her interruptions, but Mr. Childe grew increasingly testy and finally Hugo waved her into silence when she broke into a particularly convoluted explanation of the banker's.

"Save your questions until later, lass. Otherwise we'll be here all afternoon."

"But will you be able to answer them?"

"I'll try."

"But—"

"That'll do, Chloe."

The sharpness took her aback and she subsided, knotting her fingers in her lap, closing her lips firmly.

Hugo cast her a sideways glance. She was looking distinctly aggrieved, but he had no intention of offering encouragement for further interruption.

"One last matter, Sir Hugo. Will you be continuing the yearly payment to Sir Jasper Gresham?" the banker asked, resting his clasped hands on the pile of documents on the desk.

"What?" This ejaculation of Chloe's went unadmonished.

"For the past ten years Lady Gresham had instructed us to pay Sir Jasper three thousand pounds a year." The banker pointedly addressed her guardian. "Her will contained no instructions to us to continue the payments."

So that was how Elizabeth had protected herself and her daughter from the Greshams. Hugo tapped the tips of his fingers together as the pieces fell into place. Three thousand pounds a year was a tidy sum; Jasper wouldn't take kindly to its cessation.

"What was Mama paying Jasper for?"

"How should I know?" Hugo lied. He couldn't say *your safety,* although he was certain that had been uppermost in Elizabeth's mind.

Jasper would have tried to take control of the heiress to his stepmother's fortune. With Elizabeth drifting through life in a laudanum haze, he could have taken Chloe under his own roof and exerted his own inimitable influence over the child. She would have been married to Crispin at sixteen whether she wanted to or not. Elizabeth had managed to protect her daughter into adulthood by removing her completely from Shipton, and by bribing Jasper. She would have hoped that if Chloe reached adulthood untouched by her half-brother's authority and therefore unafraid of him, she would have the strength to resist the pressure he would bring to bear on her once her mother was no longer around.

And to give her an extra advantage, Elizabeth had called upon the memory and obligation of an old love and aligned Jasper's greatest enemy on her daughter's side.

"No," he said. "If Lady Gresham left no instruction, then the payments should lapse."

"Good," Chloe declared. "I fail to see why Jasper should have *my* money."

"That's a most unnecessary statement," Hugo said repressively, seeing the banker clearly scandalized by this unladylike young lady.

Elizabeth really would have helped him in the task she'd set him if she'd managed to instill some conventional manners into her daughter.

He stood up. "Well, that seems to be everything, Mr. Childe. We'll take up no more of your time."

"What about my allowance?" Chloe reminded him.

Hugo frowned and said off the top of his head. "A hundred pounds a quarter should be ample."

"Four hundred pounds a year!" Chloe exclaimed. "When Jasper was getting three thousand, and it wasn't even his money."

Mr. Childe's little eyes seemed to pop in his red face.

Hugo, who felt that Chloe had a point for all its reprehensible presentation, said quickly, "We'll discuss it later. Come." He extended a hand in farewell to the banker and drew Chloe forward with the other. To his relief, she made her farewells very prettily, thanking the banker for his time and apologizing for having been a nuisance.

It was hard to withstand her smile and Mr. Childe was somewhat mollified. He patted her hand, then accompanied them to the door. "Will you be informing Sir Jasper about the change in payment, Sir Hugo?"

Hugo shook his head. He intended to have no dealings whatsoever with Stephen's son. "No, I'll have Lawyer Scranton notify him."

Outside, Chloe said again, "Whyever would Mama have paid Jasper all that money? She detested him."

"It doesn't matter," her companion said shortly, beginning to walk down the narrow cobbled street.

"Are you vexed?" Chloe looked up at him, a hint of anxiety darkening her blue eyes. "I know I shouldn't have said that about Jasper and I suppose I shouldn't have objected about my allowance, but it all took me by surprise."

"I must endeavor to keep you from surprises in future," he said dryly. "Childe was scandalized, and I don't blame him."

"I was only expressing an opinion."

"There are some opinions that should not be expressed before strangers, however legitimate they might be."

"Ah, so you *do* agree with me," she said with a little skip of triumph.

He stifled a grin, stepping over a pile of ordure in the kennel. "That's beside the point. However, you're not getting an allowance of three thousand pounds a year, so don't think it."

"But in London I'll need enough to maintain my horses as well as my wardrobe."

Hugo stopped as they emerged from the narrow alley into a broader thoroughfare. "I told you I didn't want to hear any more of that," he stated. "Are we going to continue this errand to the milliner's or not?"

Nothing would be gained by depriving herself of new clothes. Chloe shrugged and said with an accepting smile, "Continuing, please."

Hugo cast her a suspicious glance to which she returned a dazzling smile of such innocence, he knew his suspicions were justified. He shook his head in resignation and resumed walking.

The city's milliners and drapers were gathered together on one street. Hugo was not a frequent customer of such shops, but from a lifetime's acquaintance with Manchester, he knew the names of the most reputable and had a particular establishment in mind. Chloe, however, was utterly and indiscriminately entranced by every display in every bow-fronted window. She pranced from one side of the lane to the other, drawing his attention to gowns and hats as they caught her eye.

To his dismay, Hugo realized that she had not the slightest idea about what was either tasteful or appropriate. As he listened to her rapturous praise of a gown of violet sarsenet embroidered with paste sapphires and a tulle hat of the most ludicrous proportions, he realized he was going to have to revise his plans for the remainder of the afternoon.

He had intended leaving her in the charge of the dressmaker while finding some much-needed liquid refreshment in a nearby tavern. Now it became apparent that he couldn't trust her judgment, and knowing how determined she could be, he was fairly certain the modiste would be unable to guide her choice. The bottle of burgundy would have to wait.

He fortified himself again from the hip flask and turned into the doorway of a discreet establishment displaying a dainty gown of sprigged muslin in the window. "In here."

"That looks very ordinary." Chloe wrinkled her nose. "I much preferred the other shop—the one with the flame redingote."

"Yes, I'm sure you did. However, we are going in

here." A hand on the small of her back urged her through the door.

The modiste bustled out of a back room at the sound of the bell. Sharp black eyes examined Chloe and saw through the hideous, ill-fitting serge to the beauty beneath. She bowed to the gentleman, shrewdly assessing his worth. It was hard to tell. He was respectably dressed, the cloth of good quality, but there were no obvious signs of wealth—no jeweled pins or fobs, or even rings. But he was clearly a man whose tastes ran to the very young when it came to setting up a mistress. Although this very young lady was a diamond of the first water.

Smiling, Madame Letty asked how she could be of service. Her smile became calculating as the gentleman explained that to start with, his ward required a riding habit and at least two afternoon dresses.

"Suitable for a debutante?" she inquired, nodding with satisfaction. This promised to be a lucrative transaction. Guardians did not normally accompany their wards shopping, but the nature of the relationship made no difference to profits.

"Exactly so." Hugo had a fair idea of the construction the modiste had put on her customers, but so long as she knew her job, she could think what she pleased.

Madame Letty called sharply, and a girl of about thirteen came into the shop. She curtsied, twisting her work-reddened hands, keeping her eyes down. At her employer's instruction she fetched gowns from the back room, laying them out for the customers' inspection.

Chloe was unimpressed. The afternoon gowns were all of sprigged muslin or cambric, demurely cut, trimmed with lace. Something caught her eye on a rack in the corner of the room. Abandoning the display, she wandered over to the rack and pulled out a gown of peacock-blue taffeta, lavishly adorned with silver thread.

"This is lovely." She held it up in front of her. "Isn't it the most beautiful gown?" Her hands caressed the material. "I love the way it shines in the light."

Hugo winced and Madame Letty cleared her throat. The little maidservant covered her mouth with her hand to hide a grin.

"I think Miss would be more comfortable in muslin," Madame said.

"Oh, no, I don't want any of those boring dresses," Chloe declared with a dismissive gesture at the previous offerings. "I like this. I want something that stands out."

"Well, you'd certainly stand out in that," Hugo said.

"May I try it on?"

The modiste looked in appeal at the gentleman, who nodded infinitesimally. With obvious reluctance she gestured to a fitting room. "If Miss would like to come this way, Mary will help you."

Hugo sat down on a couch and waited for the apparition to appear. He had the faint hope that once Chloe saw for herself how ridiculous she would look in a dress made to appeal to the pretentions of a high-class whore, the issue would resolve itself.

The hope was not realized. Chloe emerged from a dressing room, beaming, rustling across the floor toward him. "Isn't it lovely? I feel so grand." She twirled before the cheval glass. "It's a little big, but I'm sure it could be altered." She adjusted the neckline of the décolletage with a tiny frown. "It does reveal rather a lot though, doesn't it?"

"Far too much," Hugo declared.

"I could always wear a fichu," she said cheerfully. "I'm going to have this gown. Oh, and you know what will look beautiful with it, that tulle hat we saw in the milliner's down the road."

Hugo closed his eyes and prayed for strength. "That hat would make you look like a squashed pumpkin. It's far too big for your face."

Chloe looked dismayed. "I'm sure it wouldn't. How can you know until I try it on?"

Hugo had somehow assumed that women were born with a dress sense as they were born with ten fingers and ten toes. But apparently it was an acquired talent . . . one that had not been acquired by this practically motherless child who'd grown up behind the high walls of a seminary, smothered in brown serge.

The situation required drastic measures. He stood up. "Would you excuse us for a minute?" he said to Madame Letty. "I'd like a word in private with my ward."

The modiste hustled the maidservant out of the room and Hugo took a deep breath. Chloe was regarding him with an air of earnest inquiry.

He came over to her, took her by the shoulders, and turned her to face her image in the mirror. "Now, listen to me, lass. This gown is made for a woman who lives on Quay Street."

"What kind of women live on Quay Street?" She frowned at him in the glass.

"Whores," he said succinctly. Her eyes widened. "Look at yourself." Reaching around, he plucked at the loose neckline. His arm brushed her breast and he drew a sharp breath but doggedly continued. "To wear a dress like this, you need to be rather more lavishly endowed than you are. You also need to paint your face, wear a great deal of trumpery jewelry, and be at least ten years older than you are."

Her face fell. "Don't you like it?"

"That's an understatement. It's an utterly tasteless garment and makes you look ridiculous." Brutal, but he adjudged it necessary.

She bit her lip, tilting her head as she examined herself in the mirror. "It would look better with the right shoes and hat."

Hugo closed his eyes on another fervent prayer. He rested his hands lightly on her shoulders. "If I can't convince you, Chloe, then I'm going to exercise a guardian's right of command."

"You mean I may not have it?" Her chin went up and her eyes darkened with anger.

"That's exactly what I mean." He began swiftly to unhook her. "Try on one of the others and I'm sure you'll see how much prettier you look."

"I don't like the others," she said flatly. "I want to look different, not ordinary."

"My dear girl, there is not the slightest possibility that you could ever look ordinary," he said with conviction.

She continued to look at him in the mirror, assessing the strength of his determination as she had in the stable the previous night. But this time she had no master card up her sleeve.

"I am resolved, lass," he said softly. "Looking daggers at me isn't going to change anything."

He turned to the gowns over the chair, sorting swiftly through them. "This one goes with your eyes," he cajoled, holding up a sprigged muslin gown with a cornflower-blue sash and blue ribbons.

"It's so demure," Chloe muttered.

"It's so suitable," he retorted, and called the modiste. "Miss Gresham will try this gown."

With as good a grace as she could muster, Chloe submitted to being divested of the peacock-blue taffeta and buttoned into the muslin. Madame Letty tied the sash around the slender waist and stood back with a smile.

"Beautiful," she said. "Mary, fetch that chip straw hat, the one with the matching ribbons. It will look exquisite."

Chloe was unconvinced and rather glumly stepped out of the dressing room to show her guardian.

A slow smile spread across Hugo's face as he examined her. "Come here." He beckoned her and turned her to face the mirror again. "Now, that, lass, is a vision to delight the most jaded eye."

"Is it?" Chloe looked longingly toward the glitter of the discarded taffeta.

"Trust me."

When they left Madame Letty's an hour later, Chloe possessed three gowns, a velvet cloak, the chip straw hat and a well-cut but unexciting riding habit of dark blue broadcloth. Hugo had allowed her a tricorn hat with a silver plume to go with the habit, but otherwise had ruled the selection with an iron hand. Chloe was quiet as they walked back to the George and Dragon, and Hugo tried to think of something to make up for her disappointment.

Suddenly, Chloe was gone from his side. With a shout of outrage she darted into the road, dodging in front of a curricle driven tandem by a young blood in a caped driving coat with a dozen whip points thrust into the buttonholes.

His leader reared, snorting, as Chloe ducked, jumped sideways, and plunged into the center of the traffic-filled thoroughfare.

Hugo, without looking at the driver, seized the leader's harness, holding his thrashing head as he stared across the street anxiously for some sign of Chloe. The young man filled the air with profanity.

"For God's sake, man, stop swearing and look to your horses," Hugo said impatiently, his eyes still searching the gathering throng for Chloe, even as he continued to hold the horse.

Without responding, the driver cracked his whip, catching the leader's ear. The horse leapt forward and

Hugo jumped aside just in time. At the same instant he recognized the stolid features and flat brown eyes of the curricle's driver. Chloe had run in front of Crispin Belmont's horses.

He watched the curricle's plunging progress up the steep street at the behest of its evil-tempered driver. Maybe not Jasper's son by birth, but certainly by temperament. A small crowd had gathered on the opposite side of the road, voices raised in fervent argument. With considerable foreboding Hugo crossed the street and pushed through the crowd.

Foreboding was justified. Chloe bore no resemblance to the disconsolate girl of the dress shop. A diminutive firebrand, she was violently berating a large man sitting on the driver's seat of a cart filled with turnips.

Hugo took one look at the horse between the shafts and understood. The sorry-looking animal hung its head, its hide ridged with scars from old weals, blood streaking from fresh whip cuts, its ribs painfully visible, its chest heaving as it struggled to gather strength for the rest of its uphill journey.

"Brute! I'll have you taken up by the magistrates," Chloe yelled. Her hands, unbuckling the animal's harness, were deftly efficient despite her fury. "You should be pilloried!" She released the bit and launched a new tirade at the condition of the animal's mouth, cut by the cruel curb.

The turnip seller jumped from his cart with surprising agility for such a large man. "What the 'ell d'ye think you're doin'?" He grabbed Chloe's arm. She spun around like a top and kicked him in the groin.

The crowd gasped as the man doubled over as if the air had been punched from his body. Chloe turned back to the horse, unbuckling the girth.

"Chloe!" Hugo called out sharply.

She looked up impatiently, and he could see that

nothing concerned her at the moment but the horse. She was oblivious of herself, of the impression she might be making, of the gawking crowd. "Give this man some money," she said. "I'm taking his horse. Even though he's used the poor beast so dreadfully, it wouldn't be just to take it without compensation."

"You expect me—"

"Yes, I do," she fired back. "Not your money—mine!" She had finally released the animal and now led him out of the shafts, her hand stroking the hollow neck. The crowd fell back as the animal's owner tried to straighten from his agonized crouch.

"You take my 'orse and I'll—" He gave up, gasping. The crowd began to mutter, sympathy for one of their own replacing curiosity.

Swiftly, Hugo dug into his pocket and tossed two gold sovereigns to the ground between the man's feet. The decrepit animal didn't look as if it would last the night, but the crowd would be on the side of the horse's owner and he had to get Chloe away in one piece.

"Move!" he commanded under his breath.

Chloe seemed to take the point and hauled her piti-able prize through the crowd while they were still react-ing to the sovereigns.

"Thank you," she said somewhat belatedly as they reached the far side of the street.

"Oh, don't thank me," he responded with an ironical quirk of an eyebrow. "As I recall, it was *your* money."

"What's the point of having it if you can't use it for what you want?" she demanded, one hand gently strok-ing the horse's neck.

Like taffeta gowns and tulle hats, Hugo thought. The pathetic, maltreated beast seemed a fair exchange for the whore's dress. However, he wasn't sure he ever wanted to spend another such day. His zealously unpredictable ward was an exhausting companion. And he still hadn't made contact with a decent drink.

However, he was not prepared to linger in the George and Dragon while she found something else to engage her attention in this city full of unrest and potential victims. Unrefreshed, he hurried Chloe and the turnip seller's liberated nag homeward.

Chapter 6

"WHERE'S DANTE?" Chloe slipped from her pony in the courtyard and looked around, frowning. The dog's absence was conspicuous. It was inconceivable that he wouldn't have come rushing to greet her.

Hugo dismounted and yelled for Billy. The lad appeared from the direction of the kennels, swinging an empty pail. He set the pail down and came toward them, rather less lethargically than usual.

"I was feedin' the dogs, sir." He tugged a forelock and then stared in unabashed disgust at the turnip seller's nag. "What's that?"

"You may well ask," Hugo said. "Where's Miss Gresham's dog?"

Billy scratched his head. "Well, I don't rightly know." He gestured to the pump. "I 'ad 'im fastened over yonder. But 'e up an' went when I went for me dinner."

"Did he break the rope?"

Billy shook his head. "Don't look like it, sir. Rope looks like it's gone an' untied itself."

"Don't be ridiculous!" Chloe stalked across to the pump. The rope was not frayed or broken. "You must have tied him insecurely."

"He'll be back, lass," Hugo said, seeing her expression. "How long's he been gone, Billy?"

" 'Bout an hour, I reckon, sir."

"He's chasing rabbits in the wood, I'll lay odds," Hugo reassured her. "He'll be back covered in mud and starving as soon as it gets dark."

Chloe frowned unhappily. "I'll look for him when I've seen to Rosinante."

"You've christened that sorry beast Rosinante?" Hugo gave a shout of laughter. "You absurd creature."

"Rosinante was a fairly sorry animal," Chloe retorted. "Anyway, I've always liked the name. And he'll grow into it, won't you?" She scratched between the ears of the nag's hanging head. "Billy, I want you to make up a bran mash. I'm going to do something about his cuts."

Hugo turned toward the house, inquiring with a degree of curiosity, "By the by, what name does the parrot rejoice in?"

"Falstaff," she said promptly. "I'm sure he's had a thoroughly dissolute life."

Chuckling, Hugo went inside.

Chloe bathed Rosinante's wounds, fed him warm bran mash, and installed him in a stable with a lavish supply of hay.

"I'm going to look for Dante," she said, entering the kitchen. "It's getting dark."

Hugo, gratefully ensconced before a bottle of burgundy, squashed the uncomfortable conviction that he ought to abandon his wine and accompany her himself.

"Take Billy with you, since it's largely his responsibility."

"What if I don't find him?" Her eyes were purple.

"I'll go out with you after dinner," he promised. "But be back here in half an hour."

Chloe returned punctually but empty-handed and sat miserably at the table, picking at the laden plate Samuel put in front of her.

"Summat wrong wi' it?" he demanded roughly.

She shook her head. "No, I'm sorry . . . I'm not hungry."

"That's a first," Samuel remarked to no one in particular.

"Have some wine." Hugo filled her glass. "And eat your dinner. You only think you're not hungry."

Chloe chewed a mouthful of chicken. It tasted like sawdust. She drank her wine with rather more enthusiasm and by the second glass was beginning to feel more cheerful. Dante was a young, healthy dog who hadn't had too many opportunities to roam the countryside, chasing up scents.

"Wretched animal!" she exclaimed crossly, and attacked her dinner. There was no point going hungry because the exasperating creature was doing what dogs, given half a chance, did.

"That's better," Hugo approved. "What are you going to do with him when he does decide to return?"

"Nothing," Chloe said. "What could I do? He doesn't know he's doing anything wrong . . . in fact, he's not. He's just being a dog."

But the knowledge that Dante would never choose to spend this amount of time away from her obtruded through wine-induced buoyancy.

By midnight she was distraught and Hugo at point non plus. All three of them had stumbled across fields by the light of an oil lantern, trod cautiously through the tinder-dry wood, and called until they were hoarse.

"Go to bed, lass." Hugo leaned wearily against the kitchen door to close it. "He'll be outside in the morning, a picture of penitence."

"You don't know him," she said, the catch in her voice accentuated by unshed tears.

But Hugo had formed a pretty fair impression of Dante and didn't believe for one minute that his continued absence from his beloved owner's side was voluntary. However, he strove to keep that from Chloe.

"It's time you were in bed," he said again. "There's nothing more to be done tonight."

"But how can I sleep?" she cried, pacing the kitchen.

"Supposing he's hurt . . . in a trap . . ." She covered her face with her hands as if to block out the images of Dante in agony.

" 'Ot milk and brandy," Samuel declared, setting the oil lamp on the table. "That'll send 'er off like a babby."

"Heat some milk, then," Hugo said. He took Chloe's shoulders and spoke with calm authority. "Go upstairs and get ready for bed. I'll bring you up something to help you sleep in a minute. Go on." He turned her with a brisk pat on the behind. "You can do Dante no good by pacing the floor all night."

There was sense in that, and she was bone-weary. It had been a long and exhausting day after a disturbed night. Chloe dragged herself upstairs. She put on her nightgown and sat beside the hat box, trying to take comfort from the contentment of Beatrice and her now-much-prettier offspring.

Downstairs, Hugo contemplated lacing the milk with laudanum rather than brandy. But then he thought of Elizabeth, slipping into addiction. Maybe such tendencies could be passed on. He slurped a liberal dose of brandy into the beaker Samuel filled with milk and took it upstairs.

He tapped lightly on the door to the corner room and went in. Chloe was sitting on the floor. She looked up as he entered, her eyes huge in her white face. He remembered how young she was, but he also remembered fourteen-year-old midshipmen who'd witnessed death and suffered agonizing deaths of their own under his command. Seventeen was mature enough to handle the emotional stresses of a missing dog.

"Into bed, lass." He put the beaker on the table beside the bed. "In the morning, you'll be able to deal with it."

She didn't argue. "It's not knowing, that's all," she said, scrambling to her feet. "I could accept his death

. . . I just find it hard to think of him suffering alone somewhere." She pushed her hair away from her face and regarded him seriously. "You mustn't think that I count the suffering of a dog above the suffering of people. But I do love Dante."

Perfectly mature enough to handle the emotional stresses of a missing dog . . . and some. Without conscious thought, he put his arms around her and she hugged his waist fiercely, her head resting against his chest. He cupped her chin in the palm of his hand and turned her face up, lowering his head.

He had intended an avuncular kiss on the brow, or perhaps the tip of her nose. But instead he kissed her mouth. All might still have been well if it had been a light brushing of lips. But as his lips met hers, a heady, intoxicating rush of blood surged through his veins, driving all else from his mind but the warmth of her skin through the thin shift, the delicate curve of her body in his arms, the press of her breasts against his chest. His hold tightened as he possessed her mouth with a fervent urgency and she responded, her lips opening for the probing tongue, her arms gripping his waist. Her scent of lavender and clover honey engulfed him, tinged now with the spice of arousal . . . and for too long he yielded to the intoxication, exploring her mouth, encouraging her own tentative exploration, his hands sliding to her bottom, kneading the firm flesh, clamping her to the rising shaft of his body.

Too long he yielded to temptation, and when reality finally broke into entrancement, he pushed her from him with a roughness that could almost have been engendered by revulsion. For a moment he took in her swollen, kiss-reddened lips, her tousled hair, the excitement in her eyes, now the color of a midnight sky. With a soft execration he turned from her and left the room.

Chloe touched her lips wonderingly. Her heart was

pounding, her skin damp; her hands trembled. She could feel the imprint of his body on hers, his hands pressing her against him. And she was on fire, a surging maelstrom of emotions and sensations that as yet she had no name for.

Dazed, she picked up the beaker of cooling milk and drank it down, the brandy curling in a hot wave in the pit of her stomach, bringing insidious relaxation to her already heavy limbs. She blew out the candle and climbed into bed, pulling the sheet up to her chin, lying still and flat on her back, staring up into the moonlit dimness, waiting for the fire to die down, for some words to come to mind that would make sense of what she was feeling . . . of what had just happened to her.

Hugo walked slowly downstairs, cursing himself. How had he allowed himself such a piece of flagrant self-indulgence? And the memory of her eager response lashed at him even further. He was her guardian, a man she trusted. She lived under his roof, subject to his authority, and he'd taken shameless advantage of his position and her innocence.

Samuel looked up as Hugo entered the kitchen, watched as he swept up the brandy bottle from the table, and left again, the door banging shut behind him. Samuel recognized the signs, and sighed. Something had happened to send him into one of his black tempers, from which sometimes he wouldn't emerge for days.

Music drifted in from the library. Samuel listened, recognizing Beethoven's strong chords. Anger was the driving force at the moment. When the bleak despair was on him, Hugo played the most desolate passages of Mozart or Haydn. Samuel preferred the anger—recovery was usually speedier.

The library was beneath Chloe's bedchamber, and the strains of the pianoforte came clearly through her open window. She'd heard him playing the night before, a haunting melody that couldn't drown out Dante's howls. The power of this music would drown groans from hell. A wave of sleepiness broke over her, and she turned over, pulling the sheet over her head.

She didn't know how long she slept, but something brought her awake and upright in the same movement. The music had stopped and the night seemed blacker. She sat unmoving, straining her ears to catch the sound that had awakened her. Then she heard it again. It was faint but unmistakable. A dog was barking frantically.

"Dante," she whispered. She jumped out of bed and ran to the window. She listened, trying to pinpoint the direction of the frenzied barking. Her room faced the front of the house and the side opposite to the courtyard, but if she craned her neck she could see the gravel driveway winding down to the road. The sound was coming from somewhere along the driveway. But why? He must be hurt, or stuck.

She ran from the room, her bare feet making no sound on the wooden floor, down the staircase, and across the hall. She stubbed her toe on an uneven flagstone and her cry of pain, hastily bitten back, sounded loud in the creaking quiet of the house.

She listened, but to her relief it seemed that she hadn't awakened anyone. Dante had already caused enough upheaval without dragging the two reluctant men from their beds at dead of night.

She opened the door quietly and slipped outside, pulling it to gently behind her. Clouds had come up and the stars were now mostly hidden, making the night much blacker than it had been. She wondered what time it was, wishing she'd thought to look at the clock in the hall.

An owl hooted and there was a sudden screech of a

small animal's terror and pain. But the barking had ceased.

Chloe knew she hadn't imagined it. She ran lightly down the steps to the courtyard, the cobblestones cold beneath her feet. A breeze stirred, freshened with the coming of dawn, and she shivered as it pressed her nightgown to her body. She hesitated, thinking of the overcoat behind the kitchen door. But when she heard a faint yelping on the breeze, she forgot the cold and ran down the driveway, heedless of the gravel pricking the soles of her feet.

Hugo had heard her cry from the hall, but it took many minutes to penetrate the brandy stupor he had finally achieved as he sat slumped over the keyboard, a candle guttering beside him.

He raised his head, blinking fuzzily, listening, but there were only the usual night creaks of the sleeping house. He shook his head and let it drop onto his folded arm again; one finger of his free hand began picking out the melody of a piece by Scarlatti. But slowly, a prickle of unease penetrated his semi-conscious trance. He raised his head again, listening. There was still no sound, but he had the unmistakable conviction that something was missing from the house.

Chloe? She was sound asleep above him, knocked out by brandy and milk and physical and emotional exhaustion. His head dropped and then lifted again. He pushed himself off the bench and stood for a second swaying as he tried to marshal his senses. He'd go upstairs and satisfy himself that she was asleep in her bed and then perhaps he'd be able to pass out in his own bed.

Staggering slightly, he negotiated the obstacles in the library and stepped into the hall. A gust of wind blew the unlatched front door open, and he blinked at it, puzzled. Then the puzzlement left him and his head cleared somewhat.

Chloe again! Presumably, she'd gone out in search of that damned mongrel—wandering around the countryside all alone in the dead of night. Hadn't she the faintest sense of self-preservation? It was a relief to turn his anger on someone outside himself, and a relief to recast her in the image of a stubborn, exasperating schoolgirl with a proclivity for scrapes that urgently required curbing.

He strode to the door, his step becoming firmer with each one as the brandy fumes cleared. He stared down into the shadows of the courtyard. There was no sign of her. He couldn't guess how long it had been since he'd heard the first alerting noise. It could have been anything from five minutes to twenty—brandy played merry hell with a man's sense of time.

Then he heard a dog's bark, faint but frenzied, coming from the direction of the bottom of the driveway. It explained Chloe's expedition, although it didn't excuse its recklessness. Why the hell hadn't she called him?

He set off down the drive, following the sound. The trees lining the driveway formed an archway, blocking out what little moonlight the intermittent clouds let through. He peered ahead, trying to catch the sounds of her footsteps or the glimmer of her shape. The barking grew closer and the frenzied note was even more pronounced. The dog must be trapped somewhere. He increased his speed, thankful that he knew the twists and turns of the drive like the back of his hand.

He called her name several times, but there was no reply. Presumably, intent on listening to Dante's barking, she had ears for nothing else. He emerged from the avenue of trees at the bottom of the drive and then the barking ceased. A sense of foreboding sent a chill through his gut. Without knowing why, he began to run toward the crumbling stone gateposts. As he reached them, a scream, abruptly cut off, shivered on the air.

He hurtled onto the narrow lane outside his estate. Frantically, he gazed up and down the lane as a crescendo of barks deafened the night. He could make out a group of moving shadows a hundred yards down the lane. An agonized yelp interrupted the barking and the shadows wreathed in some kind of frenetic dance. The indecisive moon chose that moment to emerge, and the knives in their belts glinted.

It had to be Jasper, there was no other explanation. And then he had but one thought as he veered sideways into the undergrowth: He had no weapon. And whatever was going on, it was violent and one unarmed man would be no match for the three shapes he could make out. Three . . . no four. But the fourth was on the ground, a shapeless bundle wrapped in something.

Somehow, he had to separate them. One he could take on, but no more. He could hear their voices now and Dante's alternate barks and yelps. Then he heard Chloe's voice as furious as she had been that afternoon with the turnip seller. She was yelling at them to leave her dog alone. He couldn't see so could only guess that she'd somehow freed herself from her wrappings. Praying that she'd have the strength to distract them for a few moments longer, he crept on his belly until he was alongside the scene.

Dante caught his scent and began another frantic whirligig at the end of the rope that Hugo now saw bound him. Someone swore and turned on the dog, a knife lifted.

Chloe hurled herself across the lane and grabbed his arm, her teeth sinking into his hand. The knife clattered to the ground, six inches from Hugo.

He had it in his hand while the other two men were grappling with Chloe, flinging a blanket over her head, struggling to restrain her wildly thrashing limbs in the suffocating folds. Hugo sliced through the rope holding

Dante, and the dog leapt for the throat of one of the men holding Chloe. He went down with a shrill scream of terror.

One down, one unarmed. Hugo sprang for the third man's back. His knife sank into his shoulder. The man spun around, a look of total surprise on his face, his hand flying to his shoulder. Hugo reached forward and yanked his knife out of his belt.

He had no way of telling whether he had disarmed his opponents or whether one of them might produce a pistol. Either way, he was still one against three, and the odds, even with Dante, were not good enough to stay around and ask questions. Surprise was his last card.

Chloe was still struggling with the blanket, and he simply picked her up, maneuvered her slight weight over his shoulder, and again dived sideways into the undergrowth. He had no desire to present a running target for a pistol shot, and he had a boyhood's knowledge of the rough terrain.

Dante crashed through the bushes at his side and Hugo was capable of one grateful prayer that this time the dog didn't consider him the enemy, for all his rough handling of his mistress.

Chloe had the sense to lie still despite her shock and the violently jolting progress. Her head and arms were still buried in the stuffy folds of the blanket and she'd seen nothing of what had happened. But she knew who held her and she could hear Dante, so she lay limp and tried not to sneeze.

There were no sounds of pursuit. Hugo slowed as they broke through the underbrush onto the driveway of Denholm Manor. Chloe struggled, trying to bring her imprisoned arms up to free her head.

"Keep still." It was a curt instruction and she opened her mouth to respond, but the words were lost in a hairy mouthful of blanket. She sneezed violently.

Hugo used a word she'd never heard before and increased his pace. Until they were safely behind his own locked door, he wasn't prepared to stop to unravel her.

Dante, tail waving furiously, bounded up the steps into the house, his exuberance clearly unaffected by his recent ordeal. Hugo slammed the door behind him and threw the heavy iron bolt that he rarely used. He carried Chloe into the library. Only then did he set her on her feet and pull the swaddling blanket away from her.

"Who was it?" she said. "Why would anyone want to kidnap Dante? Do you think they thought he was valuable . . . I know he's unusual, but . . ."

For a minute Hugo was taken aback. She hadn't seen herself as the target of the attack. But then, why should she? She had almost no sense of self-importance, and it probably made better sense to her that her adored dog should be coveted than that anyone should have designs on herself.

Her face was pink and hot, strands of hair sticking to her cheeks, her eyes wide with a curious wonder rather than fear. She tossed her hair back and sneezed again. Hugo's heart turned over. She'd suffered enough rejection in her lonely life without being told that her family intended her harm . . . that she was of value to her kin only in terms of her fortune. Desperately, he resisted the urge to bundle her into his arms.

"I have not the slightest idea why anyone should be mad enough to want that ridiculous animal," he exploded. "For God's sake, just look at you! You've been told once about running around loose in nothing but your nightgown. And where the hell are your shoes? You'll catch your death of cold! And what the devil did you think you were doing anyway? Why didn't you call me when you heard Dante barking?"

At the sound of his name, Dante pricked up his ears. His tail thumped.

Chloe could never later analyze why she did what she did next. Earlier in the evening Hugo had awakened her from the chrysalis of her girlhood. Then she had been assaulted and terrorized, rage and fear coursing through her. And then she'd been rescued as suddenly and as violently as she'd been attacked. It seemed to her now that nothing ordinary could ever happen to her again.

Following blind instinct, she flung her arms around Hugo's waist and looked up at him, her head on his chest, her eyes dark with emotion. "Please don't be vexed," she begged, the catch in her voice as richly sensual as anything he had ever heard. *"Please,* Hugo."

The last tenuous thread of his resistance snapped. His arms went around her; a cupped palm molded the curve of her cheek. "I'm not vexed," he murmured, adding almost as a prayer. "I wish to God I were."

"Kiss me." She stood on tiptoe, reaching her arms around his neck, her small hands cupping his scalp, pulling his head down to her.

Hugo inhaled sharply at the soft yet insistent command, and all the preconceptions of his universe tilted as her lips locked onto his with a hungry assurance that had no place in the world of seminaries. She tasted of milk and brandy, of innocence and experience, and her body in his hands was soft and sinuous, hard and determined by turns.

He moved a hand to her breast, closing over the soft mound, his thumb stroking the hard bud of the nipple beneath her shift. She shuddered against him and her mouth opened to him, her body arching as she thrust her breast against his palm.

Chloe was adrift, storm-tossed on a wild sea of sensation. It was as it had been earlier, with that first kiss, and this time she was determined not to lose the sensation, but to follow the path to its end. Her mind held no sway over her responses as she drank greedily of his tastes and drew in the powerful male scents of his body.

He lifted her against him, his mouth still joined to hers, and placed her on the couch, coming down with her. Her nightgown rode high on her thighs. Impatiently, he pushed it to her waist, bending to kiss her belly, to curl his fingers in the silky fleece at the apex of her thighs.

Chloe cried out softly as he parted the fleece and found the core of her sensitivity. She was aware only of a wild excitement, of delight swirling and raging through her veins.

He slipped one hand beneath her, lifting her as he pulled the nightgown over her head, letting her fall back naked on the faded velvet cushions. She shifted on the cushions, her eyes half closed, glorying in the feel of her nakedness, in the pulsing stimulation of arousal.

Her arms lifted to him and he came down on top of her, his mouth closing again over hers as their tongues warred, danced, plunged in a wild spiral of passion that excluded all but the urgency of desire. Her legs curled around him, pressing her opened body instinctively against the erect shaft rising against his britches. With the same instinct her tongue darted, dancing in the corner of his mouth, running over his lips in a tingling, tantalizing caress.

Hugo tugged at the waistband of his britches, and her hands were helping him, pushing the restraining garment off his hips, then running in greedy exploration beneath his shirt, over the narrow hips, enclosing the burning, throbbing root that lifted to her touch.

There was a moment when he paused on the threshold of her eagerly welcoming body, a vague sense of unease hovering at the edges of passion. He looked down at her. Her eyes were closed, her face lost in joy. Then the thick golden eyelashes swept up, and her eyes like a midnight sky carried both appeal and a passion that matched his own.

"Please," she whispered, lifting her hand to touch his mouth.

Delicately, he guided himself within the moist, tender portal. He checked when he sensed the resistance of her maidenhead, and his muscles strained under the effort of will. But her hands went to his buttocks, gripping with urgent demand, and he yielded with a soft exhalation of release. For a second Chloe couldn't breathe as a taut fullness stretched her body, and then it gave way and her low cry was more a sigh of relief than a cry of pain.

Hugo touched the corner of her mouth, stroked her damp temples, moved his hand to her breast, sliding his thumb over the pliant, responsive peak. He felt her relax, supple and open, and he eased deeper.

Pleasure raced through her from one nerve ending to another. She began to move with him, reveling in the joy of fusion. The bud of joy began to blossom, her muscles tightened in expectation of she knew not what. Then he withdrew to the very edge of her body and she lay beneath him, taut as a bowstring. He smiled down at her, knowing how she felt, knowing how close she was to fulfillment. With great deliberation he drove to the very center of her self and the bud burst into full flower.

It was a long time before she moved beneath him, shifting on the cushions as the liquid dissolution of muscle and sinew faded and she came back to a sense of herself and the world around her. Hugo's body was heavy on hers, his head turned away from her on the cushions. She touched his back, where his shirt clung damply to his skin, feeling suddenly shy.

Slowly, Hugo sat up. He looked at her face in silence, a devastated look in his eyes that terrified her. She opened her mouth to say something . . . anything to break the silence. But the words were stillborn under that brooding green gaze. Instead, she tried to smile.

Hugo rose to his feet. He stood beside the couch, staring down at her. He saw the wanton sprawl of her naked body—the pose of a body that a man has just left. He saw the smile—the seductive smile of a lover. Her voice was still in his ears, demanding her fulfillment. He could feel her hands on his own skin, arousing, tantalizing, insistent. He saw a girl whose trust he'd violated as surely as he'd violated her innocence, but he also saw a seductress—a woman who'd had no doubt about the power of her beauty or of how to use that power.

Thoughts and images tumbled in his head. He could see Elizabeth in her daughter, but Elizabeth had had no passion, no hungers. She had been as pure and fragile as crystal despite her husband's attempts to sully her purity.

But Elizabeth's daughter was also Stephen's daughter. A man of passions and deep hungers. And it seemed to Hugo, looking at the abandonment of the woman he'd just initiated, that her father's passions and hungers ran as deeply and as virulently in the daughter.

God help him, but she would have enjoyed the crypt.

The unbidden, loathsome thought brought bile to his mouth, and black spots danced before his eyes. He snatched up her discarded nightgown. "Cover yourself."

The rasping command was so shocking after the silence that Chloe made no attempt to take the garment from him. She lay unmoving, gazing up at him, dismay chasing the soft glow from the blue depths of her eyes.

Hugo dropped the shift on her belly. "Cover yourself!" he repeated. "And then go upstairs to your room." He turned from her, pulling up his britches with shaking hands.

In shock and disbelief Chloe sat up, swinging her legs

over the side of the couch. Then she just sat there, holding her nightgown on her knees, too stunned to move.

Hugo spun around. "Did you hear what I said?" Roughly, he pulled her to her feet. "I told you to put this on." He picked up her nightgown, dropped it over her head, and pushed her arms into the sleeves. "Now go up to your room."

"I don't understand," she whispered, crossing her arms and hugging her breasts. "What have I done?" She quailed before the look in his eyes, where vipers of rage and disgust darted at her.

"Get out! *Now.*"

She ran from the room, Dante at her heels.

Hugo stood staring into the empty hearth, his mind skittering. Perhaps it hadn't happened . . . perhaps in a brandy trance he had dreamed it. Brandy played such tricks sometimes, so that one didn't always know what was true and what was fantasy.

But denial was a child's trick to escape consequences, and after a minute he went to close the door Chloe had left open. He glanced sideways at the couch. There was a dark stain on the faded velvet cushion where she'd been lying.

He sat down at the pianoforte, staring bleakly out at the dawn breaking beyond the window. Chloe had not been responsible. Her seductive behavior had been that of a young girl trying her wings. She *didn't* know her own power any more than she knew not to yield to swirling emotions and hungers she'd never before encountered. It had been his responsibility to provide the control. A sharp snub would have finished the business once and for all . . . Instead . . .

Hugo picked up the brandy bottle and hurled it against the paneled wall.

Chapter 7

"How, in the name of goodness, could three able-bodied idiots fail to lay hands on a seventeen-year-old chit?"

Jasper Gresham stared in disbelief at the three men huddled in the dawn chill of the stable yard at Gresham Hall.

"It weren't our fault, sir." Jethro Grant, the only man still standing upright, spoke now for his wounded companions. "It was that dog from 'ell, bit Jake clean through 'is arm; and we wasn't expectin' no man with a knife on the road neither." A truculent note entered his voice. "You didn't say as 'ow there'd be any guards on 'er, Sir Jasper. Ned's got a demmed great 'ole in 'is shoulder . . . beggin' your pardon, sir."

Jasper's eyes, unreadable, untouchable, slithered over the man facing him and Jethro shivered, cleared his throat, and his shoulders slumped a little.

"And whose knife did this mighty assailant use?" Jasper demanded quietly. "Don't make excuses for your incompetence. It was a simple enough task, and you botched it." He turned on his heel.

Jethro looked in panic at his wounded companions, then spoke up again, a slight shrillness to his voice. "Sir Jasper . . . sir, what about our purse? A guinea apiece, you promised."

Jasper spun around and Jethro shrank as the blank, shallow eyes seemed to flay him. "I pay for work done, not for the incompetence of a trio of fools. Get off my land."

"But sir . . . sir . . . Ned can't work with that hole in 'is shoulder, and there's kiddies to feed . . . six of 'em, sir, and another on the way."

"Get off my land, the lot of you, before I set the dogs on you!"

"Oh, Jasper, is that quite fair?" The hesitant question came from a woman wrapped in a shawl, standing to one side of the stableyard.

"Are you questioning my judgment, madam?"

Louise Gresham's rare moment of courage died as her husband looked through her. "No . . . no, of course not, sir. I wouldn't do such a thing . . . it was only—" She fell silent.

"Only what, my dear?"

She shook her head abjectly. "Nothing . . . nothing at all."

"You will catch cold out here, my dear. I'm sure you must have business to attend to in the house." His voice was silky but the command was no less clear. Louise scuttled out of the yard, averting her eyes from the three men she had tried to champion.

"Crispin, see them off the premises."

"Certainly, sir." As his stepfather walked away, Crispin pushed himself away from the wall against which he'd been lounging. He strolled into the tack room and returned, carrying a heavy whip. His eyes gleamed with amusement as the three would-be kidnappers stumbled in terror toward the gate out of the yard. He pursued them lazily, cracking the whip at their heels until they had reached the end of the long drive and stood beyond the gateposts.

"Good day, gentlemen," he said with a mocking bow, then retraced his steps, absently kicking the gravel over the blood so untidily shed by the wounded men.

His mother appeared out of the shadows as he entered the house. She thrust a handful of coins at him and spoke in a scared whisper. "Crispin, you must give this to those men. Ned's wife is about to have another baby, and if he can't work, there'll be no food. . . ."

"Don't be so soft, Mother." Crispin glanced at the small pile of coins, guessing how long it had taken his mother to amass this pathetic sum from the pin money she managed to beg from her husband when in the direst necessity. He took her hand and dropped the coins into her palm. "If Sir Jasper discovers you're trying to meddle—"

"Crispin, you mustn't tell him!" Her hands flew to her worn cheeks and she looked in terror at her son.

Crispin shook his head with a dismissive contempt and stalked toward the breakfast parlor, where he would find his stepfather.

Louise stared after him and tried to remember her son in the days when he'd been a loving little boy . . . in the days before he'd come to regard his mother through the harsh, derisive eyes of his stepfather. And not just his mother, she thought, turning to go upstairs. And not just the women they took to the crypt. The whole female sex it seemed. Poor little Chloe. She'd been such a bright, lively child despite her mother's illness and neglect. How long would it take Jasper and Crispin to break her too?

It didn't occur to Louise for one minute that her husband and son would fail in their plans for Elizabeth's daughter. Jasper wasn't going to be put off by one setback.

"Dog's come back, then," Samuel observed, lifting a steaming kettle off the fire as Hugo entered the kitchen. The back door stood open, filling the room with the brilliant sunlight of mid-morning.

Hugo winced at the dazzle and ran his hands through his hair. "Where is he?"

"Miss took him outside for a walk." Samuel glanced shrewdly at his employer and added an extra spoonful of coffee to the jug before pouring boiling water on the grounds.

Hugo swore and strode to the door. "Hasn't she got a grain of common sense? Wandering all over the countryside after last night!"

"Don't suppose she's gone far." Samuel stirred the coffee. "Not in 'er nightgown and wi' no shoes." He poured a mug of the thick black aromatic liquid. "Anyways, what about last night?"

Hugo didn't immediately answer. He turned back to the room, demanding in exasperation, "You're not telling me she's gone outside again in her nightgown?"

"Dog was in a powerful 'urry," Samuel offered in explanation, pushing the mug across the table.

Hugo took it, cupping his hands around its warmth, inhaling deeply of its fragrance. It cleared his head. "Any strangers around here yesterday, while I was in Manchester?"

Samuel nodded. "A fellow wantin' casual work. 'E fixed the 'enhouse roof . . . did quite a decent job."

"Could he have taken the dog?"

Samuel's faded blue eyes sharpened with intelligence. "Reckon so, while young Billy was havin' 'is dinner."

Hugo told him the events of the night up to the moment when he'd thrown the bolt on the front door, his ward and the dog safely inside.

"Chloe's convinced they were after the dog, but I'm not so sure it's as simple as that," he concluded. He debated sharing with Samuel his suspicions of Jasper's involvement, but to do that he would have to reveal some of the hideous tangle of the past, and he couldn't face that.

"Until I can decide what's best to do, she'll have to be watched all the time . . . but don't make too much of it. I don't see any point alarming her unnecessarily."

Samuel's sharp eyes didn't waver. He heard much that was unspoken, but he was accustomed to Hugo's secrecy and knew better than to probe.

Hugo strode back to the door. As he looked impatiently out at the walled kitchen garden, an exuberant Dante came bounding from the orchard beyond, tail flying. Chloe followed the dog, the long skirts of the kitchen overcoat trailing in the grass.

At least she'd taken the point about wandering around in a skimpy nightgown. Hugo's eyes were riveted to her bare feet. They were the most beautiful feet, long and slender with high arches, straight pink toes, and lovely rosy heels. But then, one wouldn't expect perfection to be marred even by something as insignificant as feet. His head swam. Somehow he had to forget what had happened in his brandy-sodden trance. He had to compel Chloe to forget what had happened . . . or at least to put it behind her as an aberration stemming from the excitement and confusion of the night's events.

It would never happen again, and the greatest service he could do her now would be to kill in her whatever bud of passion awaited watering.

"In future, you are not to go outside without an escort," he snapped, standing aside as she came up to the door. "In fact, you're not to go farther than the courtyard without my permission. It's completely inappropriate for you to be roaming the countryside unescorted. You're not a milkmaid."

Whatever greeting she'd been intending died on her lips and she gazed up at him, such aching vulnerability in her eyes that his heart turned over. He continued with the same harshness. "And since that damn dog gets into trouble at the drop of a hat, you are to keep him with you at all times. If you can't control him, then he goes. Is it understood?"

Hurt and confusion stood out for a moment in her eyes, and then were abruptly replaced by a flash of defiant anger, and her firm, round chin tilted. "A puzzling volte-face, Sir Hugo, since only yesterday you were forbidding Dante the house. Or am I to be confined to the stable also?"

"If you continue in that vein, my child, you will discover I have a short way with insolence," he said with the softness that Chloe knew denoted danger.

"Dante will need exercise," she pointed out, standing her ground. "A two-year-old dog can't be kept indoors indefinitely."

"Samuel or Billy will take him for a decent walk once a day." Hugo turned away with a dismissive gesture that infuriated her as much as it hurt her.

"I also need more exercise than pacing around the courtyard," she fired back.

He swung back to her, his eyes narrowed. "I suggest you occupy yourself about the house, in that case. You've cast enough aspersions on its general state of cleanliness. I should imagine you'd be happy to kill two birds with one stone. I'm certain scrubbing and polishing will be sufficient exercise."

"I thought it wasn't a fit occupation for an heiress of eighty thousand pounds," she retorted, her voice shaking with fury. She had no idea why she was being targeted in this way any more than she understood why it had happened last night, but her spirit rebelled at the injustice and at this moment she couldn't imagine ever feeling anything more than dislike for her guardian.

"You may as well make yourself useful," he said, shrugging.

Blindly, Chloe picked up the nearest hard object,

which turned out to be the breadboard, and hurled it, bread and all, across the kitchen.

Hugo ducked sideways, but the missile had been unaimed and crashed against the wall with a resounding crack. The loaf had departed in flight and fell to the floor under Dante's nose. He sniffed at it, a long tongue drooling.

Chloe sprang for the hall door and Dante, abandoning his unexpected prize, charged after her. The door slammed on their departure. Samuel bent to pick up the bread. He examined it critically. "Bit 'ard on the lass, weren't you?" He dusted the loaf off on his apron. "What's she gone an' done to get the rough edge o' your tongue?"

"Mind your own business, damn you!" Hugo flung down his coffee mug. "Just make sure she keeps that dog with her as protection, and keep an eye on her." He stalked out of the kitchen.

Samuel heard his feet on the cellar steps. He scratched his nose, frowning. In the past fourteen years he'd stood beside Hugo Lattimer under cannon fire and musket shot. He'd watched the twenty-year-old lad grow into the wisdom and maturity of a victorious commander. And he'd sat with him through the bouts of black depression over the brandy bottle during every shore leave. He'd never known what caused the blackness, although he sensed the deep self-directed anger that fueled it.

He'd accepted the moods phlegmatically, secure in the knowledge that as soon as they hauled anchor, his friend would become again the cheerful, quick-thinking, authoritative commander, secure, too, in the belief that no young man of Hugo's character and abilities could live forever under such a bitter curse of self-contempt. Something would happen to repair the breaches in his soul.

But with the return to Denholm Manor, the depressions had become more frequent and intense. Again Samuel was vouchsafed no explanation, but he guessed that it was the proximity to the past that triggered them —that and the lack of purpose in Hugo's present existence. And the brandy merely exacerbated the misery. Patiently, he'd sat it out, trusting that something would happen to put things right.

Then the girl arrived. She was a bright, lively young thing with a streak of independence and determination that would require firm handling. Samuel had hoped she'd be just the thing to take Sir Hugo's mind off his troubles.

Now Samuel was beginning to suspect that Miss Gresham had gone a lot further than that. Whether that was a good thing or not remained to be seen.

He heard Hugo's returning footsteps on the cellar stairs. They crossed the hall and the library door banged. Presumably he was shutting himself away for a long session with whatever he'd fetched up from the cellar. Samuel sighed. Clearly, at the moment the advent of Miss Gresham was *not* helpful.

Hugo opened the bottle and poured himself a drink. His head was beginning to ache and only more brandy would dull the pain. He walked to the window, staring out at the overgrown garden. A climbing rose much in need of pruning straggled across the window, tangling with a rampant honeysuckle, filling the room with their mingled scents. Chloe's special fragrance suddenly seemed to hang in the air, a tantalizing memory so vivid as to be almost real.

With a muttered oath he turned from the window and his eye fell on the couch where they had tangled with such sudden and all-consuming passion. The stain of her virgin blood glared at him in dark reproof.

Sweet Jesus! What if she'd conceived a child? How

could he ever have permitted such a thing to happen? How could he ever have been so blind to the consequences of his drunken folly as to have taken not even the most elementary precaution against conception?

There were things that could be done to avert such a consequence. But they were methods practiced by harlots and the Society women of his past—those who dallied without affection, who deceived lovers and husbands without a qualm as they bolted down the barren paths in search of something that would give pleasure or purpose to their lives.

To provide Chloe with such a means would put her in the same category as those women . . . would ally her with his haunting, bitter past. But what choice did he have?

He drained his glass and refilled it. He'd taken her maidenhead—the act of a cur. Would he now, having satisfied his rutting urge, run off like a cur in an alley, leaving her to bear the fruits of that urge?

He mentally lashed himself, choosing the most despicable images his fevered brain could create, and when he'd done with it, he went to the stables for his horse.

Chloe was in the kitchen with Samuel, eating breakfast with a remarkable lack of appetite, when the library door opened. She sat up, all attention, a look of hope and expectancy in her eyes. But with the slamming of the side door, her shoulders slumped and the light died out of her eyes.

"Don't mind 'im," Samuel said gruffly. "When he gets these moods on 'im, there's nowt anyone can do 'til it's over."

"But I don't know what I've done wrong," Chloe said, lethargically spearing a grilled mushroom. A light blush mantled her cheek. She could guess where the trouble lay, although not why, but she could hardly confide in this bluff sailor with his gold hoop earrings and rough tongue.

"Leave well alone," Samuel advised. "It's best not to go near 'im when the mood's on 'im."

"But I don't see why I should put up with it," Chloe stated, pushing her plate from her. "It's unjust that he should attack me without telling me why. It wasn't my fault Dante got loose, and I don't see how he could have expected me to ignore him when he was barking."

Samuel shrugged as if the subject had ceased to interest him. Hugo was keeping his own counsel on the subject of last night, and Samuel wasn't going to be drawn into anything. He'd keep an eye on the girl and a closed mouth, as he'd been instructed. "There's a pig's liver in the pantry for that cat of your'n."

Chloe managed a smile of thanks and wandered out to the courtyard. She sat on the upturned rain barrel in the corner, lifting her face to the sun. Dante flopped down at her feet with a breathy sigh.

The sun was warm on her closed eyelids and a soft red glow soothed her eyes as Chloe tried to puzzle her way through her hurt confusion. She had enjoyed what had happened in the library with a pleasure uncomplicated by regret or guilt. She was well aware that society's rules decreed that lovemaking should be confined to the conjugal bed, but in her experience, such rules had no meaning when applied to the reality of her life. This seemed just such an instance. She wasn't injured in any way by what had happened, quite the opposite. She felt opened to the world for the first time, as if she had crossed the threshold that separated the dreary confines of her girlhood from the vibrant, exciting realm of adult experiences.

But what had Hugo found so disturbing about it? Even in her inexperience, it had been obvious that his bodily pleasure had matched her own. Knowing this had augmented her own pleasure, released her from inhibition, allowed her to give herself without reserve or fear of embarrassment.

But he'd turned on her afterward with a bitterness that had tarnished the purity of her pleasure. Mortified, she had fled the library and had lain awake, wondering why he should have unloosed such a flood of contempt. And this morning he had spoken to her with the harsh authority of the severest guardian . . .

Ah! Chloe's eyes shot open as she began to see a path through the maze. Just because *she* didn't feel guilty didn't mean that Hugo didn't. He was her guardian and he probably had some antiquated notion about the way guardians should behave toward their wards. He'd certainly become quite prune-faced at her suggestion that they dip into her fortune to benefit both of them. Perhaps he didn't yet understand that Chloe had her own plans for her future and wasn't inclined to sit passively while things happened to her. She had made last night happen much more than Hugo had. *She* was responsible. How absurd for him to blame himself.

Suddenly much more cheerful, Chloe slipped off the rain barrel and went to the stables to check on Rosinante. The nag looked as sorry as ever, notwithstanding warm bran mash and a bale of fresh hay.

"A bullet'd be the kindest thing, I reckon," Billy opined, shaking his head.

"Maybe," Chloe said. "If he doesn't improve in a few days, I'll ask Sir Hugo to put him out of his misery." She ran her hand over the painfully thin rib cage, and her mouth tightened. "I know whom I'd like to put a bullet through!" Then she looked up at Billy, asking casually, "By the way, do you know where Sir Hugo went?"

Billy shook his head. "Just wanted 'is 'orse saddling."

"Did he say how long he'd be?"

Again Billy shook his hand. "Nah. No reason why 'e should. None o' my business."

"I suppose not." Chloe left the stable deep in thought. It seemed it was up to her to put matters right. She must simply reassure Hugo and persuade him that they had done nothing wrong. In fact, maybe the best way to do that would be to make it happen again.

She gave a little skip on the mired cobblestones at the thought. She suspected that there was much more to the business of lovemaking than last night had vouchsafed, and the prospect of further experiments sent little prickles of anticipation coursing up her spine.

In her bedroom she examined the gowns from Madame Letty hanging in the armoire. It hadn't occurred to her to dress in anything but the brown serge that morning—it had been a rather brown serge kind of morning—but sunlight seemed to be running in her veins again as she planned her campaign, and the crisp, dainty muslins looked most appealing . . . not as dramatic as peacock-blue taffeta, of course. But there was no point dwelling on battles already lost.

She tossed aside the brown serge and slipped the sprigged muslin with the cornflower-blue ribbons over her head, twisting to fasten the hooks at the back before tying the sash. There was no mirror in the room, but she remembered seeing a swing mirror on a dressing table in one of the other bedrooms. She went off to find it in a dark and gloomy chamber smelling of mice, where the dust lay thick on the oak floor and faded velvet curtains blocked the light from the mullioned windows.

She pulled back the curtains to let in the light. She tried to lift the mirror from the dressing table, intending to carry it back to her own room, but it was far too heavy with its mahogany frame. So she had to examine herself in parts, standing on a low stool to see herself from the waist down.

The clumsy half boots that went with brown serge looked ridiculous with the pale filmy muslin, but there'd been no time yesterday to visit a shoemaker. Chloe kicked off her shoes, pulled off her stockings, and wriggled her toes in the mirror. The barefoot effect was rather alluring, she decided, like a milkmaid or shepherdess. It was to be hoped her guardian found pastoral images enticing.

She peered at her face in the dust-coated mirror, licking her finger and stroking her eyebrows into a tidy curve, experimenting with her hair, drawing it first into a knot on top of her head, then pulling it away from her face, held at the nape of her neck. In the end she decided it looked more pastoral tumbling unconfined over her shoulders and went back to her own room to brush it until the guinea-gold radiance rippled and shone.

Falstaff watched with his head cocked and one beady eye fixed on the rhythmic sweep of the brush, maintaining a soft stream of obscenities throughout. Beatrice abandoned her sleeping litter for a few moments and stretched herself in the sunlight on the windowsill, warming her flanks. Dante looked expectant, his feathery tail thumping the floor periodically.

"I wonder what you'll all think of London," Chloe remarked absently, threading a cornflower-blue ribbon through her hair. "We won't be able to go until you've weaned the kittens, Beatrice." A feline ear pricked. Dante sighed heavily and flopped to the floor, clearly deciding that nothing noteworthy was about to happen. "But then, I expect it'll take that long to persuade Sir Hugo to agree and to make all the necessary arrangements," she mused, sitting on the window seat, careful not to crease her dress.

It was an hour before the lone horseman appeared on the driveway. Chloe sprang to her feet, closed the door firmly on a disconsolate Dante, and ran to the head of the stairs, from where she looked down into the great hall.

Hugo strode up the steps and into the house, his face set, lines of fatigue etched deep around his mouth and eyes. His red-rimmed eyes were lightless, like dull green stones in a face drawn beneath the sun's bronzing.

He threw his crop onto the table and ran his hands through his hair, massaging his temples with his thumbs in a gesture that Chloe was beginning to find familiar. It spoke of such utter weariness that she longed to comfort him, to find some way to bring him peace. What must it be like never to sleep?

Hugo glanced up suddenly to where she was standing stock-still at the head of the stairs. "Come down to the library," he said in a flat voice.

Chloe's optimistic assurance faltered at his tone. She hesitated, one bare foot raised to take the first stair.

"Now!"

She gasped and ran down the stairs as if there were a whip at her back, but he'd already turned toward the door leading to the kitchen.

"Wait in the library," he instructed her curtly, and went through the door.

Chloe obeyed slowly, all her earlier confidence evaporated. He hadn't seemed to look at her properly, let alone notice her appearance. She stood in the library door, looking around the room where so much had happened. It seemed as gloomy and unfriendly now as it had the first time she'd entered it in search of Lawyer Scranton's letter.

Her feet led her to the couch, and she gazed at the rumpled cushions, at the rusty smudge on the shabby velvet. She'd been bleeding a little when she'd reached her own room, but in the shock of Hugo's violent rejection on the heels of euphoria she'd paid no attention beyond a superficial mopping up before crawling into bed. She bent to touch the dark mark of her body, trying to reconnect with the joyous moment that had created it.

At this moment Hugo walked into the library, a glass in his hand. His stomach plummeted with renewed self-condemnation.

Chloe whirled toward him, her eyes wide with anxiety. "I was only . . . I was only . . ." she stammered, trying to find the words for what she had been thinking.

"I want you to drink this," he said, brushing the stammered attempt aside, refusing to see what lay in her eyes. He held out the glass.

Chloe took it and looked at the cloudy liquid it contained, her nose wrinkling at the powerful aromatic fumes. "What is it?"

"Drink it," he said.

"But . . . but what is it?" She gazed up at him in bewilderment. "Why won't you tell me?"

"It will ensure that there are no consequences from last night," he stated, his voice cool and even. "Drink it."

"What consequences? I don't understand." Her soft mouth quivered in a tentative smile of appeal, the blue eyes turning as purple as the heather on a Scottish moor. "Please, Hugo." Her hand drifted toward his arm, and he jerked away as if from a burning brand.

"Naive little fool!" he exclaimed. "I cannot believe you don't know what I'm talking about." He swung away from her to the brandy bottle and glass—ever-ready succor. He gulped down a shot and felt the warmth settling in his belly. The tremor in his hands steadied. He drew a deep breath and turned back to face her.

"A child. That is the consequence. You may have conceived a child. What's in that glass will ensure that it doesn't happen."

"Oh." Her expression became grave. "I should have thought. I didn't mean to be such a simpleton." She

spoke clearly and distantly. Then she tilted the contents
of the glass down her throat, closed her eyes against the
unpleasant taste, and swallowed. "Does it work?"

"Yes, it works." He walked to the window.

His first time in the crypt, he'd learned about the potion. The woman had asked him for it in the dank drear
light of dawn, when the hallucinatory euphoria of the
night was fading and the spirit felt cold and dark. He
hadn't known what she'd been talking about, and she'd
laughed at his naivete, a harsh and unkind laughter that
had lacerated his youthful dignity. She'd called to Stephen and laughed with him at her young lover's inexperience. But Stephen had not taunted him. He'd been
sympathetic and understanding and had taken the
youthful initiate to the cupboard where all the strange
substances were kept. He'd explained how to mix the
contraceptive herbs and a few days later took him to the
charcoal burner's hut in the forest where the herbalist
plied her trade.

Hugo had listened as Stephen and the old woman
discussed what new supplies were needed. He watched
as Stephen paid in gold for the leather pouches and the
alabaster jars. And the next time the cupboard needed
replenishing, Hugo ran the errand himself.

The herbalist still lived in the charcoal burner's hut.
She'd recognized Hugo, even after fourteen years, and
to his eyes she hadn't changed much, maybe a few
more lines on the wizened face, and the gray-white hair
was thinner and more unkempt. But her eyes were as
sharp and her price as high.

Chloe put down the empty glass and stepped toward
Hugo as he stood staring out of the window. She took a
deep breath, then reached up and touched his face over
his shoulder. "Hugo, I—" But she got no further.

He swung around, slapping her hand away with a
violence that made her cry out. "Don't touch me!" he

snapped. "Don't *ever* touch me again, do you understand?"

She nursed her smarting hand and stared up at him in shocked silence.

He took her by the shoulders and shook her once. "Do you understand?"

"But why?" Chloe managed to say.

"Why!" he exclaimed. "You ask why? After last night."

"But . . . but I enjoyed last night, it was lovely, I felt so wonderful. And if you feel guilty about it, you mustn't." She spoke with fervent urgency, her eyes burning with intensity. "There's no reason for you to feel bad about it. There's nothing to regret—"

"You presumptuous little girl!" he exclaimed. "You have the audacity to tell me what I should or should not regret! Now, you listen to me, and you listen very carefully." The bruising grip of his curled fingers on her shoulders made her wince, but she could no more move than she could tear her eyes away from the piercing green gaze that held her own.

"What took place last night occurred because I was drunk. If I'd been sober, it would never have happened. Do you think I'm mad enough to find a naive schoolgirl irresistible?" Another sharp shake punctuated the question.

"I did not know what I was doing." He enunciated the brutal words with a cold clarity. "And from now on you will stay out of my way unless I summon you. And I swear on my mother's grave that if you ever try your temptress tricks on me again, it will be the sorriest day of your life."

He released her shoulders abruptly, pushing her from him. "Now get out of here."

Chloe stumbled out of the library, too numb for tears. She didn't seem able to breathe; it was as if she'd been plunged into an icy lake, and she stood in the hall, forcing the air into her lungs until the piercing pain under her ribs diminished. Then instinctively she moved toward the open door, questing the warmth and sunlight of the courtyard to caress her icy flesh and breathe life into her frozen spirit.

Chapter 8

C HLOE TOOK HER usual seat on the rain barrel and
sat numbly, staring into space.

Vaguely, she wondered why she wasn't crying,
but the wound was too deep for something as simple as
tears. She wanted to run from this place, from the man
who could cut so deeply, but she had nowhere to go,
no one to turn to. Except Jasper. She disliked her half
brother, but he was the only kin she had. Her mother
had feared him, Chloe knew, just as she knew what was
said about him in the district, that he was a hard man to
cross. But he'd never really taken much notice of his
little half sister and she couldn't remember receiving any
overt unkindness from him. She'd had much more contact with Crispin.

The sound of hooves on the driveway beyond the
courtyard penetrated her bitter musing, and she looked
up incuriously toward the archway. As if in response to
her reflections, Crispin Belmont rode into the courtyard.
He was alone and astride a black gelding of impeccable
pedigree. He looked around, saw Chloe on her rain barrel, and raised his curly-brimmed beaver. He offered her
a small bow that seemed to invite a shared joke at this
formality.

Chloe stood up slowly. "Good day, Crispin. What
brings you here?"

"That's not much of a welcome," her visitor said with
a jovial heartiness that struck a slightly false note to
Chloe's ears. "I come with all goodwill and friendship,
Chloe." His gaze flickered over her and a spark of inter-

est enlivened his features as he took in the rippling mass of shining hair, the slender waist accentuated by the sash of her flowing muslins, the rounded bosom, and the gentle flare of her hips. This Chloe was very different from the grubby, brown-serge schoolgirl eating bread and ham the other morning.

He dismounted, looping the reins over his forearm, and smiled at her. "Do you always walk around barefoot?"

Chloe glanced down at her feet and shrugged. "I felt like it." She stood waiting for him to reveal the purpose of his errand.

Crispin struggled to overcome his annoyance at this cool reception. He had a task to perform and was in all things obedient to his stepfather's commands. The new plan, hatched over the breakfast table, was to be initially conducted single-handedly by the intended bridegroom. He now swallowed his anger, reminding himself that eighty thousand pounds compensated for many an insult. Besides, such disrespect wouldn't survive under Jasper's roof.

He smiled again and held out a parcel. "My mother sent you some gingerbread. She was remembering how much you loved it when you used to come up to the big house as a little girl. I think there's something else in there too. Ribbons or some such frippery." He laughed in self-deprecation. "Ladies' trifles, my dear."

"Oh." Chloe took the parcel, looking rather nonplussed. "Well, please thank Lady Gresham for her kindness." She half turned away.

Crispin was searching for some way to hold her attention, when Samuel appeared on the steps of the house. Samuel had been watching from an upstairs window and, mindful of the need to keep Sir Hugo's ward under constant surveillance, hastened downstairs.

"A word wi' ye, miss," he called.

"Excuse me," Chloe said with offhand politeness, and went over to Samuel.

"Who's 'e?" Samuel wasted no words.

"Crispin, my brother's stepson. Why?"

Samuel scratched his head. He could see no harm in a conversation in the courtyard with a relative, and the sharpness of her tone was belied by the sadness in her eyes.

"Where's that dog of your'n?" he asked. "Sir 'Ugo said you was to keep 'im out of trouble."

"He's shut up in my room. I forgot to let him out." The defiant sharpness faded from her voice. She had had very good reasons for thinking Dante might be an unnecessary addition to the scene she had planned in the library.

"I'll let 'im out." Samuel turned back to the house. "But don't you go leavin' the courtyard."

Chloe walked back to Crispin, still standing beside his horse.

"Rather peremptory for a servant, isn't he?" Crispin frowned.

Chloe shrugged. "He's not an ordinary servant, more a kind of confidant."

Dante came bounding down the steps, barking joyfully. He stood on his hind legs and put his front feet on her shoulders, licking her face. "Would you believe someone tried to steal this silly animal?" Chloe said, laughing as she pushed him away, forgetting her dismal mood for a minute. "He's such a commoner, surely no one could imagine he'd be worth anything."

"He's unusual," Crispin said noncommittally, trying to ignore Dante, who sniffed at his boots and pushed his nose into his crotch in a most embarrassing fashion. "And there are so many poachers in the area. There's no knowing but that one of them saw him and took a fancy to him. He might make a good rabbiter."

"Oh, I'm sure he would," Chloe agreed. "He's extremely intelligent . . . Dante, stop that." She toed him away from Crispin.

"Where's your guardian?" Crispin glanced casually around the disheveled yard.

Drinking himself into a drunken stupor. Chloe bit her lip hard, keeping both the words and the tears at bay. "In the house somewhere," she said. "I have to go in now. Things to do . . ." She gestured vaguely. "Thank you for calling, and please thank your mother for the gingerbread." She turned and ran lightly up the steps without waiting for Crispin's responding farewell.

The young man remounted and trotted out of the courtyard, perfectly satisfied with his progress so far. If Sir Hugo believed the dog to be the object of the attack, then he was more of a fool than Jasper thought him, but whatever he believed, he had no proof. And Chloe, at least, was not suspicious. And he'd made a small step toward disarming her. Jasper would be pleased.

Chloe wandered into the kitchen, averting her eyes from the closed library door as she passed it. She put the gingerbread on the table and began to unwrap it. "Fancy Lady Gresham remembering how I used to like this," she said, selecting a piece.

"Now, don't you go eatin' that before nuncheon; it'll spoil your appetite," Samuel said sharply, scooping up the parcel.

Chloe frowned. "I don't suppose it would, but I don't really want it anyway." She broke off a corner of the piece she had in her hand and held it out to Dante.

"Samuel!" Hugo spoke suddenly from the kitchen door. Chloe, unthinking, spun around toward him, then turned away, flushing. "I'm going into Manchester," Hugo said, his eyes unfocused, his voice heavy. "I don't know when I'll be back."

"Runnin' out of brandy, are we?" Samuel said.

"Damn your insolence, Samuel!" The door slammed on his departure.

"Why's he going to Manchester?" Chloe asked.

"Always does when the devils is bad," Samuel observed.

"But what does he do?"

"Drinkin' and whorin'," Samuel said flatly. "E'll be gone for days, I shouldn't wonder." He put a round of cheese on the table. "Sir 'Ugo's fightin' some powerful demons, miss. Has been ever since I've known 'im, since 'e was nobbut a lad of twenty summers."

"And you don't know what they are?"

"No." Samuel shook his head. "E's never said a word, not even when the drink's on 'im. Most men babble like a Bedlamite in the drink, but not 'im. Close-mouthed 'e is. Like a oyster." He cut into the cheese. "How d'ye fancy a morsel of toasted cheese?"

Chloe shook her head. "No, thank you. I think I'll go upstairs and lie down. I feel rather tired."

When Crispin Belmont appeared in the courtyard the following morning, Samuel called Chloe down from her room. "Ye've a visitor, miss."

"Oh? Who?" The question was lethargic and Samuel silently cursed his employer, who had to bear the responsibility for the girl's heavy-eyed pallor. She'd also returned to the brown serge, which didn't improve matters. A diversion of some kind would do her a world of good.

"That relative of your'n." He gestured with his head to the open door.

"I'm not sure I want to see him," she said, turning back to the stairs.

"Don't be foolish," he said roughly. "It'll do ye good. Can't mope around up there all the livelong day."

"I don't see why not."

"Oh, don't you?" Samuel abruptly decided that his

role as watchdog needed expansion. "Now, you get along out there, miss, an' talk to your relative. Downright rude it is to refuse to see a visitor. I don't know what Sir 'Ugo would say."

"And we're not likely to find out," Chloe muttered, but she went out to the courtyard.

Crispin had already dismounted and held a large bouquet of wildflowers. He offered them with a smile as she came up to him.

Not accidentally, he'd hit upon a happy choice. Cultivated flowers found no favor with Chloe, but the natural melange of color in the bunch of foxgloves, pimpernel, bindweed, and bugloss drew a cry of delight from her.

"Oh, they're lovely. Did you pick them yourself?"

"On the way here," he said. "Do you remember making daisy chains? You once made me a crown and collar."

Chloe frowned. She didn't remember—in fact, from what she did remember of Crispin, it seemed rather unlikely. However, she was prepared to give him the benefit of the doubt and said, "Vaguely."

She felt sufficiently in charity with him to consider inviting him into the kitchen, and then remembered Hugo's voice telling Jasper he wasn't welcome in his house. Presumably, the prohibition applied to Crispin also.

"Would you like a cup of water?" she offered, gesturing to the pump. "It must have been a hot ride." It was the only hospitality available to her, but Crispin looked as neat and cool as if he hadn't ridden the seven miles from Shipton.

"Thank you no," he said. "But I'd like to walk with you. How about we take the dog across the field?"

Dante heard the magic word and emitted a short, excited bark, his tail waving.

Chloe frowned. "I'll have to ask Samuel."

"The servant? For permission?" Crispin sounded genuinely shocked.

"He runs the household," she said. "While Sir Hugo is . . . is away."

"Oh. Where's he gone?" Crispin asked casually, bending to pat Dante.

"Into Manchester," Chloe said.

"How long will he be away?"

Chloe realized she was not prepared to admit she didn't know. "Just a day," she said. "I'll go and talk to Samuel."

Crispin watched her run into the house and wondered why she'd reverted to the hideous serge and the clumpy boots. He didn't much fancy a walk through the fields with quite such a dowdy companion. But his instructions were clear, so he waited for her return with an eager smile pinned to his lips.

Samuel's negative had been unequivocal and Chloe returned disconsolate. "He has to obey Sir Hugo," she explained. "It wouldn't be fair to press him to do otherwise."

Crispin put a good face on it. "Let's sit in the sun, then." He led his horse over to Chloe's rain barrel and hitched himself boyishly onto the low wall beside it.

Crispin kept up a cheerful flow of friendly conversation for half an hour before taking his leave. Chloe was thoughtful as she returned to the house. There was something about him that jarred on her—a false note somewhere—but she couldn't put her finger on it, and it seemed ungenerous to look for faults when he was going to so much trouble to entertain her. And if anyone needed entertainment and something to divert her thoughts, *she* did.

·   ·   ·

Hugo stirred heavily in the deep featherbed. He drew in the stale reek of beer and bodies as he rolled onto his back. Groaning, he flung his arm over the soft mound of flesh beside him. Betsy snuffled and turned her plump body sideways, burrowing deeper into the feathers. Still only half conscious, Hugo smiled in vague warmth and gave her a couple of friendly pats before making more purposefully suggestive movements.

Betsy moaned in halfhearted protest but lent herself as she always did. It was her job, and this customer was gentler and more regular than most, and paid with a generous hand.

Afterward, Hugo lapsed once more into unconsciousness, coming to an hour later with a horrid jerk into heavy-limbed, aching wakefulness. Betsy had left the bed and was lighting the candles. "Time to go, luv," she said.

Her petticoat was grubby, barely covering her ample breasts and riding high on her chunky calves, but her smile was friendly. "Got other customers. Can't make a livin' lyin' 'ere with you 'til mornin', now, can I?"

Hugo closed his eyes, filled with a terrifying emptiness. If he was alone, the void would swallow him.

"Come back to bed," he said. "I'll pay you for the rest of the night."

"Can't," Betsy said firmly. "The bed's promised to Sal now. We takes it in turns, and now it's my turn for the street corners. It's not so bad in summer, but it gets right parky on a winter night." She chuckled expansively and bent to the tarnished copper plate that served as a mirror, pulling a comb through her tangles. "Fair do's, luv. Sal an' me 'ave worked it like this for a year now."

Hugo struggled up. His hands shook and the iron band around his head tightened ominously. He looked around the room with a flash of desperation.

" 'Ere." Betsy handed him a brandy bottle in instant

comprehension. "There's a drop in there. It'll keep the crawlers at bay."

Hugo downed the contents and his hands steadied, the incipient pain died. "Come home with me." There was a pleading note in his voice. "I can't be alone, Betsy. I'll pay you for the night and it'll be a lot more comfortable than street corners." He attempted a cajoling smile, but all his facial muscles were stiff.

"And 'ow'll I get back then?" Betsy frowned at him.

"I'll make sure you do," he promised. "Please, Betsy. I promise you won't lose on it."

She shrugged plump shoulders. "Well, why not. But I'll want a guinea for the 'ole night. And some extra for the inconvenience, mind."

"Whatever you say." He stood up slowly, ready for the violent swinging of the room around him. It steadied and he picked up his coat, hanging over a chair, feeling through the pockets. "Here, be a good girl and buy another bottle of that gut rot from your friend downstairs while I get dressed."

Betsy took the coin and went out in her petticoat. It wasn't her business if a customer chose to drink himself into an early grave.

Hugo pulled on his britches, concentrating hard on every little movement. If he didn't allow his mind to wander from the minute details of the present, the void wouldn't swallow him.

Betsy came back with the brandy and he took another deep swallow. He felt stronger immediately and a happy tingle of warmth spread through him, sending the demons back where they came from.

He escorted Betsy, his arm around her shoulders, down the stairs and to the mews where his horse was stabled. "You don't mind riding pillion, do you, Betsy, my love?" he said with a chuckle, slapping her ample rear in friendly punctuation.

"I don't, but the 'orse might," Betsy responded with an answering chuckle. " 'Elp me up, then."

Hugo heaved her upward and then mounted in front of her. The horse was well rested and stood firm beneath the combined weight. Hugo pulled the bottle from inside his coat and took a long pull, then clicked his tongue and nudged his mount's flanks. He couldn't remember how long he'd been away from Denholm. Several days, he guessed. But it hardly mattered.

It was a brilliant night, the air mild and soft, the white road to Denholm winding ahead of them. Betsy began to hum a ribald taproom song and Hugo joined in, taking occasional pulls from the bottle. The void no longer threatened. There was emptiness, but it was a comforting emptiness. No demons lurked; he could remember nothing in the past and couldn't care less about the future. He existed only in the capsule of the present with Betsy's warm, welcoming body against his back, the horse moving between his thighs, the brandy curling in his belly. Hugo Lattimer was happy.

Samuel heard the horse's hooves on the cobbles beneath his open window. He heard Hugo's deep chuckle and a feminine giggle. With a resigned sigh he rolled over and composed himself for sleep. At least Sir Hugo was back and in one piece. There was always the fear that during one of these orgies in the stews when Hugo forgot who he was and what he was, he'd fall victim to some assailant intent on robbery and murder. Somehow, though, he always came through unscathed. Probably because even when he was drunk he didn't lose the power and stature of a man who'd commanded one of His Majesty's ships of the line. There was an indefinable authority about the man that transcended even the uncoordinated merriness of a drunkard.

Hugo managed to put his horse in the stable, fumbling with saddle and bridle and stirrup leathers as he unsaddled him. But he got the job done and turned to Betsy, standing in the doorway, still humming her ribald song. As he turned, his eye fell on an unfamiliar shape in a neighboring stall. He frowned, shaking his head, wondering how a strange beast had found its way into his stables. The shadow of the answer seemed to be there, but it wouldn't take shape. It was supremely irrelevant; everything was supremely irrelevant at the moment. Flinging his arm around Betsy, he hustled her into the house and into the library.

Chloe hadn't heard Hugo's arrival in the courtyard, since her chamber was at the other end of the house, but Dante, stretched out across the end of the bed, pricked up his ears as the master entered the house. He listened for a minute, then, satisfied that nothing out of the ordinary was happening, dropped his head back onto Chloe's feet with a heavy sigh.

The sound of the piano drifting up through her open window woke Chloe. She lay listening as the music filled the darkness. It was a cheerful, rollicking tune unlike any she'd heard Hugo play before. Together with her relief that he'd returned safely came a flicker of hope that if the demons had left him, he'd revert to the man he'd been before his cruel rejection of her.

The music stopped after a while, and she tried to go back to sleep. But gradually, as the possibility of an end to her wretched loneliness and confusion grew, she began to feel a return of her usual strength of purpose. Her life was still hers to manage. And there were fences to mend before her future could be arranged.

She was out of bed before she realized she'd made any decision. Dante jumped down and shook himself, going to the door.

"No, stay here," she said. "I won't be long." She slipped out into the corridor, closing the door quietly behind her. The dog whined.

It was only when she was halfway down the stairs that Chloe realized she was again running around the house in her nightgown. But there was no one to see and she wasn't going outside. At the library door she paused with a flicker of uncertainty. He'd told her she wasn't to approach him unless he summoned her . . . but that had been when the demons had been with him, when he'd been a different person. The man who'd been playing that merry tune couldn't possibly be the same man who'd thrust her from him with such rough unkindness.

She lifted the latch and pushed the door open. A silvery thread of moonlight lay across the worn Turkey carpet. There were soft sounds in the room, puzzling sounds that stirred her with a strange mixture of apprehension and curiosity. She stepped into the room.

The entwined figures lay in the moonlight, rustling with muffled whispers and heavy breathing. Chloe stared in shock, seeing plump white thighs gleaming in the moonlight, enclosing the long, hard body of Hugo Lattimer. His chestnut hair flopped over his forehead as he gazed down at his partner, moving himself rhythmically within the generous welcoming maw of her body.

With a small chuckle of pleasure he threw his head back, tossing the long lock of hair away from his brow. His eyes opened.

The sight of the girl standing in open-mouthed shock in the doorway hit Hugo like an icy waterfall. He'd forgotten about her. He'd forgotten about everything that had driven him into the brandy lake of amnesia and into the hospitable arms of an amiable whore. And as he took in the slight figure outlined by the candlelight from the hall behind her, the gleaming hair tumbling about her shoulders, bitter bile burned in his throat and the brandy in his stomach turned sour. He tried to tell her to go away, to avert her eyes from this shameful sight, but he couldn't form the words.

And then she'd gone, the door closing quietly behind her.

"Eh, what was that?" Betsy demanded. "What's 'appened to you, then?" It was very clear her partner was no longer either interested in or capable of completing their coition.

Hugo disengaged and stood up. He felt queasy and horror-struck. He looked down at Betsy sprawling on the rug at his feet and saw only the degrading vulgarity of her position, the white slabs of flesh beneath the rucked-up grimy petticoat. With a muttered curse he turned from her.

"Get dressed and go."

"Eh, now, what's all this?" Betsy sat up, shaking down her petticoat. "All night, you said. You're not turnin' me out of 'ere like that!"

"It's almost dawn," he said, pulling up his britches. "The carrier's wagon passes the bottom of the drive at six o'clock. He'll give you a ride into Manchester." He went over to the desk in the corner, pulled open a drawer, and took out a strongbox. "Here, take this."

Betsy stared at the three gold sovereigns winking in the fading moonlight. It was as much as she could expect to earn in two months, and it had been earned without much effort and no discomfort. "You're a rum 'un, you are," she said, taking the money with an easy shrug. "I'll be off, then."

Hugo made no response. He went to the window and stared out into the graying night, waiting while Betsy hooked herself into her dress, pulled on her cheap cotton stockings, and thrust her feet into her wooden clogs.

"All right, then," she said, hesitating at the door. "I'm off."

The rigid figure didn't move a muscle. With another

shrug she went into the hall, closing the door behind her.

"Who are you?"

Betsy jumped at the soft question. She turned to look at the small figure sitting on the bottom stair. "Bless my soul! And what's it to you, might I ask?" She approached and examined the white-faced girl curiously. "Was it you just came in there, then?"

"I didn't know," Chloe said in a flat voice. "Are you a friend of Hugo's?"

Betsy laughed, a rich chuckle from her belly. "Bless you, no, dearie, not what you'd call a friend exactly. It's my business to cheer gentlemen up and I does what I can." The coins chinked in her skirt pocket. "But what's a kiddie like you doin', prowlin' around in the middle o' the night, seein' things you shouldn't?"

"I'm not a child," Chloe said. "And I wasn't prowling."

Betsy peered closer. "Reckon as 'ow you're not such a babby after all," she agreed with a note of sympathy. " 'Ad a bit of a shock, did you, dearie?"

The library door opened before Chloe could respond. Hugo stepped into the hall. "Go up to your room, Chloe," he directed, his voice without expression.

Chloe stood up slowly. "I'm sorry I interrupted you," she said with an ironic courtesy. "Please forgive me. I didn't realize you had a visitor." She turned and ran up the stairs without a backward glance.

"That's a pickle, an' no mistake," Betsy observed wisely as Hugo opened the front door for her. "You'd do best to keep your little entertainments out of the 'ouse, if you wants my advice."

Hugo said nothing, simply closed the door on her. He went back to the library and steadily gathered up all the bottles scattered around the room, the full, the half full, and the empty. He took them into the kitchen, then went upstairs and woke Samuel.

Samuel listened to his instructions in complete silence. When his employer had finished, he said, "Reckon you can do it?"

"I must," Hugo said simply, but there was quiet desperation in his voice and eyes. "Keep Chloe away from the library at all costs." As he left the room, he added with a tinge of humor that surprised them both, "She has the devil's own facility for appearing in the wrong place at the wrong time."

"Mebbe so, but then, mebbe not," Samuel mused as he got out of bed. Maybe this time she'd appeared in the right place at the right time.

Hugo went back to the library and closed the door. He sat down in the cracked leather wing chair beside the empty grate and stared sightlessly into the graying light of the room as he waited for the long, slow descent into hell to begin.

Chapter 9

CHLOE DIDN'T GO back to sleep. She sat on the window seat, watching the sunrise, Dante's head on her knee, Falstaff preening his raggedy feathers with a peacock's pride. Beatrice climbed out of the hat box, stretched, yawned, arched her back, and glided purposefully to the door. Chloe let her out. The cat knew her way in and out of the house by now.

Chloe examined her emotions with an almost distant curiosity. She discovered that she was no longer hurt or confused; she was, very simply, angry. She supposed it was none of her business whom her guardian chose to bed, but the supposition did nothing to cool her indignation. He'd banished her from his presence and taken a fat whore in her place! Maybe she was a *kind*, fat whore, but a whore nonetheless. From now on she was going to have nothing to do with Sir Hugo Lattimer beyond the absolute necessities engendered by his guardianship. She'd been hurt and humiliated enough, and the sooner she made arrangements to leave his roof, the better it would be for everyone. The only question was where she should go.

And then she remembered Miss Anstey. Why shouldn't she set up an establishment with Miss Anstey? Presumably her fortune could pay a companion at least as much as she'd be paid by Lady Colshot. She would write first to Miss Anstey, and if she received a favorable response, then she would lay out the plan in a formal letter to her guardian. He'd made no secret of his anxiety to be rid of her, and it was so like the plan he'd had himself that he'd surely jump at it. But she would insist on establishing herself in London.

Thus resolved, Chloe went down to the kitchen to fetch a jug of hot water. The library door was closed as she passed it, and she stuck out her tongue at it in a childish gesture that nevertheless relieved her feelings.

"You'll be wantin' your breakfast," Samuel observed as she entered the kitchen. In full possession of the facts now, he cast her a shrewd glance, assessing her state of mind. The leaden depression of the past few days seemed to have left her, although the light in her eyes didn't strike him as particularly joyful.

"I'd like a bath more than anything," Chloe said, surprising herself with the realization. She ran her hands through her hair. "I'd like to wash my hair."

"Long as you don't mind the kitchen," Samuel said. "I don't relish carrying jugs of 'ot water up them stairs. There's a tub somewhere in the scullery." He went into the small back kitchen, reappearing with a tin hip bath. He set it down in front of the range. "Reckon ye'll need a screen or summat."

"There's that fire screen in the library," Chloe said, moving to the door.

"I'll get it, miss. You're not to go in there, you understand?" The sharp urgency of his voice arrested her.

"I've seen him drunk before," she said acidly. "And rather more than that."

"I know," Samuel said. "But what's goin' on in there now is between Sir 'Ugo and 'is own self. You put one finger on that door, and you'll be answerin' to me."

Chloe blinked at this unlooked-for ferocity from the usually phlegmatic Samuel. "What's he doing, then?"

"Never you mind. None o' your business." He stomped to the door. "I'll set that bath up for you straightaway."

Chloe sat at the table, thoughtfully picking at the crust on a loaf of bread. Now what was going on?

Samuel went quietly into the library. Hugo was still sitting in the chair, his hands clenched on the arms, the knuckles bloodless. Sweat shimmered on his forehead.

"Bring me some coffee, Samuel."

"Right you are." Samuel picked up the heavy fire screen. "Miss is goin' to 'ave a bath in the kitchen."

"Well, watch young Billy," Hugo said. "I wouldn't put it past him to play Peeping Tom."

It was an attempt at levity, and Samuel smiled tightly in response. "You want anythin' to eat?"

Hugo just shook his head.

Samuel returned with a pot of coffee and set it down beside Hugo. He filled a beaker and silently held it out. Hugo took it carefully, his hands curling around the warmth, the aromatic steam hitting his nostrils. "Thanks."

"Anythin' else?"

"No, just leave me."

The door closed behind Samuel, and Hugo took a sip of coffee. His stomach revolted and a wave of nausea broke over him. He set the mug down and closed his eyes. He'd been blind drunk for four days, in a constant state of semi-intoxication for several years, and it was going to get a lot worse before it got better.

While Chloe bathed, she tried out her plan for Miss Anstey's companionship on Samuel, who was peeling potatoes beyond the screen, keeping a watchful eye out for unexpected visitors.

"I should think Sir Hugo would approve," she concluded, pouring a jug of water over her hair. "If he ever sobers up enough to listen, of course."

"There's no call for talk like that," Samuel reproved. "Don't go meddlin' in what you don't understand."

"You mean the demons?"

"Reckon so."

"But you don't understand them either. You said so."

"No, I don't. And so I don't go throwin' stones."

Chloe was silenced. She stood up and reached for the towel hanging over the screen. "I wish I did understand," she said finally, twisting the towel around her wet hair. "Then maybe I wouldn't be so angry." She shrugged into a dressing gown and came out from behind the screen. "I could stick a knife in his ribs, Samuel!"

Samuel smiled his tight smile. "I wouldn't recommend tryin' it, miss. Not with Sir 'Ugo. Drunk or sober, 'e's a hard man to tangle with."

Chloe went upstairs to dress. As she selected one of her new gowns, she found herself wondering if Crispin would pay her another visit. The prospect surprisingly was rather pleasing. Not least because she suspected Hugo would be annoyed by it.

A man who amused himself in drunken sport with fat whores deserved to be annoyed.

She was in the stable yard, examining Rosinante's wounds when Crispin arrived, leading a roan mare of elegant lines.

"What a disgusting beast," he said without thought as he took in the turnip seller's abused nag. "It should be fed to the crows."

Chloe laid a strip of gauze over one of the still-oozing wounds on Rosinante's flanks before saying in a deceptively neutral tone, "Oh, do you really think so?"

"I know so." Crispin dismounted. "It's not even worth a bullet. Why are you wasting your time and good medicine on such a travesty?"

Chloe turned and surveyed her visitor. The look in her eye caused Crispin to take an involuntary step backward. "You always were a brute," she declared, fire and ice in her voice. "Too good for a bullet, is it? This pitiable creature has been tortured throughout its life, and when it can't endure anymore, it's to be fed to the crows? That attitude makes me sick, Crispin." She turned back to the patient.

Crispin flushed a dark red at this vigorously uncivil castigation, and it took the certainty of his stepfather's wrath and the promise of eighty thousand pounds to keep him from rewarding her insolence with the back of his hand.

"It was a manner of speaking," he said at last. "There's no need to fly into the boughs, Chloe. And I must say"—he laughed, a feeble and unconvincing attempt—"I must say, to accuse me of always being a brute is a bit much, you know."

Chloe continued with her ministrations in silence for a minute, then said, "You used to pull the wings off butterflies."

Another unconvincing little laugh. "Oh, come now, Chloe. Boys will be boys, you know."

"No, I don't know," she said shortly.

"Well, I don't do it anymore," he said somewhat lamely.

"No. But do you still bring your hunters back from the field bleeding and foundered? A hunter with broken wind isn't worth much either, is it? But I expect you'd do it the kindness of a bullet."

This bitter, passionate speech left Crispin for a moment dumbfounded. The attack seemed to have come out of nowhere, and he floundered around, trying to find a way of recovering his equilibrium. Chloe had suddenly reduced him to the status of an unpleasant little boy. His gloved hands flexed as he held himself on a tight rein.

"If we could change the direction of the subject of horseflesh, Sir Jasper has sent you a present," he said stiffly.

"Oh?" Chloe turned, squinting up at him against the sun.

He gestured to the horse he was leading. "This is Maid Marion. She's out of Red Queen by Sherrif. Your brother thought you might like a good riding horse."

"Oh, I remember Sherrif," Chloe said. "A magnificent stallion. No wonder she's such a pretty lady." She accepted the change of subject with the rueful reflection that her attack on Crispin had rather gone to extremes. "But I couldn't possibly accept her."

He'd been warned to expect this and had his answer ready. "Why not? It's perfectly customary for brothers to give their sisters gifts."

Chloe blew softly into the mare's nostrils. Maid Marion wrinkled her velvety nose and rolled back her lips in a horsey smile. Chloe stroked her neck and said as neutrally as she could, "Perhaps so, but I really can't accept her as a gift. Maybe I could borrow her one day though."

It would achieve the same purpose. Crispin relaxed and asked lightly, "Will your guardian permit you to ride with me?"

Chloe frowned. Hugo had forfeited all rights to dictate to her. There was not the slightest reason why she shouldn't spend time with her own family. It wasn't as if she had a surfeit of caring friends and relatives around her. She swallowed hard, castigating herself mentally for self-pity. She knew instinctively that Hugo would not permit her to ride with Crispin, but the reasons had nothing to do with her; they belonged to whatever lay between Jasper and Sir Hugo. She failed to see why her happiness should be sacrificed.

"I shan't ask him," she said. "But it can't be today. I'd have to plan it."

Crispin couldn't hide his satisfaction and asked eagerly, "When, then?"

"Let me think about it and we'll make plans when you come tomorrow. . . . If you come tomorrow," she added.

"You'll have to promise to receive me with more courtesy," Crispin said. He tried to make his voice teasing, but his eyes were hard and he bent to pat the ever-present Dante, hoping to conceal his expression. The dog moved away.

"If I was rude, I apologize," Chloe said. "I sometimes speak out of turn when I'm angered . . . and I do become very angry when animals are maltreated." She shrugged as if such a response were only to be expected. "Poor Rosinante. Can't you imagine what it must have been like, unshod, starved, and beaten, and forced to haul impossibly heavy loads?"

"Not being a horse, I'm afraid I can't," Crispin said. He offered a wry grin and Chloe, whose sense of humor was never far from the surface, half smiled in response.

"I suppose I do become rather obsessive," she conceded. "But you did pull the wings off butterflies."

Crispin raised his hands in a disarming gesture of defeat. "But I was very young, Chloe. No more than nine or ten. I've reformed, I promise."

"Oh, very well," she said, laughing. "We'll consign it to the dim and distant past."

"And you really won't let me leave Maid Marion with you?"

Chloe shook her head. "Thank Jasper for me, but I can't possibly accept such a gift. I'd be happy to buy her though," she added. "Sir Hugo said we would purchase a good horse for me, once—"

"Once?" Crispin prompted when she seemed disinclined to continue.

"Oh, once it's been decided where I should live and in what manner," she said with another dismissive shrug.

"And when will that be decided?"

When and if my guardian is ever sober enough to think about it. "Soon, when Sir Hugo's looked at all the options."

"And what are the options?"

For some reason, despite her newfound charity with him, Chloe discovered she didn't want to confide her plans to Crispin. "Oh, I'm not sure yet," she said casually. "I have to prepare a fresh poultice for Rosinante, so . . ."

"I have to be on my way." Crispin took the hint. He reached for her hand and raised it to his lips. "Until tomorrow, then."

"Tomorrow," Chloe agreed, retrieving her hand in some surprise. She hadn't expected gallantry from Crispin. So far, in the arena of gallantry, she'd experienced only the stammers and fumbles of the curate and Miss Anne's nephew. The butcher's boy didn't really count.

And neither did what had happened between herself and Hugo. That hadn't been gallantry. What had it been?

She waved good-bye as Crispin rode out of the courtyard, leading Maid Marion. What had it been? It had been magical, but it had far transcended the games and rituals of gallantry. It had not been play. There had been nothing playful about it at all.

That night she heard the pianoforte again. But there was nothing merry or rollicking about the music—in fact it wasn't music. It was a harsh melange of discordancy, the notes beaten from the keyboard with a desperation that chilled her. It was a cry of pure anomie—a despairing statement of aloneness. The agonized cry of a man who'd lost his grounding in his own world.

Chloe could find no words for the pain described in the sounds coming through her window. But she felt the pain as if it were her own. She got up and sat on the window seat. Dante was shivering against her and Beatrice had curled around her kittens, her body and her warmth a protective arc.

Chloe heard Samuel's tread, heavy on the stairs. She heard the library door open and she drew a ragged breath. Samuel would help him as she knew she could not. The depths of her own ignorance, her own inability to grasp such pain, stunned her.

The discordant music ceased. She exhaled slowly, feeling the tension leave her body.

When Samuel's callused hands covered Hugo's on the keys, Hugo's head dropped onto his chest. "I don't know if I can do it," he whispered.

"Aye, you can," Samuel said softly. "You need rest."

"I need brandy, damn you!" Hugo held out his hands. They shook uncontrollably. "My skin's on fire," he muttered. "I feel as if I'm shoveling fuel on Satan's fires already. Eden in hell." His crack of laughter was mirthless. "Seems appropriate, doesn't it, Samuel? You want to join me there? I promise you the road is paved with every debauchery known to man. The question is—" He shook his head slowly. "The question is, Samuel, whether the joys of the road are worth the hell of its destination."

"Come upstairs," Samuel said. "I'll put you to bed—"

"No, damn you!" Hugo pushed away his helping hands. "I can't sleep. I'll stay here."

"You need to eat something—"

"Samuel, leave me alone." The sentiment was savage, the voice quiet.

Samuel left the library and went back to bed. Chloe heard him come upstairs and crept back beneath the covers of her own bed, encouraging Dante to leave her feet and come up beside her. His breath was damp and warm on her face, his heavy body like an extra blanket, and finally she fell asleep.

In the library Hugo kept up his lonely vigil of endurance.

Crispin didn't come the following morning, and Chloe, who had already worked out a plan for evading her custodian's sharp eyes, was more disappointed than she cared to acknowledge. Restlessly, she decided to take Hugo's advice and divert her energies into housekeeping. She took down the hangings and curtains in her bedchamber and washed them, hanging them to dry in the courtyard. With Samuel's grumbling assistance, she hauled the Elizabethan rug outside and beat the clouds of dust from it, then swept and polished the oak floor and the heavy wooden furniture in the bedroom. By sundown she was exhausted but satisfied. Dante, who'd had a long walk in Billy's charge, was equally at peace and flopped muddy and breathily at her feet in the kitchen.

Samuel was preoccupied, his grizzled, beatling eyebrows drawn together in a frown of anxiety as he clattered copper pots on the range. He'd been in and out of the library all day, bearing pots of coffee, bowls of soup, all of which he'd brought back untouched.

Chloe was well aware of this, but when she asked what was going on with Sir Hugo, Samuel told her it was none of her business and changed the subject. All her speculations led back to the assumption that he'd drunk himself into unconsciousness and Samuel was waiting for him to come to. She contemplated going into the overgrown garden and peering in through the library window, but quailed at the thought of what would happen if Hugo caught her and this time could justifiably accuse her of prying.

She lay in bed, waiting for the haunting sounds of the pianoforte, but Hugo had gone far from the solace of his music into a world where nothing could express his anguish. His body was racked with pain, every muscle and joint aching with the single-minded concentration of his will. It would be so easy to put a stop to his agony. One swallow and he would begin to feel better, but he fought on even when he saw shapes in the corners of the room, felt creeping things on his arms, and his spine was terrifyingly alive with myriad tiny feet he could neither catch nor see. He prayed for the gift of sleep, for just an hour of surcease from his torments, but he remained wakeful, sweating, staring into the room, visited by every evil memory and every shame of his past.

There was no sign of Crispin the next morning, and Chloe decided that she'd mortally offended him. She minded more than she felt she should, and the realization didn't sweeten her temper. By late afternoon she was on the verge of defying prohibition and taking herself off for a long walk across the fields, when Crispin rode into the courtyard.

His absence had been carefully calculated and had achieved the desired result. Any doubts Chloe might have had about playing truant in Crispin's company had been defeated by the prospect of losing the opportunity for truancy.

She greeted him with a warmth she'd not shown before.

"I give you good afternoon, Chloe," he said with a slightly smug smile as she came swiftly toward him, ready words of welcome on her lips. "Or is it evening? I'm sorry I couldn't come before, but Sir Jasper had some business he wanted me to transact for him in Manchester." He dismounted carefully, holding a small lidded box against his chest. "I have a surprise for you."

"Oh?" Chloe took the box. Instantly, she knew it held something living. Gently she lifted the lid, where air holes had been bored. "Oh," she said again. "Poor baby. Where did you find it?"

A baby barn owl lay in a nest of straw, its dark eyes unblinking in the heart-shaped face. Its plumage was ruffled, one buff wing oddly angled.

"It must have fallen out of its nest," Crispin said. "I found it near the ruined belfry of Shipton Abbey. I think it's broken its wing."

"Yes, I'm sure it has." Delicately, she touched the awkward-looking wing. "If it's a simple break, I believe I can splint it. How clever of you to find it, Crispin."

"And even cleverer to bring it to you," he said with another complacent smile. "I trust I've made up for my unkind remarks about that pathetic nag."

Chloe laughed. "Indeed, you've earned your pardon."

"Sufficiently for you to come on a picnic with me?" He slapped the reins in the palm of his hand, watching her reaction through narrowed eyes.

"Certainly," Chloe said promptly, gently stroking the bird's breast. "I have it all planned. I will meet you at the bottom of the drive. But it would be best if we made it early in the morning. Samuel's busy then, helping Billy in the stables."

"Tomorrow?"

"If you like." She was too absorbed in the wounded owl to look up at him. "About eight o'clock."

"Then I'll be at the bottom of the drive with Maid Marion. But I can see you've got more on your mind than chatting with me at the moment, so I'll leave you to your doctoring." He remounted. "Until tomorrow, Chloe."

"Yes," she agreed absently. "Bye, Crispin." She hurried into the house with her prize without waiting to see him go.

Crispin rode out of the courtyard well satisfied. By

this time tomorrow Chloe Gresham would be safely secured in her half brother's charge.

Chloe carried the bird into the kitchen and set the box on the table.

"What you got there?" Samuel asked, coming in through the back door with a basket of apples.

"See for yourself," Chloe said distractedly. "I'm going to warm some milk and mix it with bread to make pellets for it. It'll do for food for the moment, since I don't think I'm capable of regurgitating mice."

"Lord love us," Samuel muttered, peering at the bird. "What's the matter wi' it?"

"Broken wing. I have to find two very light, thin pieces of wood to act as splints. Do we have any thread?"

"Reckon so." He watched with a resigned curiosity as she mixed bread and milk into tiny pellets and sat down, holding the bird in the palm of one hand, patiently opening its beak to pop the food inside. After two pellets the baby owl was opening its mouth without assistance.

"There, that's better now, isn't it?" she crooned, laying the bird back in its box. "Now, for a splint."

She was working intricately with two shavings from the log basket wrapped in thread when Hugo came into the kitchen. He leaned against the door jamb and said tranquilly, "Good evening."

Chloe was painstakingly straightening the broken wing and made no response. Samuel, however, sighed in audible relief and beamed, scrutinizing the haggard figure in the doorway. Hugo's face bore the ravages of four sleepless days and nights and the deeply etched lines of endurance. His eyes were red-rimmed, the paper-thin skin beneath swollen, a week's worth of stubble on his chin. But he exuded an air of peace, a sense of being purged, of being washed up on a calm shore after shipwreck.

"Come you in." Samuel rubbed his hands together, his eyes shining with pleasure. "What can I get ye?"

"Coffee first, then food," Hugo said. He surveyed Chloe's rigid back and said, "Good evening, lass." Again there was no response. He raised his eyebrows interrogatively at Samuel, who shook his head and set the kettle to boil on the range.

"What are you doing, Chloe?" Hugo tried again.

Chloe ignored him, concentrating on the exquisitely delicate operation of binding the splint to the owl's wing.

Hugo came over to the table. "Didn't you hear me, lass?"

"I should have thought it was obvious what I was doing," she muttered. "I'm splinting a broken wing."

Hugo watched her fingers and pursed his lips in admiration at their precision. He decided to ignore the issue of blatant discourtesy and sat down opposite her.

His first draft of coffee was a revelation. He'd taken nothing but water since incarcerating himself in the library. Anything else had made him violently nauseated. Now the hot liquid seemed to bring renewed life to every crevice of a body that seemed as sore both inside and out as if it had been passed through a mangle. He was famished and exhausted. But he was cleansed, his body freed of poison and his mind clear, his spirit somehow healed, as if in those long hours of endurance he had finally expiated the past.

Now he had to address the problem of his beautiful ward from whom anger and resentment radiated in almost palpable waves. He knew he had hurt and confused her. From now on they would conduct their relationship on the friendly practical basis of guardian and ward, and Chloe would soon forget what had passed between them in his drunken madness. And he would make up for it in whatever ways he could without compromising his authority.

"The problem now is where to put you," Chloe said, examining her handiwork with a critical frown. "Somewhere dark and quiet . . . and safe from Beatrice. Although she's fairly occupied with the mice," she added.

"A mouser, is she?" Samuel tossed sweetbreads in a skillet over the range.

"Yes, I just wish she wouldn't play with them before she kills them," Chloe lamented, sniffing hungrily.

"It's the nature of the beast, I suppose," Hugo remarked.

Chloe flicked him a look of supreme contempt, as if he'd said something idiotic, and pointedly addressed Samuel. "So, do you have any suggestions, Samuel, about where I could put him?"

"Why don't you use the old stillroom?" Hugo persevered. "It's dark and there's a key in the door, so you can be sure it won't accidentally open."

"Where will I find it?" Chloe continued to address Samuel, as if it had been his suggestion.

"End of the north corridor upstairs," Samuel provided. "Full o' cobwebs, prob'ly."

"Then he'll feel quite at home." She picked up the box and left the kitchen.

"Oh, Lord!" Hugo groaned, resting his head in his elbow-propped hands.

"Reckon as 'ow some fences need mendin' " was Samuel's laconic response. He put a loaf of bread and a crock of yellow butter on the table.

"An understatement . . . but I haven't the energy to do anything about it tonight."

"Now, don't you let Miss trouble ye," Samuel advised with a touch of asperity. "You just get rested." He scraped the contents of the skillet onto a plate and set it before Hugo. "Get that down you, Sir 'Ugo. Do ye a power of good. And there's a nice brook trout to follow. Caught it this mornin'."

"And what are you going to feed the lass?" Hugo asked with a slight smile. "It's not going to sweeten her temper if I eat her dinner."

"She'll 'ave ham an' eggs like me an' be thankful."

Chloe had no fault to find with ham and eggs and cast no envious glances across the table at her guardian's dinner. She had, however, been shocked at his spent appearance on her one surreptitious examination, although the green eyes, despite their red-rimmed exhaustion, were clearer than she'd ever seen them. The memory of that dreadful music knocked at the carapace of anger she was fiercely preserving. If he hadn't been drinking during the long days and nights in the library, and he obviously hadn't, what had he been doing?

"How's Rosinante getting along?" Hugo asked, laying down his fork with a sigh of repletion.

Chloe shrugged. "All right, I suppose." She'd have liked to have discussed the animal's condition, but perversely denied herself the opportunity for a second opinion.

Hugo pushed back his chair. "I'm dead on my feet, Samuel. I'm going up to bed. Don't wake me."

"Wouldn't dream of it," Samuel declared.

Hugo came around the table and stopped at Chloe's chair. Catching her chin, he lifted her face. The deep blue eyes glared, but he could read the deeper emotion the belligerence was masking.

"I grant you the right to punish me this evening," he said evenly. "But tomorrow morning, lass, you'll accord me ordinary civility at the very least. Is that clear?"

"I am not uncivil," Chloe replied, trying to pull her chin free of his fingers.

"Oh, yes, you are. Abominably so, and I won't have it

after tonight. We have a lot to discuss, and I don't intend to conduct the discussion with a monosyllabic brat." He softened the words with a weary smile because she was heart-stoppingly beautiful despite the truculence of her expression. Then he remembered where contemplation of that beauty led and abruptly released her chin. "I bid you both good night."

The kitchen door closed on his departure. Chloe brushed her chin where the imprint of his fingers still lingered.

Chapter 10

C HLOE WAS AWAKE at cockcrow, filled with a sense of adventure that she knew arose from the forbidden nature of the day's plan. In any other circumstances the prospect of a ride with Crispin would have left her unmoved. He was hardly a stimulating companion. But she was sick to death of being confined in a dusty, falling-apart manor house at the bidding of a man who couldn't get his own head together. After ten years locked up in the Misses Trent's seminary, it seemed to add insult to injury. Besides, the sun was shining and there was a world awaiting.

There also seemed little point in having a new habit and a tricorn hat with a silver plume if one was denied the opportunity to wear them.

She ran down to the kitchen and let Dante out into the kitchen garden, taking an apple from the basket and following him into the orchard. She perched on the low wall encircling the orchard and looked across Shipton valley, where an early mist curled, promising another hot day.

She'd already decided to make her escape by climbing over the wall and skirting the orchard to come out halfway down the driveway. There was much less chance of discovery than using the courtyard exit.

She ate her apple while Dante chased up hares in the dew-wet grass, then returned to the kitchen. She couldn't go adventuring without leaving a note of explanation. They'd be angry enough as it was without scaring them both out of their wits, wondering what had happened to her.

The kitchen dresser yielded paper and a lead pencil. She took them up to her room to compose a suitable missive.

At seven o'clock Chloe heard Samuel's heavy tread on the stair. He'd put the kettle on the range and go to the hen house to collect the eggs. Then he'd make tea and porridge for himself and Billy. When they'd breakfasted, they'd go to the stables to see to the dogs and horses.

She dressed swiftly and read through her note. It was hardly poetry, but it was clear and said she'd be back in the afternoon. In afterthought she scrawled an addendum. Dante would have to be shut up while she left, since Crispin's plans might go awry if a dog joined them. Samuel would have to release him once she'd gone.

That done, she left her bedroom, tiptoed to the end of the corridor, looked in on the sleepy Plato, in the stillroom, who blinked at the crack of light but seemed peaceful and so far hadn't disturbed the splint.

The kitchen was empty, as she'd expected, the back door standing open. She propped the note against the coffeepot on the table and darted outside. Across the kitchen garden, through the orchard, over the wall, and she was home free.

Crispin was waiting in the lane at the bottom of the drive. He held Maid Marion on a leading rein and had a wicker hamper strapped to his saddle.

"Good morning," Chloe called as she ran through the gate. "Isn't it a lovely morning?"

Crispin dismounted. "Beautiful. No one knows you're here?"

"Not a soul," she said cheerfully, rubbing Maid Marion's nose. "But I left them a note so they won't worry."

Crispin paled. "You left them a note?"

"Yes, of course. . . . Will you help me mount? Without a mounting block, I find it difficult."

Crispin took her booted foot in his palm and tossed her up. She landed gracefully in the sidesaddle, hitched her right knee over the pommel, and adjusted her skirts, offering her companion a brilliant smile. "Where are we going?"

"It's a surprise." Crispin mounted his own horse. "What did you say in your note?"

"Oh, just that I was going for a ride with you and we would be back sometime this afternoon." She looked at him askance. "Is something troubling you?"

"No, why should there be?" But his mouth was tight and his eyes hard. "How soon before they find your note?"

"Oh, half an hour, I should think," Chloe said. "Why?"

Crispin shrugged and touched his spur to his mount's flanks. The horse broke into a canter and then into a gallop. Chloe, taken by surprise, followed suit, the roan's stride lengthening as she established her pace.

It was fifteen minutes before Crispin slowed, and by then Chloe was enjoying the ride so much, she thought no more about that sudden burst of speed. Crispin still refused to say where they were going, so she just relaxed into the pleasure of the bright morning and the feel of a powerful mount beneath her and the heady sense of a whole day of freedom ahead.

Samuel saw the note as soon as he returned to the kitchen from the stables. He unfolded the sheet of paper and puzzled at the scrawled letters. His reading was severely limited and his writing nonexistent, but he could make out the signature and it filled him with foreboding. Further mental contortions yielded the fact that she'd gone somewhere.

On occasion Samuel could produce a string of profanity to impress His Majesty's entire navy. This was one of those occasions. Clearly, he had no choice but to wake Sir Hugo from the first decent sleep he'd had since God knew when.

Women were pesky creatures . . . never anything but trouble. He stomped upstairs and knocked at Hugo's door. There was no immediate response, and he lifted the latch.

"Beggin' your pardon, Sir 'Ugo—"

"What is it, Samuel?" Hugo was immediately wide awake although for a second disoriented, believing that he was back commanding a ship and Samuel was waking him in the night watch with urgent news.

"It's Miss," Samuel said, stepping up to the bed. "Left this on the kitchen table." He held out the paper.

Hugo snatched it from him. He took in the contents and closed his eyes briefly. "Why the *hell* would she go anywhere with Crispin? She said she couldn't stand him."

"That relative of 'ers?" Samuel asked with an uneasy frown. "The one what's been 'anging around the last few days?"

"What!"

"Well, she was down, like, Sir 'Ugo, and he seemed to cheer 'er up. They never went out of the courtyard, I swear it. An' I was watchin' all the time. Brought 'er the owl, I'll lay odds." A ruddy flush stained Samuel's weather-beaten cheeks as he gazed anxiously at his employer. "Did I do wrong?"

"It wasn't your responsibility, Samuel, it was mine." Hugo's lip curled in disgust. "I thought it could wait until I'd pulled myself together. Jasper said he was more than a match for a drunken sot . . . and by God he knew what he was talking about." He pushed aside the sheet and stood up. "How long could she have been gone?"

" 'Alf an hour, p'raps."

"Could be worse." He pulled his shirt over his head and stepped into his britches. "I'm damn sure I told her she wasn't to leave the estate without permission . . . or is that another fond hope born out of my drunken imagination?"

"No, Sir 'Ugo, I was there when you told 'er," Samuel said stolidly, handing him his boots.

"Ahh. In that case, Miss Gresham had better be prepared for some serious trouble when I get my hands on her." He sat on the edge of the bed and pulled on his boots. "Tell Billy to saddle the horses. There's only one road and they could only have gone one of two ways. I'll take the Manchester road to Shipton and you go toward Edgecombe. Someone along the road will have seen them and can put us right."

He stood up again and buckled on his belt. "I want my knife, Samuel, and my pistol."

Samuel handed them to him and hurried downstairs to give Billy his orders.

Hugo ran a finger down the blade of the knife before thrusting it into the sheath in his belt. He primed the pistol before dropping it into the deep pocket of his coat.

He hadn't confided his suspicions about the Greshams to Chloe, so perhaps she couldn't be held entirely to blame for accepting Crispin's company. He was a part of her childhood, and she had no reason to suspect him of perfidy. However, she *had* been told to stay close to the house, and by ignoring that instruction had walked straight into the lion's den and was causing him a great deal of trouble . . . not to mention waking him prematurely from the almost-unremembered luxury of a deep sleep and driving him out of the house, unshaven and breakfastless. If he'd summoned the energy to rid himself of a week's beard before he'd gone to bed, he'd look less of a vagabond.

Hugo was in no charitable frame of mind as he strode downstairs. But neither was he in the least anxious about retrieving her. He never fretted about the outcome of a venture when in the midst of it.

Would they have taken her to Shipton? Or somewhere farther afield? He'd start at Shipton anyway. If Jasper wasn't there, the chances were fairly high that someone could be induced to impart some information. A knife and a pistol in the hands of a man unafraid to use them were potent persuaders.

He emerged into the sunny courtyard, drawing on his gloves. "If someone saw them pass on your section of the road, Samuel, stay on their tracks. If you draw a blank, then follow me as fast as you can. I'll do the same." He swung onto his horse.

"Right you are." Samuel mounted and followed him down the drive to the road, where they went their separate ways.

Crispin pressed his horse onward over the dry, rutted surface of the Manchester road. They were nearing the city now and the post-chaise would be waiting at the crossroads. He glanced impatiently behind him. Chloe was now dawdling, examining the hedgerows, stopping to look at a hovering hawk, and he didn't know how to hurry her up. If they only had half an hour's start, he had to get her into the chaise and across the city without delay.

Fuming, he reined in his horse and waited for her to come up with him. "You're so slow, Chloe."

She looked surprised. "But we aren't in a hurry. We

have all morning. . . . Don't you think there are a lot of people on the road?"

It was true. The Manchester road was getting busier by the moment, with carts and horsemen and pedestrians, whole families of them in some cases, straggling along the grassy verge, children darting and squealing in and out of the throng. There was an air of excitement but also a holiday atmosphere, as if they were going to a fête on this sultry Monday morning.

If Chloe resisted entering the chaise, it would create the devil of a scene on this public highway. Nothing was going right, and Crispin wished his stepfather hadn't put the success of this venture squarely on his shoulders. Control seemed to be slipping through his fingers, and he didn't know how to adapt the plan to changed circumstance.

"Come on," he said, looking around impatiently.

"I'm hungry," Chloe stated. "I only had an apple for breakfast. Why don't we turn off the road into the field and have some of our picnic? You did say we were going to have a picnic?"

"Yes, but not here."

"Well, what have you got in the basket? There must be something I could nibble while we ride."

Crispin had a sudden memory of his companion as an infuriatingly persistent little girl of seven, demanding to know the meaning of a word she'd heard in the stable yard at Gresham Hall. He'd not known himself, beyond the fact that it was grossly improper, but having pretended he knew, he'd been stuck. Chloe had persisted, although she'd guessed he didn't know, nagging at him until he'd slapped her. The urge to do the same now was becoming overpowering.

"Wait a few more minutes," he said tightly. The crossroads was around the next corner, and he gazed anxiously ahead, as if he could make it materialize sooner.

Chloe frowned, both puzzled and annoyed. The attentive, generous Crispin of the past few days seemed to have disappeared. Her present companion was much more like the peevish, self-centered boy she remembered from their childhood.

They rounded a corner in the road and she felt Crispin stiffen in his saddle. Curiously, she glanced at him. He had an air of nervous expectancy. He edged his horse closer to hers until their flanks were almost touching. The mare, uncomfortable, whinnied and tried to sidestep. Crispin leaned forward and took hold of Chloe's rein.

"It's all right," she said. "I can manage her perfectly well. Your horse is crowding her."

When Crispin's hand remained on her bridle, she felt a flash of unease. She looked ahead.

A post-chaise stood at the crossroads, three men on the ground beside it. They were looking down the road toward the approaching riders. Chloe suddenly knew that something was wrong and that she was in danger. She held herself very still for a second, gathering herself together, like a gazelle scenting the lion.

Then her whip hand lifted and flashed down, catching Crispin across the back of the hand holding her rein, biting through the soft leather glove. He gave a cry of pain, snatching back his hand, and in the same instant, Chloe touched Maid Marion's flanks and the mare plunged down the road. As they passed the chaise, one of the waiting men gave a shout and leapt into the road after them. Chloe leaned low over the roan's neck and whispered encouragement, urging her on. The shouts continued behind her, and she could hear the pounding of Crispin's hooves in pursuit. The stallion was faster than the mare—longer-legged and with a more powerful chest—and she knew she wouldn't be able to hold her lead.

A crowd of banner-waving men and women ahead straggled across the road, and desperately Chloe rode straight into the middle of them. They closed around her like two halves of an oyster around the pearl, and she reined in the mare, afraid she'd trample one of her unwitting escort. Crispin would never be able to get through. And even if he did, it was hard to imagine what he could do in the midst of such a multitude.

The crowd swelled and bore her onward toward the city. She couldn't escape the throng even if she wanted to, so she allowed herself to be carried forward even while she wondered what they were doing and where they were going.

Hugo was informed by a hedge-cutter that a young man and woman had ridden by on the Manchester road about an hour previously. Satisfied that he was on the right track, he pressed his horse into a gallop. The question was: Had they turned off toward Shipton or continued toward the city? Luck was on his side, however, and at the turning a small boy fishing in the ditch with a worm on a bent pin volunteered the information that a geezer on a black horse and a lady on a roan had gone by toward Manchester. He remembered them because the lady had slowed her horse and asked if he'd managed to catch anything yet.

It sounded like Chloe. But what the devil had they in mind? Were they going to hide her in the city? It would be easy enough to do.

Hugo hesitated for a moment, wondering if he'd do better to go to Shipton anyway and pry what information he could out of its inhabitants. But there was still the faint chance that he could catch up with them before they reached the city. Something could have happened to delay them. Hoping fervently that Chloe would continue to dawdle by the roadside, exchanging greetings with avid young fishermen, he rode on.

The crowds on the road slowed him, but he assumed they would have slowed his quarry also. Vaguely, he wondered what was going on, but he was too intent on pursuit to give it much thought. And then he saw Crispin.

The young man was fighting his way against the crowd, amazingly riding toward Hugo. Hugo pulled his horse into the side of the road in the relative concealment of a massive oak tree and sat calmly waiting for him to come abreast. Since Chloe was not with Crispin, it was to be assumed she'd already been dispatched to her destination. Had they put her in a carriage?

The question was only mildly speculative, since the answer was fast approaching as Crispin slashed with his whip to the left and right, freeing himself from the mob's embrace.

He finally broke out and heaved a sigh of relief. It was short-lived. Hugo Lattimer materialized on the road in front of him.

"A happy meeting, Crispin." Sir Hugo was smiling at him, but it was a smile that sent shivers up Crispin's spine. There was something ineffably menacing about the set of his unshaven jaw; the green eyes had fire in their depths. Although Hugo's mouth smiled, Crispin had the horrible sensation that he was about to be devoured.

Crispin raised his whip to strike his mount's hindquarters. At the same instant Hugo leaned over in an almost leisurely motion and caught his wrist. Crispin gasped at the pain as the gloved fingers tightened. The whip fell to the ground.

"Now," Hugo said, still pleasantly, "let us move out of the road, Crispin. I don't believe we can have a tranquil chat in all this brouhaha." He released his wrist and took his bridle instead. Perforce, Crispin sat his horse as he was led into the shadow of the oak tree.

"Do dismount."

The invitation was delivered with the same smile but cut with a razor's edge.

"I protest—"

"No . . . no, Crispin, such a waste of time," Hugo said, swinging off his horse, hooking Crispin's bridle over his arm. "Do you care to dismount with my assistance?" He drew off his gloves with a threatening purposefulness and stood slapping them in his palm, still smiling.

Crispin felt as powerless as if he were back at school, facing the absolute power of authority. Almost mesmerized, he swung obediently from his horse.

"Wise," Hugo commented, shaking off the bridle and leaning against the trunk of the oak with an appearance of nonchalance. But the physical force emanating from the large frame made Crispin feel like a midget.

"Now," Hugo said, "to points, Crispin. Where, pray, is my ward?"

"Chloe?"

"The very same."

"How should I know?" Sullenness was the best he could muster.

"Well, I should rather imagine you would know since she was obliging . . . or perhaps prudent . . . enough to tell me that she rode out with you earlier this morning." The smile had vanished and the green eyes now burned with a glacial glitter.

"This is absurd." Crispin tried bluster. He turned back to his horse. "I don't know what you're talking about, Sir Hugo. Chloe is your responsibility, not mine, and if your hand isn't strong enough on her bridle, then it's hardly my fault." He gasped as two hands closed around his throat from the back.

"Oh, make no mistake, my friend. My hands are strong enough," Hugo said softly.

Crispin could feel Hugo's breath on his neck. He tried to move his head, but the long, white fingers tightened . . . and tightened.

"Where is she?"

He choked, shook his head. The pressure increased on his windpipe. He was suffocating, his chest heaving.

"Where is she?" The inexorable question was breathed into his ear. Black spots danced before his eyes, and he felt as if his chest were about to burst. "Where is she?"

His shoulders slumped as he struggled to speak. Mercifully, the pressure lessened and the question was asked again.

"Don't know," he choked out.

The vise tightened again, and Crispin thought his head would explode with his lungs. A red mist threatened to swallow him. "Truly," he whispered. "Please."

"Explain." The hands relaxed just enough for him to do so. In a heaving gasping whisper he said that Chloe, for some unknown reason, had left him and bolted with her horse toward the city.

Hugo removed his hands from Crispin's throat and dusted them off with a grimace. "I'm sure you know the reason, but it can wait. You may leave. And you may tell Jasper that it's the mark of a coward to hide behind the ineffectual incompetence of his minions. If he wants to do battle, then I'm ready and waiting . . . I have been for fourteen years," he added. "Tell him, Crispin."

He stood back and watched as the young man remounted, his face red and mottled, one hand unconsciously stroking his throat where the finger bruises purpled on the delicate skin.

Crispin's throat was too sore for a reply even if he'd been able to think of one. For one terrifying moment he had faced his own death by strangulation. He had never imagined such power in a man's fingers. He rode off, bending low over his horse.

Hugo thoughtfully flexed his fingers. A musician's fingers. Delicate and sensitive. A smile of satisfaction touched his lips, then he remounted and turned his horse toward Manchester, where presumably Chloe was to be found, caught up in the crowd. But what the hell were they all up to?

And then he remembered. It was Monday, August sixteen. The day Orator Hunt was to address the Reform Meeting at St. Peter's Fields. The demand was for manhood suffrage and the magistrates would be prepared for the worst.

He turned his horse off the road and rode across country, skirting the crowds in his haste to reach the city.

Chloe stayed with the crowd as it surged onto St. Peter's Fields. The excitement was infectious, and she pushed speculation about Crispin and the post-chaise to one side for the moment. It was all very interesting, and clearly she'd have to discuss it with Hugo, but there wasn't much to be done about it now.

People continued to pour onto the field, a torrent of humanity waving banners and shouting. An air of good humor pervaded the mass, with children playing and tumbling underfoot and young couples, arms entwined, exchanging surreptitious kisses. The hustings were hung with brightly colored flags, others waved gaily from flagpoles. The crowd jostled and chanted on the field, gazing eagerly toward the platform where Orator Hunt would soon step up to speak.

Chloe sat her horse on the outskirts of the throng. She had a clear view over the crowd to the hustings and watched as a party of men climbed onto the platform. A great roar of welcome went up from the gathering and the chant of "Votes for workers" swelled on the sultry summer breeze.

A man in an unusual white top hat stepped to the edge of the platform and the crowd roared louder. The man who'd told them about the Reform Meeting that day she and Hugo had come to Manchester had worn a white top hat, Chloe remembered. Presumably it was some kind of membership insignia.

Orator Hunt's voice rose above the crowd, which fell into a murmuring quiet. But whenever the speaker paused for effect, they roared approval and chanted his name.

Chloe's blood stirred as she strained to hear the orator over the crowd, and then she became aware of a different sound, a strange murmuring coming from one section of the meeting. She swiveled in the saddle and looked toward a church at the far side of the field.

"It must be the folks from Blackburn comin'," a burly man in a cobbler's apron declared from the ground beside her. There was a murmur of agreement as people stood on tiptoe to peer over heads to see what was causing the disturbance.

"It's soldiers," Chloe said. A troop of cavalry in blue and white uniforms trotted around the corner of a garden wall. The sun glinted on the unsheathed blades they held. Wheeling in formation, they lined up in front of a row of houses overlooking the field and facing the hustings.

A shout went up from the crowd, but it sounded perfectly good-humored to Chloe, more of a welcome than anything. And then it happened.

The cavalry rose in their stirrups and waved their sabers over their heads. Someone shouted an order and with a cry the soldiers spurred their horses and charged the front ranks of the throng, slashing right and left with their swords.

Chloe stared in horrified disbelief as the front ranks swayed before the cavalry charge and the air was rent with screams. Around her people were shouting, "Stand fast . . . stand fast." The crowd stood its ground and the soldiers fell back for a minute, unable to force their way through the compact press of humanity to reach Orator Hunt. Then they charged again, their swords chopping and hacking at the people blocking them. Chloe could see spurting blood, and the screams grew agonized, interspersed with groans and cries of terror.

"Break!" someone yelled. "They're killing them and they can't get away." And the cry was taken up. "Break . . . break." The crowd held still, as if drawing breath, and then with a rumbling roar surged and broke apart. It was like a tidal wave, immense and unstoppable. Maid Marion whinnied with fear as the mass of people eddied around her, and Chloe knew she would have bolted if she could have pushed through. Holding tight to the reins, desperate to prevent her from rearing and causing even more havoc to the hapless foot traffic around her, she struggled to guide the mare out of the crowd. All around, people were being trampled in the mob's terror-struck frenzy. The yeomanry charged through them wherever there was an opening, hewing at heads and hands and arms as they forced their way to the hustings and the man they'd come to arrest.

A child fell to the ground and screamed in terror as feet pounded around him. Chloe flung herself from Maid Marion, sweeping the child up. Leading the horse, she clutched the boy against her, stumbling as the mob propelled her forward.

She reached the relative safety of a garden on the outskirts of the field. Maid Marion was sweating and trembling, her eyes rolling, the whites glaring. Chloe set the child on his feet. He stared at her for a moment in shock and then picked up his heels and ran.

Presumably he knew his way home. Chloe felt sick with a rage greater than any she had known. The mob teemed past the garden and suddenly it was quiet. The field, which ten minutes ago had been a maelstrom of humanity, was almost deserted. The hustings were a wrecked heap of broken spars, the remnants of flags fluttering on the flagstaffs, torn banners lying crumpled in the dirt. And beneath the pitiless glare of the August sun, bodies lay as they'd fallen, one on top of another, crushed and suffocated, trampled and cut. The dry grass was littered with the bright fragments of clothes, hats and bonnets, shoes, that had been ripped from bodies in the stampede.

Chloe tied the mare to the garden gate and moved out onto the field. The yeomanry had dismounted and stood around, wiping their sabers, loosening the girths of their horses. The humid air was alive with groans emerging from the mounded bodies and the whinnies of the horses as they pawed the earth and smelled blood.

Other people now appeared on the field, bending over bodies. Chloe knelt beside a young woman, bleeding from a sword cut to her breast. She was alive, though, and her eyelids fluttered. Chloe lifted the skirt of her habit and tore a strip from her petticoat, using it to staunch the blood. Two men passed by, carrying a dead man. An elderly man staggered along, leaning on the arm of a young lad. His lips were blue in his waxen face and he was wheezing painfully.

"I'll take 'er now, miss," a voice said softly. A man bent and picked up the young woman. "Thankee kindly." His eyes were blank, his voice flat.

Chloe wandered over the battlefield, helping where she could as people lifted bodies off bodies, releasing the survivors and the wounded from the suffocating press of flesh.

They were all stunned, moving as if in a trance, saying little or nothing. Out of the sixty thousand peaceful people at St. Peter's Fields that afternoon, four hundred had been wounded and nine men and two women killed by a troop of yeomanry ordered by the city magistrates to arrest Orator Hunt.

Chapter 11

HUGO WAS RIDING fast down Market Street in the eerily deserted city when the rumble, like low thunder, reached him from St. Peter's Fields. His horse started, lifting his head, nostrils flaring. Then the screams came and ice water ran in Hugo's veins. He turned down Cross Street, spurring his horse. People surged toward him, screaming "Cavalry" in warning and explanation as they ran.

The magistrates must have panicked, as he'd been afraid they would. But how the hell would he ever find Chloe in this mob? He rode on against the tide of humanity, searching the crowd. He turned the corner by the church, reaching the field as the last of the fleeing throng rushed past him. He sat his horse, feeling sick as he took in the carnage on the littered field. Was Chloe somewhere at the bottom of one of those misshapen mounds of tangled limbs? She was so tiny, she couldn't possibly survive such a crush.

He dismounted and tethered his horse to a post by the church. Then he walked onto the field. He saw her almost immediately, on her knees beside a prone body. She had lost her hat and her hair was escaping from its pins. It threw off the sun's radiance in a luminous glory of luster and color that was almost shocking against the grimness of the scene.

"Chloe!" He yelled her name across the space that separated them, his knees abruptly weakening with relief.

She looked up, then scrambled to her feet and ran

toward him. "Oh, Hugo!" She fell into his arms, clutching him around the waist with fierce need in a gesture that flooded him with memories to stir his body and set his blood racing.

She was crying and her eyes were like drowned cornflowers.

"Are you hurt?" he demanded roughly.

She shook her head. "No . . . no, not really . . . but I'm so angry. How could they have done such a thing? What possible justification? It was the most terrible . . . terrible . . . wicked thing, Hugo." Her voice caught on a gulping sob.

"Hush." He stroked her hair and pulled out his handkerchief. "Dry your eyes . . . and your nose is running." He mopped the tears and wiped her nose with a briskness that concealed his emotion and enabled him to see her as he wanted to see her—a distressed child in need of comfort.

"I've lost my hat," she said with forlorn irrelevance.

"There are other hats."

"But I was most particularly fond of that one." She looked around the field and said with another cry of outrage, *"Why?* Why would they do such a thing?"

"Fear," he said quietly. "France has taught the power of the mob. They're terrified of a popular uprising."

"I'd guillotine the lot of them," she said fiercely. *"And* knit while their heads fell into the basket . . . except that I can't knit." Her eyes filled with tears again and abruptly she sat on the ground.

"What is it?" Alarmed, Hugo bent over her.

"I don't know," she said. "My legs are shaking. Perhaps it's because I haven't had anything to eat all day except for an apple."

Hugo lifted her to her feet, sure that rather more than her customary complaint of hunger lay behind the sudden faintness. However, satisfying such a basic need might help to distance the afternoon's horror for her. "That's easily remedied." He took her hand. "There's nothing more you can do here."

Chloe glanced around the field. The citizens of Manchester were looking after their own, the field slowly clearing as the wounded were carried off by friends and family.

The anger still burned, but it was true she wasn't needed. Her own concerns could come to the forefront now.

"Crispin was supposed to bring a picnic. . . . Oh, I have to tell you about Crispin." She sniffed and wiped her nose with the back of her free hand as Hugo led her off the field.

"I already know." He handed her back his handkerchief.

"How?" She blew her nose vigorously and offered him the crumpled ball.

"Keep it," he said. "I came across him and he was . . . uh, induced, shall we say, to tell me that you had left him in some haste. He affected not to know why."

"There was a post-chaise and I had the strangest feeling they were going to force—induced?" She looked up at him, momentarily diverted. "Did you hurt him?"

"Not much."

"I wish you had."

For such a healing soul and champion of the underdog, she could be remarkably ruthless, Hugo thought. "Crispin is just obeying your half brother," he told her. "Like the men the other night. I've known that all along, and I don't believe in wreaking vengeance on minions."

"The men the other night?" Chloe stopped and turned to look up at him. "You mean . . . they wanted *me*, not Dante?"

Hugo's lips curved a fraction at her astonishment. "Strange as it may seem to you, lass, I believe that you're rather more valuable a prize than that mongrel . . . not that I'm casting aspersions on Dante's lineage, you understand . . . but . . ."

The teasing remark lifted the shadows somewhat on the somber countenance. "What would they want with me?"

"You're a wealthy young woman. Jasper would like to keep your fortune in the family."

"By marrying me to Crispin," she asserted. She kicked at a loose pebble, her mouth hardening. "He can't *force* me to marry him?"

"No, not if I have a say in the matter," Hugo agreed calmly. "But if he got his hands on you, he'd have a damn good try."

Chloe absorbed this in silence. They reached the garden where she'd left Maid Marion and she withdrew her hand from Hugo's.

"Where are you going?"

"To fetch my horse . . . or, rather, Jasper's horse. You didn't think I was riding Dapple, did you?"

Hugo realized he hadn't given the matter any thought. And when he saw the animal she led over, he whistled in admiration. "Beautiful lines."

"Yes, she's out of Red Queen by Sherrif . . . I know the stallion but not the dam. Sherrif's the pride of Jasper's stud." She stroked the mare's neck. "She's highly strung, but she seems quieter now."

Hugo frowned. "She'll have to be returned to Shipton."

"I told Crispin to tell Jasper I couldn't accept her as a gift, but I *would* purchase her," Chloe informed him.

"Oh, did you now?" He raised his eyebrows. It seemed an appropriate juncture to initiate the new regime and assert his seriously diminished authority with his headstrong ward. "And just who gave you permission to make such a major decision? Permit me to remind you, Miss Gresham, that your fortune is in my control and *I* will decide how it's to be spent."

"But that's silly when we both know this horse is a good buy and I don't—"

Hugo silenced her with a raised forefinger. "You may not be aware of it, young Chloe, but you are already in a good deal of very hot water. I shouldn't compound your position if I were you. You've enough explaining to do as it is."

Chloe bit her lip. "I didn't think you'd be vexed after what's happened here."

"What happened here has nothing to do with how and why you happen to be in the middle of it." He caught her waist and lifted her onto the mare. "We'll discuss it in the quiet of Girton's Coffee House."

"But I did leave you a note so you wouldn't be worried," she ventured as he mounted his own horse.

"I will take that into account," he said. "But how much it will weigh against my having to leap from my bed and chase after you without so much as a mouthful of coffee or a moment to shave, I don't know."

It didn't sound too promising to Chloe. She cast him a sideways glance. He did look uncomfortably in need of hot water and a razor. "I did save myself," she pointed out.

"If you'd done as you were told, it wouldn't have been necessary."

Chloe lapsed into a somewhat apprehensive silence.

Girton's Coffee House was empty of custom. The entire city seemed to be in shock, people gathered in dazed knots on street corners or huddled in doorways. Mr. Lampton greeted his guests without ceremony, asking immediately if they'd been at St. Peter's Fields. Hugo told him what he knew.

"Eh, but it's 'ard to credit," Lampton said, shaking his

head. "It'll set the cat among the pigeons, you mark my words."

"They've arrested the orator." A man appeared in the doorway, his face drawn, a cudgel in his hand. "Folks is gatherin' at the Mitre." Announcement made, he vanished to stop at other doors down the street.

"Not me," Lampton said, shaking his head again. "There's trouble enow. What can I get for you folk?"

"A pot of chocolate for the lady, coffee for myself, and whatever you can provide in the way of nuncheon," Hugo readily informed him.

A tureen of potato soup and a cold chicken appeared in short order, and Hugo waited until they'd both satisfied their hunger. Then he leaned back in his chair, crossing one booted leg over the other, and bent a stern eye on his ward.

"Well?" he said.

Chloe shifted uneasily but took up the offensive, meeting the green eyes with a defiant light in her own. "I didn't know Crispin meant me any harm. You didn't say anything about suspecting Jasper of wanting to kidnap me. If you had, of course I wouldn't have gone with him."

"I may not have shared my suspicions with you, but as I recall, you were most expressly forbidden to leave the estate without permission."

"I've known Crispin all my life. We used to play together as children. I couldn't see anything wrong with going for a ride with him."

"If you didn't see anything wrong with it, why didn't you simply ask me?" He raised his eyebrows. "You could have presented such a convincing case quite eloquently."

"You weren't there to ask," Chloe retorted. "And Samuel said I wasn't to go into the library."

He shook his head. "That won't do, lass. You had only to ask Samuel to consult me."

Chloe could think of nothing with which to counteract this truth.

"It couldn't have been because you decided I didn't warrant consulting, now, could it?" he mused. "It couldn't have been that you simply decided to flout my authority because you were out of temper with me?"

Chloe decided she knew what a pinned butterfly must feel like as the green eyes fixed her with a steady and uncomfortably knowing look.

Hugo nodded slowly when she said nothing. "I thought as much. So, what am I going to do with you, Miss Gresham?"

Chloe broke the hold of that mesmerizing gaze and decided it was time to defend herself with the biggest guns she had. She put up her chin. "Yes, I was out of temper with you. And with very good reason . . . if you can remember." A slight flush blossomed on her cheek, but she continued to meet his eye steadily.

"That brings us to something else we need to discuss," he said. His voice was crisp and level, but he didn't change his relaxed posture. "I am going to say this just once and then the subject will not be referred to again by either of us. I regret what happened more than I can say, Chloe. But it happened and it's over. I was, God forgive me, not in my right mind. I took advantage of your innocence and of my position—"

"But I wanted—"

"No!" He swung forward, his hands coming to rest on the table between them, his face close to hers. "No, Chloe. You will not say it. You're far too young to know what you could have wanted. It was an aberration, the product of a diseased mind . . . mine. And it's finished."

It wasn't. She could feel it in every bone and sinew of

her body, the knowledge flowed with her blood through her veins. It was no more finished for Hugo than it was for herself. But argument wouldn't convince him. It would need something much more potently persuasive.

"And let's just get one more thing straight while we're about it." He sat back again, as if satisfied that her silence indicated acceptance. "I may have given you the impression that I'm somewhat lax, careless about conventions, and easygoing enough to be treated without undue attention. To an extent that's true. But I have my limits, and if you find them, lass, I can safely promise that the discovery will prove most uncomfortable."

He drew on his gloves and stood up, beckoning to the server. "Bring my reckoning, lad."

He pulled Chloe's chair back for her and said in much the same tone, "Since we're beginning this relationship on a new footing, we'll not on this occasion revisit the past, but it'll be worth remembering from now on that I have an inconvenient need to be obeyed by those in my charge."

There seemed no obvious response to a statement that sounded all too convincing. She stood aside as he paid the reckoning. He ushered her outside in customary fashion with a hand between her shoulder blades and lifted her onto the mare.

"Don't look so disconcolate, lass," he said, suddenly smiling. "I'm no ogre and I'm certain we'll deal extremely well together from now on. And if you wish to keep the horse, then I'll send payment to Jasper." He chuckled. "It's a nice twist that'll have him spitting, I'll lay odds."

His ward managed a smile, but she was feeling too chastened to enjoy properly the prospect of her brother's reaction to such a table-turning. It was one thing to plan the seduction of the easygoing, insouciant

Hugo she'd assumed sobriety would return to her, quite another to make such plans with the stern, composed guardian he'd now become.

They rode out of the city and met Samuel on the road. "Oh, thank God ye're safe," he said, his weather-beaten face twisted with anxiety. He turned his horse to ride beside Hugo. "I got no news of Miss and the young man on the road to Edgecombe, so turned back to follow ye. But the crowds was summat awful. Couldn't 'ardly get through. And what the 'ell's goin' on in the city?"

. Hugo explained. "Chloe was in the middle of it," he concluded.

Samuel cast her a sharp glance, taking in her pallor. "Y're not 'urt?"

"No." She shook her head. "But it was wicked, Samuel. Evil! They just charged the crowd with their swords."

"Damn yeomanry," Samuel muttered. "You wouldn't think they w'd do that to their own kind."

"No," Chloe agreed. "Any more than you'd think my own brother would try to kidnap me and make me marry Crispin. But I still don't see how he could *force* me into marriage, Hugo."

Hugo saw Jasper as he had been in the crypt . . . Jasper holding down a feebly struggling young woman whose eyes were glazed with drugs and liquor; Jasper raising his hand to a cringing serving maid who'd had the misfortune to drop a plate at his feet; Jasper taking a dog whip to a hound that had displeased him. Not images he would share with his ward.

Chloe was chilled anew by his expression. She'd seen it before—a mask of anger and contempt, carved and immobile, his eyes the haunted eyes of a man who looked into hell.

And then his face cleared. He shook his head briskly. He'd reached some accommodation with his memories in the dreadful hours in the library and, while they'd never leave him, their power was lessened.

"He's not going to get the chance, Chloe," he declared. "From now on you are going to stay within eyesight and earshot of the house at all times unless you're with me or Samuel . . . even if I have to tether you."

Chloe offered no argument. Apart from the fact that she was more shaken than she cared to admit by the ruthlessness of her brother's plotting, it would suit her own plans to stay close to Hugo. Once she'd overcome the awkward attack of conscience that had hit him with his newfound sobriety, she could pursue her London plan. It was a plan she was convinced would benefit them both. Hugo was wasting his life in his neglected house on the Lancashire moors, and if he wouldn't save himself from such a desolate and meaningless existence, then she'd have to do it for him.

An idea glimmered and a spark of cheerfulness penetrated the bleakness of the day's memories. "I wonder if that woman you had in the library the other night was in the crowd," she remarked casually. "I hope she wasn't hurt. She seemed very nice."

Hugo drew breath sharply. She was looking at him with an imp of mischief dancing in her eyes and a wicked little curve to her mouth. His world tilted. Grimly, he brought it back on an even keel. He glared at her and said in soft warning, "I should be very careful if I were you, miss."

Chloe put her head on one side as if considering the advice, then said in a puzzled tone, "But I only said I thought she was nice. Rather plump, of course, but some men like that, I believe. And she had a kind smile and seemed very cheerful."

Samuel choked and Hugo realized just in time that by responding in any way at all to these outrageous remarks, he would fall into a pit of depthless indignity.

Ignoring her observation, he turned to Samuel with a comment on the afternoon's mayhem.

Chloe nudged the mare's flanks and took off down the road at a mad gallop, her hair flying out behind her, the warm air whistling past her ears. The speed seemed to clear her head of the day's confusions, tensions, and agonies, and her body relaxed, moving fluidly with the roan's long, graceful stride.

She had decided how to broach the citadel of Hugo Lattimer's conscience. Constant provocation. She would keep him whirling with one challenge after another. She *knew* instinctively that he wanted to respond to her as he had done once. And since that one experience had aroused in her a vortex of curiosity and yearnings, she could see no bar to bringing about the satisfaction of their mutual interests. And once that was achieved, then she could set about arranging a future that would haul Hugo from his self-imposed renunciation of the world and put her well beyond her half brother's reach.

Chapter 12

WHEN CHLOE CAME down to the kitchen the following morning, Hugo was sitting at the table in buckskins and top boots, a white linen cravat tied neatly if without great artistry at his throat.

"Are you going to visit someone?" Chloe filled a beaker from the milk churn and drank deeply.

"Your half brother," he said, pushing his plate away and leaning back in his chair. "To settle the matter of Maid Marion. You did say you wanted to keep her, didn't you?"

"Oh, yes, of course." She regarded him thoughtfully, and he caught himself thinking that her eyes were like gentians in the sun. "Will you be discussing anything else?"

Hugo shook his head. "I'll play it by ear, but I hardly think it'll be necessary to spell anything out, lass."

"No, I suppose not," she agreed, trawling her fingers through a bowl of gooseberries on the table until she found a particularly succulent one.

"Jasper's not obtuse . . . although I'm not sure the same could be said of Crispin." She popped a berry into her mouth and punctured the skin with her front teeth, closing her eyes in unconscious pleasure as the sharp juice squirted down her throat and the lush round fruit yielded its flesh. "Are you going alone?"

Hugo was for a minute riveted by the sheer sensuality of her expression and missed the careful deliberation of the question. How could such a vibrant creature so full of earthly hungers have grown in Elizabeth's pure, pale womb? But she'd also sprung from the loins of Stephen Gresham. The black thought came and went with surprising lack of pain.

He stood up. "I'll only be a couple of hours. If you care to ride out with me this afternoon, lass, I have to do a long-overdue survey of the estate. It'll give Dante a decent walk too."

"That'll be nice," Chloe said somewhat absently. "Are you leaving now?"

"Shortly." He strode to the door. "Samuel, I think it's time young Billy got off his backside and cleaned up the courtyard. He's been getting away with murder."

"Right you are," Samuel said. "I'll tell 'im." A pleased little smile lit up his creased countenance as Hugo left the kitchen, and he nodded to himself with secret satisfaction. "You want coddled eggs, lass?"

"Oh, no, thank you, Samuel." Chloe was on her way out of the kitchen. "I don't think I want any breakfast." On which extraordinary statement, she whisked herself out of the door, closing it firmly on Dante, left inside.

"Lord love us," Samuel muttered. "Now what's she up to?"

In her room Chloe threw off her gown and hastily donned her riding habit. She flew down the stairs and waited in the hall until she heard Hugo ride out of the courtyard. Then she ran to the stable. "Billy, help me saddle the mare."

The stable lad shrugged but offered a lethargic helping hand. Chloe led the horse to the mounting block and sprang into the saddle. "Tell Samuel that I've gone with Sir Hugo," she instructed. "Tell him right away, Billy."

She waited just long enough for the lad to round the corner to the kitchen door and then trotted Maid Marion down the drive. Samuel wouldn't worry if he knew she was with Hugo.

On the road she encouraged the roan to a gallop toward Shipton. Hugo had perhaps ten minutes start, and he wouldn't be making particular speed since she doubted he was in a hurry. She should catch up with him very soon.

Hugo heard the pounding hooves behind him and at first took no notice. It was a relatively busy highway. When they were almost beside him, he glanced incuriously over his shoulder.

Chloe beamed at him, drawing rein as she came up with him. "I thought you might like some company."

"You thought what?" He was for a moment completely taken aback.

"I thought that you'd probably regret deciding to go alone," she said, still beaming. "And there you'd be, riding along, feeling lonely, with no one to talk to. And I don't mind at all bearing you company, so here I am."

The bare-faced effrontery of this sunnily artless justification rendered him momentarily speechless. Chloe continued to chatter, commenting on the warm morning, the beauty of the hedgerows, a red squirrel.

"Quiet!" he demanded when he'd finally gathered his forces. "You have a very short memory, Miss Gresham. I told you only yesterday that I do not tolerate disobedience from those in my charge."

"Oh, but I'm not disobeying," she said earnestly. "I was most particularly careful not to ask you if I could accompany you, so you haven't told me that I may not. If you remember, I only asked you if you intended to go alone."

Hugo closed his eyes briefly. Of all the scheming little foxes!

"And then, as I said, it occurred to me that no one would truly wish to be alone on such a beautiful morning, and if you were regretting it, then—"

"I heard you the first time," he snapped. "And it was no more convincing then than it is now."

"When you've stopped being vexed, you'll realize how much pleasanter it is to have my company," she said with utter confidence, still smiling. "And I can't come to any harm from Jasper and Crispin when you're there to protect me. And I know exactly how we should behave. It'll be most diverting. We'll behave as if nothing happened yesterday . . . as if we don't suspect anything. We'll just say we've come to buy Maid Marion, and I'll say that I was sure Crispin would like to know how Plato—"

"Plato?" He was betrayed into the interjection.

"The owl," she said impatiently. "I'm sure Crispin will like to hear that he's doing so well. Or at least, that's what I'll tell him. But I'm sure he doesn't really give a damn."

"You're sure he doesn't *what*?" He seemed to be reeling from one outrage to another.

"Give a damn."

"That's what I thought you said. I refuse to believe the Misses Trent can have taught you such language."

"Of course not," she said cheerfully. "I expect I learned it from the poacher or the grooms at the livery stables."

"Then you will oblige me by unlearning it immediately."

"Oh, don't be stuffy. You say it all the time."

"*You* will not."

"Oh." Her nose wrinkled at this, then she shrugged and said equably, "Very well. If you don't wish it. But what do you think of my plan with Jasper and Crispin? I can't wait to see Jasper's face when we trot up to his door . . . all smiles and politeness."

Hugo privately admitted that the scheme had a certain appeal. However, he was not going to give his manipulative traveling companion any such satisfaction, and set about dampening her confident high spirits. "This is not a matter for childish games-playing, and your presence is as inappropriate as it's unwelcome. My business with Jasper most emphatically does not need your input."

"Oh." Chloe seemed to consider this, then she said, "I suppose I could go back, but it's quite a long way, and I know you don't want me riding alone."

"And just what, pray, were you doing to get here in the first place?"

The sarcasm ran off her like water on oiled leather. "But that was only a few minutes. I galloped like the wind to catch you up."

Hugo gave up. He wasn't going to send her back on her own. He could take her home, of course, but it would be a waste of a morning. He rode on, maintaining a severe silence.

Chloe seemed to feel it was her duty to entertain him. She filled his silence with a cheerful commentary on their surroundings, some reflections on the events of the previous day, and anything else that popped into her head.

He interrupted a minute description of all six of Beatrice's kittens. *"Must* you talk so much?"

"Not if you don't wish it," she said, instantly accommodating. "I want to be exactly the companion you would wish, so if you prefer to be quiet, then I won't say another word."

A sound halfway between a strangled sob and a choke of laughter came from her companion.

"Have I amused you?" Her eyes were brimful of merriment as she looked at him.

"I am rarely amused by nuisances. If you value your skin, Miss Gresham, you will refrain from all conversational sallies until we get home," he declared, managing to school his features with some difficulty.

When they turned up the driveway to Gresham Hall, Hugo wasn't expecting his own reaction. It had been fourteen years since he'd set foot in this place, and Elizabeth, his unattainable love, had been young and alive. The ruined edifice of Shipton Abbey stood out against the summer sky in a clearing to the right of the driveway, halfway between the road and the house.

He averted his gaze, then forced himself to look at it, to see in his mind's eye the steps that led to the crypt. The dank smell of corruption was suddenly vivid in the soft summer air, overlaying the rich scent of honeysuckle.

"What is it?" Chloe asked in a near whisper, all raillery and mischief gone from face and voice.

He wrenched his gaze from the scene of past evils. "Painted devils."

"You said that once before. What are they?"

"None of your business, Miss Poke-nose. It's time you developed some respect for other people's privacy."

"That's unjust," she said with quiet force. "And you know it is."

It was. He sighed. "Since you're bearing me company against my wishes, it would be tactful, not to say prudent, to intrude on my consciousness as little as possible."

"Oh, pah," Chloe said. "If you're unhappy, then of course I'd try to help."

"Of course you would," he murmured. "I can't think how I could have thought otherwise. However, you may set your mind at rest. I am not unhappy . . . merely annoyed with you."

Chloe clearly didn't think this worth a response. "I haven't been here since Mama's funeral," she observed next. "Louise was very kind, but then Jasper and Crispin weren't around, so she wasn't afraid."

Hugo turned sharply toward her. "Afraid?"

"Most people are afraid of Jasper," she said matter-of-factly. "Or at least those people he has power over."

"Are you afraid of him?" He looked at her closely.

Chloe wrinkled her nose in thought. "I don't think so," she said. "Or at least until yesterday I wasn't. I just disliked him heartily. But since he doesn't have any power over me, I don't have any reason to fear him, do I?"

"It's to be hoped not," he said neutrally.

Chloe seemed to accept this and changed the subject. "Are we going up to the front door?"

"I don't know how else one would approach when paying a social call."

"I always went through the side door . . . because I'm a relative, I suppose."

"Well, on this occasion you'll do as I do."

"Of course," she said demurely as they trotted onto the gravel sweep in front of the house. "Shall I bang the knocker?"

"If you wish," he said, giving up his attempt to maintain his severity. It was impossible to stay annoyed with her for more than a minute, and pretending was clearly as much a waste of effort as it was tedious.

Chloe slipped from her horse and ran up the steps, seizing the great brass knocker and banging it with gusto.

The door was opened by a footman in a baize apron. He blinked at the visitor.

"Good morning, Hector. Is Sir Jasper in?"

"Well, well, if it isn't my little sister." Jasper spoke from behind the footman. "That'll be all, Hector." He stepped into the doorway and looked down on Chloe, one eyebrow raised. "So what brings you?" His eye flickered over her head to where Hugo still sat his horse, impassive on the drive.

"I've come to buy Maid Marion," Chloe informed him.

"I told Crispin I couldn't accept her as a gift, but I'd like to purchase her."

Jasper put his hands on her shoulders and moved her out of his way. He walked slowly down the steps to Hugo. Chloe followed, not a whit put out by being ignored.

Crispin came around from the side of the house, and she called out to him. "Good morning, Crispin. We came to buy Maid Marion, and I thought you might like to know how the owl is recovering. The splint is holding nicely." Her smile embraced the three men with an ingenuous confidence that fooled none of them.

Hugo's eye caught hers in acceptance of the scene she was setting. "Stop prattling, Chloe," he said with feigned exasperation as he dismounted. "Jasper, how much do you want for the mare?"

"I'm not sure she's for sale," Jasper said.

"Oh, but she must be!" Chloe cried. "You were going to give her to me, so you can't say you want to keep her. And I so enjoyed riding her yesterday. I couldn't bear to give her up." She turned the brilliance of her smile on Crispin. "It was such a pity we weren't able to have our picnic, Crispin, but I became caught up in the crowds going into the city for the Reform Meeting, and I couldn't turn back."

Crispin put a hand to his throat. A starched cravat hid the finger bruises from his audience, but the involuntary gesture spoke for itself to Hugo and Jasper.

Jasper's eyes narrowed to slits as he looked between his stepson and Hugo Lattimer. "It's to be regretted you missed your picnic, little sister," he said blandly. "Crispin had gone to a great deal of trouble to ensure your pleasure."

"Yes, I was aware," she replied. "I was desolated to spoil his efforts."

Hugo decided that it was time he joined the fencing

match. Chloe seemed to be running away with herself. "Chloe, I asked you to stop prattling. Jasper, do you have a price for the mare?"

"Three thousand pounds" was the prompt response. "Since my sister won't accept the gift, then I'd be a fool not to ask a fair price."

"A fair price!" Chloe squeaked. "Three thousand—"

"Hold your tongue!" Hugo put a heavy hand on her shoulder. "This immoderate behavior is most unbecoming."

"Yes, but—"

"Quiet!"

Chloe subsided, glaring at her half brother. His cold eyes slid over her, and for the first time she read menace as well as the usual dislike in their depths. Then he turned to Hugo, a sardonic smile on his thin lips.

"Three thousand pounds. Since I now find myself short by such a sum . . ."

"Quite," Hugo said in perfect understanding. He had stopped Elizabeth's payments to Jasper and was now being required to make up for it. Chloe's slender shoulder was rigid beneath his hand, and he could feel the currents of tension running through her. Clearly she, too, understood what her brother was demanding. But if he expected her to rush into ill-considered speech at this realization, he was mistaken.

"We have to see the dam," she said as calmly now as she'd been fervent before. "I know Sherrif, but I'd like to inspect Red Queen."

Jasper inclined his head in acknowledgment. "Crispin, take Chloe to the stables and show her the Queen. I'm sure she'll be satisfied." He turned back to Hugo. "Shall we conclude this business in my book room, Lattimer?"

"I doubt it's a business to be so easily concluded,"

Hugo commented with an oblique smile. "But by all means let's discuss terms. However, you'll understand if I don't accept your hospitality. Since I don't extend my own, it would be a trifle hypocritical, wouldn't you say?"

He turned to his ward, who'd made no move to accompany Crispin to the stables. "Chloe, if you intend to inspect the dam, I suggest you do so."

He and Jasper waited until Chloe and Crispin had disappeared around the side of the house.

"She always was an ill-mannered brat," Jasper said with clear venom.

Hugo raised an eyebrow and said quietly, "Too ill-mannered to make a suitable wife for your stepson, Jasper? Or would her fortune compensate adequately for any faults in character?"

Jasper's florid complexion deepened, but his eyes were almost opaque as they skidded away from Hugo's direct gaze. "Are you trying to say something, Lattimer?"

Hugo shook his head. "What would I be trying to say, Jasper?"

Jasper smiled his thin smile again and observed with soft insult, "Something seems to have sobered you up, Hugo. I wonder how long it'll last."

"Long enough to see you in hell," Hugo responded pleasantly. He turned his back and remounted his horse. "I'm not interested in the mare at any price. I'm not interested in *any* dealings with you, Jasper . . . unless you should be foolish enough to meddle again in my bailiwick."

Jasper's tongue flickered over his lips. "You are mistaken, Hugo. It's you who are meddling in *my* bailiwick. You did it once before, and I'll be doubly avenged, make no mistake."

Hugo nodded. "So we understand each other. It's always as well to be certain of that."

Chloe and Crispin reappeared, and he called her sharply.

She hurried over. "Are we leaving?"

"Yes, but without the mare." He held down his hand. "Up you come. Put your foot on my boot."

Chloe showed neither surprise nor disappointment at this abrupt, unexpected conclusion to the negotiations. She took his hand, put her foot on his, and sprang upward as he pulled her. She settled on the saddle in front of him.

"Good day, Jasper . . . Crispin." She smiled down at them with such friendliness, one would believe only pleasantries could ever take place between them. "Thank you for lending me Maid Marion . . . and for showing me Red Queen. She's beautiful."

"And to think your brother called you an ill-mannered brat," Hugo remarked with a dry smile as they rode off. "When it suits you, you can be impeccably polite."

Chloe chuckled. "I wouldn't give them the satisfaction of thinking I was disappointed. I'm sorry about Maid Marion, but I certainly wouldn't have paid three thousand for her."

"I'm relieved to hear it, since I had no intention of doing so."

"Would he not negotiate?" A hint of wistfulness crept into her voice.

"I didn't attempt it."

"Oh. I suppose you had your reasons."

"I did, lass. But we'll buy you a horse this afternoon. Squire Gillingham has a good stud in Edgecombe. I'm sure he'll have something suitable."

His arm encircled her lightly as he held the reins, and she leaned back against him, fitting herself into his shoulder as naturally as if she always rode in such fashion. The seeming artlessness of her proximity produced a riot of confused and confusing responses in both mind and body, and Hugo had the unnerving suspicion that Chloe was quite aware of her effect. Every time he persuaded himself she had to be protected as an ingenuous young innocent on the verge of womanhood, she did or said something that proved beyond doubt that in all important matters she had crossed the line long since.

Samuel came out to the courtyard as they rode in. "Took me by surprise, you did," he said gruffly. "I didn't know Sir 'Ugo 'ad said you could go along wi' him."

"I hadn't," Hugo said, dismounting. He reached up to swing Chloe down from her perch.

"He didn't say I *could* go with him, Samuel," Chloe explained with a sunny smile. "But he didn't say I couldn't either."

Samuel stared at her in bemusement, shaking his head like a dog with a flea in his ear, his mouth ajar as he looked for words.

"Don't even try, Samuel," Hugo said with a wry grin. "When it comes to logic-chopping, the lass can produce the finest examples since Eve ate the apple."

Hugo was playing the pianoforte before dinner that evening when Chloe came hesitantly into the library. He turned as the door opened, offered her a smile of greeting, and continued with his playing. It had been a long time since he'd played simply for the pleasure of it . . . a long time since he'd been sufficiently at peace to enjoy the music for its own sake.

Chloe curled into the big wing chair by the window, where she could watch his face as she listened. She was enthralled by the play of emotions flitting across his face as the long, slender fingers drew deep feeling from the notes, bringing the music alive in the room. Dusk encroached as the sun left the last corners of the library, and his face fell into shadow, but she could still see the mobile mouth, relaxed and half smiling, the long lock of hair flopping over his wide brow.

It occurred to her that there was more than one Hugo contained in that powerful frame. She'd enjoyed the easygoing, humorous companion; she'd felt the sting of the authoritarian commander; and once she'd known the man of passion. Now there was Hugo the musician. Perhaps it was in this form that all the others came together and found expression.

Hugo stopped playing and turned toward her, resting one forearm on the top of the instrument. "Did they teach you to play at that seminary?"

"Oh, yes. I have all the accomplishments," she assured him earnestly.

Hugo stifled his smile. "Well, let me hear you." He stood up and gestured to the bench.

"But I couldn't play that piece," she said, rising with great reluctance.

"I wouldn't expect you to. It's my own composition." He struck tinder and flint and lit the branched candlestick, then moved it so it would fall over the keyboard. "I'll find you something simpler." He riffled through a pile of sheet music and selected a familiar folk song with a pretty lilting melody. "Try this."

Chloe sat down, feeling as if she were on trial as he placed the music on the stand. She flexed her fingers. "I haven't practiced in ages."

"It doesn't matter. Relax and do the best you can." He sat in the chair she'd vacated and closed his eyes, prepared to listen. He opened them very rapidly after the first few bars and his expression became inscrutable.

Chloe finished with a flourish and turned to face him with a smile of triumph. It had been easier than she'd expected.

"Mmm," he said. "That was a slapdash performance, lass."

"It was perfectly correct," she protested. "I know I didn't play a wrong note."

"Oh, no, you were note perfect," he agreed. "Your ability to sight-read is not at issue."

"Then what was wrong with it?" She sounded both hurt and aggrieved.

"Couldn't you tell? You raced through it as if the only thing on your mind was to get it over with as soon as possible."

Chloe chewed her lip. She was not enjoying this, but honesty required that she admit the criticism. "I suppose it's because at the seminary we had to practice until we got a particular piece right. Then we could stop."

Hugo pulled a disgusted face. "So practicing was punishment for failure. Good God, what a criminal way to teach." He stood up. "Your mother was a most accomplished musician. . . . Move up."

"Was she?" Chloe shifted along the bench as he sat beside her. "I never heard her play." His thigh was hard and warm against the thin muslin of her gown, and she kept her leg very still, knowing that the minute he became aware of their proximity he would move away. And that was the last thing she wanted.

The laudanum must have killed the artist as effectively as it killed the mother, he thought sadly, too engrossed in music and his train of thought to be aware for once of the slight, fragrant body so close to his. "She was a harpist as well as a pianist, and she sang like an angel."

"*I* can sing," Chloe said, as if this might compensate for her lamentable performance at the keyboard.

"Can you?" He couldn't help smiling at this anxious interjection. "In a minute, you may sing for me, but now we're going to improve on your rendering of 'Larkrise.'

Listen to this." He played the opening bars. "There's a bird in there . . . not a herd of rogue elephants. Try it."

Chloe produced a faithful rendition of his pauses and tones as he took her through the piece stave by stave. "There's nothing wrong with your ear," he commented at the end. "We'll just have to cure the laziness."

"I am not lazy," Chloe protested. "But no one taught me properly, you said so." Her expression was one of half-laughing indignation as she turned her face toward him in the candlelight. "You can teach me."

His breath caught. Such heart-stopping beauty didn't seem possible. She shifted on the bench and her thigh pressed against his, sending a jolt of arousal through his loins.

"Stand up," he commanded sharply. "You can't sing sitting down."

Chloe didn't move for a second, and her eyes were filled with awareness as they searched his expression. A smile quivered on her lips . . . a smile of pure sensual invitation.

"Stand up, Chloe," he repeated, but evenly this time.

She did so slowly, still smiling, her skirt brushing across his knees, her hand resting lightly on his shoulder as if in support. "What shall I sing?"

" 'Larkrise,' " he said, clearing his throat. "The tune will be familiar. You can read the words as I play."

Her voice was true but untrained, lacking Elizabeth's power and intensity, and she still had a tendency to rush. He wondered as the last note died whether it would be interesting to see how he could improve on what nature had given her.

"There, I told you I can sing," she declared. "Wasn't that pretty?"

"My child, you lack discrimination," he said, embracing the role of mentor and tutor with relief. It gave him much-needed distance. "There's nothing wrong with your pitch, but your voice is weak because you don't breathe properly. Why were you in such a hurry?"

Chloe looked somewhat crestfallen and, as he'd intended, the sensual invitation was quite vanished from both face and posture. "I didn't think I was."

"Well, you were. But we can do something about it if you'd like to."

"You would teach me?" A speculative look was in her eye, but she was looking down at the music and he didn't see it. She was thinking that music lessons would of necessity involve more of this closeness; and the closer they became, the sooner she would be able to overcome his inconvenient sober prudery.

"If you'd like me to," he repeated. "You have to do it because you want to. And that means practicing because you want to and not because I tell you you must."

"How long would I have to practice every day?" she asked cautiously.

Hugo threw up his hands. "As long as you feel it's necessary to achieve what *you* want to achieve."

"But what if I don't achieve what *you* want me to achieve?"

"Then the lessons will cease, since clearly you won't be interested."

"Oh." She frowned. "How well did you know my mother?"

It was a legitimate question, one he'd been expecting at some point. He made his voice matter-of-fact. "Quite well. But a long time ago."

"Why didn't you see her recently? You lived so close and she had no friends. But she must have counted you as a friend. She wouldn't have made you my guardian otherwise."

He'd prepared his answer to this during the long night watches of the insomniac. "She withdrew from the world after your father's death. You know that yourself."

"So, she didn't want to see you?"

"I don't think she wanted to see anyone. But she knew she had my friendship, regardless."

"I see." Still frowning, Chloe wandered over to the window. The evening star had appeared, hanging over the valley. "You must have known my father, then."

He stiffened. All the preparation in the world couldn't prevent his blood from racing or his palms from sweating. "I knew him."

"How well?"

There was only one honest answer. "Very well."

"I don't remember him at all. I was three when he died, you'd think I'd have some vague memory . . . a smell, or an impression, or a sensation. Wouldn't you?"

Stephen had had nothing to do with his daughter. Hugo doubted he'd laid eyes on her more than a couple of times in those three years. He had a son, and the son had a stepson, and only they were important in his scheme of things. If Elizabeth had given him a son, it would have been different. The child would have come under the father's influence from his earliest moments. A girl child was of considerably less interest than the hunters in his stable.

"He was in London a great deal," Hugo said.

"What was he like?"

Evil . . . unimaginably evil . . . corrupting all who fell under his influence with the devil's enticements.

"Not unlike Jasper to look at. A bruising rider, a clever man, very popular in Society, which is why he spent so much time in London, I believe . . . he and your mother were somewhat estranged."

"And then he died in the accident," she stated flatly. "I'm surprised a bruising rider should have broken his neck on the hunting field."

It was the official explanation, one that protected the

Congregation's secrets. Stephen Gresham was buried in the family vault, the victim of a riding accident.

"Supper's ready." Samuel appeared in the open doorway.

With relief Hugo ushered his immediately diverted ward out of the library.

Chapter 13

C RISPIN HAD BEEN watching his stepfather throughout dinner. He knew from the signs that Jasper was in one of his more fearsome rages. The morning's visit from Hugo Lattimer and Chloe had put bellows to the smoldering ashes of his fury at the failure of the previous day. When Crispin had returned empty-handed and with the marks of Hugo's fingers on his throat, Jasper had held back his wrath at his stepson's failure. Now Crispin was afraid that the reprieve was to be short-lived. Someone would have to pay for whatever had happened between Lattimer and Jasper that morning.

Louise also recognized her husband's mood. She sat trembling throughout the meal, terrified that a servant would fumble, or a dish would not be hot enough, or his wineglass wouldn't be refreshed quickly enough. Any domestic derelictions, however minor, would be visited on her. There would be first the icy request that she correct the fault immediately. Later that night would come the punishment. He would humiliate her with his body while his voice softly taunted until he grew bored with her weeping and he would go to his own bed.

The servants knew their own danger and tiptoed around the gloomy, silent dining hall, keeping their eyes on the floor and standing as far away as possible from their master when they served him.

Jasper looked up suddenly. "What's the matter with you, my dear wife? You look as blue as a gaffed carp."

Louise jumped and tried to find something to say.

"Oh, nothing . . . nothing at all, Jasper. Nothing's the matter . . . not at all . . . at all . . ."

"I take your point," Jasper interrupted with heavy sarcasm. "There's no need to belabor it, my dear. However, surely you must have some conversation with which to enliven the dinner table. Some detail of domestic trivia to impart, perhaps . . . or some piece of news from a friend . . . but, I was forgetting, you don't have any friends, do you, my dear?"

Tears filled his wife's eyes. Desperately she blinked them away, knowing that any sign of distress would only goad him.

Crispin shifted in his chair, wishing his mother weren't so pathetic. It seemed to him she invited his father's displeasure with her nervous twitching and stammering.

"Not even the vicar's wife," Jasper continued, his shallow eyes skidding over his wife's pale countenance. "It strikes me as odd that the vicar's wife should not call upon the wife of the chief landowner. Have you offended our neighbors in some way, my dear?"

Louise pressed her hands together tightly in her lap. Jasper had done the offending, as well he knew. The ungodly goings-on in the crypt, while not known in any detail, were widely speculated upon. And the whole neighborhood knew that Sir Jasper was a bad man to cross. No one would willingly and knowingly set foot across his boundaries.

"I await an answer," he said silkily, half smiling at the effigy at the other end of the long table. He picked up his wineglass and sipped, his eyes glittering over the lip of the glass.

Louise took a deep breath. Her mouth worked and she pressed her handkerchief to her lips. Her voice shook as she said, "I don't believe so, Jasper."

"You don't believe so? Well, I wonder what the explanation could be. It's quite a puzzle."

Louise pushed back her chair. "If you will excuse me, I'll leave you to your port." She fled the room with a pitiable lack of dignity that not even the servants could miss.

"Put the decanters on the table and get out!" Jasper said savagely to the butler, who obeyed and left with a degree more sangfroid than his mistress had shown.

Crispin hid his apprehension as he waited for the ax to fall on him now. He knew his only hope was to appear unafraid. Casually, he poured himself a glass of port as his stepfather slid the decanter toward him on the polished surface of the table.

"So what are you going to do, sir?" He asked the question almost nonchalantly, leaning back in his chair, crossing his legs, taking a sip of his port, hoping that by bringing the issue into the open he would avert an explosion.

Jasper gave a sharp crack of laughter. It was not a pleasant sound. "Maybe *you* have a suggestion, dear boy, since you signally failed to bring off mine."

"That was hardly my fault, sir." Crispin defended himself as he knew he must. "Chloe took off before I knew what was happening. If the crowds hadn't been so thick, I wouldn't have lost her. If she hadn't been riding Maid Marion, I might have caught her."

"So it was my fault, was it?" Jasper stared morosely into the ruby contents of his glass. "Somehow, I don't believe she would have escaped me. Maid Marion or not."

"But you weren't there." He was daring much, but if anything would work, it was courage.

"No." Jasper sat back. "For the simple reason, my asinine stepson, that Chloe would go nowhere with me willingly. God knows why she holds me in such dislike

. . . to my knowledge, I've always treated her with kid gloves."

"She's not afraid of you."

"No . . . not yet," Jasper agreed. "But that will come, make no mistake." He twisted the stem of the glass between finger and thumb and his mouth thinned to a vicious line.

"So what do we do now?" Crispin knew he was no longer in danger.

"Intimidation," Jasper said. "I'll be revenged on Lattimer, and that little sister of mine is going to begin to feel the smart of fear."

"How?" Crispin sat forward, the candlelight falling across his sharp face, his small brown eyes eager pinpoints in his sallow complexion.

"A little arson," Jasper said softly. "And I believe one of those ridiculous creatures my sister loves so much must be constrained to suffer a little."

"Ahh." Crispin sat back again. He remembered the stinging rebuke she'd administered when he'd commented so carelessly on the condition of the nag. It would be very satisfying to avenge the insult in such appropriate fashion.

For the next two days Chloe played her game discreetly. She entered with enthusiasm into the music lessons but offered Hugo no seductive smiles, and whenever she stood or sat beside him she was careful to behave as if she were unaware of his closeness. When she touched him she made it seem like an accident. But she could feel Hugo responding to every brush of her hand, to every move she made when she was close to him. She knew he watched her when she seemed to be absorbed in the music, and she knew that much of the time he was not watching with the eye of a tutor or of a

guardian. And the more she affected ignorance and behaved with the natural ease of a girl who'd never tumbled with him on the faded velvet cushions of the old
couch, the more relaxed he became in his responses.

They rode out together around the estate, Chloe on
her new horse, a spritely chestnut gelding that almost
made up for the loss of Maid Marion. Hugo found her an
attentive and intelligent companion as he went about
the dreary business of listening to the universal com-
plaints of his tenant farmers, dismally examining the
tumbledown cottages, the leaking barn roofs, the broken fences, desperately trying to think of some way to
raise the funds to make the necessary repairs.

He sat up late in the kitchen after their ride, the sleeping house creaking quietly around him. His body was
tired, but his mind, as always, wouldn't take a backseat.
His first sober overview of his estate had shaken him to
his core. He'd allowed an already neglected property to
go to rack and ruin in the past years, while he wallowed
in brandy-induced self-pity. It was a painful realization
and one that prevented all possibility of sleep.

Several times his eye and his mind drifted to the cellar
steps. He could picture the racks with their dust-coated
bottles of burgundy and claret, madeira, sherry, and
brandy. It was a magnificent cellar acquired by his father and grandfather. He himself had added little . . .
he'd been too busy depleting it.

That lash of self-contempt kept him away from the
cellar for half an hour. Then he found himself on his
feet, inexorably crossing the kitchen, lifting the heavy
brass key off its hook by the cellar door. He put the key
in the lock and turned it. It grated in the lock and the
door swung open with a complaining rasp. The dark
flight of stone steps stretched ahead. The cool earth
smell of the cellar, overlaid with the musty scents of

wine, teased his nostrils. He took a step down, then realized he had no lantern.

He turned back. Abruptly he slammed the door shut at his back. The violence of the sound jarred the night. He turned the key, hung it back on its hook, extinguished the lamps in the kitchen, lit a carrying candle, and went up to bed.

The bang awoke Dante, who leapt from the bed with a growl. Chloe sat up. "What is it?" Dante was at the door, snuffling at the gap beneath, his tail waving joyously in recognition of the familiar.

It must be Hugo coming to bed. Chloe wondered what the time could be. She seemed to have been asleep for hours, but it was still darkest night beyond the window. Was he once again unable to sleep?

She slipped from bed and quietly opened the door onto the corridor. Hugo's apartments were at the far end, beyond the central hallway. She could see the yellow glimmer of light beneath his door. She waited, shivering slightly, for the light to be extinguished, but it remained for hours, it seemed, much longer than it would take someone to prepare for bed. Thoughtfully, she went back to bed and lay down. Dante settled on her feet again with a sigh that expressed relief that these strange nighttime wanderings had ceased.

Sleep wouldn't return. She lay gazing up into the darkness that her now-accustomed eyes could easily penetrate. Not for the first time, she wondered what it must be like never to know that once night fell, one would sleep and wake refreshed. She could see Hugo's face in repose, when the vibrancy no longer concealed the deeply etched lines of fatigue around his eyes and mouth, the purple shadowing in the hollows beneath his eyes.

She thought he'd slept better since he'd emerged from the days in the library. He looked less depleted, his eyes clearer, his skin supple. But what did she know about the way he spent the long, dark hours of the night?

She jumped out of bed and went back to the door. The light still glowed beneath the door at the far end of the corridor. Suddenly, she had the unmistakable sensation of pain . . . of some kind of struggle in the air around her. Was he drinking again? *Please, no.*

Her hands shook as she lit her carrying candle, then she flew like a wraith along the corridor, down the stairs to the library. She was acting on impulse now as she fumbled across the room, her candle flickering on the massive dark furniture and throwing eerie shadows on the heavy paneling.

She knew what she was looking for: the backgammon board she faintly remembered seeing the first time she'd entered this room. She found the hinged board on an inlaid chest against the wall. The pieces and dice were in a carved box beside it.

Clutching the heavy board and box to her chest with one arm, she made her way back to the hallway, holding her candle as high as she could. Dante, now resigned to these untimely peregrinations, trotted at her heels as she carefully negotiated the stairs and turned down the corridor to Hugo's chamber.

She knocked on the door.

Hugo was sitting on the window seat, drawing deep breaths of the cool night air. His hands were clenched in tight fists against his face, leaving a bruising imprint against his cheekbones.

When the knock came at his door, he started and for a minute was disoriented. Then, assuming it was Samuel, he said wearily, "Come in."

Chloe stood in the doorway, something clutched to her breast, a flickering candle in her other hand. Her hair tumbled in sleep's unruly tangles over her shoulders. Her eyes were blue velvet as they gazed anxiously at him. "I thought perhaps you couldn't sleep again," she said, stepping into the room and closing the door behind her. "I thought perhaps you'd like a game of backgammon."

"Backgammon! For God's sake, Chloe, it's three o'clock in the morning!"

"Is it? I didn't know." She advanced farther into the room. "You haven't been to sleep yet." It was statement rather than question. Somehow, she knew Hugo was in trouble tonight and every line of her body, every movement of her features, evinced utter determination to help him.

"Go back to bed, Chloe," he said, running his hands through his hair.

"No, I'm not in the least sleepy." She set her candle down and opened the board on the bed. "I'm sure you'd like some company. Shall I set up the pieces?"

"Just why is it that you're always so sure about what I want?" Hugo demanded. "For some reason, you keep popping up beside me, informing me that I must be lonely and in need of *your* company."

"Well, it's true," Chloe said with that recognizable stubborn twist to her lovely mouth. "I know it is." She perched on the bed and began to set up the draftsmen.

Hugo knew that an hour's distraction would save him. He didn't know how Chloe knew it, but know it she did. He came over to the bed and sat down on the edge opposite her, saying with a resigned sigh, "This is madness."

There was a scratching at the door and Dante whined. "Oh, dear." Chloe jumped up. "I shut the door on him. You don't mind if he comes in, do you?"

Hugo shook his head in dumb surrender to an unmovable force.

Chloe was not wearing a dressing gown yet again,

and her slender frame moved fluidly beneath the thin cambric of her nightdress as she opened the door.

It was one area in which he could assert himself. Hugo went to the armoire and drew out a brown velvet robe. "Come here." Taking her arms, he thrust them into the long sleeves, spun her around, and pulled the voluminious sides across her body, tying the girdle at her waist with a firm jerk. "How many times, Chloe . . . ?" he demanded in not entirely feigned exasperation.

"It's not cold, so I don't think about it," she said.

"Well, I suggest you start thinking about it if you're going to continue to roam around in the middle of the night." He turned back to the backgammon board on the bed.

Chloe hopped up and sat cross-legged in front of her half of the board, arranging the folds of her borrowed robe around her. "Why does it bother you?"

Hugo looked sharply at her and read the mischievous invitation in her eyes. His world took that familiar tilt again as the need for brandy was abruptly joined by one with even more potential for trouble. If he let her see it, however, he'd be tacitly acknowledging the invitation.

"Don't give me that pseudo-naivete, lass," he said mildly, throwing the two dice. "It doesn't bother *me* particularly. But you know perfectly well it's not appropriate for a young girl to wander around half dressed." He moved a draftsman.

Not fooled, she threw the dice in her turn. A questioning miaow came suddenly from the door she'd left ajar. Beatrice stood in the doorway, a tiny bundle of fur gripped by the scruff of its neck between her teeth.

"Oh, she's bringing the kittens for their first outing," Chloe said, extending her hand in welcome to the advancing cat. Beatrice leapt on the bed, deposited the kitten in Chloe's lap, and went out again. Five more times she came and went as Hugo watched in a kind of dazed disbelief. When all six kittens were settled in Chloe's velvet lap, Beatrice curled on the coverlet and gazed unwinking at the tableau.

"We lack only Falstaff and Rosinante," Hugo observed. "Oh, I was forgetting Plato. Perhaps you should fetch them."

"You're funning," Chloe said. "It's your throw."

"Funning? Whyever should I be funning?" He tossed the dice. "I have a profound dislike of domestic animals, and yet at three-thirty in the morning I'm playing backgammon in an animal house that used to be my bedroom."

"How could you dislike them?" Chloe stroked one of the fur bundles with the tip of her finger. The kitten blinked its newly opened eyes at Hugo.

"Forgive the indelicate question, but are they housebroken? I have to sleep in that bed."

"Beatrice cleans up after them," Chloe informed him serenely.

"Oh, how very reassuring." Laughter swelled from some deep well in his chest, and he realized that the desperate tension of his brandy craving had left him. His hands were steady, his stomach at peace.

Chloe looked up from her intent concentration on the board and laughed happily as she examined his face. "You're better?"

He looked sharply at her. "Yes, how do you know?"

"I can feel it when people are hurting," she said. "Just as I can feel it when the pain goes away. Will you ever be able to drink again, do you think?"

The question surprised him. He hadn't expected someone with so little experience of the world to understand his agony so completely. She was regarding him intently, the mischievously seductive playmate transformed into a solemn, caring companion.

"I don't know, I'll have to wait and see," he answered as seriously as if she were of his own generation. "But I'm not stupid enough to put it to the test yet awhile. It's too damn difficult to resist at the moment."

"I'll help you." Reaching over, she laid her hand over his and it startled him more than any of her previous intimacies. It was a simple human gesture of support and friendship.

"You already have," he answered quietly.

The silence in the room grew to enclose them, and he felt as if he were slipping into the deep blue depths of her eyes. Then, with a supreme effort of will, he hauled himself out of entrancement and broke the spell.

"Come on, it's time you went back to bed." He scooped the draftsmen up and put them in the box. "You've done what you came to do, and I'm very grateful, but now I'd like my own room back. How are you going to transport that litter?"

"I'll fetch the hat box." She moved the nest of kittens from her lap and slipped off the bed, hiding her disappointment. Struggling with the unwieldy folds of the robe, she went to get the box. When she returned, Hugo had cleared away the board and pieces, shooed Dante off the bed, and was staring somewhat nonplussed at Beatrice, who lay fast asleep, unimpressed by the busyness around her.

"She looks as if she's settled for the duration," he said as Chloe put the box on the bed.

"She'll follow the kittens." She picked them up and put them in the box. "I can't carry them without tripping over your robe, so if you don't mind, I'll take it off." She shrugged out of it, laying it over the foot of the bed. "Good night." Her voice was flat.

"Chloe?"

"Yes?" She paused at the door.

He came up behind her, turned her, and gently kissed

her brow. "Thank you. You were a great help." She quivered under his hands, her rounded shoulder warm in his palm beneath the thin nightgown, but she said nothing, and he released her. She left, Beatrice and Dante streaking ahead of her down the corridor.

Hugo lay down fully dressed on his bed, wrinkling his nose at the faint lingering smell of warm animal.

Something had to be done before the situation became completely out of hand. He would have to send her away somewhere. But where? Where would she be safe from Jasper if he himself wasn't there to protect her? One thing he knew with absolute certainty: The three of them couldn't go on living together in this dangerous intimacy. Each day he drew closer to breaking faith with Elizabeth. If he yielded, he would ruin a sweet-faced innocent who didn't understand the consequences of what she was offering—and such a prospect belonged amid the depravities of the crypt.

Down the corridor, Chloe lay in bed, unaware that her thoughts were in one respect an echo of Hugo's. Something had to be done. But in her case, she searched for a way to bring her plan to a swift conclusion. She was a prey to such tormenting fires and dreams and only one thing would quench the one and fulfill the other. She sensed it needed one firm push to propel Hugo over the edge of restraint. But what form should the push take? She'd tried gentle maneuvering and soft insinuations, hoping he'd pick up on the initiative. Perhaps it was time to do something utterly outrageous. But what?

She yawned and closed her eyes as a wave of sleepiness washed over her. The opportunity would present itself if she was on the lookout for it.

Chapter 14

"WHERE'S THE LASS this morning?" Hugo came into the kitchen, yawning, rubbing his flat palms over his face. His clothes were more than usually rumpled.

"She 'ad breakfast about an hour ago. Said she was goin' t' put nag to grass in the orchard." Samuel cast a sharp look at his employer. It was mid-morning, unusually late for Sir Hugo to rise unless he'd been drinking heavily. But apart from looking as if he'd slept in his clothes, he seemed clear-eyed and refreshed.

Samuel poured coffee. "We need supplies, so if ye've got a few pennies, I'll take the cart."

Hugo grimaced. "How much is a few pennies, Samuel?"

Samuel shrugged. "A couple o' guineas'll prob'ly do for a bit o' flour an' coffee an' the like. But the pig'll 'ave to be stuck soon if there's to be bacon for the winter, and Colin likes 'is money on the dot. An' there's the farrier to pay."

"Won't Colin take payment in kind? A side of bacon?"

"Aye, 'e might. Things is 'ard for 'im at the moment. 'Ard for everyone, what wi' wages bein' cut at the mill."

"Mmm." Hugo drank coffee. "And there'll be no reform meetings for a while. Henry Hunt's been sentenced to two years in prison."

"Just makes 'em more riled. They'd see the magistrates swing soon as look at 'em." Samuel set a plate of ham in front of Hugo. "That do ye?"

"Amply, thanks." Hugo cut into the meat. "Take what

you need for the supplies from the strongbox in the library."

He remembered with a guilty pang the three gold sovereigns he'd given Betsy . . . not to mention the two he'd lavished on the turnip seller for Rosinante— more than enough to pay the farrier and the pig sticker and keep them in flour and coffee for a month. Chloe had insisted it was her money he was spending, but he couldn't see himself recouping the outlay from his ward's pin money.

"I could do with a bath, Samuel," he said, diverting his thoughts to a more easily remediable situation.

"I'll set it up for ye in 'ere," Samuel said. "Like I did for the lass. Ye'll be wantin' to use the screen, I reckon."

"Yes, I'd better," Hugo said. Until Chloe's advent, he'd been accustomed to bathing without such niceties, usually under the pump in the courtyard, in clement weather. But they were no longer an all-male household.

Half an hour later, he was ensconced in the hip bath before the range and behind the fire screen, luxuriating in the hot water that steamed gently around him. Toward dawn, he'd finally fallen into a deep sleep and he was now filled with a sense of physical well-being. He had fought his addiction last night and won, and the sense of achievement was sweet. Chloe's part in the victory had to be acknowledged and he contemplated what he could do to please her that wouldn't involve him in vast expense. Another trip to Manchester . . . and perhaps he'd bite his tongue when she demanded some hideous monstrosity and let her enjoy her purchase. But then again, remembering what tended to appeal to her, perhaps not. He closed his eyes, flexing his toes over the edge of the bath, idly slurping water over his chest.

The water was cooling slightly, and he thought he

heard Samuel in the kitchen. "Before you go, Samuel, bring me another jug of hot water."

Chloe stood in the open doorway, looking around the deserted kitchen. She was about to tell the disembodied voice of her guardian that Samuel wasn't in the room, when a hot tide of excitement washed over her, sending a jolt to the pit of her stomach that made her knees weak. Here was the opportunity . . . and a golden one at that.

She approached the screen, where a line of copper jugs stood waiting to replenish the bath. Did she dare? It was about as outrageous as anything ever could be.

"Samuel?" Hugo's voice was slightly impatient as he repeated his request. "Pass me another jug of hot water, please."

Chloe hefted the nearest jug, marshaled every last fiber of courage, and rounded the screen. "Good morning, Hugo."

"What the . . . ?" He stared in momentary disbelief and then realized she was gazing with unabashed curiosity at his lower body, only partly submerged in the water. He opened his mouth to say something . . . anything . . . when she emptied the contents of the jug she was carrying over his chest.

Chloe had been so intent on her plan, so blinded with excitement, she'd grabbed the first jug to hand. It was the one that contained ice cold water from the pump.

Hugo bellowed like a wounded ox and leapt to his feet, frantically shaking water off his body. "You . . . you *brat!*" he roared. He sprang out of the tub, grabbing a towel hanging over the screen.

Chloe shrieked in mingled fear and excitement and fled. Hugo came after her, knocking over the screen, wrapping the towel around his waist. "Come here, you obnoxious brat," he yelled, beside himself with rage. "Just wait till I get my hands on you."

"You'll have to catch me first." Chloe dodged behind the kitchen table, her eyes shining as she delivered her challenge.

Flinging a chair aside, Hugo dived around the table. Dante, who for some reason seemed to sense nothing threatening to his beloved mistress in this wild scene, barked excitedly. Neither pursuer nor quarry paid him any attention.

Chloe escaped Hugo's grasping hands by a hair and bounded for the door. She raced headlong across the hall and paused for a split second. If she ran into the courtyard, Hugo wouldn't be able to follow her, not in that skimpy towel loincloth. And if he didn't follow her, he wouldn't catch her.

She veered toward the stairs, taking a flying jump at the first two. Hugo threw himself forward, and for a heart-stopping second his fingers circled her ankle, but she was moving too quickly for him to grasp her properly and his hold slipped away. She leapt upward, her heart juddering with a fearful hectic turbulence, her blood swirling hotly in her veins. She was lost in a world of purely visceral responses, her mind no longer controlling her body's decisions. At the head of the stairs she hurtled down the corridor leading to Hugo's apartments.

Hugo was on her heels as she flung open the door and sprang inside. He slammed the door shut as he hurled himself after her. Dante jumped back with a startled yelp as the door banged in his nose.

The wild chase had fanned the flames of Hugo's shocked fury. His breath came swift and ragged and the water was cold on his skin. "By God, you stand in sore need of a sharp lesson, miss," he declared. "Come here!"

"Catch me!" She laughed at him, bright-eyed, and

jumped backward onto the bed. His anger excited her, though she had no idea why it should.

Hugo lunged for her as she danced across the bed, and this time he caught her ankle and hung on. He jerked hard. Chloe shrieked as she tumbled facedown on the bed, her free foot waving wildly in the air.

He seized the other ankle, his fingers gripping as tightly as any fetter. He hauled her toward him across the wide expanse of coverlet, her skirt rucking up as he dragged her. Distantly he noticed that the soles of her bare feet were grass-stained, that her smooth calves were stockingless, that the hollow behind her knees was deep and satiny, that her small round bottom was clad in serviceable linen drawers, unadorned with frills or lace.

Even as he struggled with his suddenly reeling senses that had driven all clarity of purpose from his mind, Chloe twisted onto her back, so he now held her by crossed ankles. Her eyes were dark liquid pools of sensuality, her lips were slightly parted, her cheeks flushed, golden wisps of hair escaping from her braids in a lustrous mist around her exquisite countenance. The sweet swell of her bosom rose and fell with her swift breath. Her skirt was hiked to her waist, and the legs of her drawers were pushed up on her thighs. His eye ran over the flat stomach, the sharp points of her hipbones pressing against the linen undergarment, the long, creamy length of exposed thigh.

"Sweet heaven," he whispered in the despairing recognition of imminent surrender. He opened his hands.

Chloe sat up in a deceptively lethargic movement, her eyes never leaving his face, triumphant certainty lurking in the cornflower depths as she sensed his capitulation. Leaning forward, her eyes narrowing with deliberation, she plucked the towel from his loins. His body sprang free in hard readiness, and with the same deliberation she touched him, kneeling up on the bed, holding him with one hand, her fingers exploring in the wiry tangle of hair as she learned the feel of him while her other hand moved upward over his chest, brushing his nipples. Her head was bent, watching the effect of her hands' intimacies, her eyes intent on his body as if seeing it for the first time. And indeed, that night in the library, she had seen little of him, had been too lost in her own sensations to be aware of much outside herself.

Hugo threw back his head with a soft, almost helpless groan of pleasure. His hands caressed her bent head, palming the delicate shape of her skull beneath the untidily braided hair. She slipped her hands around his hips, her fingers digging into the firm muscles of his buttocks, increasing the scope of her voluptuous exploration.

He turned her face up and bent his head to kiss her mouth. Her lips parted eagerly and her tongue joined with his in a mischievous dance before his hands gripped her face more firmly and he drove deep into her mouth, possessing its sweetness in rough and delightful plunder, and Chloe finally yielded the initiative. Her hands fell from his body, and she arched backward on her knees, her thighs opening in involuntary response, her body's cleft moistening and throbbing as he ravaged the softness of her mouth.

Hugo drew back and looked at her face, one finger delicately tracing the line of her jaw, her reddened lips, the small, tip-tilted nose. His gaze held no humor, but a hunger and single-minded determination that sent answering thrills of anticipation over her skin, lifting her scalp, rippling in her belly.

Bending over her as she still knelt on the bed, he laid his flat palms on the insides of her opened thighs and exerted firm pressure, pushing them wider. She let her palms rest on the bed beside her knees as her body was slowly, inexorably opened and she could feel the aching vulnerability of her core begging for his touch. With the same slow deliberation he laid his hand over the throbbing furrow and she jumped as if touched with a burning brand.

"Be still," he said quietly. "Be still and let your body speak." His fingers worked through the dampening linen of her drawers until she moaned, biting her lip as the pleasure built in a tight spiral in the pit of her stomach. She felt she was being split asunder, leaning backward on her hands, her body pressing urgently against the magic of his fingers. And then the coil burst and she was flooded with a sensation that rocked her entire body, that curled her toes and brought tears of startled joy to her eyes.

He took her face again and kissed her with the hard, possessive demand of before. She clutched at him, her arms circling him, her hands stroking his back, feeling the turgid shaft of his flesh pressing against her stomach as she reached against him.

He released her mouth and took a step away from her. "Take your clothes off . . . all of them . . . quickly." The green eyes were narrow slits of passion as his voice rasped the command.

With fumbling fingers she pulled loose the sash at her waist and tore at the hooks at the back of her gown. She dragged it over her head while she still knelt on the bed, transfixed by the green-eyed gaze, afraid she wasn't being fast enough to please him, wanting only to pleasure him as he had pleasured her. The tiny buttons of her sleeveless chemise were resistant, and one broke off as she struggled with it, but finally she pulled the garment over her head and tossed it to the floor. Kneeling upright, she unfastened the tie of her drawers and pushed them off her hips, sitting down hastily to kick them free of her feet.

"Now your hair," he said.

She pulled the already loosened braids out of their ribbons and ran her fingers through her hair, flicking it over her shoulders.

"Stand up."

She rose slowly, vaguely aware that her knees were weak, her body in ferment; all-consuming desire thrummed in her veins. She stood still, her hands at her sides, gazing into his face as he looked at her in a long, lingering appraisal that sent a violent jolt through her loins.

"Turn around."

She turned as if in a dream, looking down at the bed, her back and buttocks prickling with the knowledge of his eyes roaming over their damask curves. She felt him come up behind her, and his body pressed warm against her back, his hands moving around to caress her breasts, holding their roundness in the palms of his hands, circling her erect nipples with the pad of his thumbs. His lips brushed her ear, his breath warm on her neck.

"Please." The whispered plea for she knew not what was the first word she'd spoken since it had begun, and it reached Hugo through the mists of his own consuming arousal . . . an arousal that had arisen out of his anger with such suddenness, he hadn't attempted to take ahold of it but had allowed it to take them both where it would.

"What would you like?" he murmured now against her ear. "You have only to tell me."

She shook her head, unable to find words for what she didn't understand. Her hands moved behind her to clasp him more tightly against her body, her feet shifting on the bare floorboards.

"Let me see if I can guess." There was the faintest hint of understanding humor in his voice now. He took a step forward, half lifting her, and they tumbled together onto the bed.

Hugo rolled sideways, keeping her flat on her belly with a warm palm in the small of her back. Propping himself on one elbow, he kissed each pointed shoulder blade before nipping and nuzzling down her back, his lips brushing across the flare of her hips, blazing a trail down her thighs, his tongue dipping into those silky hollows behind her knees. She squirmed and moaned in soft delight as he revealed her to herself, showing her what pleasure her body could afford her. And when he'd finished with her back, he flipped her over and began his downward journey from the pulsing hollow at the base of her throat.

"Did I guess correctly?" he murmured with a tiny smile of satisfaction as he moved up her body again, feeling how alive she was, every square inch of her skin sensitized. Her head moved in inarticulate answer and her eyes met his with such a richly sensual glow of demand as her hips moved with urgent expression that the reins on his own tightly harnessed passion finally snapped. Using every skill garnered from experience, he'd held himself in check while he taught the tender novice an educated response to match her impulsive, unlearned eagerness, but he could wait no longer.

Slipping his hands beneath her arching buttocks, he lifted her higher as he eased into the moist, welcoming sheath of her body. She shuddered around him, instinctively tightening her inner muscles so that he drew breath with sharp pleasure. Holding her on the shelf of his palms, he moved within her until she picked up his rhythm and the warm-muscled roundness he held clenched and released in harmony with his movements. He drew her legs onto his shoulders, and her eyes widened in surprise as the sensation changed and she felt his flesh deep within her own.

He held her gaze, watching her face change, reveling in the candid openness as expressions chased themselves across her features, registering every shift in sensation. He knew she was capable of no artifice; she could no more feign pleasure than she could disguise it, and the knowledge deepened his own pleasure in a way he wouldn't have believed possible, releasing him in some way from the dark, furtive games of his sexual past.

"No, don't close your eyes," he whispered as the thin, blue-veined lids veiled them for a moment. The long-lashed lids swept up immediately, and she smiled at him with such radiance, he thought he was going to drown in her beauty.

He knew the moment she was almost at the pinnacle. Deliberately, he moved his hand to touch the exquisitely sensitive bud at the point of their fusion. Chloe cried out, her body convulsing around him, her spine arched, and tears again filled her eyes that still locked with his, drawing him into her moment of bliss, submerging him in the midnight-blue depths.

With a wrenching gasp he withdrew from her body the instant before his own climax rushed upon him. He gathered her to him as the tide took him on its tumbling ride of ecstasy and held her until he was tossed to shore. He fell backward, still holding the slight body against him, until his heart slowed and his head cleared.

"Oh, Chloe," he whispered. "What wicked magic did you brew?" He rolled sideways, still holding her, and smudged the tearstains on her cheeks with his thumb. He'd had many women, but never had he seen a woman cry at the climactic moment. This diminutive bundle of passion had twice wept with joy.

Chloe blinked, smiled, and stretched out along the length of his body. "No magic."

"Yes, magic," he disagreed with a rueful headshake. "That was not the lesson I intended teaching you."

"But it *was* the lesson I intended to learn," she said with more than a hint of smugness.

He laughed and lay on his back, pulling her with him so she lay atop him. He pushed the tumbling hair back from her face and examined her countenance. "It would seem I've been boarded and taken for a prize."

"Is that what they do with ships?"

"In wartime."

She lowered her head and kissed the corner of his mouth, a delicate butterfly kiss that barely brushed his lips. "But this isn't war."

"No," he agreed. "You're a piratical minx, but you're not built for warfare."

"A pirate?" She gave a little gurgle of laughter that entranced him anew. "I think I shall make an expert pirate."

"Heaven help us both, but I think you will too," he murmured. There was a power here too strong for one man to resist on the grounds of scruple. Somehow, he'd steer a path through it.

"But I don't like it when you withdraw at the end in that fashion," she said suddenly, a crease appearing between her brows. "If it was so that I won't conceive, I would prefer to take the potion."

Hugo stiffened and abruptly rolled her onto the bed beside him. Leaning over her, he spoke with soft vehemence. "You will not ever again take that filthy stuff, Chloe."

"Why not?"

The crypt rose in its dank evil, its smell filling his nostrils. Stephen Gresham's voice rang in his ears. The man's vicious hungers spread themselves on the carpet of memory. This girl was his daughter. A creature with all the appetites, vital and glowing with a devouring lust for life's pleasures.

"What is it?" She saw him go from her, back to the world of his painted devils, and in fear she touched his face. "I'm sorry, Hugo. Please. Whatever I did, I didn't mean it."

He pulled himself back to the sunlit room and the reality of the woman he'd just loved with such shared joy. He spoke evenly. "There are many things you don't understand, lass. You will have to trust me to know what's best in these matters."

"I do . . . I will," she said hastily. The bright morning seemed to have dimmed somewhat. "But you're not sorry, are you? You don't regret what happened?"

How could he regret such pleasure, or deny the spur of unstoppable passion? He was not harming Chloe, he knew that now. She was an equal partner for all the disparity in their ages. And maybe he was the best person to guide the vast appetite she had for life in all its earthly facets. Perhaps Elizabeth had sensed that too. Even in her laudanum trance she would have had a mother's recognition of her daughter's nature. Had she been afraid that once free of the restraints of her girlhood, her daughter would follow where her appetites and her stellar beauty led? Unguided, they would lead her to ruin. Had Elizabeth recognized Stephen in their daughter?

She was still regarding him with anxiety, and he saw the ingenuous girl again. He remembered the openness of her responses. Appetites as such were not wrong if they were not governed by evil. The sins of the father should not be visited upon the child.

"No," he said. "I don't regret it, lass."

Chapter 15

"I'M SURE THERE'S a simple answer to this, lass, but just why do you never wear shoes these days?" Hugo regarded his ward's bare feet as she came into the kitchen from the orchard. The memory of her grass-stained soles of the previous day was still vivid.

"Because I don't have any," she responded simply, taking an apple from the basket and rubbing it against her skirt.

"What do you mean, you don't have any? Of course you have shoes."

"Only brown serge kind of shoes," she explained, scrunching into the apple. "Clumpy half boots that look silly with this dress."

"The dress looks as if it could do with a wash," he observed. "It looks as if you've been mucking out the stables in it."

"Oh, it's just from Rosinante and the dust from the stillroom," she said, flicking carelessly at a smudge on her muslin skirt. "I was trying to encourage Plato to eat one of Beatrice's mice, but I think he's too young. I'll have to dig up worms for him."

"That will certainly improve the condition of your gown," Hugo said dryly. "However, I think we'd better have another shopping trip to see about shoes."

"And a riding hat," Chloe reminded him. "I lost the other one at St. Peter's Fields. I've a mind to purchase a shako. I saw a woman wearing one in Bolton once. It looked very dashing."

"A shako!" Hugo groaned. "You're far too small for such a style, lass."

"Stuff," Chloe declared. "It'll make me look taller. Are we to go this morning?"

"We might as well get it over with," Hugo said.

"Then I'll change into my habit."

"Give me strength," Hugo muttered as the door closed on her energetic departure. "A shako! What the hell's she's going to come up with next?"

"Reckon as 'ow ye'll be able to steer 'er right," Samuel observed, biting off a length of thread. He held up the shirt he'd been mending and shook his head. "Ye'd do as well to buy yerself a new shirt. This one's more patches than anythin'."

"Not with the farrier to pay," Hugo said, getting to his feet. He sighed. "Ah, well, into the breach, I suppose. Wish me luck, Samuel."

Samuel gave him a dry smile. "If'n ye think ye needs it."

Hugo's answering smile was rueful. "Oh, make no mistake, Samuel, I'm going to need all the luck in the world to steer a safe path through this maze."

Neither of them was referring to the shopping expedition. Hugo rarely had to tell the old sailor anything directly. His friend missed little of what went on around him.

"Tell the lass to bring down that gown and I'll wash it while yer gone."

"I hardly think it's your place to do her laundry," Hugo said, frowning.

"Right 'andy she is wi' the animals," Samuel said, "but I don't reckon they taught 'er much about washin' an' flat irons in that seminary. She 'ad enough trouble washin' the curtains from 'er room . . . and she didn't know one end of the iron from t'other, as I recall."

"No, I don't imagine an heiress with eighty thousand

pounds would have been expected to learn the finer arts of domesticity," Hugo said. "But then, I don't imagine such an heiress would expect to be living in quite such spartan surroundings either."

"She's 'appy enough," Samuel said gruffly.

"Are you talking about me?" Chloe's clear voice came from the doorway and both men turned toward her.

"Yes, we were," Hugo said calmly. "Samuel is offering to wash your gown."

"Oh, no, I couldn't let you do that." She crossed the kitchen.

She danced rather than walked, Hugo thought, watching as she bent and kissed Samuel's cheek. And what an amazing capacity for love and friendship, a capacity until now starved of recipients except the lonely, injured, and unloved of the animal kingdom.

"Nonsense," Samuel said, his ruddy cheek glowing. "Just fetch it down 'ere and then get along wi' ye. I've enough to do wi'out all this argumentation."

"Do as he says, lass," Hugo said. "And then let's get moving."

"Purple shoes with gold rosettes and three-inch heels, Samuel!" Hugo flung himself into a chair at the kitchen table. "And the hats . . . you would not believe how many milliners we had to visit before we found a hat that the lass liked and I was prepared to tolerate."

He shook his head, massaging his temples. "There was a cartwheel of straw and tulle . . . you have never seen its like . . . but the shako . . . Dear God, I thought we were going to come to blows over that. Can you imagine what such a minute creature would look like in purple shoes and a foot-high shako with a monstrous dyed scarlet plume?"

"The shoes were lovely," Chloe said indignantly.

"Don't take any notice of him, Samuel. They were the most beautiful shoes I've ever seen, and Hugo is the stuffiest, primmest, most . . . most old-fashioned stick-in-the-mud!"

Perched on the table, she extended one dainty foot and examined with a grimace of disgust the bronze kid slipper enclosing it. "Look at this, it's so *boring.*"

"It's tasteful," Hugo said. "And elegant."

"It's boring, isn't it, Samuel?"

"Don't bring me into this," Samuel said, stirring the contents of a pot on the lugpole. "I don't know nothin' about such flimflam."

"And I don't like the hat nearly as much as the one I lost." Chloe glared at her guardian. From her point of view, it had not been a successful shopping expedition, and Hugo had shown a dismaying propensity to behave as if their relationship had not changed dramatically as a result of the previous morning's activities.

"Well, you shouldn't have lost the other one, lass," he said, refusing to be drawn. "No one forced you into the midst of a melee, as I recall."

"Oh, yes, they did! Crispin and Jasper did."

"But who chose to be so forced?" His eyebrows lifted and his smile was slightly mocking.

"Oh, you make me so cross sometimes!" Chloe jumped off the table. "I'm going to feed Plato."

"Hey! Not in those slippers," Hugo protested as she stalked to the kitchen door. "You are not going to dig up worms in kid slippers. They cost a small fortune."

"The sooner they're ruined, the sooner I can buy a new pair."

The silly challenge fell into a stony silence, and Chloe bit her lip, her cheeks warming as she heard her petulance. In a subdued voice she said, "I'll put on my clunky boots."

As she passed him on her way to the hall door, Hugo

reached out and caught her around the hips, drawing her close to his chair. "Don't be cross, lass. I really do know better than you." He smiled up at her, his eyes crinkling with amusement and something else that she couldn't yet read with fluency.

"But you don't know what I like better than I do."

"Oh, I think I might take you up on that later," he said softly. "You might well be surprised."

Her knees were suddenly weak, and the day's irritations faded as if they'd never been. His arm tightened around her, his hand flattening on her thigh, and she drew a shaky breath.

"I do like surprises."

He laughed and released her with a light pat. "Find your clunky boots and see to that owl. Samuel's dinner won't wait."

Chloe recovered her good humor with habitual speed and, Plato having been fed, came to the table with a ready hunger. Samuel carved a leg of mutton, ladled boiled potatoes, green peas, and parsnips onto her plate and set it before her as she took her usual seat at the side of the long table.

"Would you like a glass of wine with that, lass?" Hugo raised a questioning eyebrow as he was about to take his own seat at the head of the table.

Chloe shook her head and gave him a quick smile. "No, thank you, just water."

"I think Samuel's dinner deserves accompaniment," Hugo said calmly. "Fetch two glasses." He took the cellar key from the wall and went down.

Chloe looked anxiously at Samuel, who shrugged slightly and said, "Do as 'e says, I should."

She took two wineglasses from the dresser and then stood at the table, uncertain where to place them.

Hugo came up with a bottle of claret. "You and Samuel, lass," he said with a slight smile, pulling the cork.

Deliberately, he examined the cork, sniffed it, nodded, placed it on the table, and filled their glasses. Then he sat down and began to eat.

A collective easing of tension rippled around the table. Hugo had set himself a test and had passed it.

Chloe helped Samuel with the dishes while Vivaldi filled the house from the library; they could both hear the harmony in Hugo's soul as it flowed from his fingers.

Afterward she went into the library and stood behind him, one hand lightly clasping his neck. He looked over his shoulder and smiled at her. "You're tired. You had a long ride. Why don't you go up to bed?"

"I'm not tired," she denied, spoiling the effect with a deep yawn.

Hugo laughed. "No, of course you're not. Go on upstairs." His voice softened. "I'll come up and wake you later."

Some instinctive wisdom told her that she couldn't insist that he accompany her, nor could she stay with him until he was ready. Hugo had too dense a thicket around himself for such a new relationship to penetrate. She had no rights of possession, no right to intrude on his privacy. His age and experience demanded that she respect his ruling on the time, the place, and the manner in which they conducted their liaison.

"Promise?"

He reached up, cupped the back of her head, and pulled her face down to his, kissing her firmly. "Promise. I'll play you a lullaby."

"But I don't want to go to sleep yet."

"Didn't I say I'd wake you?"

She nodded and left, the soft strains of a nursery lullaby, cleverly varied by the pianist, accompanying her up the stairs and drifting through her open window as she undressed.

She hadn't expected to fall asleep, but the music worked its magic and within minutes she was sleeping peacefully.

Samuel took himself to bed soon after, and Hugo continued to play for himself, softly now so as not to disturb the sleepers, enjoying the quiet of the house, the knowledge of the sleeping girl waiting for his waking touch, the satisfaction of another day's battle fought and won.

Across the courtyard, three dark-clad figures ran in a huddled crouch, hugging the shadows. The side of the house overlooking the courtyard was in darkness, and they couldn't hear the now-muted strains of the piano from the library, where only a single candle cast its light.

Silently, one of the three lifted the latch on the stable and they crept inside. A horse shuffled in the straw, whickered in alarm at the scent of strangers. The three moved fast, piling straw in a corner of the building. Flint scraped on tinder, a yellow flare lit the cobwebbed corners, threw an outsize shadow of a horse's head on the wall.

The yellow flare was put to the pile of dry straw. A horse whickered again, a panicky sound as the smell of burning filled the confined space.

The three figures backed out of the building, latching the door behind them. Then they flew across the courtyard, no longer worrying about hugging the shadows, and disappeared into the underbrush along the driveway.

The straw caught, but it burned slowly at first. Thanks to Billy's lack of husbandry, it was mixed with wet straw that had been moldering in the kennel.

Hugo caught the faint smell of smoke from the open library window at the same time one of the horses screamed in terror. The scream woke Chloe instantly, and as instantly she recognized the sound.

She was out of bed and down the stairs without thinking. Hugo was already wrenching at the locks on the side door as she raced across the hall.

"What is it?"

"Fire," he said curtly.

"What the 'ell's goin' on?" Samuel, pulling on his britches over his nightshirt, hopped down the stairs.

But Hugo had the door open and was out in the courtyard. Smoke poured thick and black through the open stable window and wreathed under the door. The stamping of hooves and the high-pitched, terrified screaming rent the air in a horrific cacophony.

"Get back!" Hugo bellowed as Chloe bobbed up beside him. "And stay out of the way!"

Chloe jumped back obediently as he wrenched open the door, leaping to one side as he did so. Flame licked out at them, and the roaring and crackling of the straw pile added a hellish din to the already ear-splitting noise of terror.

Hugo covered his face with his arm and plunged into the smoke. He knew where each of the horses was stabled. The bolts on the stalls were too hot to touch, and his fingers blistered as he hauled them open. The animals were not tethered, but they were too terrified to find their own way through the smoke and flame.

He grabbed the mane of his own black stallion and dragged the terrified animal out of the stall, praying one of the powerful hooves wouldn't fell him as the beast reared and plunged. But as he smelled the fresh air, he charged forward, knocking Hugo to his knees as he raced into the courtyard.

Samuel was beside Hugo now, wrenching at the bolts of the other stalls. It was impossible to see anything now, and they were guided by the screams and stamping hooves. Hugo could smell his own hair singeing, his skin was burning, his nostrils like cinders, his lungs heaving with the lack of air.

Dapple was released. Samuel was struggling with one of the two hunters, both of which were too terrified to find their way out of the stalls. Suddenly Chloe was beside him. She had the hunter by the mane and was leading him around, her voice, choked with smoke, speaking to him with a desperate urgency that was still somehow quiet and soothing. She pointed him toward the opening and slapped his rump.

As he lunged forward, she left Samuel and was stumbling down the aisle, her head buried in the sleeve of her nightgown. Her chestnut was at the far end of the aisle, with Rosinante. She could free only one of them.

The chestnut was young and inexperienced. He resisted all her efforts to lead him. By now her head was about to explode, her lungs were on fire, and she knew she was going to lose consciousness. With a last effort born of desperation, she scrambled halfway up the scorching wooden rail of the stall and fell forward on the gelding's back. Somehow, she got one leg over and kicked hard with her bare heels against his flanks, steering him out of the stall. The gelding exploded out of the stall and out of the stable into the courtyard.

Hugo was staring frantically around the courtyard as the released horses milled and stamped and whinnied. It was a bright night, the moon hanging full and round, low in the sky. Billy had appeared now, his face white in the moonlight, his usually vacuous expression a terrified blank. But Chloe was nowhere to be seen.

"Chloe!" Hugo bellowed in desperate fear just as the chestnut hurtled out of the burning building, his eyes rolling, lips pulled back over great yellow teeth.

"Goddammit!" Hugo yelled, his fear turning to rage. He grabbed Chloe by the waist and swung her off the horse, holding her in midair. Her eyebrows and the wisps of hair on her forehead were singed, and black tears of pain and desperation streaked down her smoke-blackened cheeks.

"Of all the lunatic, reckless things to do," he raged. "I told you to stay back." He shook her as he held her off the ground, beside himself with terror-induced fury.

"I had to rescue Petrarch," she cried as impassioned as he. "Petrarch was still in there! I couldn't leave him."

"Petrarch?" For a moment he was bewildered, then he understood. The damn chestnut had finally been christened. "I was just going in for him," he declared, setting her on her feet with a jarring thump.

"But he couldn't wait!" she cried, rubbing her tears with the back of her hand, smudging her face with black. "I couldn't wait for you. . . . And Rosinante . . . he's still there." She dived suddenly beneath his arm and raced to the stable, ignoring everything he'd just said.

"Chloe! Come back here!" He lunged and caught her arm, spinning her away from the burning building. "Didn't you hear a word I said?" He almost threw her backward into Samuel's arms. "Don't let go of her!" Then he dived once more into the smoke-filled stable, stumbling down the aisle, crouching low to the ground. By the time he reached the end stall, his lungs were about to burst and he was blinded with smoke. The heat was so fierce, he could feel his clothes beginning to smolder, scalding his flesh.

Somehow, he grabbed the mane of the enfeebled nag. The hair was burning to the touch and he could smell the animal's scorched hide. He hauled him backward out of the building, thankful that the years of deprivation had reduced the beast to a weight that he could physically control.

He staggered into the yard just as his lungs were

about to yield to the smoke. Rosinante buckled at the knees and fell to the cobbles, where he lay on his side, his flanks heaving, foam bubbling from his mouth, his eyes rolling.

Chloe dropped beside the nag, tears still pouring down her cheeks. She laid a hand on the animal's tortured flank and then looked up at Hugo. "Put him out of his misery. He can't breathe. He'll never recover from this."

"I'll fetch your pistol," Samuel said.

He was back in a few minutes and silently handed the pistol to Hugo. Chloe was still crouching beside Rosinante, murmuring to him as if she could somehow reach him through his agony.

"Go into the house, Chloe," Hugo commanded brusquely, bending to lift her to her feet. "Right away!"

"It's all right, I don't need—"

"Go! And put that kitchen overcoat on while you're about it." He knelt to place the pistol against the animal's head. The shot rang out and Rosinante jerked once and was at peace.

"I'll kill Jasper."

The soft-spoken ferocity of the statement brought Hugo to his feet in one movement. Chloe was standing to one side, out of his line of sight as he'd shot the horse. But she was still coatless and had clearly remained in the courtyard.

"I told you to go into the house!"

"I didn't need to," she said, her mouth taking on the stubborn line he was beginning to know.

"Go and put a coat on!" he ordered her in clipped accents. A battle royal with his willful ward would have to wait until the fire was under control.

Chloe went for the coat without further protest and then ran to join them at the pump, where they were frantically filling buckets.

"I'll work the pump," she said, seizing the handle from Billy.

Half an hour later, the blaze was under control. The stable was solidly built of lime-washed stone, and while the straw and the wooden partitions of the stalls burned merrily, the flames finally exhausted the fuel.

Chloe was drenched with sweat from pumping the handle, her hands blistered, her nightgown beneath the overcoat torn and black with smoke, her face and hands and feet as filthy as a coal miner's. But without flagging she turned to calming the horses and settling them in the barn, where the stench of charred wood and burned straw wouldn't reach them. While she was thus occupied, the three men heaved Rosinante onto the cart and buried him in the far field.

It was past four o'clock before Billy went to his bed in the loft above the old dairy, and Hugo, Samuel, and Chloe staggered into the kitchen.

"Cup o' tea won't come amiss, I reckon," Samuel declared, setting the kettle on the range.

"I'm parched," Chloe agreed, shrugging out of the overcoat. She rubbed her stinging eyes with the heels of her palms.

"Come here, you." Hugo took her by the waist, lifted her, and sat her on the table. "You and I need to have a little talk, my ward. Leaving aside that inexcusable piece of arrant interference over . . . over whatever you call him"—he clutched at the air—"Petrarch . . . I gave you two direct instructions, which, on both occasions, you chose to ignore."

"But you'd forgotten about Rosinante," Chloe protested. "I had to go in after him." Her position on the table meant that she was obliged to look directly at her guardian as he stood in front of her. It was not a comfortable exercise. Hugo was as filthy and as weary as she, but his eyes were dauntingly severe and his jaw was set in an uncompromising line.

"You did *not* have to," he said forcefully. "I had just forbidden you to go anywhere near the fire, and you weren't going to take a blind bit of notice. Do you think I say these things just to exercise my vocal chords?"

"I couldn't think about anything but the horses. And you *had* forgotten about Rosinante." Seeing him for a moment without a response, she rushed on in swift self-defense. "And I didn't need to go inside when you shot Rosinante. I'm not such a milksop. It was the least cruel thing that had ever happened to him, poor soul." She sniffed and wiped her eyes with her filthy sleeve. The lace edging was torn and unraveling, and she began to pull at it. It gave her the opportunity to look down and away from that unwavering scrutiny.

Hugo put a finger under her chin and tilted her face. "In ten years at sea," he said deliberately, "no one ever, *ever* disobeyed an order of mine."

"Too interested in keepin' a whole skin," Samuel observed, measuring tea into a pot. "Powerful 'ard the navy is."

It occurred to Chloe that Samuel was on her side. "But this isn't the navy," she pointed out.

"No, it's not, for which you may thank your stars." Hugo lifted her off the table. "In view of the circumstances, I'm going to let it go this time, but you'd be making a great mistake to assume any precedents."

The storm seemed to have blown over. Chloe shifted the subject to good purpose, saying with the ferocity of before, "I'd like to stick a knife in Jasper."

"So you've said." Hugo sank into a chair with a weary groan. "What makes you think your brother's responsible?"

"It's obvious. It has his mark all over it," she said. "He

never forgets an insult or an injury, and he doesn't scruple what methods he uses to get even."

" 'Ere, get this down ye." Samuel put a mug of tea in front of her. "A tot o' rum in that wouldn't do 'er any 'arm," he said to Hugo.

"There's a crock in the pantry, isn't there?"

"Reckon so." Samuel fetched the stone jar of rum and poured a dollop into Chloe's tea. He doctored his own similarly and sat down in his usual chair by the range, closing his eyes.

"Once, when a man offended Jasper . . . he wouldn't sell him a horse or something . . . Jasper arranged to have the stream that watered his orchard diverted. And I know he poisoned old Red Biddy's drinking trough and poisoned her cow because she'd cursed him once."

"How do you know these things?" Hugo sat up, no longer weary. He'd put nothing past Jasper, but he hadn't realized that the man's evil was so well known.

Chloe shrugged, sipping her tea. "Jebediah, the poacher, told me. He knows everything that goes on."

"Mmmm." Hugo sipped his tea in silence, a deep frown corrugating his forehead. Jasper had taken up the gauntlet with a vengeance, it seemed, and the duel would continue until one of them was defeated. Chloe had to be protected first and foremost. Only when she was safely beyond her brother's reach could Hugo turn his attention to the more personal vendetta that this had now become.

Chloe Gresham needed a husband . . . and soon.

"So what are we going to do?" she said. "We're not just going to let him get away with it, are we?"

"What do you suggest?" He smiled slightly at her intent, ferocious expression. "I doubt he'll let you come close enough to stick a knife in his ribs."

"Burn his hay ricks," she said promptly. "What's

sauce for the goose is sauce for the gander . . . but *we* won't hurt anyone," she added, tears suddenly sparking anew in her eyes. "What if you'd been asleep, or if we hadn't woken? Or if we were too late?"

"None of those things happened," he said soothingly. "Don't dwell on might-have-beens, lass."

"It was too late for Rosinante."

"It had been too late for Rosinante for a long time." Suddenly, he stood up and his voice took on a completely new tone. "You look like a chimney sweep. You can't possibly go to bed in that condition."

"What do you mean?" But he'd already left the kitchen.

Chloe lapsed into a fatigued trance, sipping the comforting brew in her mug until she tipped it up, draining the tea, and yawned. "I can't stay awake another minute."

"You can stay awake long enough to clean up." Hugo spoke from the doorway. He carried the brown velvet robe she'd worn before, a thick towel, and a cake of soap. He beckoned. "Come on, lass. It'll be a bit chilly, but we'll get it over with quickly."

"What are you talking about?" There was something about the gleam in his eye that made her uneasy.

"You'll soon see," he said, and the gleam intensified, his lips twitching with a secret amusement that increased her suspicion.

Samuel stood up. "I'll be off to me bed," he said deliberately.

"No, don't go, Samuel." Chloe put out a hand to stop him.

He glanced at her and shook his head. "Sir 'Ugo's right. A proper little sweep you are. Wouldn't 'ave happened if'n ye hadn't gone into the stable."

"But I thought you were on my side," Chloe wailed.

Samuel, chuckling, left the kitchen.

"Come on, lass." Hugo beckoned again. "It's bath time."

Chloe stood her ground, holding on to the back of the chair, regarding Hugo with the deepest suspicion. "I don't want a bath."

"Oh, you're mistaken, lass. You want a bath most urgently." He walked toward her with soft-paced purpose and she backed away.

"What are you going to *do*?"

"Put you under the pump," he said readily, sweeping her easily into his arms.

"But it's freezing!" Chloe squealed.

"It's a warm night," he observed in reassuring accents that Chloe didn't find in the least reassuring.

"Put me down. I want to go to bed, Hugo!"

"So you shall . . . so you shall. All in good time." He carried her out to the courtyard. "In fact, we'll *both* go to bed very soon."

Chloe stopped wriggling at that. Despite fatigue and the events of the night, she realized she was far from uninterested in what such a statement might promise.

"Why can't we heat some water and have a proper bath," she suggested carefully.

"It would take too long." He set her down beside the pump, maintaining a hold on her arm. "And it would not convince you of the consequences of headstrong, willful behavior. If you dash into the midst of an inferno, you're going to come out like a chimney sweep." Releasing her arm, he pulled the nightgown over her head so she stood naked in the moonlight.

"And chimney sweeps go under the pump," he declared, working the handle.

A jet of cold water hit her body and Chloe howled. He tossed the soap toward her. "Scrub!"

Chloe thought about dashing out of the freezing jet and into the house, but the filth pouring off her body under the vigorous application of the pump convinced her that she had no choice but to endure this punitive bath. She danced furiously for a few moments, trying to warm herself, then bent to pick up the soap and began to scrub in earnest.

Hugo watched her with amusement and rapidly rising desire. The gyrations of her slender body, silvered in the moonlight, would test the oaths of a monk. She was in such a frantic hurry to get the job over and done with that her movements were devoid of either artifice or invitation, which he found even more arousing.

"I hate you!" she yelled, hurling the soap to the ground. "Stop pumping; I'm clean!"

He released the handle, still laughing. "Such an entrancing spectacle, lass."

"I hate you," she repeated through chattering teeth, bending her head as she wrung the water out of the soaked strands.

"No, you don't." He flung the thick towel around her shoulders. "Rarely have I been treated to such an enticing performance." He began to dry her with rough vigor, rubbing life and warmth into her cold, clean skin.

"I didn't mean to be enticing," she grumbled somewhat halfheartedly, since the compliment was pleasing.

"No, that was part of the appeal," he agreed, turning his attentions to the more intimate parts of her anatomy. "But I trust that in future you'll think twice before you fling yourself into whatever danger presents itself, my headstrong ward."

Chloe knew perfectly well that given the set of circumstances, she would do the same thing, but it seemed hardly politic or necessary to belabor the issue, particularly when he was doing what he was doing. Warmth was seeping through her in little ripples, and, while her skin was still cold, her heated blood flowed swiftly.

Finally, Hugo dropped the towel and wrapped her in

the velvet robe. "Run inside now and pour yourself another tot of rum. You can dry your hair at the range. I'm going to clean myself up."

"Oh?" Chloe raised an eyebrow. "I'm sure it would be easier for you if I worked the pump." She turned up her blistered palms. "I've had a deal of practice already . . . and besides, I'm entitled to my revenge . . . or do I mean *my* pleasure."

Hugo smiled and stripped off his clothes. "Do your worst, then, lass." He faced her, his body fully aroused, his eyes gleaming with challenge and promise.

With a gleeful chuckle she sent a jet of water over him, careful to circumvent that part of his body that most interested her. Hugo was unperturbed by the cold, having enjoyed many baths under the deck pump of one of His Majesty's ships of the line. The secret was to know it was coming. The other morning, when Chloe had chucked a jug of the icy stuff over him in the bath, he'd been expecting the benediction of steamy liquid warmth.

With the utmost seriousness he washed himself as she continued to work the handle, but deliberately he offered himself to her wide-eyed gaze. She worked the pump with breathless enthusiasm, her tongue peeping from between her lips, her eyes sparkling with anticipation.

"Enough!" Finally, he held up his hands, demanding surcease. "The show's over. Pass me the towel."

Chloe grinned and continued to work the handle for a few more minutes. Hugo leapt out of the stream and grabbed the damp towel. "You're asking for more trouble, young Chloe." He rubbed his hair and abraded his skin.

"Inside with you, unless you want to go under again." He took a menacing step toward her and with a mock scream she ran into the house, but instead of going to the kitchen she went into Hugo's bedroom, diving beneath the sheets.

When he came in five minutes later, she was lying in his bed, the sheet pulled demurely up to her chin, her cornflower eyes filled with the rich sensuality that never failed to overwhelm him.

"Good morning, Sir Hugo." She kicked off the cover, offering her body, naked, translucent in the pearly dawn light.

"Good morning, my ward." He dropped the towel from his loins and came down on the bed beside her.

Chapter 16

"I F WE WENT to London and you married a rich wife, then you could repay whatever of my fortune you had to use to make your house habitable." Chloe's tone was casually conversational. "You wouldn't have to repay what we spent on my come-out, of course. Clothes and balls and things like that . . ."

She twirled a silky chest hair around her little finger, her head resting in the crook of his shoulder. She'd never managed to get this far without being cut off before.

"There must be lots of rich women in London—widows or some such—who'd love to marry you. You're handsome and clever and—"

"Enough flattery." Hugo interrupted at last. "As it happens, I'm not in the least interested in rich widows, although I'm deeply complimented that you should imagine ranks of them falling at my feet."

"Oh, but you have to be sensible," she said earnestly. "It's possible that they won't be pretty . . . or even very young . . . but if they're rich—"

"What have I done to deserve being leg-shackled to an ancient widowed antidote, Chloe! You really have a low opinion of my charms, don't you?"

"No! I do not!" She sat up, her expression genuinely horrified that he should have thought such a thing. "I said you were handsome and clever and kind. But wouldn't a young, rich, pretty woman expect to marry a title and a fortune? I thought that was what happened." She frowned down at him. "Did I hurt you?"

"No, you silly child, of course you didn't." Smiling, he reached up and twined his hands into the radiant cascade of hair falling around her face. "I am well aware of my handicaps on the marriage mart—elderly baronets in straitened circumstances are considered poor catches."

"You are not elderly!" Chloe laughed at this absurdity. Emboldened by the absence of the customary brusque interdiction on the subject, she went on. "But if you won't marry a rich widow, then why can't we pay to put your house in order as part of the expenses of my come-out? I have to live somewhere while I find a suitable husband."

"Very well," Hugo said.

"What?" Chloe sat back on her ankles, blinking in disbelief. "Did you just say we could go to London?"

"That would be a correct interpretation," he agreed solemnly.

"But why . . . when . . . did you change your mind?"

"Why should that interest you?" he teased. "Isn't it enough that I said yes?"

"Yes . . . no . . . yes . . . but . . . but up to now you wouldn't even entertain the idea. I expected it to take weeks to soften you up!"

"Soften me up!" He pulled her down on top of him. "Of all the unscrupulous, sly little foxes!"

She was malleable satin, her body sweetly molding to the contours of his as he parted her thighs and entered her with a slow twist of his hips.

Her eyes widened as she absorbed the very different sensations of this novel position. "I didn't know you could do it this way."

"There are many ways, sweetheart." He stroked down her back.

"And we'll do them all," she declared with a smile so like a contented cat that he burst into laughter.

He'd never before made love with a partner so deliciously full of uninhibited joy. She was always eager, seizing on each new experience and sensation with hungry passion. And what he loved the most was the way she told him what she wanted even while she demanded he tell her what he wanted of her. She told him what she was thinking throughout, what pleased her both about what he did to her and what she did to him. It made lovemaking the most shared and sharing experience he could ever have imagined, and when he was with her in this way, the tarnished memories of the travesties in the crypt lost their bite.

"If I do this," she now said, moving her body over and around him, her teeth clipping her bottom lip, a frown of concentration drawing the fine eyebrows together, "does it feel nice for you?"

"Wonderful," he said, smiling at her through narrowed eyes, as entranced by her expression as he was by her movements.

"And this"—she leaned backward over her ankles, arching her body, and then gasped—"oh . . . perhaps I shouldn't do that just yet."

"Whatever and whenever you wish, lass," he said, holding her hips. "The conductor's baton is in your charge this afternoon."

"But it has to be right for you too," she said seriously. "You always make sure it's right for me."

He smiled again and reached for one perfect round breast; the small firm swell fit his cupped palm neatly. "Such a bundle of love you are, young Chloe."

Half an hour later, Chloe gathered her scattered attentions together again and returned to the subject uppermost in her thoughts. "How will we travel to London? It's a dreadfully long way."

"Two hundred miles," he agreed. "We'll hire a postchaise."

"And change horses along the road," she said with a knowledgeable little nod. "Miss Anstey was to do that."

"That reminds me, we have to find you a duenna," he said, hitching himself up against the pillows. "You can't live in London alone in a bachelor household without scandalizing society."

"But you're my guardian."

"You still need a female chaperone . . . someone to accompany you to parties, to help you receive visitors, to shop with you."

"I had thought of asking Miss Anstey if she'd like to be a companion if I set up my own establishment," she said thoughtfully, a fingertip tracing the coiled serpent on his chest. "When you were being so horrid to me and I thought I couldn't bear to stay with you."

He caught her wrist, trying not to let her see how he hated her touching the mark of Eden. "Was I horrid enough to drive you to that, lass?"

"Yes, but not for long. Shall I write to Miss Anstey?"

"No, a governess won't do," he said. "You need a chaperone of some social standing."

"But who?"

"Leave it to me." He swung out of bed and stretched. "What a shameless way to spend an afternoon."

"It was a lovely way," Chloe disagreed. "And it's still pouring with rain. What else could one do?"

Hugo regarded her quizzically. "There are many useful things to be done on a rainy afternoon, lass."

She shrugged. "But none so pleasant, I'll lay odds."

"No, there you have me, I have to admit." He pulled on his shirt.

"So when shall we go?" Chloe made no effort to leave his bed, snuggling farther under the covers.

"As soon as I've talked to Childe at the bank, hired the chaise, arranged matters here. A week maybe."

"That soon!" Her indolent posture vanished. "But Beatrice won't have weaned the kittens by then."

"No!" Hugo said, stepping into his britches. "No and no and no." He came up to the bed. "I repeat, Chloe: *no*. I am resigned to Dante, but I will not journey to London with a cat, six kittens, a one-legged parrot, and a barn owl."

"Of course we won't take Plato," she said, as if the very idea were ridiculous. "He belongs here and his wing is almost healed."

"I'm relieved," he said dryly. "However, neither will we be taking the rest of the menagerie."

"I should think you'd be glad of Beatrice and her litter if your London house has as many mice as this one."

"No. No. No. Must I say it again?"

Chloe stared past him, apparently gazing with unwarranted interest at the rain-drenched windowpane.

Seven days later, two fascinated postilions watched as one of their passengers busily ensconced a basket of mewling kittens and a bird cage inside the chaise. The occupant of the bird cage offered a ripe opinion on this change in his circumstances and then cackled with the appearance of self-satisfaction. A tortoiseshell cat leapt into the chaise after the kittens and curled on the squabbed seat by the window. A huge brindled mongrel ran, barking excitedly, around the chaise, his feathered tail flailing all and sundry.

Hugo stood supervising the securing of Petrarch to the rear of the chaise. He had no idea how it had happened. He couldn't even pinpoint the moment when he'd yielded. His ward had the most obdurate will, one that simply ignored opposition. She had behaved as if he couldn't possibly have meant his prohibition and somehow he'd come to believe that he hadn't.

But, dammit, he had! The prospect of a two-hundred-mile journey with that circus was hideous. No less so was the thought of arriving at his deserted and neglected house on Mount Street accompanied by a menagerie.

With a helpless frown he listened to Chloe's cheerful reassurances as she bestowed her family within the chaise. She seemed to be extolling the virtues of travel by post-chaise and all the excitements to come their way. Judging by Falstaff's response, they were not wholly impressed.

"Don't fancy travelin' with that lot," Samuel muttered, appearing at Hugo's side. "I've 'alf a mind to ride along wi' you."

Since Samuel was not much of a rider, rolling decks suiting him more than the rolling gait of a horse, the possibility was indicative of the depths of his feelings on the matter.

"I'm sorry," Hugo apologized, shaking his head. "I don't know how it happened."

"Won't take no for an answer, that's 'er trouble," Samuel pronounced.

"But what's mine?" Hugo demanded.

Samuel cast him a shrewd look. "Reckon ye know that as well as anyone." He stomped around to the open door of the chaise and peered doubtfully within. "Any room in there for me?"

"Yes, of course," Chloe said. "I'll sit with Beatrice and Falstaff and the kittens, and you can have the whole opposite seat to yourself."

"What about the dog?"

"He'll sit on the floor . . . but I expect some of the time he'll want to run along beside the carriage."

Samuel sighed heavily and clambered in. Chloe smiled warmly in welcome and scrunched herself up against the squabs as if to make herself even smaller than she was.

"You do have enough room, don't you?" she asked with anxious solicitude as he settled down.

"Reckon so," he said with a grudging sniff. "But it'll smell to 'igh 'eaven in here, soon enough."

"It won't," Chloe insisted, trying to make Dante diminish as he leapt exuberantly into the carriage and bestowed his breathy grin on his fellow travelers. "They're very clean. And we can have the window open."

"Drafts is bad for me neck."

"Oh, Samuel, please don't mind." She reached over and placed a hand on his knee.

As always, he was not proof against the beguiling charm of her appeals. He grunted in half-acceptance. The whole expedition struck him as lunacy. He was Lancashire born and bred, and apart from his years at sea had never been out of the county. He had never been to London and had never wanted to go. He didn't want to now. It seemed to him they had enough to do at the manor, and now that Sir Hugo had come out of the doldrums, life could jog along quite smoothly. But where Sir Hugo went, he went too, and if Sir Hugo believed this crazily uncomfortable disruption of their lives was necessary, then Samuel would bite his tongue.

Hugo swung onto his horse, and the chaise moved out of the courtyard. He cast a glance behind him at his home. He had never been fond of it, not even as a boy, and had left it without regret when he'd joined the navy. Since his return, its proximity to Shipton and Gresham Hall had destroyed any desire to make a permanent home there. He'd stayed, attached by some fantastical umbilical cord to the one pure love of his life . . . and because it was as good a place as any other to drink himself into an early grave.

But all that was behind him.

Now he was caught up in a convolution to which he had to find a solution. And the only solution was a husband for Chloe. No suitable husband could be found if she remained at Denholm Manor. He couldn't establish her on her own without exposing her to Jasper's machinations. So it had to be London under his protection. *Quod erat demonstrandum.* The Latin tag from schoolboy geometry was somehow appropriate in its absolute truth.

And maybe in London they would find the distractions that would lessen the spell that diminutive bundle of love had cast over them both. Until the spell was broken, Chloe wouldn't be truly free to follow the conventional paths that Elizabeth would have wanted for her. She would find friends, activities, a social whirl that the sheltered girl could never have imagined. And as she became absorbed, so would the ties to himself lessen.

As for himself—once he had found London a hypnotic treasure chest. There were members of Society who would remember him . . . there were distant relatives who knew no worse of him than that he'd gone somewhat precipitately to fight Napoleon. He had friends at the Admiralty . . . men who existed on half pay rather than sell out at war's end. Once he'd been gregarious, there was no reason he shouldn't become so again. The shadow of the Congregation of Eden could be thrown off.

And in the pursuit of these distractions he would be able to withdraw gracefully from the unnatural . . . no, not unnatural, but utterly improper and disgraceful liaison with his seventeen-year-old ward.

And once she was respectably married, she'd be free of Jasper's threat, and he would be free to leave England and make some kind of a life for himself on the Continent.

He knew one thing, it was a knowledge that came from the marrow of his bones rather than his brain. He couldn't endure to live close to Chloe once she was married . . . in love . . . lost to him for all the right reasons. He'd ached in the wilderness for her mother. He wouldn't do it again for the daughter.

Chapter 17

"**H**UGO LATTIMER, isn't it?"

At the quiet question, Hugo looked up from the shelf of music books he was perusing in Hatchard's. He frowned for a second at the black-eyed man who'd addressed him, then his expression cleared as recollection came.

"Carrington," he said, holding out his hand to Marcus Devlin, Marquis of Carrington. "It's been many years."

"At least fourteen," Lord Carrington agreed, shaking hands. "We were both a pair of striplings. You joined the navy, I believe."

"Yes, for the duration. I sold out after Waterloo."

"And what brings you to London? The joys of the Season?" Carrington's voice was faintly sardonic. He was not an aficionado of Society's social whirl.

Hugo shrugged easily. He remembered some old story about a broken engagement that had soured Marcus Devlin's view of Society's pleasures. "I've acquired a ward," he said with a smile. "And it seems orchestrating a come-out lies within the duties of a guardian."

He glanced around the crowded bookshop. "She's here somewhere, searching for Miss Austen's posthumous publication; *Persuasion,* I believe it's titled."

"An interesting lady, Miss Austen," Marcus observed. "A painfully sharp wit and no patience with fools and their foibles."

"No," Hugo agreed. "Pride and prejudice . . ."

"Sense and sensibility," Marcus continued promptly.

"Well, if you'll excuse me, Lattimer . . . I'll see you in White's or Watier's perhaps?"

Hugo inclined his head in vague acknowledgment. He was still a member of both clubs, but he had neither the resources nor the inclination for gaming—the major activity in the exclusive clubs of St. James's—and no desire to draw attention to himself by refusing to join in the heavy drinking that accompanied social intercourse in those bastions of male privilege.

The marquis left the bookshop and stood on the street, looking up Piccadilly, waiting for his tiger to bring the curricle whose team he'd been walking while his lordship made his purchases.

He barely noticed the raucous commotion from a group of lads on the corner of an alley behind him, until a slight figure hurtled out of the bow-windowed shop, racing past him with a cry of outrage. Curiously he turned to watch, and suddenly the figure spun around and ran back to him.

"Your whip?" she demanded, her eyes crackling with passion. "Please, quickly." Impatiently, she extended her hand for the long driving whip he held loosely at his side.

Marcus didn't think he'd ever beheld a more exquisite countenance or an angrier one. She blazed with the pure fire of righteous rage. Before he could say anything, however, she had snatched the whip from him without further ceremony and was racing back to the noisy group on the corner.

He watched in stunned amazement as she plunged into the middle of the group, slashing savagely from side to side with his whip with a complete indifference to the shrieks of those she struck.

"What the hell . . . Chloe!" Hugo Lattimer appeared on the pavement. "I do not believe this," he exclaimed.

"I turn my back for two minutes and she's embroiled in some melee again."

"Happens often, does it?" Marcus inquired, as amused as he was intrigued.

"When it comes to abused animals," Hugo replied shortly. He strode over to the disintegrating group, where quite a crowd was gathering.

Fascinated, the marquis followed.

Chloe Gresham emerged victorious from the melee as the whipped youths slunk away into the alley. She held something clutched to her breast. Her hat was crooked, her skirt muddied, a streak of dirt down one cheek. Her eyes blazed with a mixture of fury and triumph.

"Just look!" she demanded of Hugo, the catch in her voice as always accentuated by emotion. "They were baiting him with pointed sticks."

"Dear God," Hugo muttered, staring at Chloe's prize. "It's a bear!"

Marcus could well understand the other man's dismay. Nevertheless, his shoulders shook slightly as Chloe said, "It's a baby . . . it can't be more than two months old . . . and they were torturing it. I thought bear baiting was against the law."

"It is," Marcus said. "I beg your pardon, but I don't seem to have had the honor . . ."

"My ward," Hugo said with a sigh. "Chloe Gresham. Chloe, allow me to present Lord Carrington."

"Enchanted, Miss Gresham." Marcus bowed, his black eyes brimful of amusement and more than a little admiration. For some reason, the streak of dirt seemed to accentuate the peaches and cream complexion, emotion darkened her eyes to an indescribable depth of blue, and the angrily quivering lip merely served to underline the full perfection of a lovely mouth.

"Oh, your whip, Lord Carrington. Thank you, and I

beg your pardon if I snatched it from you." She held it out to him.

"Not at all," he murmured. "I would have offered to help, but such an offer seemed somewhat superfluous." He cast a glance of complicit amusement at Hugo Lattimer, who returned it with a resigned shake of the head.

"Come here, lass. Your hat's crooked." Careful to avoid the bundle in her arms, he straightened the chip straw hat, affording Marcus a more thorough glimpse of a lustrous golden head.

Taking out his handkerchief, Hugo licked the corner and wiped the streak of dirt from her cheek. "Now, would you mind telling me what you intend doing with a bear cub. I doubt Dante will appreciate him . . . it . . . not to mention Beatrice."

"Dante?" queried Marcus, fascinated. "Beatrice?"

"Oh, my household resembles a circus," Hugo informed him. "So far we have seven cats, a massive, obsessively devoted mongrel, a one-legged parrot with the foulest mouth you've ever heard, and now, it appears, a bear . . . oh, and in the past we've also had a barn owl and a much-abused nag liberated from a turnip seller. They all rejoice in the most erudite of names."

"You exhibit much fortitude, my friend," Marcus commented.

"You're laughing at me," Chloe accused, looking between them.

"Heaven forfend." Hugo threw up his hands. "What could be less amusing than a bear?"

"It's only a baby," she said again, bending her head to look at the mangy bundle of fur in her arms. A pair of bright eyes looked out at her and a black snout snuffled.

"But what are you going to do with it?"

"I wonder if bears can be housebroken—"

"*No!*" Hugo exclaimed.

"You don't think they can?" She looked up, frowning, her head on one side.

"I should think it's highly unlikely." Marcus weighed in on the side where fellow-feeling seemed to place him. "The stables seem the most appropriate place . . . at least until he . . . it . . . grows up." His voice quavered as Hugo groaned audibly, and they both envisaged a fully grown brown bear in situ in a London establishment.

"Well, I'll see," Chloe said. "When I've had a chance to see if he's badly hurt and how undernourished he is. I may have to keep him inside for a while."

"I wish I didn't have to go," Marcus murmured, "before you resolve the issue, but unfortunately I have an appointment." He extended his hand again to Hugo. "You must be blessed with remarkable forbearance, Lattimer. I don't know whether to offer you my congratulations or my condolences."

"I'll accept either or both," Hugo said wryly. He barely knew Marcus Devlin, but there was something about his reaction to the situation that created an easy familiarity. But then, Chloe tended to have that effect on most people. "I only wonder which Society will offer."

"With that beauty," Marcus said, softly enough for Chloe not to hear. "She'll bring the town to its knees, my friend."

"And eighty thousand pounds," Hugo said as softly, although Chloe was far too intent on her new acquisition to pay attention to this low-voiced conversation.

Marcus's lips pursed in a soundless whistle. "You'll have to beat them from your door, Lattimer."

He turned back to Chloe. "Miss Gresham, pray accept my compliments, you are quite out of the common way. I know Lady Carrington will enjoy meeting you. I shall suggest she call upon you . . . in Mount Street, isn't it?" He looked inquiringly at Hugo.

Hugo confirmed it, reflecting that Chloe seemed to have done herself some good by this unlooked-for meeting. If the Marchioness of Carrington interested herself in Chloe, then her entrance into the first circles was assured. However, he was aware that embroiling herself in a street brawl could have had the opposite consequences. If Marcus Devlin had chosen to be disgusted by such an outrageous display from a debutante, she could have found herself ostracized by all but the most inveterate fortune hunters.

Marcus climbed into his now-waiting curricle and drove home to Berkeley Square. He found his wife in the nursery.

"I have just encountered the most exquisite little rogue," he said. "But not as exquisite a little rogue as my Emma." With a soft smile he bent to pick up his daughter, clamoring at his knees. He swung the toddler into the air, and she squealed excitedly, grabbing at his nose with a dimpled fist.

Judith Devlin leaned back in her chair, cradling her infant son, smiling as she watched her husband with the little girl. Marcus was a devoted father.

"So?" she prompted, when he'd stopped playing with the child and settled her on his hip. "What about this encounter?"

Marcus bent to examine his son, who lay placidly, sucking his thumb in his mother's arm. "Edmund looks bigger today."

"Nonsense," Judith said with an indulgent laugh. "He's no bigger this morning than he was last night." She lifted her face for her husband's kiss. "Are you ever going to tell me?"

"Oh, yes. Rarely have I been so richly amused." He described the bear's rescue and, as he'd expected, the ready amusement sprang to his wife's tawny eyes. It was a story to appeal to the unconventional, and Judith had ever been that.

"Hugo Lattimer and I came into Society at the same time," he said, setting his wriggling daughter on her feet. "But he ran with a wild set in those days . . . oh, that is a splendid house, Emma." He took the sheet of paper she was pressing at him.

"There's Mama." She jabbed at a stick figure. "Wiv' your horse."

"Very lifelike," he said solemnly, critically comparing his wife with the facsimile. "Anyway, lynx, I engaged that you would call upon the girl. She must be Stephen Gresham's daughter. Lattimer was much involved with his set." He grimaced. "The Greshams are bad blood, if all the rumors are true, but it's hard to imagine bad blood running in the veins of such an exquisite creature. And she struck me as quite without artifice."

"She's closer to Harriet's age," Judith said. Her sister-in-law was five years younger than herself.

Marcus shook his head. "True enough, but you know as well as I, my love, that Harriet's tastes don't run to the unconventional. She wouldn't know what to make of Miss Gresham."

Judith laughed slightly. "No, I suppose you're right. Anyway, Sebastian tells me that she's expecting again. She always suffers so badly from nausea, poor love, I don't know why they keep having babies."

"Because it suits them," Marcus said. "Your brother is even more besotted with his children than I am."

"Yes, and he spoils them abominably. And Harriet is incapable of saying no. Little Charles created havoc in here yesterday, and as for young Peter . . ."

"Well, you're the only person Sebastian will listen to, including his wife," Marcus pointed out with perfect truth.

"I've told him," she said. "And he won't listen. I suppose he wants to give them all the things he never had. A childhood spent racketing around the capitals of the Continent in the train of an impoverished gamester left out a lot."

"It didn't do either of you any harm."

"Oh, you were not always of that opinion," she said, her eyes narrowing. "There was a time when you expressed yourself most vehemently on the subject."

"A lot of water's flowed since then," her husband said equably. "If the girl's Gresham's daughter, why isn't her half brother her guardian, I wonder? Lattimer's no relation . . . although . . ."

"Although?" Judith prompted when he paused.

"Well, there was something about the way he treated her," Marcus said slowly, remembering how naturally Hugo had straightened her hat and wiped the smear on her cheek. "A rather particular intimacy . . ."

"Ohh . . ." Judith said. "What do you suspect?"

"Nothing." He shrugged. "Lattimer's all of thirty-four and the girl's barely out of the schoolroom. I expect he was being avuncular. . . . Anyway, will you call on her?"

"I can hardly wait."

Two days later, Lady Carrington drove herself in her high-perch phaeton to Mount Street.

It was clear from the moment the door was opened to her by a sturdy man in leather britches and waistcoat, sporting two gold earrings, that she was in no ordinary household.

"Is Miss Gresham in?" She drew off her gloves, looking around the square hall. The smell of fresh paint hung in the air.

"Aye, I reckon so," the unusual butler said. "Last I knew, the lass was pesterin' that Alphonse in the kitchen. Mind you, what we want wi' a cook, I don't know, specially one what calls 'imself some fancy Frenchie name when it's as plain as day he's no more of a Frenchie than I am. What's good enough in Lancashire ought t' be good enough 'ere, I says."

Judith was somewhat at a loss as to how to respond to this confidence, when a swinging baize door at the end of the hall flew open and a brown bundle exploded into the hall, followed by an enormous dog.

"Dante! Come here!" A slight figure whirled through the door on their heels, brandishing a wooden spoon. "You are the worst-behaved animal! Leave Demosthenes alone."

Judith jumped out of the way as the brown fur bundle lumbered past her at a surprising speed, the dog yapping at its heels.

"Miss Gresham?" she inquired.

"Yes," Chloe said distractedly. "I beg your pardon, but I must catch Demosthenes. If Hugo finds him loose in the house, there'll be terrible trouble."

"Demosthenes?" Judith said feebly. She rarely felt feeble.

"Well, Bruin's rather boring, don't you think," Chloe said, lunging for the bear cub. "Samuel, can you catch Dante?"

Samuel grunted and grabbed Dante by the collar. The dog sat down, panting. The bear had retreated beneath an inlaid console table and a pair of bright eyes gazed out from the shadows.

Judith sat down on a chair and burst into a peal of laughter. "Marcus said you were refreshing," she gasped. "But I don't believe he knows the half of it."

"Marcus?" Chloe, who was on her knees in front of the console table, looked over her shoulder.

"My husband, Lord Carrington. I understand you met him the other day."

"Oh, yes, he was kind enough to lend me his whip." Chloe dropped forward onto her hands and knees, sticking her nose under the table. "Come on, you silly animal. I only want to dress that cut."

It was at this moment that Hugo sauntered into his house through the still-open front door. Dante greeted him exuberantly, and he didn't at first see their visitor on her chair by the wall. His attention was immediately caught by Chloe's upturned rear as she peered under the table.

"What are you doing?" He swung his crop lightly at the inviting behind.

"Ouch!" Chloe backed out hastily. "I was hoping you wouldn't come back until I'd captured Demosthenes. Dante jumped at him while I was stirring the poultice in the kitchen and all hell broke loose."

"All what?"

"Oh, well you know what I mean. Oh, this is Lady Carrington. She came to call." She gestured toward Judith.

"I seem to have picked a rather inconvenient moment," Judith said, wiping tears of laughter from her eyes. "Sir Hugo."

"Lady Carrington." He bowed formally over her hand but his eyes twinkled at the ready laughter in the golden-brown eyes of his guest. "Sometimes I wonder if there is ever a convenient moment in this circus. Allow me to give you a glass of sherry to restore your shattered nerves." He gestured toward the library, saying over his shoulder, "Chloe, you will remove that wild animal forthwith, and if I ever catch him in the house again, it will be very much the worse for both of you."

Chloe watched the two of them disappear into the library and muttered one of Falstaff's more inventive phrases.

It was twenty minutes later before she was able to

join her guardian and his guest in the library. Lady Carrington and Hugo were laughing as she entered and seemed to be getting on famously. For some reason, this made her feel put out. She examined the visitor with more attention and saw a vibrant, beautiful woman in her mid-twenties, radiating assurance and confidence, conversing with Hugo as if she'd known him all her life.

Hugo's public rebuke still stung, and Chloe, feeling uncomfortably young and rather grubby, had the sense that she'd wandered uninvited into an adult's domain.

"May I have a glass of sherry?"

"Of course, lass." Hugo poured her a glass and re-filled Lady Carrington's. "Where's the beast?"

"In the stables." She took the glass and sipped. "I must apologize, Lady Carrington, for not welcoming you properly."

"Oh, don't apologize," Judith said, chuckling. "An escaped bear is more than sufficient explanation."

"Where's your chaperone?" Hugo inquired of his ward, explaining to Judith, "My late mother's cousin, Lady Smallwood, resides with us as Chloe's duenna."

"She's lying upon her bed with her smelling salts," Chloe said, her eyes suddenly sparkling with mischief. "I'm afraid Falstaff upset her again."

Judith demanded to know the identity of this character and left soon after, still laughing. "I am having an evening party on Thursday," she said. "You will come, both of you . . . and Lady Smallwood, of course."

That evening, as Judith was dressing for dinner, she remarked to her husband, "You're right about Harriet, Marcus. She won't be able to make heads or tails of Chloe Gresham. But Sebastian will enjoy her enormously. Her beauty is astonishing, of course, but it's that roguish personality that really appeals. She's completely without artifice; I don't even think she knows that she's beautiful. I intend to make her the toast of the Season. What do you think?"

"I don't see how you can fail, if you've a mind to." Marcus took the emerald necklace from the maid, fastening it himself around the slender column of his wife's throat. "With a fortune of eighty thousand pounds and a face and figure to rival Helen of Troy, all she needs is the right patronage."

"Then she shall have it. She'll need a voucher for Almack's, so I'll introduce her to Sally Jersey on Thursday. She's so good-natured, she won't disapprove of Chloe's easy ways, where Princess Esterhazy might."

"I still wish I knew why Hugo Lattimer has her in charge and not Jasper Gresham." Marcus shrugged. "Did you notice anything about them?"

"Only that she can clearly twist him around her little finger," Judith said. "For all that he plays the exasperated guardian on occasion."

"Intriguing."

"Very. There's a Lady Smallwood in residence as chaperone. His late mother's cousin."

Marcus nodded. "Lattimer's mother's family were Beauchamps. Impeccable background. Lady Smallwood will have the right cachet . . . although I understand she's not entirely sensible."

"Since when has that mattered to Society?" Judith asked tartly.

Her husband laughed. "Never. And perhaps the less sensible she is, the more it suits Hugo and his unconventional ward."

"He certainly runs an unconventional household."

"Intriguing," Marcus said again.

"Very," Judith agreed.

Chapter 18

T HE GIRL'S EYES were fixed on the shadowy vaulted ceiling. Vaguely she was aware of the warmth of candle flame on her bare breast as she lay on a bier in the center of the crypt, her body lit by altar candles ranged along the table.

A masked face hung over her, and she turned her head in weak protest as a goblet was presented to her lips.

"Don't be foolish," the man said harshly. He lifted her head with one hand and pressed the goblet against her mouth.

The girl opened her mouth and the aromatic contents were tipped down her throat. She fell back on the white pillow. The muzziness filled her head, and a great warm lethargy spread through her limbs. She had no idea how long she'd been lying naked in this shadowy cavern. She couldn't remember how many times the goblet had been pressed upon her. She had only vague memories of the pouch of gold that had changed hands in her uncle's cottage some time . . . a long long time . . . ago. Her uncle had pocketed the gold and the strange man with the black mask had taken her away.

She felt hands on her body, stroking, smoothing— pleasurable little touches that made her stir and moan. Far away in some recess of her brain she connected the drink with these strange feelings of excitement. When her thighs were drawn apart, she offered no resistance, floating now in a dream world of shadowy figures and shadowy sensations. The sharp pain that accompanied the penetration of her body was a dream, and the swift rhythmic pounding deep within her seemed to have nothing to do with her and yet paradoxically to be intrinsic to her flesh.

Crispin closed his eyes on a surge of pleasure as he possessed the pale body, lying so still beneath him. The eyes of the others were on him, watching him in this rite of initiation under the flickering candles in the cold vault. Behind his closed eyes he saw Chloe lying beneath him, submitting, bound to his pleasure, her arrogant insolence forever subdued as he used her in front of the eager lusting eyes of the Congregation. Jasper had promised it would happen. And Jasper always kept his promises as he always made good his threats.

Jasper leaned back against a pillar, his arms folded, his eyes behind the loo mask skidding over the tableau vivant on the bier. Like his stepson, he was mentally substituting another body for the peasant girl's. Hugo Lattimer had deprived the Congregation of Elizabeth Gresham, but her daughter would make up the deficit. And there would be no interference this time. He would avenge every insult Lattimer had thrown at him by taking the girl and her fortune. Not only would Lattimer suffer the humiliation of failing to fulfill the dying wishes of the woman he had loved with such a besotted, infantile, sentimentalized love, but he would watch while the daughter took the place intended for her mother fourteen years before. And when it was over, Hugo Lattimer's blood would water the granite tombstone slabs of the crypt as Jasper avenged his father's death.

Stephen Gresham had known of Hugo's passion for his wife. He had been intending to give Elizabeth to Hugo in the crypt—a vicious gift, one that he would have found deeply satisfying. Hugo was bound by the oaths of the Congregation to absolute obedience to its leader. He would have been forced to violate the object of his mawkish compassion and idealistic fantasies and thus would have relearned the most important lesson of the crypt: Nothing is sacred.

Instead, Hugo had broken his oath and killed the leader to whom he was bound in obedience. And the leader's son had devised the perfect punishment.

Jasper's eyes roamed around the faces surrounding the bier as they awaited their turn with the ravished virgin. His gaze lingered on the young, fresh face of Denis DeLacy. The youth's eyes were unfocused, his lips parted with eager lust. He was ready to do anything to earn his spurs in the Congregation and he had all the right qualifications for the task: youth, good looks, an accepted place in the Fashionable World, and a respectable fortune.

Jasper pushed himself away from the pillar and walked over to the young man. He tapped him on the shoulder. Denis turned immediately. His face fell as he understood that he was to be deprived of his turn on the bier. But he followed Jasper with the alacrity of an acolyte into one of the smaller chambers in the crypt.

"I was the most amazing success tonight, Samuel." Chloe pranced into the hall as Samuel opened the door. "Lady Jersey has promised to send me a voucher for Almack's, and I didn't have to sit one dance out, and I had so many partners no one could dance more than once with me." She twirled, setting her cream silk skirts swirling.

"And it's a swelled 'ead ye'll be gettin' if you goes on in that fashion," Samuel remarked, closing the door.

"It is most unbecoming, dear," a very fat lady said, shivering in her cashmere shawl. "It's lovely that you should have had so many partners, but you'll lose them all quickly if you don't behave with due modesty."

"Oh, pah," muttered Chloe.

"I'm most dreadfully fatigued," her chaperone said with a wheezing sigh. "Not that it wasn't a most elegant affair . . . most elegant, wasn't it, Hugo? Lady Carrington certainly keeps a good table . . . such lobster patties, such scalloped oysters . . ." She passed a hand over her rotund stomach in an unconscious gesture of corporeal recollection. "Oh, and the trifles—did I mention the trifles—I had two dishes . . . or was it three?" She frowned with the utmost seriousness.

"Six," said Chloe, sotto voce.

"I beg your pardon, Chloe dear?"

"I said they were delicious," Chloe said with a sweet smile. "And the syllabubs also. You seemed to enjoy those equally, my dear ma'am."

"Oh, yes, indeed. I was forgetting the syllabubs." Lady Smallwood sighed with pleasure. "How could I have forgotten the syllabubs."

"Very easily, with everything else one was obliged to sample," Chloe said, still smiling sweetly.

"Oh, yes, there was so much to choose from. Some people consider such varied choice to be a little vulgar, but I'm not one of them."

"No," Chloe agreed.

"I do believe it shows respect for one's guests to set a good table for them."

"Yes, I'm sure you're right, Dolly." Hugo spoke up before Chloe could continue with her wicked asides. "I'm glad you were tolerably amused."

"Well, as you know, I'm not a great one for socializing . . . not since my dear Smallwood passed on," Lady Smallwood said with a sigh. "But I said I'd do my best for the child, and I will. You won't find me shirking my duties." She waddled toward the stairs. "Now, if you'll excuse me, I'll retire. Come along, Chloe. You don't want to be fagged tomorrow. You'll lose your looks if you're peaky . . . and that would never do."

"But I'm not in the least fatigued, ma'am."

"Lady Smallwood knows best, lass," Hugo said earnestly. "Think how humiliating it would be to see your success slip away from you before you've had a chance to savor it."

Chloe put her tongue out at him but followed her chaperone's mountainous figure up the stairs.

Hugo grinned and shook his head. "What an evening! I foresee we're going to be inundated with bewitched young men in the next weeks, Samuel. You couldn't get near the lass from the minute she walked into the room."

"It's to be 'oped that duenna of 'er's doesn't cotton to the fun she makes of 'er," Samuel said. "I'm 'ard pressed to keep a straight face most o' the time. Right wicked, she is."

"I know, but it is irresistible." Hugo followed Samuel through the swinging door to the kitchen. "I'll put a curb on her if she gets too outrageous." He sat down beside the fire and stretched out his legs, examining his satin knee britches with a frown. "Lord, Samuel, I never expected to be dressing like this again, dancing attendance on vapid ladies at insipid gatherings."

"That Lady Carrington seems a fine woman," Samuel observed, setting a mug of tea beside Hugo.

"Oh, she is," Hugo agreed. "Actually, it wasn't that bad. It's just that I thought I was done with all that nonsense. Instead . . ." He sighed.

Samuel laced his own tea with rum and sat down opposite. "Get her married and off yer 'ands an' we can get back to Denholm."

"That's the object of this exercise," Hugo said dryly,

sipping his tea. A kitten jumped onto his lap, knocking his hand. Tea slurped over his white waistcoat.

"Damnation!" He glared at the kitten, who merely settled purring into his lap. "Which one is this?"

Samuel shrugged. "No idea. Couldn't pronounce it if'n I did know."

Hugo laughed reluctantly. "I suspect it's Ariadne, but I wouldn't swear to it." He leaned back in his chair, closing his eyes.

Samuel smiled to himself and sipped his tea. It was a nightly ritual, the time they had together in the kitchen, no longer the domain of the churlish Alphonse, whose running battles with Chloe over the animals' nutritional needs caused daily upheavals.

Samuel subjected his friend to a close covert scrutiny. Hugo, for all his vociferous dislike of Society's round, looked younger and fitter than at any time since he came ashore at the end of the war.

But Samuel suspected that trouble lurked around the next corner. Hugo was happy. Whatever feelings he held for his youthful ward, they gave him deep pleasure. But beneath it lay the knowledge, the certainty, that it could only be temporary. Once Chloe had gone from his life, would he go back to the wasteland?

Samuel knew that Hugo's strength grew with each successive day that he triumphed over his addiction. Sometimes the old sailor prayed that the relationship would continue for as long as possible, and then he thought that the sooner the end came, the better. The longer it lasted, the harder it would be to break the chains that bound him to the girl.

Hugo put down his cup and yawned. "I'm for bed." He picked up the kitten, holding it aloft in one hand. "No," he said, squinting, "definitely not Ariadne. You must be Aeneas." He set the creature on the floor. "Go back to mama." The kitten merely set to grooming itself with leisurely grace.

Hugo laughed and stood up. "Good night, Samuel."

" 'Night, Sir 'Ugo."

Half an hour later, Hugo was in bed, when his door opened stealthily and a bright head popped itself around the corner, a pair of cornflower-blue eyes twinkling mischievously. "Oh, good, you're not asleep."

Hugo put down his book. "No, having become accustomed to your habits, I was waiting for you. Are you going to bring the rest of you in here?"

Chloe slid into the room, closing the door behind her with exaggerated care, one finger to her lips. "Mustn't wake Milady Smallwood from her dreams of syllabub."

"You are a disrespectful wretch! Have you no respect for your elders and betters?"

"I do if they *are* my betters," she responded. "But I fail to see why simple age should qualify for uncritical submission."

She pulled her nightgown over her head, tossing it over a footstool, then walked over to the cheval glass and stood in front of it, examining her image with a tiny frown.

She was completely without inhibition, Hugo thought, not for the first time, as he enjoyed vicariously her own examination of her body. She lifted her breasts, touched her nipples, turned sideways, running a hand over her flat stomach, scrutinized her back view over her shoulder.

"What are you looking at, lass? Or is it for?" he asked, a quiver of desirous amusement in his voice.

"Well, I've never looked at myself before," she said seriously. "I think I have quite an elegant figure, don't you?"

"You'll pass."

"Is that all?" She extended one leg, flexing her ankle.

"All those men tonight seemed to think it was more than that."

"Samuel's right—you are going to get a swollen head."

Chloe ignored this. "And they only saw my face," she mused, peering closely at her features in the mirror.

"Only half the story," Hugo agreed, wondering where this was leading. "But in my character as strict guardian, I have to tell you, lass, that it's most improper to speculate on the effect your naked body might have on prospective suitors."

Chloe ignored this too. She turned back to him. "Do you find me attractive?"

"I'd have thought I'd made that clear by now."

"Yes, but I was the only woman around," she pointed out. "You didn't have anyone to compare me with in Lancashire."

"What the hell are you getting at, Chloe?" It occurred to him that amusement was not going to be the appropriate response to whatever this was.

"Nothing really." She stood, frowning down at the threadbare carpet. Hugo's renovations had been strictly limited to the public rooms of his house, and his household staff was at the barest socially acceptable minimum.

"Out with it, lass."

"You find Lady Carrington attractive, don't you?"

Hugo leaned back against the carved headboard, a slight frown in his eyes now. "What makes you say that?"

"I can tell from the way you look at her when you're talking to her," she replied. "She is very beautiful and very witty. And you seem to like talking to her."

"I do enjoy talking to her."

"And she flirts," Chloe said, raising her eyes from the carpet. "Doesn't she?"

Hugo smiled. "Yes, she does. Women in her position often do. It's a game."

"A game you like to play."

"Yes," he agreed. "A game I enjoy playing with Lady Carrington."

"Mmmm. Would you like to make love to her?"

Hugo pulled at his chin, trying to work out what was going on. "Judith Devlin is a married woman, lass. And from what I can see, a very happily married woman."

"Yes, I'm sure that's so. But it doesn't answer my question. Would you like to make love to her?" She was standing at the end of his bed, holding on to one of the posts, now completely oblivious of her nakedness.

He debated and decided on an honest response. "Yes," he said evenly. "I could imagine making love to Lady Carrington with a great deal of pleasure."

"I thought so. I expect she would know much more about it than I do."

"You learn very fast, lass," he said, trying to lighten the mood. "Come here." He stretched out a hand in invitation.

Chloe remained where she was. "But I'm not worldly or . . . or up to snuff, like Lady Carrington."

"Come here." Hugo leaned forward, caught her around the waist, and toppled her onto the bed beside him. "No, you are not worldly, and it would be quite wrong for you to be so. Why on earth are you comparing yourself with a woman some ten years older than you? If you must make comparisons, then do so with other debutantes."

"But you're not interested in debutantes," she said, lying rather stiffly against him. "And I'm comparing myself with women you are interested in."

"Ahhh." He sat up. It seemed a moment for plain speaking. "I think we'd better clarify a few things, Chloe. This London scheme was of your devising, as I recall. You wish to acquire an accommodating husband so that you may have control of your fortune and thus the ordering of your own life. Isn't that so?"

He looked down at her as she lay still on the bed. Her eyes were tightly closed. "Chloe, open your eyes and sit up."

When she didn't immediately comply, he pulled her into a sitting position. She opened her eyes, since keeping them shut while sitting up seemed absurd.

"Isn't that so?" he repeated.

"It was," she said. "But why can't you marry me and then—"

"Of all the absurdities!" Hugo interrupted. "I've never heard such moon-mad nonsense. I am thirty-four, my dear child, and thirty-four makes a poor husband for seventeen—even if I wanted such a thing."

"You wouldn't want to marry me?" It was a soft question, but her eyes had darkened with the expectation of hurt.

"I have no intention of marrying *anyone,*" he stated. "As I've told you before. We are here because you wished it—and because it keeps you out of your brother's orbit. You will enjoy your come-out like any other seventeen-year-old in her first Season, and if your reception tonight was anything to go by, you will have more offers of marriage than you can handle. We'll both have our work cut out making the right choice for you."

"But what about us?"

"What *about* us?" he demanded with sudden harshness, realizing the slipperiness of this slope. "I am breaking every honorable rule of conduct in the book, Chloe. I was weak enough to allow you to engineer this, but I have sworn you will not be harmed by it. You will marry and put this behind you, hopefully as an interlude that brings you only pleasant memories. You will tell *no one* about it, ever."

"But I don't want it to stop." She looked at him with painful candor and put a hand on his thigh. "Please, Hugo, why must it ever stop? I'll try very hard to be a good wife, and I can learn how to be like Lady Carrington—"

"For God's sake, Chloe, stop it! I don't want you to be like Lady Carrington. I do not want a wife, do you understand?" He put his hands on the slender shoulders and gave her a little shake. "I am not getting any deeper into this mess than I am already. The sooner you find yourself a husband and start leading an appropriate life, the happier I will be. Do you understand that?"

"You would be rid of me?"

"You are twisting my words."

"I don't think I am." She slid away from his hands and stood up. "You said it was a mess." She bent to pick up her nightgown.

Hugo sighed, passing a hand over his eyes. "And so it is. Can't you see, little simpleton, how grossly improper this is? There are those who would say I have debauched my ward, and many would agree with them."

"But you don't believe that?" Her head appeared from the folds of the nightgown and her eyes fixed on his face.

"It is the bald truth," he said flatly. "But bald truths are not always the whole story."

"Why don't you wish to marry anyone?"

"This catechism grows tedious." He sounded suddenly bored.

"But I want to know," she declared, coming over to the bed. "I think I'm entitled to know."

"Oh, do you now?" He was genuinely annoyed, as much by her truculence as by the unwelcome persistence in an area he preferred to keep dark even from himself. "And just where, my impertinent brat, does this entitlement lie? Are you assuming that your presence in my bed gives you the right to poke and pry in whatever private thoughts and feelings I might have?"

Chloe flushed scarlet. "I didn't mean that."

"Then what did you mean?"

"I don't know," she said. She had meant exactly that, but it sounded dreadful when put in those bluntly contemptuous terms. Feeling like the brat he had called her, firmly put in her place, she turned to the door with a mumbled "Good night."

Hugo made no attempt to stop her. He swore under his breath, a short barnyard oath, wondering why he hadn't foreseen such a damnable complication in an already impossibly convoluted situation.

He had convinced himself she was simply trying her sexual wings and he was giving her the opportunity to do so safely. His own feelings were kept rigorously battened down. But if Chloe was beginning to envisage some kind of future to their liaison, then he'd have to take serious measures to disabuse her.

She had put the method into his hands, he realized. If she saw him engaging in light flirtation with the sophisticated worldly women who would seem so much more in his social sphere than herself, she might take the point more effectively than with simple words. It would lessen the intensity of their relationship and would certainly help him to conceal from his willful ward the passionate, tormenting, obsessive nature of his desire for her.

How could he tell her that the bars to their marriage were manifold? He was her father's killer; he had loved her mother, who had trusted him with her daughter's future, and anything but the destiny to which her beauty and fortune entitled her would be a gross betrayal of that trust; he was twice her age and a poor man; he was her guardian and by any ethical rule therefore banned from taking advantage of that relationship to improve his own circumstances.

He had done many despicable things in his life, but tying an eager, passionate innocent to a man twice her age, a man who had played in the crypt and had killed her father, stuck even in *his* craw.

He leaned over to blow out the candle and lay back in the dark, waiting to see if sleep would be kind to him. After a while he relit the candle, hitched himself up against the pillows, and resignedly picked up his discarded book. Within a few minutes, his door opened.

"Do you want to play backgammon?"

Chloe stood in the door, a diffident little smile on her lips that was impossible to resist. He'd employed enough severity for one night.

"Bad one," he scolded. "Why aren't you asleep?"

"I can't." Taking his tone as invitation, she closed the door and came farther into the room. "I was unhappy. I didn't mean to be impertinent and poke and pry."

He put his book aside. "Come here."

She sat on the bed beside him, still with that diffident air and an aching question in her eyes. "Are you still angry?"

"No, but I want you to listen to me very carefully. That kind of talk is utter foolishness. If you mention such a thing again, then the only contact you and I will ever have afterward will be purely as guardian and ward. Is that clear?"

Chloe nodded.

"From now on I want you to enjoy everything London and the Season have to offer," he continued, slipping an arm around her. Immediately she cuddled into his embrace with a little sigh of relief. "I want you to make lots of friends, to flirt, to dance, to go to picnics and parties; to surround yourself with admirers, to become surfeited with all the amusements available. All right?" He flicked her cheek teasingly with a lock of guinea-gold hair.

"All right," she said, delicately brushing his nipples with a fingertip. "If I must."

Hugo laughed. "I have just given you permission for unbridled pleasure and that's all you can say: if I must."

She bent her head and touched her tongue to his nipples. "So long as I have permission to do this." She turned her head on his chest to look up at him, and he read only sensual mischief now in the eyes previously so full of hurt. "Or would you prefer to play backgammon?"

When she regained her own bed some considerable time later, Chloe lay sleepless, watching the dawn through her uncurtained window. She had decided that she was going to marry Hugo Lattimer. The only question was how to arrange it.

She had decided they would become lovers and had managed to arrange that in the teeth of his vigorous opposition, so she couldn't see any reason why this next step shouldn't be similarly accomplished.

But she would have to lull him into a false sense of security, as she had done over the other issue. She would obey his orders to the letter, fling herself into whatever pleasures and adventures might come her way, encourage suitors, and be as careless of convention as she chose. Hugo would soon relax again and forget she'd ever brought up the subject of marriage.

She would drive him to distraction with deviltry. He would never know what she was about to do next, and the last thing on his mind would be worrying about whether she still cherished the notion of their marriage. And then, at the right moment . . .

With a leisurely stretch Chloe yawned and snuggled down under the quilt. At the right moment she would spring it upon him and carry the day. Hugo didn't know what was best for both of them, so she'd just have to prove it to him.

Chapter 19

"WE HAVE HAD the most satisfying shopping expedition." Chloe burst into the library, her nose just visible over the armful of bandboxes. "Shall I show you what we bought? . . . Oh, I do beg your pardon." Quietly, she placed her packages on the sofa and sat down to listen as Hugo finished the Haydn sonata.

"I am so sorry," she said when the last notes had died. "I didn't hear as I came in and—"

"No matter," he said, turning on the bench. "But on that subject, I haven't heard you playing for a day or two."

"I've been very busy," Chloe offered in lame excuse. "The knocker is always sounding, and there was the balloon ascension, and all this shopping."

"Perhaps this afternoon?"

"Yes, this afternoon . . . only—"

"Only?" he prompted with a quizzical raise of his eyebrows.

"Only I had promised to go riding in Hyde Park with Robert and Miles and Gerald."

"And your chaperone, of course?"

Chloe went into a peal of laughter at the thought of Lady Smallwood's wobbling rear on horseback. "No, but Robert's sister is coming, so it will be quite unexceptionable."

"I am relieved."

Chloe grimaced at the dry tone. "Are you cross about the music?"

"Disappointed, rather," he said, shrugging. "But I told you the decision would always be yours."

"Oh, now I feel horribly guilty." She looked so stricken, he couldn't help laughing.

"That was my intention, lass."

She threw a cushion at him just as Lady Smallwood rolled into the room. "Child!" she exclaimed. "Hugo, you really shouldn't permit—"

"I don't, ma'am," he interjected, bending to pick up the cushion. "But my permission wasn't asked." He threw the cushion back at Chloe. "My ward's a shameless, lazy, self-indulgent, hot-tempered chit."

Lady Smallwood sank into a chair with earpieces and fanned herself vigorously with her hand. "You may laugh, but it's no way to go on in Society . . . throwing cushions at people. Whatever next?"

"Oh, I do beg your pardon, ma'am." Chloe leapt up and kissed her chaperone with the genuine affection that never failed to disarm her most crusty critics. "Hugo was taking me to task for not practicing my music."

"Well, goodness me, that's no reason to throw cushions," her ladyship said, shaking her head. "Either of you!"

"How right you are, Dolly." Hugo rose from the piano bench. "Let me pour you a glass of ratafia. I'm sure you need it if you've been shopping with Chloe. Lass, you may have sherry if you wish."

He filled two glasses and then sat down again. "So, let me see the fruits of your expedition."

Lady Smallwood's intake of breath was portentous. His heart sank. "Ma'am?"

"I have to say, Hugo, that I approve of *nothing* . . . *nothing* that Chloe has bought. I was unable to influence her to the least degree." She took a sip of her ratafia and dabbed at her lips with her handkerchief.

"Oh, pah," Chloe said with her customary lamentable

lack of ceremony. "I have bought the most beautiful spencer and a net purse, and a spray of artificial flowers. Oh, and a bonnet, *and* an evening gown—you wouldn't believe how elegant it is, Hugo."

"I'm sure I wouldn't," he muttered gloomily, but Chloe was rushing on.

"Unfortunately it had to be altered, so I couldn't bring it home, but the modiste promised I should have it by tomorrow afternoon, so that I may wear it at the Bellamys' soiree."

A faint groan emerged from Lady Smallwood, and Hugo reckoned with increasing gloom that it was probably even worse than his imaginings. He prepared himself for battle.

"Show me what's in the boxes."

"This is the bonnet." Chloe lifted the lid of a hat box and drew out an enormous confection of ruched and padded scarlet and black silk. She set it on her head and tied the black silk ribbons with a flourish. "Isn't that fine? And the spencer goes with it." The spencer was of black striped satin with scarlet piping to the sleeves.

Hugo stared at the black and scarlet vision before him. While there was nothing vulgar about the hat or the spencer—only, he suspected, because in the establishments patronized by Lady Smallwood vulgarity wouldn't show its face—they utterly drowned Chloe's exquisite fresh beauty.

"Black is not a debutante's color," he said finally.

"Oh, pah," Chloe declared again. "It's sophisticated. I don't care for all the niminy-piminy *à la jeune fille* colors. These are the flowers. I thought they'd go well with the spencer." She held an elaborate spray of gilded orchids to her bosom. They completely obscured the soft, perfect swell of her breasts.

Hugo said carefully, "Describe this evening dress if you will, Dolly."

Vixen 279

"Oh, it's lovely—"

"I didn't ask you, Chloe." He cut her off smartly. "I'm sure you consider it to be lovely. Now, ma'am . . . ? As accurate as you can make it."

Lady Smallwood shuddered. "It's purple and turquoise stripes embroidered with jet beads . . . and I believe there's a braided fringe at the hem and a matching fringe at the neckline . . . falling over the shoulders in place of sleeves. I could imagine it would look most striking on some women, but not on Chloe, and it's quite unsuitable for a debutante."

"It's dashing," Chloe said. "I wish to look dashing."

"Not while you're in my wardship," Hugo stated flatly, getting to his feet. "We are now going to return the spencer and the bonnet and the flowers, and we are going to visit the modiste and cancel the evening dress. You may choose something more suitable under my guidance, since you reject that of your chaperone."

"No!" his ward exclaimed, fired to more than usual vehemence. "I won't take them back. Why should you know better than I do, Hugo?"

"I wish I knew," he said, sighing. He addressed his cousin. "Ma'am, I should beat a retreat if I were you; I have a feeling this is about to become ugly."

Lady Smallwood looked from Chloe's set face and indignant eyes to Hugo's calm but determined features and took the advice. She had found Chloe's will impossible to bend and her views utterly resistant to guidance. So it was with relief that she handed the matter over to the clearly stronger hands of the girl's guardian.

"Hugo, why must you be so stuffy?" Chloe broke out as soon as the door closed on her chaperone. "Why can't I wear what I wish to wear?"

"Because what you wish to wear, lass, is completely unsuitable," he said. "I do not understand why you should have been born without the first inkling either of what suits you or is socially appropriate, but sadly it seems to be the case. Therefore you must learn to accept the judgment of those who know better."

"I don't," Chloe said mutinously, stroking the silk sleeves of the spencer. "I think I look very sophisticated in this . . . and I will *not* cancel the evening dress and buy some wishy-washy pastel thing, whatever you say."

"Oh, Chloe, don't throw down the gauntlet," he said, cajoling. "It will make everything so uncomfortable." He held out a hand. "Come, kiss and make up, and we'll go out and choose a truly beautiful gown. It doesn't have to be wishy-washy."

Chloe stood unmoving, her dislike of quarreling with Hugo warring with her absolute resistance to submitting to him over this. She'd been long enough in London now to know what sophisticated women wore, and it didn't suit her plans for Hugo to insist upon seeing her as a youthful debutante. He had to realize she was quite mature enough and sufficiently up to snuff to make him a perfectly suitable wife despite the difference in their ages. She was no fluttering virgin, after all. So why should she dress like one?

"I don't see why I should have to suffer your interference in something as personal as my wardrobe," she said finally. "I spend all my life in brown serge, and then I ought to be able to buy whatever I like, and everything I like you tell me I can't have. It's not just."

Hugo sighed and gave up conciliation. "Just or not, lass, it's the way it is. While I hold the reins, I'm afraid you'll run as I choose, in this as in everything. Now, let's be on our way." He went to the door, leaving Chloe fighting chagrin in the library.

She stomped after him into the hall, where he was instructing Samuel to bring around his curricle. "I don't see why you need me to go with you, since I'm not allowed to have an opinion. It's just a waste of my time."

Both Hugo and Samuel blinked at her unusually petulant tone. Then Hugo said blightingly, "Don't be such a brat."

Chloe flushed and turned away, swallowing tears as her tone and words replayed in her head. It was no wonder Hugo refused to consider marrying her. What grown man would want to marry a petulant brat?

Hugo regarded her averted back and drooping head with a slight smile. Castigating a seventeen-year-old for being seventeen seemed hardly just. "Hey!" he said softly.

She turned slowly to face him. "I'm sorry."

"Go and fetch your hat and we'll do some proper shopping. I promise you won't be disappointed."

"I shall be," she said, but with a clear effort to make it sound humorous.

Resigned, Chloe accompanied him outside to where his curricle waited at the curb. Hugo had agreed to purchase a curricle and pair, and a barouche and pair for Chloe and her duenna. Society would look askance at anything less in a fashionable household, but he was very uncomfortable with his own extremely expensive acquisition paid for from his ward's fortune.

He was just handing her up, when a shout of greeting came from two horsemen farther up the street.

"Oh, it's Gerald and Miles," Chloe said, waving. "I forgot we were going riding."

The two young men drew rein, bowing from their mounts. "Good afternoon, sir." They greeted Hugo punctiliously, but their eyes were on Chloe.

"Miss Gresham was kind enough to agree to ride in the park," one of the two said somewhat disconsolately. "Have you changed your mind, Chloe?"

"I'm afraid her guardian is decreeing a prior claim,"

Hugo said with an easy smile at the two youngsters. They wore impossibly starched cravats and shiny curly beaver hats and they were fresh-faced and glowing with health and energy.

A fleeting thought of himself at that age crossed his mind. He'd been taking his pleasures with the Congregation. No fresh-faced innocent he. Haggard and heavy-eyed most of the time, his mind smudged with the herbal substances and alcohol, his body surfeited with sensual excesses.

"We have to go shopping," Chloe was explaining. She glanced at Hugo, and that chill crept up her spine again. He had the look she dreaded. She laid a hand on his arm and he seemed to haul himself back from whatever grim territory he inhabited at those times.

"Necessary errands, I'm afraid," he said, nodding at the two horsemen. "I'm sorry to disrupt your plans."

"Oh, not at all, sir," Miles Payton said, although he didn't sound convinced. "Perhaps tomorrow, Chloe?"

"Yes, tomorrow afternoon," Chloe said. "And I shan't permit anything to prevent it . . . not even Sir Hugo." She looked up at them through the thick fringe of her eyelashes, her mouth curved in an entrancing and utterly inviting smile.

Hugo reflected that while he'd told her to flirt, he hadn't somehow expected her to take to it with such alacrity, or to evince such expertise. He wasn't in the least surprised at the melting looks of her two prospective swains.

"Up you get," he said, putting a hand under her elbow.

Chloe jumped into the curricle with a speed that did nothing to diminish the grace of her movements. "But I'll see you at Almack's tonight," she called as Hugo gave his horses the office to start.

"You promised me the first waltz," Gerald said, mov-

ing his horse alongside the curricle as they trotted down
the street.

"No, you promised it to me," Miles said hotly, ranging
himself on the other side.

Hugo raised his eyebrows, wondering how long he
was going to have this rivaling escort. "You'd better settle the dispute quickly, lass, before we turn onto Park
Street. It's too narrow for outriders."

"I really can't remember," she said, laughing. "Why
don't you toss a coin and I'll accept the result, as I trust
you will."

They turned onto Park Street and their escort fell
back. "Shame on you," Hugo said amiably. "Of all the
flirtatious moves, offering two men the same dance is
quite the most unseemly."

"Oh, but I'm sure I didn't," she said with a complacent smile. "They're always quarreling over me. Anyway, I thought my suggestion was a very fair one."

"Very fair," he agreed. "I'm glad to see you've recovered your good humor."

Anxious to make amends for her earlier shrewishness,
Chloe offered no resistance to Hugo's selected replace-
ments. She did cast one longing look at the striped
evening gown, but when the modiste produced a
cherry-red taffeta over a half slip of rose pink embroidered with seed pearls, she was constrained to admit
that it did look satisfactorily dashing.

They left Three Kings Yard very much in charity with
each other and turned onto Brook Street.

"What's going on?" Chloe leaned forward as Hugo
uttered one of his short naval words and checked his
horses.

A small mob was coming down the street toward
them, waving staves and shouting. They stopped in
front of one of the tall, double-fronted houses and a
stone flew through the air and crashed against the front

door. The mob surged up the steps, and their shouts grew louder. Another stone flew and a first floor window shattered. A stave hammered against the front door.

"They're attacking Lord Douglas's house," Hugo said. "It's been happening all over the city."

"Lord Douglas?"

"Cabinet minister," he told her abstractedly as he tried to decide whether he would do better to turn his horses or drive straight past the crowd.

They were angry but not wild, he judged. But how would they react to two members of the hated aristocracy driving straight past them? These small mob attacks on the houses of government ministers had become frequent in the past months. The massacre at St. Peter's Field, now universally christened Peterloo in ironic comparison with Wellington's great victory, had fanned the disaffection, as well it might. There were many members of the government as horrified by that panicked savagery as were its victims and the members of the reform movement. But the hungry workingclass victims of repressive labor laws and harsh employers drew no distinction between their government sympathizers and those who would grind them even deeper into the dirt of powerless poverty.

"Go on," Chloe insisted. "They won't hurt us, and I want to hear what they're shouting."

"I've no intention of exposing you—"

"I was at Peterloo," she interrupted. "I'm on their side."

While he still hesitated, she suddenly sprang down and ran up the street toward the crowd.

"Chloe!" He thrust the reins into the hands of his tiger and leapt to the street, chasing after her. She had dived into the middle of the mob by the time he reached its outskirts.

"Eh, what's wi' you, guv?" a burly man demanded. "Slummin', are ye?" He waved his stave, and his beery breath wreathed around Hugo.

"No more than you are," Hugo said shortly. The milling throng seemed to have little direction. A few more stones were thrown, a few more jeers hurled, and then the mob eddied and broke.

Chloe was sitting on the steps of the minister's house as the crowd fell back. She had her arm around a shivering girl.

"The next time you shoot off on frolics of your own, Chloe, you are going to taste the full measure of my displeasure," Hugo declared furiously. "I am sick to death of these darting forays into the middle of some disturbance."

"She was knocked over," Chloe said as if none of this speech had penetrated. "And she's having a baby, but she's only a child herself. Look how thin she is, and she's so cold." She rubbed the skinny shoulders vigorously.

Hugo recognized defeat. He had early in his experience of warfare learned when the odds were insuperable. The child Chloe held was perhaps thirteen, although she looked little more than ten. Her swollen belly pushed against the threadbare material of her striped petticoat, her only protection against the sharp autumnal wind. Her lips were blue in a painfully thin, ashen face, and her feet were as bare as they'd been at her birth.

How Chloe had found this piece of society's flotsam, he didn't bother to question. They seemed attracted to her like iron filings to a magnet . . . or was it the other way around? Either way, he knew they would be housing the girl and saw no point in bootless discussion.

"Come along." He strode back to the curricle that his tiger had brought level with the house.

Chloe helped the girl to her feet, murmuring softly to her as she encouraged her to the curricle.

With a sudden exclamation of terror the child pulled back as Hugo moved to help her up. "I ain't goin' in there. Where you takin' me? I ain't done nuthin' wrong . . . I ain't goin' to no Bridewell." Her eyes wide with fear in her thin dirty face, she struggled, kicking out as Hugo tried to hold her.

"Hush," Chloe said, taking her hand. "No one's going to hurt you. No one's going to take you to Bridewell. I want you to come to my home, where you'll be warm and can have something to eat. When did you last eat?"

The girl's struggles ceased and her eyes darted between them, suddenly sharp and focused. "Dunno."

"I promise we won't hurt you," Chloe repeated. "When you've had something to eat and I've found you some warm clothes, then you can go anywhere you wish. I promise."

"You one a them do-gooders?" the girl demanded. "I bin wi' the likes a them. All preachin' and nuthin' to eat but a bite a bread and a bit a gruel . . . an' you don't get that 'n you don't say as 'ow yer a fallen' woman an' sorry fer it."

"Oh, I'm a fallen woman too," Chloe said cheerfully, oblivious of Hugo's sharp intake of breath. "So you'll be quite safe from any preaching. And I detest gruel, so we don't have any of that in the house."

Hugo closed his eyes in despair. "Not another word!" he snapped, conscious of the tiger's big ears. "You have not a grain of discretion. Get up!" Releasing his hold on Chloe's new prize, he caught his ward around the waist and swung her into the curricle. "Are you coming?" He turned back to the pregnant girl, who hadn't taken advantage of her freedom to run.

" 'Spose so," she said. "But we're not goin' to no Bridewell?"

"No!" Hugo said impatiently. "We are not."

The girl scrambled into the somewhat overcrowded curricle with Hugo's helping hand.

"Let go their heads," he said curtly to the fascinated tiger as he took up the reins.

"Right you are, guv." With a cheery grin the lad released the team and dashed for his perch at the rear of the curricle as it took off down Brook Street.

Chloe scrunched up on the seat to make room for the girl beside her. It put her in very close contact with Hugo, who glanced down at her with a look that guaranteed retribution. She offered a tentative smile and squiggled closer so that her thigh was pressed hard against his. Hugo's expression didn't soften.

Chloe turned her attention to the girl. "What's your name?"

"Peg."

"How old are you, Peg?"

"Dunno."

"Where do you live?"

"Nowhere in partic'ler." She shrugged her scrawny shoulders and hunched over her belly, folding her bare arms against the chill wind.

"You don't have a home?"

Peg shrugged again. "Sometimes I sleep at me nan's. She's cook in a big 'ouse, and sometimes they lets me sleep in the wash'ouse. But the 'ousekeeper's a right tartar an' if she found me, she'd 'ave me nan turned off wi' no character."

"What about the baby's father?"

"What about 'im?"

"Well . . . well, where is he?"

"Dunno. Dunno who 'e is."

"Oh." Chloe was silenced at the ramifications of this statement.

Hugo drew rein outside his house and jumped down.

He helped his passengers to alight and then followed them into the house.

"What the 'ell . . . ?" Samuel stared at the new arrival, who was transfixed with terror as Dante put his huge paws on Chloe's shoulder, licking her face in exuberant, ecstatic welcome.

"Oh, you didn't think we were going to stop at bear cubs, did you?" Hugo said sardonically. "I don't think Miss Gresham will be satisfied until she's turned my house into a lying-in ward and an orphanage in addition to an animal rescue center."

He turned back to Chloe. "See to your protégée and then come to the library. I have a few things to say to you." With which he marched into the library and slammed the door.

"Now what've you gone an' done?" Samuel said.

"It's not so much what I've done as what I said," Chloe replied with a rueful grimace. Then she shrugged philosophically. "Oh, well, I'll worry about it later. Down, now, Dante. Yes, I love you too, but you're frightening Peg." She smiled with warm reassurance and introduced her protégée. "This is Peg, Samuel."

"Oh, is it?" Samuel regarded the girl without much enthusiasm. "And no better than she ought t' be, I'll lay odds."

"An' what business is it of your'n, I'd like to know?" demanded the belligerent Peg. But even Samuel could see the pathetic, undernourished scrap of humanity beneath the aggression.

"She's hungry," Chloe said. "I'll take her to the kitchen and find her some food, although I suppose Alphonse will get all hoity-toity about it. And then I think we should heat some water so she can have a bath and I'll find some clothes."

"Bath?" Peg squealed. "I ain't goin' in no bath."

"Come along wi' me, girl," Samuel said. "Mrs. 'Erridge'll know what's best for ye. If I were you, lass, I'd get meself into the library and take what's comin'. The longer 'e frets on it, the worse it'll be."

"I suppose so." Chloe still hesitated. Mrs. Herridge was the housekeeper and a woman of rather unyielding disposition. But Alphonse tolerated her in his kitchen a great deal better than he did Chloe and her various dependents. "Go with Samuel, Peg," she said. "They'll look after you in the kitchen, and when you feel better we'll talk about what you want to do next."

"You ain't takin' me to no Bridewell." Peg glared at Samuel, but there was uncertainty bordering on terror beneath the glare.

"Now, why would I go an' do a thing like that?" he said, shaking his head. "Come on, girl, let's get some food down ye. There's two o' ye goin' 'ungry at the moment."

Chloe watched as a still-hesitant Peg went with Samuel through the swinging door to the kitchen quarters, then she squared her shoulders and went into the library. Dante made straight for his usual spot on the hearth rug and flopped down with a heavy sigh.

"How dare you say such a thing?" Hugo demanded even before she'd closed the door. "How could you be so childishly thoughtless? Of all the insulting, stupid remarks I've ever heard—"

"But I just wanted to reassure her," Chloe broke in. "I thought it would make her feel at ease."

"Oh, you thought it would make her feel at ease! Dear God!" He ran his hands through his hair. "And just how do you think it's going to sound when she regales the rest of the household with your *reassurance*. A fallen woman! Chloe, I don't know what to do with you!"

That consequence had not occurred to her. "They won't take it seriously," she said uncertainly. "They'll think it was a joke, or that she misheard me."

"And what makes you certain of that?"

"Well . . . well, because it's obviously absurd," she said. "Oh, Hugo, you know it is. It wouldn't occur to anyone that . . . that . . ."

"That I debauched my ward," he finished for her with an icy snap.

Chloe realized that she'd inadvertently raised Hugo's guilt demons. In a minute he'd slip from her into the world of his painted devils . . . unless she could stimulate some other response from him.

"Oh, pah," she stated, picking up the *Gazette* and pretending to be absorbed in the first page. "I wish I knew what it felt like to be debauched. It sounds as if it might be amusing. It seems to me, if I remember aright, that if any debauching went on, it was I who did it to you. So I don't see why you should take all the credit," she added, risking a peep over the paper to gauge his reaction. The ploy seemed to have worked all too well. The bleakness had vanished from his expression, and he looked thunderous.

He plucked the newspaper from her hand and she took to her heels with a squeak of mock fright before he could grab her.

"Brat!" He leapt after her as she jumped onto the sofa and scrambled over the back. She danced behind the table and stuck her tongue out at him.

"Tell me what it feel likes to be debauched, Hugo? Please, I'm dying to know." She dodged sideways as he came around the table and sprang onto the seat of a chair, flinging a leg over the back preparatory to sliding over. The suddenness of her movement overbalanced the chair, and it toppled to the floor. Her startled shriek as she tumbled over in a swirl of skirts, stockinged legs waving indelicately in the air, brought a reluctant grin to Hugo's lips.

He swooped down on her, disentangling her from the

chair. "I'm not even going to ask if you're hurt," he declared, lifting her up and setting her on her feet. "If you are, it's only what you deserve." He smoothed down the back of her skirt with a degree of calculated vigor. "Don't let me hear any more discussion on fallen women or debauchery."

"No, Hugo," she said with a docility every bit as feigned as her earlier fright. Her cheeks were pink with exertion and what he knew was arousal, and her eyelashes fluttered as she fixed him with a melting look.

"And don't flirt with me."

"I'm not," she said truthfully. "Shall I lock the door?"

"Shall you what?"

For answer, she ran to the door and turned the key. "There now." She leaned back against the door, her breast lifting with her swift breath, her eyes dancing with invitation, the rich sensual currents flowing fast in their deep blue depths. "We could be quick. We wouldn't have to take our clothes off."

Hugo was lost anew. Vaguely he wondered if he would ever be free of her spell, ever be able to resist her when she drew him into her realm of magic in this way. She was so sure of herself, of what she wanted, of what she was offering . . . and she was so sure of his response. She was archetypal woman.

She raised her skirt and petticoat slowly, her eyes never leaving his face. "We could do it standing up. Can it be done in that way?"

"Yes, it can," he said savagely, consumed with the pure, primitive fire of lust. He crossed to her, tore loose the string of her drawers so that they fell in a silken rustle to her ankles, and unfastened his britches.

"Brace yourself." He pushed her knees apart with his own knee and she laughed . . . an exultant laugh . . . as she obeyed, holding her skirts high, bracing herself with her shoulders against the door, feeling the molding of the paneling pressing into her back.

He entered the velvet moistness of her body with one swift thrust and she drew a shaky breath, smiling at him with luminous joy. He gripped her hips with both hands, his fingers curling into the satin skin as he drove himself within her. He could feel her pleasure mounting with each thrust just as he could see it on her face. Her tongue touched her lips and she laughed again. She never closed her eyes, not since the time he'd asked her not to, and he thought he would fall into the volcano of passion that beckoned with their midnight fires.

"Now," she whispered suddenly. "Hugo, now!"

"I know, sweetheart," he said. "But wait."

"I can't."

"You can." He held himself still, deep within her. She held her breath in an agony of suspense, her body thrumming around his flesh. And then he moved and she cried out as her climax ripped through her.

Hugo's head fell against the door as his own body swirled in the vortex of delight. Only when the passion was spent and his head cleared did it occur to him that he had been outfoxed again, craftily manipulated out of his anger and taken into a world far from the sway of the painted devils. How could he suffer guilt making such wondrous love to this uninhibited, artful minx who knew a lot more about the world than he'd ever given her credit for? Or was it that she knew a lot more about himself?

Chapter 20

"MAY I OFFER YOU a glass of claret, duke?" Hugo gestured politely toward the decanters on the sideboard.

"Thank you . . . thank you." His august visitor watched as the wine was poured. "I trust you look kindly upon my suit."

Hugo bowed in acknowledgment. He could hardly look unkindly upon the suit of the Duke of Alresford. It would be a brilliant match for Chloe. The duke was no fortune hunter and a mere ten years older than herself. "The decision must of course rest with my ward," he said. "Chloe has a mind of her own." He smiled and raised his own glass of claret. He was becoming expert at appearing to drink in social situations without doing so.

"I flatter myself that she is not altogether indifferent," his grace said. It would be unspeakably vulgar to allude to his title and fortune, but his smugness was allusion enough.

"Then if you've discussed this with Chloe, duke, what more can I say?"

"Oh, goodness me, no." The duke made haste to defend himself from any possibility of impropriety. "I wouldn't broach such a subject without your permission, Sir Hugo. But I have been led to have hopes . . ." He gestured vaguely. "Miss Gresham is all condescension."

"Is she indeed," Hugo murmured. Chloe's private mockery of her pompous suitor had enlivened the dinner table on more than one occasion. However, he considered it his bounden duty to promote the duke's suit. Not that he had much hope of Chloe's bending to his will.

"Rest assured, duke, I will inform my ward of the inestimable honor of your proposal as soon as she returns from her ride."

Alresford put down his glass and took his leave. "Then I may expect a response before tomorrow."

"I believe so," Hugo said gravely, escorting his guest to the front door.

Alresford, like the rest of Chloe's increasing cast of suitors and friends, had come to accept the eccentric Samuel as butler and doorman and took his hat and cane from the earringed sailor with barely a thought about his oddity. "I await Miss Gresham's response most eagerly," he said.

"To what?" Samuel demanded, closing the door behind him.

"A proposal of marriage. The lass is being offered the opportunity to become a duchess."

"Much store she'll set by that," Samuel stated. " 'Ave you seen 'er take off 'is funny way of wrinklin' 'is nose?"

"I have. Where's Peg?"

"Sittin' by the kitchen fire with 'er feet in a mustard bath, eatin' gingerbread," Samuel informed him. "Lazy little devil, she is."

"She's entitled," Hugo said. "At least until she's had the baby. Then we'll see what's to be done with her."

"I expect the lass 'as some notion."

"I wish she'd come up with a plan for that damn bear," Hugo said grimly. "It's growing like a weed."

The sounds of laughter came from beyond the front door, and Samuel pulled it open.

"Oh, thank you, Samuel." Chloe walked in, her eyes

bright with amusement, her cheeks pinkened with cold. She was followed by three young men, also laughing.

Hugo looked in vain for some female chaperoning presence . . . one of her escort's sisters or at the very least a maid. But his ward had a lamentable habit of dispensing with such niceties. For some reason she seemed to avoid censure by all but the highest sticklers for behavior that in anyone else would be considered fast. But he'd seen her charm the severest matrons with the sweet smile and soft voice that she knew how to use to advantage. A crafty little fox was Miss Gresham.

"Hugo, you're acquainted with Lord Bentham and Sir Frank Manton?" Chloe was saying, drawing off her gloves. "But I don't know if you know Denis DeLacy. He's only recently come to town."

Hugo felt the ground shift beneath his feet. The young man was the spitting image of his father, Brian DeLacy. Brian, a close friend of Stephen Gresham's, had been a chief player in the crypt. Brian had witnessed his friend's death.

"I believe you knew my father, Sir Hugo," Denis was saying, offering a frank smile. "He died two years ago, but I seem to remember his mentioning your name."

It could be perfectly innocent. They had been friends of a kind, members of the same social set. But what if Brian had told his son that Hugo had been a member of the Congregation? Did this young man know the story of Stephen Gresham's death?

Hugo forced himself to smile and shake the man's hand. He murmured some platitude while his thoughts tumbled in his head. They were all sworn to secrecy over the duel . . . a secrecy that surely encompassed a man's son. But supposing Brian had broken his oath?

"I hadn't seen your father for many years," he said. "The war curtailed many friendships."

"I came back to fetch Dante," Chloe informed him

cheerfully, for once too intent on her own plans to notice Hugo's abstraction. "We're going to take him for a walk in Green Park."

"Did you leave your female companion outside the door?" Hugo queried, raising his eyebrows. "How very impolite, Chloe."

There was an awkward silence, then young Lord Bentham said, "Fact is, sir, m'sister was to have accompanied us, but she developed a scratchy throat this morning, and it wasn't thought wise for her to go out in the cold."

"No, I quite understand that," Hugo said. "And I'm sure you'll understand if I ask you to excuse us for a few moments while I have a little talk with my ward."

Without waiting for a response, he swept Chloe into the library and closed the door on her three escorts.

"You're going to be stuffy," Chloe stated.

"It won't do," he said firmly. "I'm sorry, I know you think it ridiculous, and so to a certain extent do I, but you may not racket around the town in the company of a gaggle of young men. Why don't you persuade one of your girlfriends to join you?"

"It's not so amusing," Chloe said with disarming candor.

Hugo was betrayed into a half-smile. He guessed that after ten years in the unrelieved company of her own sex, his ward was finding the devoted attentions of the male thoroughly diverting.

"So I may go?" she said, seeing his expression soften and drawing the wrong conclusion.

"No, you may not."

"Dante needs the exercise," she tried with a hopeful smile.

"Then you'll have to endure my dull company, lass."

"You aren't dull," she said. "But . . ."

"But I'm not three young men making sheeps' eyes at

you." He shook his head. "Go and give your swains their tickets of leave and then come back. There's something I have to discuss with you."

Disappointed but resigned, Chloe did as she was told and came back to the library.

"How would you like to be a duchess?" Hugo asked.

"Not at all," she replied promptly. "Alresford?"

He nodded. "Consider for a minute, Chloe. Apart from the title, he's young, good-looking, rich. Alresford Castle is one of the stateliest homes in the land. The mansion in Berkeley Square—"

"But I don't want to marry him." Chloe interrupted the catalogue of her suitor's virtues with the simple statement.

Hugo sighed. "And you don't want to marry Viscount Bartlett, or Charles Knightley, or the Earl of Ridgefield."

"No," Chloe agreed.

"I don't think you realize, lass, that when you have practically every eligible bachelor in the ton at your feet, you have an obligation to accept one of their offers."

"I don't see why."

"Because that's the way Society works," he said, losing patience. "You insisted on having a come-out so you could find a suitable husband, and now you reject anyone who has the temerity to offer for you. What do you want?"

You. Chloe shook her head. "I'll know when I find it."

Hugo massaged his temples. "And in the meantime, you risk ruining your reputation with hoydenish excursions in the company of lads who have more money than sense."

"At least they don't pester me to marry them," she said. "They're not interested in marrying yet. And I'm enjoying myself. You told me I was to do so."

"Don't chop logic with me, young Chloe. These unchaperoned expeditions have got to stop."

"But you can't expect Lady Smallwood to accompany me. She couldn't possibly keep up."

"I expect you to engage in the kind of activities at which your chaperone *can* keep up," he declared. "I am very serious, Chloe."

"Oh, very well," she said. "May I go now? They're waiting for me in the drawing room. We're going to play charades, since we mayn't go out."

Hugo waved her away, shaking his head in defeat. At least a game of charades, however rowdy, could be supervised by his cousin.

But what of Denis DeLacy? The latest recruit to the ever-widening circle of admirers.

Taking his hat and cane, he left the house, walking briskly as he mulled over the situation. If DeLacy knew of the duel, then it was conceivable that he would tell Chloe. But why should he? There was no reason he should bear Hugo any grudge and nothing to be gained by such a revelation. He must have been a child of four or five at the time of Stephen's death.

But what if he did tell Chloe?

Hugo walked faster down Bond Street. It was unthinkable that Chloe should hear from a stranger the story of her father's death at the hands of her guardian . . . her lover. He had her absolute trust, and he would lose that—how could he help but lose it?

So should he tell her himself? Forestall any possibility of her hearing it from someone else? But he couldn't endure the thought of laying bare such a story. He would have to tell her of the crypt . . . of the hideous ugliness of his early life. He couldn't possibly sully her innocence with such a tale.

So how great was the danger she might hear it from someone else?

Jasper might tell her. Yes, he could imagine Jasper taking great pleasure in sowing such dissension and destroying all trust between his young sister and the guardian he resented so deeply. But he could outmaneuver Jasper. There was no way Chloe was going to have anything to do with either her brother or his stepson.

Frowning, Hugo decided that a few well-placed questions should give him some idea of what young DeLacy knew. If he felt there was any danger, then he'd have to remove Chloe from the young man's orbit.

That settled, he went through the doors into Jackson's Saloon. Gentleman Jackson was supervising a couple of young bloods sparring, but left them and came over to greet the new arrival.

"Practice, Sir Hugo? Or do you fancy a bout?"

"If you'll give me a couple of rounds, Jackson."

"With pleasure, sir."

Hugo went into the changing room, well aware of the honor done him by Jackson, who sparred only with those of his clients he considered sufficiently skilled.

Marcus Devlin wandered over to watch the bout. No mean exponent of the sport himself, he was impressed by Hugo Lattimer, who managed to score several hits on the master.

"How's the beautiful philanthropist?" Marcus asked as they went together into the changing room afterward.

"Indomitable," Hugo said. "But at the moment she's making me feel old and tired. When I left, my house was filled with slavering young men playing charades."

"No suitors in the offing?"

"She won't have any of them," he said ruefully, toweling his head.

"Come to Berkeley Square and share a bottle of burgundy," Marcus suggested as they left the boxing saloon. "My wife might be able to suggest some stratagem to encourage Miss Gresham to the altar. She's really taken to Chloe. That unconventional streak rather strikes a chord." He chuckled, remembering how Judith and her brother had cut a gleeful swath through the convention-ridden world of Society on both sides of the Channel. She'd certainly turned himself, a thoroughgoing stick-in-the-mud, away from the paths of strict righteousness.

Hugo accepted the invitation readily. Lady Carrington had stood a good friend to Chloe and, he suspected, was instrumental in smoothing the ruffled feathers of the highest sticklers when her unconventional ways drew censure.

To his surprise, he found Chloe and Lady Smallwood in Judith's drawing room. True, she was surrounded by a circle of swains, including the three he'd left in his house, but there was nothing to take exception to. He greeted his ward with a brief smile and bent to kiss his hostess's hand.

Judith smiled warmly at him and patted the seat beside her. There was something about him that she found immensely attractive. It was the little lines around his eyes, she thought, and the slight world-weariness of his countenance, as if he'd seen everything and done everything and found it all wanting.

Chloe watched Hugo covertly. He and Lady Carrington were engaged in the most blatant flirtation. She glanced up at the marquis, who seemed completely untroubled by the rapport between his wife and Sir Hugo, indeed was laughing with them over some scandalous on-dit that Judith had whispered into Hugo's ear.

Chloe bit her lip, suddenly finding the conversation around her reduced to the inane chatter of a schoolroom. How could she ever hope to capture and keep Hugo's attention when such a chasm of experience divided them? Of course he would find Judith Devlin irresistible. Several of Judith's friends had joined the trio on the sofa, and to Chloe's jaundiced eyes and ears, they seemed to be enjoying themselves twice as well as the younger party around her.

She stood up abruptly and addressed her chaperone. "Are you ready to leave, ma'am?"

"Goodness me." Lady Smallwood had been having a most interesting chat with Lady Isobel Henley over a plate of honey cakes and was startled at this abrupt question. "Do you wish to leave?"

"I should return to the house and see how Peg is," she said, searching desperately for something that would make her abrupt departure less discourteous. "The baby's due any day now, and I don't believe Mrs. Herridge is an experienced midwife."

"And you are, Miss Gresham?" inquired Marcus with a half-smile.

"Well, as to that, I've never delivered a human baby," Chloe said, distracted from her discomfiture by this interesting issue. "But I've helped to deliver a calf and a foal and a litter of puppies, and of course Beatrice had six kittens, so—" She stopped, aware that the senior half of the room was in fits of laughter while the younger members of the group were staring in total disbelief.

"Why is it funny?"

Hugo took pity on her. "It's not so much that it's funny, lass," he said. "It's just rather unusual."

"Oh, I see. Well, I must say good-bye, Lady Carrington. Thank you for the tea." She bowed to her hostess, wondering if Hugo would decide to come back with her. But apart from rising courteously as she made her farewells, he made no move to take his own leave, although her circle of admirers leapt to their feet and made their own farewells to their hostess.

Judith accompanied her to the door. "Let me know if I can be of any help with your protégée, Chloe," she said, kissing her cheek. "And don't take any notice of their laughter. They're just overawed by your knowledge and don't know how else to react."

"I doubt that, ma'am, but I thank you for the kindness," Chloe said with a half-smile of comprehension. She left in the company of her attendants and Lady Smallwood.

"She's nowhere near as naive as she sometimes appears," Judith observed softly, sitting beside Hugo again. "But I daresay you've noticed that."

"I have," he agreed with a dry smile. "It's something she seems to be able to put on at will. The lass is very good at getting her own way without it seeming as if that's what she's doing."

Chloe, if she'd heard this conversation, would have profoundly disagreed with Hugo. It didn't seem as if in the only thing that mattered she was any closer to getting her own way. Hugo seemed to be his usual self, and yet increasingly he wasn't. Something indefinable was missing from his manner toward her. That very particular attention she had come to expect and to rely upon was blunted, if not completely absent.

She tried various means to regain his attention. She flirted outrageously with all and sundry and drew only laughing approval. She went out alone and bought herself the most dashing and sophisticated walking dress she could find. Hugo had simply laughed and challenged her to wear it in Hyde Park during the fashionable hour of the promenade.

Laughter, she found, was a much more potent weapon than opposition. The dress remained in the armoire.

The only area in which she sensed his close attention was in her friendship with Denis DeLacy. It wasn't obvious, but his eyes sharpened when Denis was in the house, and whenever she danced with him she could feel Hugo watching her. Was it that he realized she found Denis more appealing than her other playful suitors? Did he sense another dimension to the relationship? It was certainly there; Denis was infinitely more amusing to be with—much more entertaining and sophisticated than the other cheerful young men at her feet.

Perhaps Hugo was disturbed by that extra dimension. Perhaps, despite his behavior, he was jealous. Of course he wouldn't admit it . . . to her or to himself . . . but perhaps that was the explanation.

If it was, then all was not lost. With great deliberation she began to single Denis out for ever more marked partiality.

Hugo watched the growing intimacy closely and after a while decided that Denis couldn't know the truth. If he did, he would have behaved differently in Hugo's company. Instead of his habitual open, straightforward manner, he would surely have shown some deviousness, some shiftiness. He was far too young and inexperienced to be able to keep such a secret under Hugo's skillful probing.

Having reached that conclusion, Hugo decided he had nothing to fear from the friendship, yet for some reason he remained uneasy.

Chapter 21

"YOU ALWAYS SAID you didn't care for Almack's," Chloe said at the luncheon table when Hugo announced his intention of accompanying her to the Subscription Ball that evening.

"Oh, I don't mind," he said, carving a wafer-thin slice of ham. "Curiously, my memories of insipidity strike me as false. Perhaps my advanced years have softened me." He smiled down the table at her. Chloe lowered her eyes to her plate and toyed with a morsel of chicken.

"Well, I own I'm grateful, Hugo," Lady Smallwood declared, taking several mushroom tartlets from the basket in front of her. "It's been such a week of engagements, I'm quite fatigued. A quiet evening at home will be wonderful. I shall ask Alphonse to prepare me some of his crab patties and a Rhenish cream for dinner." She nodded with a contented little smile.

"I'm perfectly happy to chaperone Chloe, ma'am, so don't give it another thought."

He was perfectly happy to chaperone her, Chloe thought disconsolately, because he was perfectly happy to flirt and dance with half a dozen women all of whom seemed to light up when he walked into the room. They weren't all married women either. Lady Harley was a widow in her early thirties whom Hugo seemed to find very good company. And then there was Miss Anselm, who had never been married and was pronounced a bluestocking, but she and Hugo could talk for hours about music and he said she had the purest pitch. He would accompany her singing at the slightest opportunity and, even from her jaundiced perspective, Chloe had to admit that they complemented each other very well. Indeed, only the other day someone had commented in jocular fashion that it seemed as if her guardian was heading for the altar.

And to make matters worse, while he was always welcoming when she came to his room at night, he often seemed to be thinking of something else. Or someone else, she thought miserably.

"What are your plans for the afternoon, lass?" He interrupted her dismal musing.

"I don't have any."

"That's unusual." Hugo gave her a teasing smile. "No young men beating down the door for once?"

Chloe didn't respond to the smile or the comment, both of which she found supremely irritating.

"Perhaps you'd like a singing lesson," Hugo suggested. "We could practice the Irish melody by Moore that you liked so much."

"If you wish," she said.

"No, lass, if *you* wish."

It was one of Miss Anselm's favorite songs. Chloe decided she wasn't going to compete. She was trying to find an excuse that wouldn't sound childishly petulant, when Samuel came into the dining room.

"Peg's time's 'ere," he said without preamble. "Thought you'd like t' know."

Chloe leapt up, all thoughts of Hugo and his possible brides vanquished. "I'll go to her at once. We'll need hot water, Samuel, lots of it."

"Aye, I know," he said. "Mrs. 'Erridge is seein' to it."

"Oh, dear, shouldn't we summon the doctor?" Lady Smallwood said. "It's not something Chloe should be doing, Hugo. It's most indelicate for a young girl to be involved in such things . . . and with such a creature!" Peg had not found favor with Hugo's cousin.

"That's nonsense," Chloe said, her eyes flashing dangerously. "It's not Peg's fault she is who she is. And it isn't her fault she's pregnant. You should be grateful, ma'am, that God didn't choose that *you* should have been born into Peg's world." On which note she whisked herself out of the dining room.

Hugo grimaced as his cousin's color deepened, all her sensibilities outraged. "She'll apologize later, ma'am," he said. "But she does become very passionate about such matters."

"You encourage her," Dolly said.

"I don't discourage her, I agree. When someone has such a single-minded mission and such exceptional skills, it would be criminal . . . not to mention futile." He stood up. "But she will apologize for her incivility as soon as she thinks about it. And if she doesn't think about it, I will remind her," he added. "Now, if you'll excuse me, I'd better see if there's anything I can do." He paused at the door. "Peg's only a child herself, Dolly."

The house shivered throughout the long afternoon with the screams of the laboring child. Dolly retired to her bedroom with her smelling salts, trying to block out the sounds. Samuel, grim-faced, toiled up and down stairs with brass jugs of hot water and whatever else Chloe demanded. Hugo tried to find peace in his music, and when that failed paced the library as if he were the expectant father.

At four o'clock, unable to bear inaction any longer, he went up to the back bedroom Peg had been given and stood irresolute outside the door, listening to the shrieks. The housekeeper suddenly opened the door and rushed out. Hugo could see the bed and he could see Chloe bending over.

He stepped into the room. "Chloe?"

"Hold her hand," Chloe said matter-of-factly. "I can

see the head, but she's so frightened, poor mite, she's not helping to push the baby out. Perhaps you can comfort her."

Obediently, Hugo took the small, clawlike hand of the waif on the bed. Peg's screams had become a low, monotonous wail, as much through exhaustion as anything, Hugo thought, gazing with pity at the waxen countenance on the white pillow, the lines of suffering about her mouth and the drenched, terrified eyes.

"Oh, my goodness, Sir Hugo, this is no place . . ." Mrs. Herridge came back with a bowl and a pile of linen.

"I've seen worse," he said shortly. The decks of a battleship, slippery with blood, littered with the dead, the dying, the hideously wounded . . . the foul, fetid hell of the hospital between decks, where surgeons cut, chopped, amputated desperately under swaying lanterns. "Much worse," he said. "Pass me something to wipe her forehead."

The housekeeper did so without a word just as Peg screamed once more, her body convulsing.

"Here we go," Chloe said softly, her hands moving with deft competence. "Ah, Peg, it's a little girl." She looked up, her face radiant, and Hugo's heart turned over.

He struggled so hard to distance himself from her, to focus on his responsibility for her as his ward, to see her only as an eager, impulsive girl with her whole life ahead of her. And then she looked at him in that way, and his efforts were for nothing. If he'd been able to banish her from his bed, he would have done so, but his desire for her was beyond reason. He told himself that when she was no longer woven into the intimate fabric of his life he would be able to put it behind him, but for as long as she was there, opening his door at night, sliding into his bed with that wonderful uninhibited passion, he couldn't resist. Indeed, he couldn't imagine what superhuman strength a man would need to resist such a gift.

So, he tried to make a game of their lovemaking, to keep their relationship on an easy footing, one where his authority was the focus, not their loving. But now, as he looked at her face, glowing with joy in her accomplishment and in the miracle of birth, he was rocked anew by wonder at the depths of his feelings for her. It was desire bordering on obsession, but it was also love . . . not the love he had felt for her mother, but a real, solid thing he could describe, could almost shape in his mind. And it wasn't going to go away.

Chloe, far too busy to be aware of Hugo's arrested expression, expertly cut the cord and brought the baby to her mother. "See, Peg, your daughter." She laid the baby on the exhausted child's breast.

Peg gazed indifferently at the scrap of humanity to which she'd given life. Then she turned her head aside and closed her eyes.

Chloe picked up the baby, her eyes troubled as she looked at Hugo. "I suppose it would be too much to expect her to love it immediately. It's funny that humans aren't like animals."

"Give her time, lass," he said. "She's exhausted and she's suffered a lot. Let her sleep awhile."

"She'll have to feed it," the housekeeper said brusquely. "You give it to me, Miss Chloe, and I'll get the poor scrap cleaned up, then her mother can feed her while I clean her up."

"I'll help you."

"That won't be necessary, Miss Chloe. I know what to do."

"Come, Chloe," Hugo said quietly, understanding, though Chloe didn't, that the housekeeper's sensibilities were as outraged as Lady Smallwood's by the thought of

Miss Gresham's intimate attendance on a girl from the slums.

Chloe glanced down at her bloodstained hands and apron. "I'd better clean myself up. I'll come back shortly."

Hugo eased her out of the room and closed the door. Tilting her chin, he lightly kissed her mouth. It should have stopped there, but, instead, his hands slipped to grasp her head firmly and his mouth took hers, his tongue driving deeply within on a ravaging voyage of possession that surprised them both.

"Oh," Chloe said when he finally released her head. She gave him a rather bemused smile. "What was that for?"

"I'm not sure," he said. ""I couldn't seem to help myself."

Chloe's smile became less bemused and her eyes held a speculative gleam. "That usually happens to me, not you." It had been such a long time since Hugo had yielded to impulse and taken the initiative in that way. Hope sparked that perhaps his period of distraction was over, and she would reassume that most important place in his life and preoccupations.

Hugo read the speculation and pulled himself up sharply. "It was a kiss of congratulation," he said cheerfully. "You did a wonderful job. Are you tired?"

The glow died out of her eyes. "No. Not particularly."

He tried not to see her hurt and disappointment, telling himself that he had no choice. "So, you still want to go to Almack's?"

"Yes." Chloe put up her chin and gave him a bright smile, pride coming to her rescue. She must learn not to give him the satisfaction of seeing that she hoped for more from him than he was prepared to give.

"Mrs. Herridge will look after Peg and the baby," she said. "I'd better get dressed for dinner."

"Before you do, Chloe, you owe Dolly an apology, and I'd have you make it without delay. You were most uncivil." The reminder was issued with calm gravity, as if the kiss had never happened.

Chloe didn't resent the reminder itself, but the timing and the manner of its delivery were like a bucket of cold water.

That night at Almack's it was impossible to keep up with her. She shone with a stellar radiance, her chiming laughter could be heard across the decorous salons, she danced with no one more than once, and the circle of men around her deepened. Hugo kept a covert eye on her. If he hadn't known better, he would think she was tipsy. But tea, lemonade, and orgeat were all the liquid refreshments offered in the Assembly Rooms, and she'd had no more than a glass of claret at dinner. There was a brightness to the cornflower-blue eyes, a delicate pink flush to the damask cheeks, a seething energy in the slight frame that set the air around her humming and infected all who came into her orbit.

Denis DeLacy was at point-non-plus. His instructions had been precise, but they hadn't taken into account the fact that Miss Gresham, for some reason, was impervious to serious lovemaking. Oh, she encouraged his flirtation and paid him a great deal of flattering attention, singling him out from among her wide circle of suitors, but it was all done with a playfulness and a laughing enjoyment that made anything more intense impossible. *He* knew he was making no serious inroads into her affections, although everyone else assumed he was the preferred suitor.

Somehow he had to gain her confidence, sweep her off her feet.

He listened with half an ear to Julian Bentham regaling Chloe with the tale of their activities the previous evening. "It's enormously amusing," he was saying.

"Billingsgate is such an extraordinary place . . . and the people, Chloe. You wouldn't believe how fascinating they are. You can't understand a word they say most of the time, and they're always fighting. We saw at least three scraps, didn't we, Frank?"

"Oh, at the very least," his friend agreed. "And nearly mixed in with 'em too." He laughed uproariously. "But the best of all is the oysters. You just eat them standing on the street. And you can buy a pint of porter to go with 'em."

"Men are so lucky," Chloe said. "Why can't women do these things? I'd love to eat oysters in a fishmarket and watch the people, with no one knowing who I was."

"Well, why don't you?" Denis said slowly, somewhat dazzled by the brilliance of his idea.

"How could I?" Chloe turned to look at him curiously.

"Come with us tomorrow."

"How?" Her eyes were sharp with interest now.

"If you dressed as a boy," Denis suggested softly, "then you'd draw no attention at all."

Chloe clapped her hands, her face alive with amusement. "What a wonderful plan. But where am I to find boy's clothes?"

"Leave it to me," Denis said. "I'll deliver them to Mount Street tomorrow morning."

"How will you leave the house?" Frank asked, lowering his head instinctively as they huddled together.

Chloe frowned. "It depends what time you go."

"Oh, not before about two o'clock in the morning," Julian said. "That's when the carts come in with the fish for the stalls and they start unloading."

Tomorrow night, Chloe thought with contrary satisfaction, she wouldn't pay her customary visit to Hugo, she would go to Billingsgate instead. And if he missed her, all the better.

"I'll meet you outside the house whenever you say," she said.

"You'll be able to escape your chaperone's eye?" Frank asked.

"Very easily," Chloe assured him.

"But what of your guardian?" Denis watched her through hooded eyes as he waited for her response.

Chloe glanced across the room to where Hugo was dancing with Miss Anselm, both of them clearly more interested in their conversation than in the waltz. They were laughing, and he seemed to Chloe to be holding his partner unnecessarily close. He had never danced the waltz with his ward.

"There won't be a problem," she said with cheerful insouciance. In fact, she had no intention of keeping this adventure from Hugo. He expected her to amuse herself with her own circle, and she would do so. And she would show him that other things could provide as much entertainment as lovemaking . . . that one could become bored doing the same thing every night and she was no more dependent upon him than he was upon her.

"We'll be waiting for you at two o'clock, then," Denis said. "And I'll deliver the clothes in the morning. Shall you mind if they're not very elegant?" He regarded her with a half-smile that managed to convey a degree of intimacy. "The thing is, you are rather small and I don't think anything of mine would fit. But I could borrow a suit of my brother's."

"How old is your brother?" Chloe demanded, not a whit struck by any possibly indecorous slant to the conversation.

"Eleven," Denis said with a disarming grin. "And he's almost exactly your size."

Chloe laughed and lightly brushed his hand with her own. In swift response he took her hand and raised it to his lips, saying daringly, "I can't wait to see you in such a costume, Chloe."

"That," Chloe declared with mock disapproval, "is a most improper thing to say, Denis."

"But then, you are proposing a most improper excursion," he said solemnly.

"It was *your* proposal, may I remind you," she bantered.

"But I didn't notice any hesitation on your part." His eyes laughed at her and her own responded. He still held her hand and she made no move to take it away.

Denis DeLacy seemed to have taken the honors for the evening yet again, her other two suitors reflected disconsolately, each of them wishing such a daring proposal had occurred to them.

Hugo wondered if he was imagining an air of suppressed excitement in his ward when he escorted her home. She seemed preoccupied and responded to his various attempts at conversation distractedly, but the sparkle in her eyes had a distinctly mischievous glimmer to it.

He decided to postpone questions until later, when she came to him in the privacy of his bed. However, as soon as they reached home, she said she had to look in on Peg and the baby and flew upstairs with a cheerful good night.

Frowning, he went to the kitchen for his customary nighttime conversation with Samuel.

"How's Peg?"

"Wants nuthin' to do with the babe," Samuel said, pouring tea. "Doesn't seem t' know what to do wi' it. Didn't even want to put it to the breast . . . and the poor mite wailin' fit to burst."

"Seems quiet enough now." Hugo sipped tea.

"Mrs. 'Erridge wasn't standin' for no nonsense." Samuel stretched his legs to the fire's blaze. "An' Peg's too weak to fight 'er at the moment."

"I expect Chloe will sort it out," Hugo said with conviction, and soon after took himself to bed, where he waited in vain for the usual visitation.

He fell asleep eventually, trying to persuade himself that he should be pleased that his efforts to lessen the intensity of their liaison seemed to be having the desired result. But he felt bereft nevertheless and wondered how long it would be before the sense of loss diminished.

Chloe huddled alone in her bed, taking what comfort she could from Dante's weight on her feet. She wondered miserably if Hugo had even noticed that she hadn't come to him. He was probably dreaming sweetly of making love to Miss Anselm . . . or Judith Devlin.

But if her plan for tomorrow night worked out as planned, she'd be the only person on his mind, and present denial would surely make the reunion all the more glorious.

Denis himself delivered the promised parcel of clothes the next morning. Chloe, who had discovered somewhat to her chagrin that Peg responded better to Mrs. Herridge's brusque instructions over care of the baby than she did to Chloe's gentler, more understanding approach, greeted him eagerly and with even more warmth than usual.

"Did you bring them?"

"Yes. Would you like to see?" He handed her the parcel.

"I'd better not open it here," she said, glancing over her shoulder to the open library door. "Samuel has a way of popping up when least expected." She chuckled. "Of course we'd hear Lady Smallwood a mile away. But that's unkind of me. May I offer you a glass of sherry?"

"Thank you. Where's Sir Hugo?"

"I don't know," she said truthfully. Hugo had already left the house when she'd come down to breakfast and Samuel had said only that he'd had some commissions to execute.

Denis sipped his wine and contemplated his next move. Was it too soon to make any overt declaration?

"The ribbons of your gown are exactly the color of your eyes," he said, smiling. "How clever of you to choose them."

"Oh, I didn't," Chloe responded with a small moue of annoyance. "Sir Hugo and Lady Smallwood make all the decisions about my wardrobe. I consider it thoroughly interfering of them. However . . ."

Her eyes danced. "Neither of them would choose what's in the parcel, which will make it all the more amusing to dress in such fashion. It was a brilliant idea, Denis."

He bowed modestly. "I own I can't wait to see you in britches, Chloe."

Chloe felt suddenly uncomfortable. He'd said something similar last night, but it had sounded different then, more jesting. The tone and the words this morning felt like the kind of thing she could imagine a man saying to a lightskirt . . . a bit of muslin, she thought they were called. And there was something faintly predatory about his eyes that made her uneasy.

Denis recognized his mistake immediately. It was appropriate to crypt games, and Jasper had warned him that he must be subtle. The time for unsubtlety would come soon enough, when he'd receive his reward. "Forgive me," he said, extending his hand. "What a shockingly improper thing to say, Chloe . . . but I do find you most . . . well . . . I don't know how to say it. But you're not like other girls . . . you're so much easier to talk to."

"Let's talk of something else," she said, accepting his hand and the apology with relief.

He was regaling her with a wicked on-dit that amused her mightily, when Hugo entered the library. He was in riding dress, his top boots dusty, and a wash of unfocused irritation flooded him as he saw who was causing Chloe's laughter to fill the library.

"Oh, Hugo, Denis has been telling me the most scandalous story about Margery Featherstone," she said, turning her laughing countenance toward him, for a moment forgetting their estrangement. "Apparently, she—"

"I believe I've heard it," Hugo broke in, going to the sideboard. "DeLacy, may I refill your glass?" He offered the decanter.

There was a coolness to his voice that while far from impolite was also far from encouraging. The younger man declined the offer and took his leave within a few minutes. Chloe gave him her hand again, a gesture not lost on Hugo any more than he missed the impishly conspiratorial glance she accorded her guest as she bade him farewell.

The little fox was up to her tricks again, he thought uneasily. Why the hell did she have to play them with Brian DeLacy's son?

"What are you up to, lass?" he demanded without preamble.

"Nothing," Chloe denied, careful to avoid looking toward the parcel of clothes in the corner of the sofa. "Why were you so unfriendly to Denis?"

"Was I?" He shrugged. "I didn't intend to be. But neither do I consider it right for you to be entertaining a young man alone."

"Oh, stuff! The door was open," she said. "There was nothing improper about it. We were in full view of anyone crossing the hall. Anyway," she added with a hint of truculence, "how am I to find a husband if I never have the chance to engage in private conversation with likely prospects?"

Hugo hid his dismay. Was Chloe that drawn to young DeLacy? "Far be it from me to impede such a worthy aim, lass," he said amiably. "I hadn't realized your partiality for DeLacy was quite that serious."

"I find him more intelligent than most," she declared.

"Ah, but will he be sufficiently complaisant?" Hugo inquired, perching on the corner of the big desk, swinging one booted foot as he examined his ward with an amused eye that disguised his uneasy speculations.

"He'll have to be," Chloe said smartly. "Since I have no intention of marrying anyone who won't permit me to have control over my fortune."

"Then I suspect, my dear girl, that you'll have to settle for a stupid husband," Hugo said. "Because I don't see an intelligent man willingly accepting the role of hag-ridden husband."

"But I would not hag-ride . . . or whatever the word is," Chloe protested indignantly. "That's most unjust, Hugo. When have I ever hag-ridden you?"

"Never . . . and don't expect to," he said, and changed the subject. "How's the mother?"

"Mrs. Herridge manages her better than I do," Chloe said. "I don't seem to speak the right language."

"That's hardly surprising," he said gently.

"No, I suppose not." She shrugged. "So long as someone can persuade her to feed the babe, then it doesn't matter."

Casually, she wandered over to the sofa and sat down in the corner, hiding the parcel as she wondered how to remove it from the library under Hugo's eye? She couldn't leave it there alone with him either, he would be bound to notice it.

"I think I'll stay at home tonight," she said, pleating

the lace of her sleeve. "Lady Smallwood will be glad of the company."

"I'm sure she will," he agreed, smiling. "Making amends, lass?"

It was as good an excuse as any. She raised her eyes and returned his smile slightly consciously. "I thought perhaps I should."

"I applaud the self-sacrifice," he said. "Would you like me to make a third?"

"No." Chloe shook her head. "I am determined to do penance and will play backgammon all evening. Besides, Mrs. Herridge needs some time to herself and I can hold the fort for the evening. You're very dusty . . . shouldn't you change your boots before nuncheon?"

"Should I?" Hugo regarded his boots with a quizzical frown. "I've not come across a household where riding clothes were forbidden at any table but the dinner table. Do I offend you, my ward?"

"Not exactly," she said. "But judging from the rather pungent odor in the room, I suspect you have more than dust on your boots."

"I don't smell anything. However . . ." He left his perch on the desk. "I'd hate to offend that pretty little nose." He pinched it lightly as he passed . . . a carelessly affectionate guardian's gesture with no hint of a lover's fierce desire.

Chapter 22

T HE CLOTHES DID NOT make her look like a boy, Chloe decided, examining herself in the mirror late that night. Nankeen trousers buttoned onto a white lawn shirt with a frilled collar. A short fitted jacket with a double row of buttons marching from the shoulder to the waist went over the shirt. Denis had even provided white stockings and a pair of flat black shoes. The shoes needed to be stuffed with paper in the toes, but apart from that everything fitted very well . . . or at least, it seemed to. But something wasn't quite as it should be.

She frowned, turning this way and that in front of the mirror in the quiet house. Dante lay watching her through one eye while Falstaff cackled softly on his perch. The fitted jacket seemed to accentuate the swell of her breasts rather than disguise them, and her hips and backside in the trousers were much more noticeable than in skirts.

In fact, she decided, the whole effect was grossly improper. Lady Smallwood would probably fall into a dead faint from which she'd never recover, and Hugo . . . well, she'd discover Hugo's reaction soon enough. She crammed the black velvet cap on her head, pulling the brim down over her forehead. It didn't seem to make much difference to the overall impression.

The clock on the mantelpiece struck two, and she went to the door, opening it quietly. Dante whined but was now accustomed to being left behind for long periods of the night and merely sighed and curled up into a tight ball when she slipped out into the dark corridor.

Hugo was still out and Samuel would be waiting up for him in the kitchen as usual. So long as Hugo didn't return in the next five minutes, the plan would work. She sped down the stairs, across the hall, and pushed through the swing door into the kitchen.

"Samuel, I'm going out with some friends," she said cheerfully. "Tell Hugo not to worry."

"Wh-wh-what the 'ell . . . ?" Samuel woke from his doze with a start and blinked at the apparition half in and half out of the doorway. "What's that you say?"

"I'm going out," she said. "Tell Hugo I'll be back in a couple of hours. If you don't lock the front door, I won't wake anyone."

Before Samuel could get the blood moving sufficiently to bring him to his feet, she had gone. It took a minute for that unbelievable image to reform in his mind's eye, and when it did, he swore vigorously and ran out of the kitchen. The front door was closed but not locked. He hauled it open and was in time to see Chloe, in her outrageous costume, climbing into a hackney carriage with the help of a young man.

"Jesus, Mary, and Joseph," Samuel muttered, closing the door again. The fat was going to be in the fire over this one. He returned to the kitchen, scratching his head, in no doubt that Chloe had her reasons for this madcap flight.

He put the kettle on the range and was making tea when he heard Hugo's step in the hall. "Still awake, Samuel?" Hugo came in. "There's no need to wait up for me, you know."

"I know, but I choose to," Samuel said. "But I'll leave you to wait up for the lass." He put a mug on the table. "There's your tea."

"Wait up for her?" Hugo inquired, alarm bells ringing in his head.

"She's up and gone out," Samuel said, returning to his

seat by the fire. "About 'alf an hour ago, cool as you please she comes in 'ere an' says, 'Samuel, I'm goin' out. Tell 'Ugo I'll be back in a couple of hours . . . don't lock the door,' she says, so she won't wake anyone."

"Gone where, for God's sake? It's two-thirty in the morning!"

"I dunno . . . and dressed like she was I wouldn't want to guess." He gulped his tea and compressed his lips.

Hugo groaned. "Spit it out, Samuel. I can't bear the suspense."

"Dressed like a lad, she was . . . although she didn't look like no lad . . . bumps in all the wrong places," he added.

"What?"

"You 'eard. Got into a 'ackney with some of those lads that're always 'angin' around 'er."

"I knew she was up to something," Hugo muttered. "For some reason, I have signally failed to get her attention over this hoydenish behavior. It's high time I did, it seems to me."

"I must say, Chloe, those clothes don't seem to make you look like a boy at all," Julian said with a hiccup, his slightly glazed eyes staring at the slim figure on the seat opposite him. He grabbed the strap as the hackney swung around a corner, iron wheels rattling over the cobbles.

"I know they don't," Chloe said. "Are you all foxed?"

"Denis isn't," Frank told her with a skewed grin. "Sober as a judge, aren't you, Denis? While we were drinking blue ruin in Cribb's Parlor, our Denis here was doing the pretty in his mama's drawing room."

"It seems fortunate one of us is sober," Denis declared. "Otherwise, we'd never get where we're going."

He could hardly take his eyes off Chloe. Once he'd been in the crypt when they'd had girls dressed as boys. The memories sent a jolt of lust through his loins, and he shifted on the seat, thankful for the gloom within the carriage. He turned his head away from the arousing sight opposite, struggling to contain the rioting images. If he wanted Chloe in that way as reward for his success, he knew Stephen would give him permission. . . .

The carriage came to a halt, rescuing him from a train of thought that couldn't be in the least helpful to present circumstances.

"Here we are." Frank stumbled out, lost his footing on the step, and fell to one knee. Laughing immoderately, as if it were the funniest thing imaginable, he stood up again and weaved to the front to pay the jarvey.

Denis descended with an agile jump and reached up to help Chloe down. She sprang down beside him, observing cheerfully that trousers certainly made some things easier. Julian didn't appear for a few minutes; he was searching through the gloomy interior for a glove that seemed to have gone missing. Finally, however, they were all safe on the ground and the hackney pulled away.

The scene under the flickering orange and red glow of pitch flambeaux, oil lamps, and braziers seethed with life as wagons rolled across the cobbles and men and women ran to unload the wicker baskets of still-wriggling fish. The ground was wet and mired, slippery with fish scales, and Chloe wrinkled her nose at the stench of fish, both fresh and rotting.

The air was filled with a cacophony of shouts as wagon drivers urged their horses on; screams of laughter or violent oaths from women running through the crowd with laden baskets on their heads; the calls of the costermongers as they offered their wares.

"Heavens," Chloe said, listening to a particularly ripe exchange between two massive women with rocklike forearms. "They could give Falstaff a lesson."

"Who's he?" Julian asked fuzzily.

"One of those fellows in Shakespeare," Frank informed him with a knowledgeable nod. "Don't you remember?"

Julian shook his head. "Can't say as I do."

"Actually, I was referring to a parrot," Chloe said.

"Oh, no . . . not a parrot." It was Frank's turn to shake his head. "Quite mistaken, dear girl. Not a parrot, some fellow in Shakespeare, I remember it very well."

"Yes, but he's a parrot too . . . oh, never mind." Chloe gave up any possibility of having a sensible conversation with her two inebriated escorts. "Let's find some oysters."

"In that tent over there." Denis took charge, cupping her elbow lightly as he escorted her to a noisome tent pitched on a patch of grass, two lanterns swaying at the entrance, lighting the hands of a woman who was shucking oysters with a dazzling speed. She wore no gloves and her hands were thickly ridged with calluses from years of cuts from the razor-sharp shells.

"Four dozen, my good woman," Frank demanded, swaying in front of her.

"That'll be a shilling," the woman said without looking up.

"Nonsense," Denis said. "They were sixpence last night."

"What does it matter?" Chloe said in an urgent whisper. "It's not fair to short-change her. How would you like to do this night after night?"

Denis stared at her under the flickering lamplight. Her eyes were for some reason now almost purple, her mouth set in a firm line. He'd never heard anyone express such a concept before, and for a minute he could think of no adequate response.

"Chloe's right," Julian declared, fumbling in his pockets. "Quite right . . . always is, aren't you, Chlo?"

"Don't call me Chlo," she said, half laughing as he peered myopically into his pockets. "And I'm not always right. Except in matters of this nature."

"Here." Denis drew two shillings from his pocket and dropped the coins on the upturned box beside the woman. She cast a quick sideways glance at this munificence and simply nodded her head as her hands continued with their work.

Chloe, however, was more rewarding. She squeezed his hand. "Thank you. That was generous, but think how much difference it will make to her."

Denis offered a deprecating smile that hid his satisfaction.

"Porter," said Frank suddenly. "You get the oysters and I'll get the porter." He set off with a lopsided motion toward a wagon parked in the shadows.

"I don't think he needs any," Chloe observed with a grimace.

A platter of oysters was suddenly thrust at her by the oyster shucker and she took them with a smile of thanks. The smile went unnoticed, or at least without response, as the woman set to work on the next dozen.

Chloe tipped the luscious contents of the shells into her mouth, feeling the gliding slither as the fishy sensation passed over her tongue and down her throat, reveling in the purity of the taste.

"More?" Denis offered her the second plate but she shook her head, smiling.

"No, I'm not going to eat yours. But I do love them."

Frank reappeared, clutching four pewter tankards by the handles. The contents slopped under his uneven progress. "Success," he declared with a radiant smile of self-congratulation. He handed the tankards around and fell upon his own plate of oysters.

Julian had sat down on the cobbles, leaning against a wooden chest, his eyes half closed. He roused himself sufficiently to make short work of the porter and downed his own plate of oysters with a beatific smile.

"Would you like to walk around the market a little, Chloe?" Denis suggested. "It might amuse you."

Chloe shivered. The cropped jacket was not particularly windproof, and suddenly the adventure had lost its savor. "I'm cold and I think Frank and Julian need their beds."

"Then we'll go," he said promptly. "Come on." He tugged at Frank's sleeve. "Unless you want us to leave you."

Grumbling but acquiescent, the other two followed them away from the fishmarket. "We'll find a hackney on the corner," Denis said. He shrugged out of his coat of olive superfine and put it around Chloe's shoulders. "I should have thought to have provided an overcoat."

Chloe smiled up at him as she huddled into the warm folds. "I didn't think about it being cold either. Are you sure you don't mind?"

"Not in the least." He offered a gallant bow.

They had barely reached the corner, when a wavering lantern ahead caused Frank to shout, "The watch . . . I see the watch. Let's give him a run for his money."

He and Julian began running toward the watchman with his lantern on a pole.

"What are they doing?" Chloe stopped.

"Childish games," Denis said. "They're just teasing him."

Julian tipped the watchman's hat over his eyes and Frank blew out his lantern, then grabbed the pole, trying to pull it loose from the watchman's grip. The man bellowed in fury, turning around in circles as he tried to push his hat up while keeping hold of his lantern.

"Oh, stop it!" Chloe shouted, running toward them. "Stop it. Leave the man alone."

"Spoilsport," Frank said huffily, releasing the pole.

The watchman had just succeeded in freeing his eyes from his hat and now, gibbering with fury, lunged for Julian with his stick. Julian dodged effortlessly until his foot caught on an uneven cobble and he fell to his knees. The man was upon him in an instant, and Frank rushed to the rescue.

"Come on." Denis had swept Chloe out of the alley before she realized it. "Leave them to it. If you get taken up by the watch, your guardian would be justified in taking a horsewhip to me."

"To me, not you," Chloe said, running with him. "I take responsibility for my own actions, Denis . . . but of all the silly, childish . . ."

"Yes, they are," Denis agreed, flagging down a hackney. "But drink does that to people." The pious statement made him chuckle inwardly. Alcohol, as he was privileged to know, should be used to enhance pleasure and free the mind from restraint. Frank and Julian had no knowledge of its best uses. They were mere babies.

It hadn't made Hugo silly and childish, Chloe reflected as she climbed into the carriage. Just rather frightening. It was a function of maturity, she assumed, glancing sideways at her companion. Denis did not seem to lack maturity. She wondered what it was that set him apart from his peers. Perhaps it was just that extra dimension of intelligence she'd noticed before. Whatever it was, it made him a pleasant although unwitting partner in the flirtation that was supposed to pique Hugo into some response. *Supposed* being the operative word, she reflected a touch glumly. But perhaps that would change after tonight.

The hackney drew up outside the house in Mount Street. "No, don't get out," Chloe said in an urgent whisper as Denis moved to step ahead of her onto the pavement. "Just in case anyone's watching from the house." She had slipped past him on the seat and jumped lightly to the ground before he could remonstrate.

"Good night, Denis, and thank you for a splendid adventure." Standing on tiptoe, she smiled warmly at him through the window.

"I'll see if I can think of some others," he replied. "If you'd like."

"I'd like." She blew him a kiss, turned, and ran up the steps to the front door. The house seemed to be in darkness, and she stooped to peer through the keyhole. A dim glow showed in the hall. Had Samuel also left the door unlocked? Softly, she turned the great brass knob and the door swung open. She whisked herself into the shadowy hall and turned to close the door.

"I trust you had a pleasant evening."

"Hugo!" She spun around. "You startled me."

Hugo, in buckskin britches and shirt-sleeves, was leaning against the newel post at the bottom of the stairs, one foot resting on the first step, his arms casually folded across his chest.

"Somehow, my devious little hoyden, I doubt that," he said dryly. "You're not going to tell me you weren't expecting me to wait up for you? That would be a true insult to my intelligence."

When she didn't respond, he examined her with an air of mild curiosity. Samuel had not exaggerated. Her costume was utterly outrageous, every line and curve of her body shamelessly delineated. He shook his head, pursing his lips. "I just don't seem to be able to get your attention, do I, lass?"

But I've got yours. The exultant thought set her blood

leaping in her veins as she waited for his next move. She could read the arousal in his eyes as clearly as if he'd spoken it.

"Take them off," he said.

"What? My clothes?" That had startled her.

"If that's what you choose to call them."

"Here?" She glanced around the hall in disbelief.

"Here," he affirmed. "And now. Take them off, fold them up, and put them on the table."

Chloe drew a deep breath, her tongue peeping from between her lips as she contemplated this instruction. The light in the hall was dim and the house was quiet, but there was no absolute guarantee that some member of the household wouldn't appear.

"Don't oblige me to repeat myself," he said evenly.

She swallowed. The game seemed to have acquired an edge, and she was no longer sure of where it was taking them. She shot him a quick glance and was un-reassured by his expression. The arousal was still there, but ominous little flames were aflicker in the green eyes. With a mental shrug of resignation, she tossed the velvet cap onto the marble-topped console table and unbuttoned the jacket.

Hugo watched, unmoving, as she divested herself of the coat, shirt, shoes, nankeen trousers, white socks. She folded them neatly and put them on the table. Then, in her chemise and drawers, she regarded him inquiringly.

"Finish it," he instructed in the same level tone he had used throughout.

A delicate flush bloomed on her cheekbones. "Hugo—"

"I can assure you you'll look no less indecent naked than you did dressed." He interrupted her half-formed protest. "If that's what's worrying you. Although I find it hard to credit . . . you seem to have not one iota of modesty."

"It was only a game." She could hear how lame it sounded.

"Well, if I can manage to get your attention this time, maybe it'll be one you won't play again. Now, strip."

Chloe pulled the chemise over her head and slipped out of her drawers. "Satisfied?" She glared at him, half angry, half defiant.

Closing his mind to the utter enchantment of her body, the slender limbs quivering in the chill of the hall, the glowing ivory of her skin, he nodded and gestured past him. "Now you may go upstairs."

She blinked. His foot was still on the bottom step and the space between his body and the other newel post was very narrow. It did not look like a safe passage.

Oh, well, she'd just have to shoot the gap. Taking a deep breath, she leapt for the stairs, scrambled past him and upward with the desperate lithe agility of a gazelle fleeing the lion.

Hugo grinned and followed her, enjoying the view.

"My room," he instructed as she reached the head of the stairs.

That sounded more promising, as if there would be a satisfactory conclusion to what had become an uncomfortable situation. Chloe reached Hugo's room at the end of the corridor and put herself on the other side of the door with a sigh of relief. Running naked through the house was not an experience she would choose to repeat.

Hugo followed her in and closed the door. Leaning his shoulders against it, he regarded her with no hint of his inner amusement. She seemed satisfactorily uncertain, he decided, but he had no intention of letting her off lightly. By the time she went to bed, his ward was going to be thoroughly focused on the need to behave with discretion in the future.

He pushed himself off the door and strolled over to a chair by the fire. Sitting down, he beckoned her. "Come here, Chloe."

She approached tentatively, realizing that she had no idea what to expect. In any other circumstances, his awareness of her nakedness would be evident, at least in his eyes, but his expression was now unreadable. She cast a swift secret glance down his body, but there were no overt indications of arousal. Earlier, she had sensed his desire, but now she could feel no stirring of the air between them, and its lack made her more uncomfortable than anything else.

When she reached him, he put his hands on her hips and drew her between his knees. His thighs pressed hard against her bare legs, the buckskin of his britches smooth and supple against her skin.

Leaning back in his chair, Hugo looked up at her, still maintaining his hold on her hips. "Where have you been?"

"To Billingsgate for oysters." It was a relief to be able to give an honest answer. His fingers were curled warm and firm into the flesh of her hips, and her skin began to prickle. The fire spurted and she could feel its heat on her right side. Her nipples hardened and warmth spread slowly through her with the familiar sinking sensation in her lower belly and the moistening of her loins.

It occurred to her with a little jolt that she was becoming aroused by her own nakedness, made all the more aware of it by Hugo's clothed presence. His hands slid around her, kneading the satin curve of her backside, slipping down the backs of her thighs. She shivered.

"And who took you to Billingsgate?" His hands retraced their path in slow, suggestive strokes.

"I don't think I want to tell you that," she said, her voice sounding thick.

Holding her hips again, he leaned forward and kissed her belly, his tongue darting into her navel. "But I think you must," he said, blowing softly, wickedly against her stomach so that she squirmed and he tightened his hold.

"But it's not relevant," she protested weakly. "And it wouldn't be fair for you to be vexed with them. It was my responsibility."

"Oh, I'm aware of that," he said, flicking the pointy hipbones with the tip of his tongue. "Your responsiblity, lass, and your consequences. Nevertheless, I wish to know."

A flat palm slipped sideways between her thighs and she shivered again. What did he mean by consequences? But her mind wouldn't hold the thought as her thighs squeezed on his hand. In an almost distant voice she told him who had been with her.

"I see." A hot tongue stroke seared her belly. "And which of your cavaliers provided you with that indecent costume?"

"I won't tell you that," she said with as much conviction as she could muster. "It can't matter to you." She gasped, biting her lip hard as his fingers moved inside her and his thumb teased the supreme throbbing sensitivity of her sex.

"I suppose it doesn't," he said equably. "You may keep that secret, then."

Something wasn't right. Even through her swiftly mounting passion, Chloe knew it. It was in his voice, so calm and level, even while he was doing the most wonderful things to her, even as he must feel the liquid arousal of her body.

And then as the spiral of delight tightened, Hugo withdrew his hands from her body. "It's time you were in bed," he said matter-of-factly. "After racketing around Billingsgate at such an ungodly hour, you need your sleep." He pushed her away from him as he rose to his feet.

Chloe just stood and stared at him, her eyes wide with dismay.

Hugo scooped her easily into his arms and without further ado carried her back to her room. Chloe was speechless with shock, struggling to make sense of what was happening.

He set her on her feet inside her room and said cheerfully, "Good night, Chloe. I'll leave you to contemplate the consequences of behaving like a wanton hoyden."

He was laughing at her, she realized, as fury rushed into the void created by unfulfilled desire. "You . . . you . . . how could you do that to me!" She flew at him, her fists pummeling his chest, her bare feet kicking against his iron-hard calves.

Hugo caught her hands and clipped them behind her back, holding her wrists with one hand. With his other, he cupped her chin and turned up her furious face. Deliberately, he lowered his head and kissed her, pressing her against his body. He kissed her until the fight left her and she was as soft and pliable as putty. Then he raised his head and released his hold on her wrists.

"Good night, Chloe," he repeated as calmly as before.

Her eyes were dazed, her skin flushed, her lips swollen. She shook her head in bewilderment, unable to recapture her earlier fury, recognizing dimly that Hugo had utterly routed her, winning an engagement she'd intended as her own triumph. How could she ever have imagined she was a match for him? He'd exacted a fiendish penalty for her provocative adventure, leaving her miserably uncomfortable and utterly mortified. How could he possibly have remained so cool and unmoved while reducing her to quivering, desperately wanting jelly?

The door closed behind him and she heard his soft laugh. Picking up a slipper, she threw it at the paneling in impotent frustration, before thumping into bed and pulling the covers over her head.

Chapter 23

UGO BEHAVED THE following morning as if the night's confrontation had never taken place. He greeted his ward cheerfully when she appeared somewhat heavy-eyed in the breakfast parlor, and asked her if she'd like to ride with him in Richmond Park.

Chloe regarded him warily, on the watch for some sign of gloating, but his smile was warm, his eyes calm, his posture relaxed as he leaned back in his chair, one booted leg crossed over the other, the *Gazette* open on his lap.

"I have other plans," she said, turning to the chafing dishes on the sideboard.

"May I be a party to them?" Hugo folded back the newspaper, skimming the contents of the page.

"Is that a question or an order?" She turned back to the table and put down her laden plate as she sat down.

Hugo cast an amused glance at her plate. Chagrin and annoyance hadn't affected her appetite, it seemed. "I would like to know," he said neutrally.

"Well, I haven't decided yet. I'll be sure to inform you when I do." She took a forkful of bacon and carried it to her mouth, not caring that she sounded petulant at best, uncivil at worst. She had passed the most wretchedly uncomfortable night of her life and had no intention of making peace without some statement of protest.

"I'd be glad if you would," he said with careful courtesy, refusing to rise to the challenge. "Where's your duenna this morning?"

"Breakfasting in bed on tea and toast . . . although I

334

think there's a platter of sirloin in case she should recover her appetite later. She feels a touch of gout and
thinks it's because the air's damp." Despite herself, the
old mischief appeared in her previously frosty eyes and
her voice caught on a bubble of laughter. "Do you think
she can be a . . . a . . . oh, what do you call it? A
valetudinarian, that's it?"

"I think it's quite likely," Hugo said with a solemnity
belied by the laughter in his own eyes. He pushed back
his chair and rose. "Are you sure you won't ride with
me, lass?" He came around to her chair and lightly
tipped her chin. "Since your plans don't appear to be
written in stone." He flicked a toast crumb from the
corner of her mouth with a fingertip, and smiled.

It was a smile to melt the most obdurate desire to
punish. Her lip trembled in response and she tried to
hang on to her justifiable grievance, but it was feathers
on the wind. "I don't know whether I like you enough
to ride with you," she said in a last-ditch attempt, but
her eyes spoke other words.

Hugo laughed. "Cry peace, Chloe. You were in the
wrong and you know it. I won't ask you to admit it, but
I'll happily put it behind us if you will."

Not even with the best will in the world could she do
anything else. Apart from the fact that she couldn't bear
to be at odds with him, a peevish withdrawal from him
would surely make him only too glad to see the back of
her.

She reached up and clasped his wrist, her eyes darkening. "We could ride . . . but then again, we could
ride."

"In broad daylight?" he mocked, trying to disguise the
turbulent resurgence of the desire he'd fought so successfully to keep in check last night.

"It wouldn't be the first time."

"No, but this is London, not Lancashire; it's Mount

Street with a house full of servants, not Denholm Manor and Samuel."

It was impossible. Chloe sighed and accepted reality. "Then it'll have to be Petrarch and Richmond."

They spent the morning in perfect amity and that night, when Chloe came to his bed, Hugo made love to her with a fierce need that met and matched her own and restored their equilibrium, obscuring the memories of his punishing self-control. It was a night Chloe remembered for many weeks afterward as the last occasion when they made love without constraint.

Denis DeLacy seemed to be everywhere. His voice was always to be heard in the house on Mount Street, and wherever Chloe was, Denis was in attendance.

Hugo couldn't decide what to make of the burgeoning relationship. Chloe seemed impervious first to his hints and then to his outright declaration that she was singling out DeLacy and that if she wasn't to set tongues wagging, she should be a little less particular in her attentions. She had ignored his instructions, maintaining that Denis DeLacy would make a very good husband: rich enough, very well connected, amusing, easygoing, intelligent, and probably could be persuaded to accept the kind of equal partnership she had in mind. However, when her guardian pressed her to say whether she really wanted to marry Denis, she always managed to evade the issue.

But it wasn't only because Chloe was making herself the talk of the town with the flirtation that Hugo couldn't reconcile himself to the increasing intimacy. Every time he heard Chloe's laugh, saw her brush Denis's sleeve with that delicate airy gesture that he'd come to associate with their own liaison, his gut roiled.

Was he jealous of Denis DeLacy? Of course he was.

The knowledge was bitter and unpalatable, but irrefutable. At thirty-four, he was impossibly in love with an exquisite seventeen-year-old innocent, who was showing a distinct partiality for a young man of her own generation—the perfectly appropriate match he, as her guardian, had been advocating.

He had no choice but to withdraw completely from the field. For both their sakes. As long as their intimate liaison continued, he couldn't help but hinder the progress of Denis's suit. Maybe that was what lay behind Chloe's reluctance to commit herself to the final step. And only by separating himself completely from Chloe could he gain some peace of mind. He was not going to repeat the past. He was not going to be devoured by another hopeless love.

Deliberately and joylessly he set about expanding his social circle. Night after night he stayed out until near dawn, returning to the house only after Chloe had finally yielded to sleep. During the day he was to be found in Jackson's Saloon, or Manton's Shooting Gallery, or Angelo's Fencing Studio, or the Corinthian Club, where he exorcised passion in the sports that had always been his metier in the company of men, who, like himself, eschewed the insipid pursuits of the clubs on St. James's. He grew fitter and stronger and grimmer by the day.

Samuel watched, understood, and waited for the outcome. He saw not only Hugo's unhappiness but Chloe's bewildered misery beneath the bright façade she offered the world. He heard the brittle quality to her ever-ready laughter, saw the fragility of her smile, saw the longing in her eyes as they followed Hugo whenever he was in her vicinity.

Samuel was not deceived by her flirtation with Denis DeLacy and couldn't understand why Hugo seemed to be. These days, in a strange imitation of past bad times, he listened for the sound of the piano in the library. But it was Chloe who played it, using the music to express her unhappiness in a way that words could not, and Samuel learned to recognize her mood from the choice of music, as he had done with Hugo.

Chloe couldn't understand why her ploy had suddenly stopped working. For quite a while Hugo had shown satisfactory signs of disapproving of her flirtation with Denis. He had even become annoyed enough on one occasion to forbid her to dance more than one dance with him in an evening. She had defied this edict, hoping for an overt confrontation that would lead to a long and exciting night, only to find that Hugo dropped the subject abruptly as if it had lost all interest for him. Once he'd asked her if she intended to marry Denis and she'd had the feeling that her answer would matter to him; but now he no longer seemed to notice when she was in Denis's company, and in general no longer frequented the social occasions to which his ward was invited. On the rare occasions he did, he was always to be found in the company of some sophisticated woman of his own age. It seemed to Chloe that he had developed a life of his own that completely excluded her.

In her confusion and unhappiness, she flirted ever more provocatively with Denis. And he met and matched her pace with an eagerness that soon had tongues wagging and bets being laid in the clubs as to how soon DeLacy would lead the beautiful heiress to the altar.

The progress of the affair was watched with undisguised interest by two men lodging in a discreet inn off the Strand.

"Why don't we act now?" Crispin paced the private parlor between the two windows. A grayish light filled the room from the thick snow falling outside.

"Patience," his stepfather counseled, sprinkling nutmeg on the contents of a silver punch bowl. He dipped the ladle into the bowl and sampled the brandy punch with a critical frown before reaching for a saucer of sliced lemons and judiciously adding a few slices.

"But why?" Crispin demanded, staring down into the lane below the window. A dray loaded with ale barrels had come to a halt in a pile of drifting snow and a group of people had gathered around, offering vociferous advice to the driver, who lashed his straining horse and cursed loudly enough to carry to the watcher above.

"Because journeying to Lancashire in a snowstorm is hardly sensible," Jasper snapped. "Use your head, lad."

"We could keep her here. She can be as easily persuaded here as at Shipton. We could be married here." Crispin sounded sullen. It was hard to be kept in the background while Denis DeLacy had all the amusement and he was impatient for his own moment on center stage.

"Sometimes I think you've cloth between your ears, just like your mother," Jasper declared, ladling punch into two goblets. "Here, drink this, it might sharpen your wits." He held out a goblet.

Crispin took it, flushing at his stepfather's contemptuous tone.

"Where do you suggest we keep the girl?" Jasper went on in the same tone. "Somehow I don't see my little sister peaceably settling in one of the inn's bedchambers while we run to fetch a priest. Oh, and where do you think we'll find a priest in London willing to marry her against her will? And you can be damned sure she'll create blue murder however persuasive I might be. And I intend to be very persuasive," he added with a vicious curl of his lip. "Not a quiet process."

"There are things you can give her to keep her quiet," Crispin pointed out, still sullen.

"Yes, and we'll need them on the journey," Jasper

replied. "I've no intention of sitting cramped in a post-chaise for a week with that girl spitting and struggling. We stick to the plan: Denis will bring her to Finchley, where we'll transfer her to the chaise and we will all go to Shipton. There, my impatient, lusting son, old Elgar in the parish of Edgecombe will do as I tell him. He'd tie the knot between you and a sheep if so ordered. And you will spend your wedding night in the crypt."

"What about Denis?"

"He'll have his reward, but don't worry, no one will interfere with the exercise of your conjugal rights."

Jasper drank deeply of the brandy punch, feeling its warmth curling in his belly. His father had died because of Chloe's mother and Hugo Lattimer. He'd waited fourteen years for his revenge, and he wasn't going to bungle it because of the impatience of a brainless lad who thought with his loins. He didn't want Lattimer to be more than one day behind them when he began his pursuit. One day would be long enough to get the marriage over and the scene in the crypt set up. It would be an exact replica of the scene of Elizabeth's presentation, but this time Hugo Lattimer would be in no position to do anything but watch. And afterward, Jasper would kill him, bringing the blood feud full circle.

There was a knock at the door and Denis came in, shaking snow off his curly-brimmed beaver. "It's the devil's own luck," he declared disgustedly. "I had everything set up, and now this." He gestured to the window.

"Patience," Jasper counseled yet again. He ladled punch into a third goblet. "We'll lose nothing by waiting a day or two."

Denis took the goblet with a murmur of thanks. "I'm just afraid that something will happen," he said. "I've got her right where I want her . . . she'll do anything I suggest at the moment. But I have this feeling that it's like . . . it's like . . . I don't know . . . *she's* like a thread stretched so tight, it's bound to snap at any moment."

Jasper looked up sharply. "Why? What's wrong with her?"

"I don't know. Nothing that you can put your finger on, but . . . but I can feel it. There's something." He drank from the goblet and said slowly, feeling for words, "Sometimes I have this feeling that she's just using me. Sometimes I don't think she sees me at all, even when she's paying me the most particular attention."

"Oh, nonsense," Jasper said. "Fanciful nonsense. The silly chit's fallen head over ears in love with you. She's a baby with no more experience of the world than a five-year-old. I expect she's overawed by you."

Denis would have liked to believe that, but he couldn't. But he couldn't explain his conviction any clearer either, so he let the subject drop.

"Have you kissed her?" Crispin demanded with the irritability of envy.

"A peck on the cheek," Denis said. It was impossible, too, to put into words his knowledge that however willing Chloe was to play games with him, there was a line she wouldn't cross. At least, not voluntarily.

"I don't want to frighten her by being too insistent," he explained.

"There'll be plenty of time for that," Jasper said. He straightened and stretched, wandering over to the window. How long before the snow abated? It *was* the devil's own luck, a snowstorm this early in December. But it shouldn't take hold and they'd be on the road within the week.

Hugo let himself into the house that same afternoon, reflecting that this was an evening they would all spend within doors. No one in their right minds would put their horses to the shafts in these conditions unless it was a matter of life or death.

He closed the door behind him, wondering where Samuel was. Two of Beatrice's offspring playing tag raced through the hall, skittering on the polished wood as they ran between his legs before bounding up the stairs. He picked up the letters on the console table and riffled through them. After a minute, it occurred to him that the house was strangely quiet. And for once there was no evidence of Denis DeLacy in temporary residence, he thought grimly, going into the library.

The fire had been allowed to go down and he frowned, bending to throw another log on the glowing embers. Where was everyone? He didn't have a large household, but it was surely large enough to ensure that the fires could be kept in, particularly on a day like this.

He strode into the hall and bellowed for Samuel. There was no immediate response and then suddenly Chloe appeared at the top of the stairs.

"Hugo!" Her voice cracked, filled with tears, and he strode to the bottom of the stairs.

"Sweetheart, what is it?" The rarely used endearment went unnoticed by either of them.

She flew down the stairs and into his arms. "It's Peg," she sobbed against his chest. "She's gone."

"Gone . . . gone where?"

"I don't know! She can't read or write, so she couldn't leave a note . . . and she didn't say anything. She's just disappeared."

"Now, just a minute." Hugo stood her upright and pulled out his handkerchief. "I can't hear a word when you're mumbling into my chest. Start at the beginning."

"There isn't a beginning," she said, taking his handkerchief but not using it, so the tears still poured unchecked down her cheeks. "She's just gone, that's all. Out into the snow. And she's left the baby. *Why?* Why would she do something so silly, Hugo? She'll freeze to death."

"She's left the baby?" Hugo struggled to absorb this.

"Yes. Just walked away and left her."

"God's grace," he muttered. "Now I'm responsible for a foundling as well as a menagerie."

"How can you be so heartless!" Chloe exclaimed through her tears. "Peg's out there in all that snow . . ."

"Of her own free will, lass," Hugo reminded her. Taking her arm, he eased her into the library, closing the door behind them. "She wasn't happy here."

"I know, but why wasn't she?" Chloe huddled over the fire. "I don't understand it. She had plenty to eat and drink, and warm clothes, and . . . and a home. Why would she walk away from that?"

"Come here." Hugo sat down on the couch and drew Chloe backward, pulling her onto his lap. "I know it's hard to accept, but you can't save the world, not even with a heart as big as yours."

"I know I can't," she said, gulping. "I just want to save some of it."

He held her tightly for a minute, then took the neglected handkerchief from her and mopped her tears. "Blow your nose."

She did so vigorously and then leaned back against him, resting her head on his shoulder. "I wish she hadn't gone out in the snow. Why wouldn't she wait . . . I don't understand, Hugo. What could have driven her?"

"I don't really know," he said, stroking her hair away from her brow. "But people do things we can't understand sometimes. Peg lives on the streets. It's what she knows. There must be people out there she knows . . . there was a grandmother, wasn't there?"

"Her nan," Chloe said. "She said she could sometimes sleep in the washhouse . . . but why would she want to do that when she could be warm and dry here? It's not sensible."

"Impulses usually aren't. But you have to remember that Peg knows that world out there. It's her world." He traced the delicate arch of her eyebrow with a fingertip.

"I know one can't *make* people accept help," Chloe said with one of her devastating flashes of mature insight that still surprised and delighted him. "And since I don't think I was trying to help her just so that *I* would feel good, I shouldn't feel miserable just because she prefers to do something else."

She was silent for a minute, then continued rather more cheerfully. "Well, at least she left the baby. And at least she was able to have the baby safely . . . but . . ." She sat up as a thought struck her. "But you know what will happen to her. She'll get pregnant again . . . she doesn't know about potions or . . . or withdrawing . . . or things like that. She'll be pregnant again in no time. And she's so young. She told me she didn't even know how old she is." She relaxed against him again with a heavy sigh.

Hugo said nothing immediately, dwelling on the somber reflection that the diminutive philanthropist on his knee knew all too much about potions . . . and withdrawing . . . and things like that . . . as she put it, with an apparent ingenuousness quite at odds with both the sentiment and her earlier conclusions.

He hadn't held her for an eternity, it seemed, and the slight weight, so familiar to him in its contours and fragrances, filled him with an inconsolable yearning. There was nothing sensual about her at this moment. In fact, she seemed unaware of their proximity, so involved in her sorrow and bewilderment over Peg that she might be sitting anywhere instead of on his knee, leaning against his shoulder. Was she even aware of his fingers playing in the tumbling guinea-gold hair?

The door opened suddenly. "Oh, my goodness . . . oh, I didn't realize . . ." Lady Smallwood stood four-square in the doorway, blinking at the pair on the sofa. "I was looking for Chloe," she said.

"And now you've found her," Hugo said easily. "The lass is very upset about Peg." Gently, and he hoped with an air of complete naturalness, he tipped her off his knee and stood up. Dolly would think nothing of it. She would simply see a guardian comforting his unhappy young ward.

"Yes, and what a to-do," Dolly declared. "Talk about ingratitude . . . talk about biting the hand that feeds—"

"We aren't," Chloe said sharply. "We aren't talking about that at all."

Her chaperone sniffed and with customary fatal lack of tact plowed ahead. "Samuel's come back. He says he's looked all over and there's no sign of her. And good riddance, if you ask my opinion."

"I can't imagine ever doing such a thing," Chloe said, tight-lipped. "Your opinions, madam, can hold not the slightest—"

"Chloe, that'll do." Hugo stepped in before the tirade became unstoppable.

Fortunately, at this point Samuel provided a diversion. He entered the library, snow sticking to his cloak and clinging to his bushy, grizzled eyebrows. "Not a sign," he said. "An' no one's seen 'er neither. I asked up an' down the street. Not that you can see much out there," he added, going to the windows, gazing out at the dense blanket still descending.

He glanced back at the tear-streaked Chloe and said gruffly, "Now, don't you go afrettin', lass. She'll 'ave known where to go. She's no fool, that Peg. If you ask me, she's 'appy as a grig now. No baby to worry over. She 'ad the money you gave 'er, all those good clothes.

She'll be in some alehouse by now, snug and warm, an' havin' the time of 'er life."

"Until the money runs out," Chloe said, refusing to be cheered by a picture that, knowing Peg, she had to admit was quite possibly accurate. "Maybe she'll come back then."

Samuel shrugged. "More to the point, seems to me, is what's to be done with the babe."

"A wet nurse, I suppose," Chloe said. "But where do we find one in this weather?"

"Well, it just so 'appens that the 'ead groom's wife 'as just 'ad a little-un. I daresay she'd not be averse to takin' on another for a few guineas."

"Oh, Samuel, you are wonderful." Chloe flew across the room and kissed him heartily on both cheeks, oblivious of Lady Smallwood's scandalized little cry.

"Get along wi' you," Samuel said, blushing. "If ye'll fetch the babe down 'ere, I'll take it along to the mews. Ted's waitin' fer it."

"And then, when she's weaned, she can come and live with us," Chloe stated.

"It's to be hoped your husband won't be averse to taking on an infant of unknown parentage," Hugo commented somewhat aridly.

Chloe's heart skipped a beat as she realized that she had simply spoken from the forbidden assumption—an assumption that despite the present bewildering estrangement was still intrinsic to her view of their future.

She said with a slight shrug, "Oh, I'm sure Persephone will win over the most unkind heart."

"*Persephone!* Dear God in heaven! What kind of a name is that for some poor little bastard from the city stews?" Hugo exclaimed, immediately diverted from contemplation of Denis DeLacy's reaction to adoptive parenthood.

Chloe's mouth took a familiar stubborn turn. "I fail to

see why a bastard from the stews shouldn't have a pretty name."

"Hugo!" Lady Smallwood squeaked. "Oh, goodness me, whatever will she say next? If anyone should hear . . . oh, my poor heart, such palpitations." She sank onto a chair, fumbling in her reticule for her smelling salts.

Unfortunately, Hugo caught Chloe's eye, brimful of wicked merriment. Over her shoulder Samuel was grinning with unabashed amusement. Hugo developed a violent coughing fit as the only recourse.

"Well, I'll go and fetch Persephone," Chloe declared, regarding her convulsed guardian with feigned concern. "That is the most dreadful cough, Hugo."

He pulled himself together. "Must it be Persephone?"

"Yes," Chloe said simply, turning to the door. "And while I'm in the mews, I thought, perhaps, since it's such a miserable night and he'll be cold and lonely—"

"No," Hugo said.

"But I promise I'll keep him on the leash; he's very good about it. And I'll only let him in here. He and Dante like to play together and they can lie by the fire."

"No."

"Oh, Hugo, please."

"Is she talking about that wild animal?" Lady Smallwood recovered from one set of palpitations and prepared for the next. "I will not . . . absolutely not stay under the same roof as a wild beast."

"Oh, ma'am, he'll only be in the library," Chloe said. "There's no reason why you should even see him." She turned dark purple eyes on Hugo. "Demosthenes hasn't been able to play with Dante all day because of the snow. And he'll be so lonely."

It was true that the massive brindle mongrel and the bear cub had developed some kind of rapport. It was also true that the pair of them could reduce a room to ruin before a man could blink.

"No," Hugo repeated.

"But I promise I'll keep him on the leash. And if he won't be quiet, then I'll take him straight back to the stables." Tearstains still tracked down the damask cheeks, her eyes were still tear-washed, that lovely soft mouth quivered in appeal.

Hugo wondered absently why he even bothered to begin a battle that experience told him he couldn't possibly win. He'd forbidden the bear the house on innumerable occasions, but it didn't seem to make the slightest difference. Demosthenes still came in.

Shaking his head in defeat, he bent to throw another log on the fire.

"Hugo, I've been meaning to talk to you about that young DeLacy," Lady Smallwood said, abruptly recovering from her palpitations as the door closed on a triumphant Chloe. "His attentions are most particular."

"I had noticed." Hugo turned to face his cousin. "And as far as I can gather, so has everyone else."

"Chloe doesn't appear to hold him in dislike," his cousin said.

"That, if I may say so, is the understatement of the season, ma'am."

"It's a perfectly good match . . . not brilliant of course, and with that beauty and such a fortune, one would have hoped—"

"But as we both know, ma'am, Chloe refused the brilliant offers made her."

"Yes." Lady Smallwood touched her smelling salts to her nose. "It's past time she settled down. All this nonsense with wild animals and waifs and strays . . . it really won't do. It's amazing that Society has tolerated her oddities this far. But I'm convinced that once she has a husband and a house and a family of her own, then she'll leave this willfulness behind."

"I wouldn't call it willfulness," Hugo demurred. "But I take your point. What are you suggesting, Dolly?"

"That you should ask DeLacy what his intentions are," she said. "He must be brought to the point. The flirtation has gone on quite long enough, and Chloe has too little experience to know how to encourage the young man to speak up."

If you only knew. Hugo steepled his fingers and painted an expression of alert concentration on his face. "You think he needs a push?"

"Most certainly. I wouldn't be doing my duty as chaperone if I didn't give you my opinion. The child is very high-spirited and sometimes it leads her into . . . well, we won't say anything about that . . . and one can't help loving her nevertheless. I really would like to see her happily settled, and if this match is something she wants, then I think we must do all possible to promote it."

"Your advice is as always most valuable, Dolly."

The door burst open. Dante leapt excitedly into the room, sending the Turkey carpet skewing across the floor. He danced backward, barking in greeting as Demosthenes galloped at the end of his leash, hauling Chloe, a laughing but totally inadequate counterweight, behind him.

Lady Smallwood gave vent to a faint gasp and fled the room. Hugo sank onto the sofa and covered his head with a cushion. There was nothing like a quiet evening at home.

And when Chloe was happily married to Denis DeLacy, he'd never have to endure another.

Chapter 24

"IT'S NOT A VERY pleasant day for a carriage ride, Denis." Chloe's nose wrinkled as she looked out of the drawing room window onto the slushy street.

"The sun's shining," he pointed out.

"After a fashion," Chloe agreed. "But it's so dirty."

"Oh, come on, Chloe, it's not like you to let a little mud stand in your way," he cajoled. "We've all been captive within doors for three days because of the snowstorm, and now it's clearing up so nicely, I feel I have to breathe some fresh air. We'll go to Finchley Common and you can take the ribbons if you'd like."

Chloe looked down at the equipage in the street. Denis was driving a pair of high-stepping grays. It was tempting, but if the truth were told, Denis was beginning to pall on her. He had a streak of sullenness that showed through his bonhomie and, while he was quick to agree when she commented on some sorry street scene or the plight of the poor, she sensed impatience beneath the smooth appearance of empathy. She was well aware that the act was to impress her and was beginning to feel guilty that she had led him on to believe in a partiality that she didn't feel in the least. Oh, he was certainly more interesting company than most of the men of his age. He had more conversation, he had little time for the exuberant silliness of his peers, and she had never seen him the worse for drink. He viewed the drunken pranks of the others with a faint contempt with which she was completely in sympathy. Nevertheless, since their flirtation was having no effect on Hugo, there seemed little point to it. But then, there seemed little point to anything these days, and moping around the house wouldn't improve things.

"Very well," she said listlessly. "But I have to change my dress."

"Of course. I'll wait for you." Denis bowed, trying to conceal the flash of relief in his eyes. There had been a moment there when he thought she was going to refuse. And he had no wish to turn up empty-handed on Finchley Common. Sir Jasper was not a person to present with failure.

Hugo was coming up the stairs from the hall as Chloe came out of the drawing room. "Is that DeLacy's curricle at the door?" He asked the question with the casual curiosity he'd managed to perfect.

Chloe flushed slightly. "Yes, he's in the drawing room. We're going for a drive, so I have to change my dress."

"I see." Hugo frowned, remembering his cousin's advice. "You might wish to inform the young man that I expect him to request my permission before paying his addresses to my ward."

"Why should you imagine he's doing that?" Her flush deepened.

Hugo decided it was time to take the bull by the horns. "If he is not, lass, then I would certainly like to know what the devil's going on," he said sharply. "Either you bring DeLacy to the point, or I must. This shilly-shallying cannot continue . . . not if you intend to remain a member of Society. There's too much talk already, and I'll not stand by while you compromise your reputation with an intense flirtation that is going nowhere. Is that understood?"

He really wanted her to marry Denis DeLacy. It had never been said so openly before, but there was no way of misconstruing such an ultimatum. She'd hung on to the belief that Hugo loved her although he wouldn't acknowledge it because of his irrelevant scruples. She'd thought she could overcome the scruples as she'd overcome everything else. Now the fight went out of her.

"I imagine Denis will wish to speak with you after our drive," she said with careful deliberation.

"I see. Well, you may assure him he won't meet with undue opposition, lass."

He pinched her cheek and offered an affectionate smile before continuing on his way along the corridor, his heart heavy. But at least the long agony of this frustrating love affair was about to come to a close. He'd have only a few more months of endurance until he walked her up the aisle and handed her over to a man of her own kind with whom she'd live and love and have babies. . . .

Chloe stifled a sob of frustration and misery and ran up the stairs to her bedchamber. How could Hugo not feel the way she did?

But she knew how. She was too young and she was his ward. And now that even their constrained lovemaking had ceased, he had no occasion to see her in any other light. He didn't care for her in that way anymore, and without that, what was there to build on?

Why had she ever insisted on this insane London scheme? Blinking back tears, she changed into her driving dress, then splashed cold water on her face from the ewer on the dresser. But she hadn't known she was in love with Hugo Lattimer then. She'd been so immersed in her plans for the future and the excitement of the present that she hadn't stopped to analyze her feelings. And now it was all dust and ashes.

So she would marry Denis DeLacy. It would be no worse a fate than any other, since she couldn't have the only future that mattered.

She crammed a velvet bonnet on her head and adjusted the plume. It was not a hat she liked—it was too small and insignificant—but Hugo had selected it with customary firmness. Soon he'd have no say in her wardrobe, or any other aspect of her life. She swallowed, trying vainly to dislodge the lump in her throat.

She went back to the drawing room. Denis was so relieved at getting her out of the house and into the curricle that he failed to observe her unusual pallor or her absentminded responses to his attempts at conversation.

He drove fast through the fashionable streets. Absorbed in her unhappy thoughts, Chloe didn't notice at first how intently he was driving, or how he was pushing his horses. Only when they narrowly missed an oncoming coach on the approach to Primrose Hill did she jerk back to full awareness.

"Your horses are sweating," she said in surprise. It was a cardinal sin for any halfway competent whip. She glanced at him and saw the set of his jaw, the tightness of his mouth.

"What's the matter?"

He looked fully at her, and there was a light in his eye that sent a shiver of alarm through her. "Nothing, why should there be? Aren't you enjoying the drive?"

"It's colder than I thought it would be," she said, trying to sound her usual self. "It's very bad for your horses to push them so hard."

"They're my horses. I'll be the judge," he said coldly. One of the pair stumbled in a pothole. His whip curled and snapped, catching the animal's ear.

"Don't do that!" Chloe exclaimed even while she was trying to recover from the extraordinary coldness of his tone. "It wasn't his fault. If you drove with more care, he wouldn't have stumbled."

Suddenly she knew that something was very wrong. But for the life of her she couldn't imagine what. Except that Denis didn't look like the man she thought she knew and that strange, predatory light was in his eye again.

"Stop the curricle," she demanded. "I want to get out." They were almost on Finchley Common and there was little traffic on the filthy road and no pedestrians, but she knew with absolute certainty that she didn't want to travel another inch in Denis DeLacy's curricle.

He didn't respond, except to crack the whip again so his horses surged forward onto the common with a final spurt.

The wind whipped across the snowy heath, bending the gnarled, leaf-bare trees and whistling through the sere brown bracken. The rutted road wound ahead, ice glittering in the hard, dry ridges, cracking under the pounding hooves.

Chloe shivered, dreadful apprehension prickling her scalp, lifting the fine hair on her arms. Then she saw the post-chaise up ahead, pulled to the side of the road under a stand of trees. A postilion, muffled to the ears in his cloak, stood beside the leaders.

The last time she'd seen a post-chaise waiting in such sinister fashion had been on the road to Manchester with Crispin. But on that occasion she'd been riding a swift horse and had her escape in her own hands.

"What's happening?" Her voice was barely a whisper as the nameless dread crept up her spine. "Hell and the devil, Denis, what's happening?"

Without answering, he drew rein as the curricle came abreast of the chaise. The horses panted and wheezed, sweat glistening on their glossy necks. Denis leapt down just as the postilion jumped into the curricle in his place.

Chloe struggled as Denis hauled her to the ground, but she was no match for his strength. Though she kicked and punched with the blind force of desperation, he lifted her off the ground and bundled her into the chaise as the door swung open.

She fell to her hands and knees on the floor as Denis leapt in behind her. A whip cracked and the vehicle surged forward with a violent jolt that sent her sprawling again as she struggled upright. Someone laughed. It was a familiar laugh.

Pushing backward, she righted herself so that she was kneeling. She looked up at the three men, two of whom were regarding her with varying degrees of amusement. Denis, on the other hand, bore the satisfied, slightly smug air of a man who has accomplished a singularly demanding task. What in the name of all that was good connected Denis to Jasper?

"Why?" she asked him. "Why, Denis?"

"You'll discover soon enough," Jasper said. "Sit up on the seat." His pale eyes, flat and expressionless, skidded over her face.

A wild rage abruptly overtook her, banishing the fear that had been born earlier out of uncertainty. If this was the enemy, she knew it . . . or thought she did.

She sprang at her brother, moving from her knees to a flying body of fury in one neat movement. She had no idea what she hoped to achieve, or even if she expected to achieve anything. Her gloved hands reached for those flat eyes that seemed to contain no soul, and her knee came up into his chest.

The next minute she was reeling as his open palm cracked viciously against her cheek. Her ears rang and she fell backward across Crispin on the opposite seat. Still she struggled, feet and arms flailing, making what destructive contact she could with the three bodies sharing the confined space with her.

Denis grabbed her ankle and she kicked viciously into his belly.

"Leave her to me. She's mine now." A rich certainty infused Crispin's voice. Denis released his hold, watching through narrowed eyes.

Crispin wrestled Chloe's slight frame facedown across his lap, wrenching her arms behind her as he held her. Jasper pulled off his cravat and tied her wrists. Then he picked her up and dumped her into the corner of the carriage next to Crispin.

"You've a great many lessons to learn, little sister," he said, breathing rather heavily. "Fortunately, I make a good teacher . . . maybe a little short on patience, but you'll learn all the quicker, I imagine."

Chloe was too stunned to reply. Her face throbbed, her wrenched arms were beginning to ache, and the cravat was uncomfortably tight around her wrists. Instinctively, she pressed backward into her corner, in no doubt as to the reason behind this abduction.

Her eyes slid sideways to Crispin. He was smiling in the way he had when he'd pulled the wings off butterflies as a child. She had once said to Hugo that Jasper couldn't force her to marry Crispin. But then she hadn't fully understood the meaning of force.

The chaise jolted in another pothole and she fell sideways, unable to balance herself with her bound hands. Crispin pushed her upright again. She huddled backward into her corner again and closed her eyes to shut out the three pairs regarding her with the predatory interest of hunters who've finally snared their prey.

Where was Hugo? But what difference did it matter where he was? Never in a millennium would he connect Denis DeLacy with Jasper.

"Where's Chloe, Dolly?" Hugo entered the drawing room before dinner, a somewhat mournful Dante on his heels.

"Why, goodness me, I thought she was with you." Lady Smallwood put down her embroidery and blinked at her cousin. "I haven't seen her since nuncheon."

"What!" Hugo impatiently pushed Dante's wet nose away from his thigh. "How could you not have seen her? Is she in her room?"

"I assumed she was with you," Dolly repeated. "I'm not usually told when you and she go off together." There was a hint of self-righteous grievance in the statement.

Hugo spun on his heel and ran down to the hall, yelling for Samuel.

"Eh, what's up now?" Samuel appeared from the kitchen, wiping his mouth with his table napkin. "In the middle of me dinner, I am."

"Where's Chloe?"

" 'Ow should I know? I 'aven't seen 'ide nor 'air of the lass since nuncheon. Thought she was wi' you." Sensing Hugo's agitation, he looked perplexed. "You mean she's not?"

"No, she's not. I haven't seen her since early this afternoon." Hugo forced himself to think clearly, to order his thoughts. Could she have had plans for the evening she'd forgotten to impart . . . or perhaps chosen not to? Like the Billingsgate affair.

It was not impossible. But it was unlikely. Chloe was an uncomfortable and incompetent liar. Her mischievous but generally purposeful schemes were never intended to be kept secret for any length of time.

She'd been going for a drive with Denis DeLacy. Had there been an accident? The curricle overturned? A stumbling horse? A lost shoe? Highwaymen?

But it was eight o'clock. Chloe had gone driving with DeLacy at two. Six hours! No ordinary accident could have happened in that time. Usually, if she went for a drive in the early afternoon, she'd be home by five o'clock at the latest. If there'd been an accident, then they had three hours leeway in which to deliver a message of some kind. Unless she was lying with a broken neck beneath the wheels of DeLacy's curricle . . . how well did the damn youth drive? Was he reckless? All young men were reckless.

He thought of his own youth . . . of the number of times he'd driven a team when he couldn't see straight . . . of the times when he'd snatched the reins of a stagecoach from the hapless driver and careened down the road with screaming passengers, waving a bottle of burgundy over his head and shooting his pistol in the air.

Dear God in heaven! How chickens came home to roost.

"I'm going to Curzon Street," he said, taking the stairs three at a time. A few minutes later he was back, drawing on his gloves, a caped overcoat hanging from his shoulders.

Samuel, who had discarded his napkin and abandoned his dinner, was in the hall, buttoning up his own coat. "So what's at Curzon Street?"

"DeLacy's mother's house," Hugo said shortly, opening the door. "I can't think of anywhere else to start." He set off down the street almost at a run, Samuel panting along behind him.

"Go around to the mews and see if there's a pair of grays and a curricle in the stable," Hugo ordered as they reached the DeLacy mansion. Samuel went off and Hugo banged the knocker.

The butler opened the door and bowed. "The family are at dinner, sir. May I take your card?"

"Only if Denis DeLacy is in," Hugo said shortly.

"Mr. DeLacy, sir, is not in." The man stood holding the door with an air of impatient courtesy.

"Has he been back this afternoon?"

"No, sir. I understand Mr. DeLacy is spending the evening out of town with friends."

"Which friends?"

"I am not privileged to know, sir." The butler moved back, preparatory to closing the door.

Hugo put his foot in the opening. "Don't be in such a hurry, my good man."

There was something about his tone and the glitter in his green eyes that caught the butler's attention. "Sir?" he said stiffly, but made no further move to end the conversation.

"Mr. DeLacy went out in his curricle this afternoon. At that point did you know he was not intending to return?"

"I believe a message to that effect came somewhat later, sir."

"How much later?"

"At around six o'clock, I believe, sir."

Two hours ago. Clearly he didn't have to worry about an accident. What the devil was going on? Hugo removed his foot, waved a dismissive hand at the butler, and ran back to the street.

Samuel appeared around the corner from the mews. "Two grays, lookin' fair winded to me," he said, falling into step. "Someone's been pushin' 'em mighty 'ard. The 'ead groom was swearin' worse than the lass's poll parrot. Says it's been two hours since they come in wi' some job ostler who vanished as soon as he'd dropped 'em off. Groom still can't get 'em cooled off proper."

"Two hours," Hugo repeated. "So the horses came back with a message carried by a stranger that their driver was not returning. Samuel, what the hell is going on?"

"Seems to me," Samuel said slowly, "that makin' off with the lass is gettin' to be a habit with some folks."

"Jasper!" Hugo stopped dead in the middle of the street. "Jesus, Mary, and Joseph, of course. The Congregation. Why on earth didn't I think . . . ?"

If Denis DeLacy had followed his father into the Congregation just as Crispin had followed Jasper, then Denis would be bound by an oath of obedience to his leader. Hugo had been so busy worrying that Chloe would hear the truth about himself from her attentive suitor, he'd completely missed the real danger attached to any connection with the Congregation. DeLacy had seemed such an inoffensive lad . . . but then, hadn't they all—most of the time?

"Congregation?" Samuel jumped out of the path of an oncoming hackney, shoving Hugo with him. The jarvey leaned down from his box and poured forth a string of obscenities.

"It's a long story," Hugo said, his mouth grim. "A long story and an old one." He stood frowning, options and speculations chasing each other in his head.

Where would Jasper have taken her? In London, they'd have to find a priest who'd turn a blind eye to marrying a young girl against her will . . . and Chloe would make that fact very clear. She'd not go docile to the altar. It would take time to subdue her into an appearance of compliance, and Jasper didn't have that kind of time. He'd want her married and bedded without delay. Once it was done, Chloe's fortune would automatically come under her husband's control. It was the law of the land. What happened to Chloe after that probably wouldn't concern her brother unduly, although it would interest Crispin.

Hugo remembered the vicious temper Crispin had evinced that day in Manchester when Chloe had run to Rosinante's rescue. He remembered the sullen cowardice of his behavior when Hugo had squeezed the truth out of him on the road to Manchester. Such a contemptible character would enjoy revenge on a helpless captive. And if he was a member of the Congregation—and of course he was—then he would have learned by now the licentious pleasures of the drug-induced trance as he pushed out the boundaries of sensation, crossing the thresholds of evil in the crypt. He and Denis would have learned it all by now, even if they were not yet as depraved as their leader.

They would be taking her to Shipton. Hugo knew it as clearly as if Jasper had told him. In Shipton, Jasper would have his own people, who knew how to keep their mouths shut, who knew what happened if they didn't. In Shipton, he could keep Chloe shut away from prying eyes and he would have his own priest. Jasper had sowed the seeds of his influence widely, using fear, intimidation, bribery, whichever power tool worked the best in each case. He'd have a priest willing to turn a blind eye.

And they'd have the crypt.

He saw Elizabeth standing in the crypt, terror in her drugged eyes as she at last understood what role her husband had devised for her. He saw Elizabeth . . . but it wasn't Elizabeth, it was her daughter, Chloe, standing by the bier in the light of the altar candles. The daughter in her mother's place . . . the feud come full circle. How it would please Jasper. Oh, what deep pleasure it would give him to avenge his father's death in that fashion.

A wave of nausea surged through him, a momentary sense of helplessness . . . and then came the cold conviction that if he had to, he would kill Jasper as he had killed Stephen.

When they took Chloe to the crypt, he would be there.

"We're going to Shipton," he said softly to the waiting Samuel.

"Shipton!" Samuel whistled. "You reckon that brother of 'ers is mixed up in this, then?"

"Up to his filthy neck," Hugo said softly. "And I am going to break every corrupt bone in his body. They've a six-hour start. If I'm right, Jasper's plans will be centered on the crypt." He was talking almost to himself as he maintained his fierce pace back to Mount Street. "Crispin and young DeLacy will be with him."

They wouldn't hurt her until after the wedding. If it was necessary, Jasper would use drugs to keep her quiet on the journey. He wouldn't risk drawing attention to his party by marking her in any visible way.

Drawing comfort from this conviction, he said briskly, "The lass doesn't have the stamina to ride from London to Shipton, so they'll be using a chaise. We should pick up the trail soon enough."

They had reached the house now and he ran up the steps. "Samuel, are you prepared to ride with me? It's a long haul, but we'll make better time than in a carriage."

"I'm with ye," Samuel said gruffly. "We startin' out now?"

"At dawn. They're bound to stop for the night, and if we ride all night, we'll only have to rest in the day. We'll leave at first light and pick up the trail at their first halt."

They seemed to have been bumping along in the ill-sprung chaise for hours. Late afternoon had given way to dusk, and the chill in the air intensified. No one had spoken for a long time.

Chloe sat slumped in her corner, every inch of her skin crawling with the awareness of Crispin beside her. Occasionally his thigh pressed hard against hers and she knew it was no accident. How could she face being married to him . . . sharing a bed with him . . . doing with him what she had done with Hugo? She felt sick and swallowed desperately, praying her body wouldn't betray her, wishing she had her hands. She felt so helpless without them.

She forced herself to think clearly, to examine her

position, hoping that focusing her mind would ease the panic. If they forced her into this marriage, what would happen? What would Hugo do? Could he do anything? People did get divorced. The king was trying to divorce Queen Caroline, although without much success. But it wasn't unheard of. Presumably Crispin would keep her fortune anyway, so perhaps he'd be willing to divorce her.

His thigh pressed against her again and she knew with sick revulsion that she was indulging a pipe dream. Crispin wouldn't let her go until he'd had enough of her. And not even Hugo would be able to persuade him otherwise.

What did he think had happened to her? It was well past dinnertime. Would he guess? But how could he? How could he possibly connect Denis with Jasper? He'd assume there'd been an accident of some kind and that she was taking shelter somewhere. It was not unusual with the roads as bad as they were after the snowstorm. He'd wait for a message . . . how long would he wait before he'd begin to worry in earnest?

"I can't feel my hands," she said in a small, fierce voice as she fought with her tears, determined not to break down in front of her captors.

"Would you like your wrists untied?" Jasper inquired almost casually, as if he were offering her a second helping at dinner.

"What do you think?" she snapped.

Her brother merely leaned back on the opposite seat and closed his eyes.

Chloe bit her lip. The ache in her arms was becoming unbearable and the lack of sensation in her hands was frightening. "Please," she said.

Jasper opened his eyes. "You are an ill-mannered brat," he observed. Leaning over, he caught her chin and examined her face in the fading light. "However, I intend to remedy that with all due speed. If you attempt to use your hands again in that fashion, you'll journey all the way to Shipton with your wrists bound day and night, do you understand?"

Chloe nodded. There seemed no alternative.

"Untie her." Jasper leaned back again and Crispin pulled her out of her corner, manhandling her across his lap again as he unfastened the cravat. His wandering hands were on her body, and she squeezed her eyes tightly, biting her lip hard to keep herself from screaming abuse at him, struggling to prevent herself from flying at him with nails and fists and feet.

But at last he released her and she sat up, shrinking back into her corner, massaging her wrists, her hands stinging with pain as the blood flowed back. She rolled her shoulders back to ease the knot between her shoulder blades and tried to think clearly.

When did they intend the wedding to take place? Presumably not until they reached Shipton. What methods of persuasion would Jasper use to get her to the altar? And how much could she endure?

She had no idea of the answer to the latter question and dismally decided that she would find out empirically soon enough.

It was full dark when the chaise drove into the courtyard of a small inn just outside St. Albans.

Jasper leaned forward again and again took Chloe's chin with hard fingers. Holding her face steady, he slapped her cheek once. It was not a particularly hard blow, but it was completely unexpected and the tears that sprang in her eyes were tears of shock rather than pain. Denis drew breath sharply and Crispin smiled.

"That's a reminder, little sister," Jasper said softly. "You will keep your eyes on the ground, your mouth shut, and if you take one step out of line, I will give you a beating you will remember for the rest of your life."

He didn't wait for a response, simply released her and jumped to the ground. The others followed, Chloe, still numb with shock, climbing down last. Jasper put his arm around her shoulders, turning her face toward his chest so that the mark of his hand on her left cheek couldn't be seen. The other two stepped close around him as the landlord bustled out to greet them.

"My sister is unwell," Jasper said. "I need two adjoining bedchambers and a private parlor."

The landlord bowed, his nose almost touching his knees, as he assured the travelers of the best his inn had to offer. "And my wife will be glad to assist the young lady to bed, sir," he said, moving backward toward the door. "A tisane should set her up nicely. Will you be wanting dinner, sirs? There's a shoulder of mutton with red currant sauce, and a compote of mushrooms, if it would please you."

Jasper didn't trouble to respond to this, merely followed their garrulous host upstairs to inspect the accommodations. He kept Chloe close to his side, and she made no attempt to move away. Two adjoining chambers, one with two big beds, the other with only one were presented and approved.

"No, my sister needs no assistance." Jasper declined the renewed offer of the landlady's help. "Just bring hot water to both chambers and have dinner on the table in half an hour. And bring up a bottle of your best burgundy," he called as the landlord rushed off.

"All right." He turned to his companions. "You two can have this chamber, my little sister and I will bear each other company in here." He pushed her ahead of him through the connecting door into the smaller of the two rooms.

"You're going to sleep in here with me?" Chloe managed finally to find words.

"Yes." It was a flat affirmative. Jasper glanced around the room and went to the window. The ivy was thick outside, certainly thick enough to bear Chloe's slight weight. "I'm not letting you out of my sight."

"I will not marry Crispin," Chloe said, finding her courage. But she flinched as Jasper crossed the room toward her.

He stopped in front of her and she tried to keep still, to meet his eye. But it was impossible to hold his gaze as his eyes slid over her. Her knees shook as she waited for another blow. Jasper read her expectation and then laughed.

"You'll do as I bid you," he said almost indifferently, turning away from her as a servant came in with the portmanteau that had been strapped to the roof of the chaise, followed by a maid with a jug of hot water. He waved them away impatiently, cutting off their offers of further assistance. "Just bring the burgundy."

"You'll find all the necessities in there," he told Chloe, gesturing to the portmanteau. "You may use the screen for privacy."

Chloe found tooth powder, hairbrushes, clean linen, and a nightdress in the portmanteau. The servant brought the burgundy while she was gathering together what she needed. She stood uncertainly, looking at her brother as he poured the wine. The connecting door between the two chambers was also open and she could hear Denis and Crispin moving about.

"Are you going to stay in here?"

"I told you you may use the screen," Jasper said, sipping wine. His eyes ran over her, and he said with a slight smile, "For as long as you behave yourself, I'll grant you that privacy for the rest of the journey. But don't test my clemency too far."

"Could you at least close the door?" She must keep calm, sound reasonable, refuse to be either intimidated or enraged by Jasper.

He glanced carelessly toward the open door. "What are you afraid of, little sister?"

"I'm not afraid," she declared stoutly. "But I'm accustomed to closing my bedroom door."

"Well, you may have to become accustomed to many new experiences." Jasper shrugged. "If you don't wish to refresh yourself, then I will do so myself."

Her need was too pressing to make a stand. Chloe whisked behind the screen. There was a commode and dressing table with mirror, basin, and ewer. Telling herself it was no more public than the retiring room at Almack's, she used the commode, bathed her face in warm water, brushed her hair, and smoothed down her dress. The marks on her cheek had faded, but there was a welt around her wrists where the cravat had bitten deep.

She couldn't afford that to happen again. Jasper had made it very clear that he would hurt her without compunction if she gave him an opportunity. The other two were acting under his authority, and she didn't sense that they would do anything unilateral, although when she thought of Crispin holding her down in the carriage, of his hands moving over her, she shuddered with a bone-deep revulsion. Jasper had permitted that. It was clear that she would have to endure some degree of humiliation, but if she pretended it wasn't happening, then she could manage not to react . . . she hoped.

Emerging from the screen, she asked neutrally, "May I have a glass of wine?"

"Certainly." He poured it for her. "Now, take it into the other chamber so Crispin and Denis may keep an eye on you while I refresh myself."

She shrugged with an appearance of nonchalance

and strolled into the connecting room. "Your pardon for disturbing you, gentlemen, but I understand you're to keep watch over me while Jasper is otherwise occupied."

Crispin and Denis were drinking wine by the fire. Unconsciously, Denis rose as she entered as if he were still in a fashionable drawing room. Crispin chuckled and Denis sat down again, flushing.

"Come here," Crispin commanded, snapping his fingers.

"I'm not a dog," Chloe said, deciding that Crispin could probably safely be defied . . . at least for the moment.

"I owe you a lot," Crispin said quietly, his hands going to his throat, remembering those steely fingers squeezing the life from him. "And I can promise you, Miss Gresham, that you will get everything that's due you."

"I don't doubt your intention, Crispin," she said coldly, leaning against the doorjamb as she sipped her wine. "But forgive me if I doubt your powers."

Crispin sprang up with an exclamation. She stood her ground, knowing that if she kept total silence, offered total submission, she would lose the will to endure. And when the time for true endurance came, she would need every fiber of will.

He gripped her shoulders and brought his mouth down on hers, grinding her lips against her teeth with savage violence. She tried to wrench her head sideways, tried to create enough space between their bodies to bring her knee up.

Then abruptly he let her go, looking sheepishly over her shoulder to where his stepfather stood in the doorway. Chloe gasped for breath, her lips stinging, every inch of her body throbbing with the sense of violation.

"She is insolent," Crispin declared with an air that

reminded Chloe of a schoolboy telling tales to escape censure.

"Really," Jasper said, holding up his wineglass to the light, subjecting the contents to an interested examination.

"Insolence goes without its dinner," he murmured indifferently. "But you will leave disciplinary measures to me in the future. Is that clear?"

Crispin flushed. "Yes, sir."

"Then let us go in to dinner . . . even those of us who will not partake." He took Chloe's arm and pushed her ahead of him across the corridor to the private parlor. "Sit down." He pulled out a chair for her in a parody of chivalry.

The promised shoulder of mutton sent up the most enticing aromas from the sideboard, filling the air with the scent of fresh rosemary. The compote of mushrooms, a bowl of red currant sauce, and a dish of roasted potatoes sat in the center of the table.

It was past nine o'clock and Chloe had eaten nothing since noon. It was one thing to be deprived of her dinner, she thought, battling with tears of rage and disappointment. Quite another to have to sit and watch while others consumed. The tormenting aromas set her saliva running, her stomach cleaving to her backbone.

Leaning back in her chair, she closed her eyes, folding her hands neatly in her lap, and took her mind out of the parlor and away from the company of her captors. It was not an entirely successful ploy from her own point of view, but at least it ensured her companions didn't have the satisfaction of her obvious discomfort.

But the ordeal was over at last. Back in their bedchamber, Jasper locked both doors and pocketed the keys. Chloe prepared for bed behind the screen. When she emerged in her nightgown, Jasper was standing in his britches by the fire. He'd pulled off his boots and was now unbuttoning his shirt. He tossed the garment aside and strode toward the bed.

Chloe stared at his chest . . . at the tiny coiled snake pricked into the skin above his heart.

"What the hell's the matter with you?" Jasper demanded, struck by her arrested expression. "I suppose you haven't seen a man without his shirt before. Well, you needn't worry, little sister, you stand in no danger from my bare chest."

"That—" Chloe said, her voice sounding strangled. She pointed at the device. "That . . . that snake . . . Hugo . . ."

"What?" Jasper gave a sudden crack of laughter. "Oh, so you've seen your esteemed guardian in a state of undress, have you? I suppose it's not surprising that drunken sot failed to observe the proprieties."

"Don't call him that!" Chloe said fiercely. "He is *not.*"

"Such a vehement defense." Jasper's voice was suddenly very soft, his eyes narrowed. "Now, whatever could Lattimer have done to earn such violent championship?"

"He was kind to me," Chloe stated, praying she wouldn't blush, that nothing would be revealed in her expression. Rushing her words, she demanded, "But why do you both have that snake?"

"Ahh, so Hugo didn't think to let you into his little secret," her brother mused. He gestured to the bed. "Get in."

"Are we sh-sharing the bed?"

"You will sleep in it, I will sleep on it," Jasper said impatiently. "Now, hurry up."

Chloe pulled back the sheet and slid between the covers. She lay on her back, very still.

Jasper lay down on the cover beside her. "Give me

your wrist." He had his belt in his hand and quite calmly fastened one end around Chloe's wrist and the other around his own.

"Now," he said softly, "I'll tell you a story, little sister. A bedtime story . . ."

Chapter 25

WHEN JASPER'S MESSENGER arrived at Mount Street at eight o'clock the following morning, Hugo and Samuel had been on the road for four hours. The letter with its seemingly innocuous information that Chloe was safe and sound in her brother's charge and on the way to Shipton lay on the hall table to await Hugo's return. Jasper was leaving nothing to chance. He wanted Hugo to pursue Chloe to the crypt, and if drink had addled his brains to such an extent that he failed to put two and two together on his own, his ward's captor would help him out.

Chloe had said almost nothing since she'd awakened, disoriented, in the cold dawn. For a few seconds she had no idea where she was. Her arm was stretched out away from her body and she tried to pull it back. Something tightened around her wrist. It all came back then. She turned her head on the pillow. Jasper seemed to be asleep beside her, but the belt was wound several times around his wrist and the tie clasped in his clenched fist.

She lay still again, remembering everything he'd told her last night. She had the secret now to Hugo's painted devils. Why hadn't he told her himself of the desperate part he'd played in her own life . . . how inextricably he was bound up in the coils that had determined her lonely childhood. Hadn't he trusted her enough? But of course she knew the real answer. He hadn't loved her enough. He hadn't loved her enough to trust her with his soul.

The manner of her father's death didn't overly trouble

her. Judging by Jasper's description of the Congregation's activities, Stephen Gresham's death was no great loss to the world. She minded much more about her mother . . . that Hugo hadn't told her he'd loved her mother with a love so deep and abiding that he was prepared to risk his life for her. If he'd told her everything, told her about her father—the kind of man he was —then she would have understood about her mother's withdrawal from the world. She would finally have understood why Elizabeth had seemed to reject her daughter. There would have been a reason for the bitter loneliness Chloe had endured throughout her childhood in the hands of indifferent caretakers, and she would have been able to lay to rest the bleak assumption that there was something lacking in herself that had made her unsuitable company for her mother.

But he hadn't cared enough for her to see that.

And it was all irrelevant now. Once she was wedded to Crispin, nothing would matter anymore. And Jasper was going to make that happen unless she could escape. But she felt small and powerless and knew herself to be so when pitted against the combined strengths and resources of her brother, his stepson, and Denis.

Feeling sick with hunger and in serious need of the commode, she pulled tentatively on the belt, hoping to wake her companion without giving him the impression she was trying to escape. She was not prepared to do or say anything that might result in the loss of her breakfast.

Jasper sat up in one movement. He was not disoriented. "What the hell do you think you're doing?"

"I'm sorry to wake you, but I need the commode," she said meekly.

He glanced at the clock. "It's time we were moving anyway." He released the belt from their wrists. "Hurry up and get dressed."

An hour later Chloe stood in the freezing courtyard, her breath steaming in the frigid air as they waited while the horses were put to the chaise. Denis stamped his booted feet and blew on his hands, rubbing them together for warmth. Crispin leaned against the wall of the inn, his mouth thinned with impatience at the fumbling of the ostlers' frozen fingers.

Chloe glanced toward Denis. For an instant his eyes lifted and met hers. Then he turned away with an abrupt movement of his head. This was the man with whom she'd danced and laughed, flirted and played silly games. And now he wouldn't even meet her eye. Guilt at his betrayal? Somehow Chloe doubted it. He was a member of the Congregation. He and Crispin would both have the snake pricked into the skin above the heart. Guilt was not something they would feel.

Escape would be impossible with all three of them watching her. Perhaps, if she offered no resistance or hint of provocation, even to the loathsome Crispin, she would lull them into complaisance. But she knew this was a forlorn hope.

She looked toward her brother. Jasper was not going to relax his vigilance. His mouth was a thin slash in the slight heaviness of his face, his jaw jutting aggressively as he cursed the slowness of the ostlers, slapping his silver-knobbed cane into the gloved palm of one hand.

Chloe shivered, and immediately he shot her a swift, appraising glance from his pale, shallow eyes. He knew she was frightened; even though she pretended she'd shivered with cold and huddled into her cloak, she hadn't deceived him. His mouth quirked with a sardonic satisfaction.

"Get in," he ordered, gesturing with his head to the chaise.

Chloe obeyed without an instant's hesitation and sat

in her corner, pulling the hood of her cloak over her head to cover her cold ears.

Jasper watched her through half-closed eyes. He hadn't expected her to be so compliant so quickly. From what he remembered of her as a child, she'd been stubborn and quick to anger; a passionate girl whose emotions were easily roused. He didn't think she'd changed that much, so this meek acceptance of her fate was interesting. He hadn't hurt her much. A few threats, an empty belly, and a couple of slaps were not enough to intimidate such an obstinate and emotional creature. Since severe physical punishment wasn't possible on such a public journey, when they were frequenting inns, he had intended to keep her sedated if necessary. No one would question a drowsy young woman being carried from a chaise. But so far she was making such a precaution unnecessary.

Chloe closed her eyes again. For some reason she felt less vulnerable, less exposed to them with her eyes shut. What did Hugo think had happened to her? Had Persephone taken to the wet nurse? Dante would be pining . . . had anybody remembered to let Demosthenes off his chain for a run in the yard? The stable hands were all terrified of him. . . . The desolate litany went around and around in her head as the chaise bore them north.

Hugo and Samuel picked up the trail at St. Albans at mid-morning. The landlord of the Red Lion, where they stopped for breakfast, informed them that three gentlemen and a young lady, the sister of one of the gentleman, had lodged overnight and left at eight o'clock that morning.

"How did the young lady seem to you?" Hugo gazed

into his coffee cup as if the question were of little importance.

"Quiet," the innkeeper said, filling a tankard of ale for Samuel. "She'd not been feelin' too well . . . them coaches can give a bumpy ride. But she ate an 'earty breakfast this mornin'."

"With anyone else, that'd be a good sign," Samuel remarked to no one in particular.

Hugo smiled faintly. Samuel's companionship was keeping him on an even keel. "When the horses have baited, we'll be on our way." He cut into his platter of sirloin.

"We'll likely catch 'em by nightfall," Samuel said quietly as the innkeeper bustled around the taproom. "If we change the 'orses in a couple of hours, we'll make much better time than a chaise."

"True enough, but I don't want to catch up with them," Hugo said.

"Oh?"

"I don't intend to catch them at all," Hugo said slowly. "It's time this tale came full circle, Samuel. Jasper and I have a meeting ahead and a long-delayed vengeance." His voice was quiet, the words without emphasis, but his companion felt the ice of conviction, the force of purpose, and he knew that this was the last thing remaining to restore Hugo Lattimer to full health and sanity.

"You're not afraid for the lass?"

"I know the role they have in mind for her," Hugo responded, his mouth hard, his eyes green glaciers. "They'll not harm her before then."

They stayed on the heels of the chaise all the way to Shipton. For all Hugo's apparent confidence that Chloe was in no immediate danger, Samuel noticed how drawn his face became when he asked the routine question at each stage of the trail: Had the young woman seemed well?

The answer was invariable. Quiet, travel weary, but nothing untoward.

As they rode into Lancashire, the air took on its familiar crisp clarity, the moorland stretched on either side of the road, the bleak winter brown hidden beneath a glistening coat of snow.

Samuel visibly relaxed as the terrain became familiar. His chin came up out of the folds of his muffler and his body moved more easily with the gait of his horse. Hugo, in contrast, tightened like a bowstring. He sniffed the air, his eyes moving restlessly from side to side as if on the watch for some predator.

They had kept two hours behind their quarry, staying in neighboring inns, so that at all times he felt close enough to Chloe to keep his anxiety in check. The knowledge that he only had to put spur to his horse and he would reach her enabled him to keep his head clear as he formulated and refined his plan.

It was four o'clock in the afternoon of the seventh day when they reached the turnoff to Shipton on the Manchester road. Hugo continued on the road to Denholm.

"Thought we was goin' to Shipton," Samuel commented.

"Tomorrow" was the short answer. Tomorrow night was Friday. Only on Fridays was the crypt used. Jasper wouldn't wait for another week. He'd be assuming that Hugo would at some point put two and two together and he'd want Chloe irrevocably tied to Crispin before there could be any possibility of interference.

The chaise drew up on the gravel sweep before Gresham Hall. The surge of energy that went through the three men was palpable to the still figure, huddled in her cloak in the corner of the vehicle. Terror threatened to overwhelm her. There had been no opportunities for escape. She had been watched constantly and each night slept tethered to her brother. At least Crispin had kept his distance and she'd managed to avoid further punishment at Jasper's chillingly insouciant hands.

But now they were on Jasper's land, surrounded by his people. There were no strangers to tell tales, no reins he need put upon his actions.

The footstep was lowered and Jasper jumped down. "Out!" he beckoned Chloe.

She moved to obey. Crispin unnecessarily put a hand in the small of her back and pushed her so she half fell down the steps. Jasper caught her, and it occurred to her with a fresh surge of terror that only he stood between herself and Crispin's unbridled appetite for cruelty. Jasper was vicious, but it was purposeful. Crispin enjoyed inflicting pain for its own sake.

She hadn't been inside Gresham Hall since she was a child, but it seemed as oppressive as ever when she stepped into the hall. The air was musty. Though Denholm Manor had also been unkempt and neglected, it had felt different. Or perhaps it was only her experiences of the two houses that was so different.

"Jasper . . ."

A tentative voice came from the shadows behind the stairs, and Louise moved hesitantly into the dim afternoon light. "Chloe . . . I didn't know . . ."

"Don't be a fool, of course you knew," her husband snapped, pulling off his gloves. "I told you to have the west attic chamber prepared."

"Yes . . . but . . . but you didn't say why." Louise wrung her hands, gazing at the still figure of her half sister-in-law. "Chloe dear . . ." She held out her hands in a ludicrous gesture of welcome.

"Louise." Chloe inclined her head in brief acknowledgment. She knew no evil of Jasper's wife, but then, she knew no good of her either. A passive partner in evil was still an enemy.

"You must make your farewells to Denis, little sister," Jasper said, mockery lacing his voice. "You'll not see him again until your wedding night. After such a close friendship, I know you'll wish to bid him farewell with all due courtesy."

Chloe didn't deign to reply, but she stared full into Denis's eyes, hoping that he could read her contempt. He had that rather smug smile on his face again and an anticipatory gleam in his eye that brought a resurgence of the cold fear she fought so desperately to keep below the surface of her thoughts.

"Crispin, take her up and lock her in." It was a sharp order.

So now Crispin was to come into his own. Chloe swallowed hard and stiffened her spine as Crispin seized her arm. "I don't need help," she said clearly. "I'm quite capable of mounting the stairs alone."

"Move." He twisted her arm behind her back and she bit her lip on the pain, moving ahead of him without another word.

"Come straight down." Jasper spoke from the hall when they were halfway up the stairs, and relief washed through her. Jasper had not yet abdicated control.

The west attic chamber was a small room under the eaves with a grimy round dormer window. The other attics in the west wing were all used for storage, and when the sound of Crispin's feet had faded from the passage, Chloe could hear no signs of life at all.

The room held a poster bed, a dresser, an armless chair. There was cold water in the ewer, a chamber pot beneath the bed.

So now what? She sat down on the bed and wished she had Dante with her. She'd never felt as alone as she did now. Even in the lonely wasteland of her childhood there'd been animals . . . always someone worse off than she was. Now there was nothing.

Tears tracked down her cheeks, and for a while she indulged them. Then she heard steps in the corridor outside. She hastily rose to her feet, splashed water on her face, and sat in the chair, her face turned toward the window so the traces of tears wouldn't be immediately visible to whoever entered.

It was Jasper, accompanied by a servant, who put down the portmanteau she'd used on the journey. He left immediately, closing the door. Jasper turned the key and stood regarding his sister for a moment.

"Louise will find you a change of clothes," he said. "Otherwise, you have everything you need."

"Thank you," she said, hearing how ridiculous it sounded.

"Let me make a few things clear to you." He came over to her chair. "Stand up."

Chloe did so. What choice did she have?

"Look at me."

That was harder. She didn't want him to see the tracks of her tears. Then Jasper made it simple. He slapped her face again and any tears could be easily explained. She raised her head and looked at him.

"That's better. Tomorrow evening, you will be married to Crispin—"

"No!" She winced in expectation of another blow, but it didn't come.

"Don't interrupt," he said in an almost bored tone. "As I was saying, tomorrow evening you will be married to Crispin. Afterward, you will be presented in the crypt, as your mother was. What she failed to do, you, her daughter, will make up for. It is the way of the Congregation," he added with a rich note of conviction. "We do not leave things unfinished, and I've waited nigh on fifteen years to fulfill the obligation.

"After that . . ." He shrugged. "That's for Crispin to decide. Your fortune will pass into his hands, and thus into my hands, as it should have done on the death of my father. Somehow, your mother managed—" He stopped abruptly, but the ugliness of his expression remained. Elizabeth, the innocent, the fool, had somehow outmaneuvered both her husband and his son.

"You will take your mother's place," he resumed, "and fulfill your mother's obligations with one difference. It will be the consummation of your marriage and Crispin will take your virginity. That is all." He turned from her.

"Not quite," Chloe said, unsure why she was speaking except that she had a desperate need to puncture her brother's calm assurance. "Crispin cannot take my virginity. It's not there to be taken."

"What!" Jasper spun around, his expression astounded. "What the hell are you talking about? You've been living in a goddamned nunnery since you were seven." A speculative gleam appeared in the cold eyes. "And since then you've been safe and sound in the care of Hugo Lattimer, haven't you?" he said slowly.

Throwing back his head, he laughed with rich enjoyment. "So that explains your vigorous championship. No wonder you know about the snake on his chest. Well . . . well . . . well . . . the self-righteous drunkard isn't so pure after all. He debauched you, did he? The innocent maiden left to his care by the woman he'd sworn to love to eternity."

"He did not debauch me." Chloe's voice was low but fierce.

Jasper shook his head, still chuckling. "He hasn't changed at all. Well, that does add a fascinating dimension to tomorrow night's revels. Lattimer's interest will be all the keener when he watches your initiation."

Chloe had paled. "Watches . . . ? What do you mean? How can he watch when he's not here."

"Oh, he will be," Jasper assured her with calm conviction. "If he left as soon as he received my message, he should arrive hotfoot at the crypt just as the ceremony begins. And we shall have a pleasant reception for him . . . and a most unpleasant and utterly final conclusion." His mouth smiled, but the pale eyes were voids. He left her.

Chloe paced the small space. She was not frightened for herself anymore, she realized. Instead, she was filled with a surging energy and determination to do something to effect her escape. She'd been passive for too long. If Hugo was coming—and he would be if he knew where she was—then there was hope, but also the desperate need now to ensure that he didn't fall into Jasper's trap. She had to escape and warn Hugo before he reached Shipton. But how?

Her eyes searched the room for inspiration. The attic was too high up for escape through the window, even if she could squeeze through the tiny aperture. Perhaps she could start a fire, and when they opened the door, she could slip out under cover of the smoke? But supposing they didn't smell the smoke? How long would it take for a fire in this isolated part of the house to become noticeable downstairs? Too long. She'd be suffocated by the time they reached her.

The only chance was to escape when the door was opened. If she could win enough time to get out into the corridor and lock the door behind her, then she'd have a chance. It was a slim one, but all that was available.

The only object heavy enough was the chair. She lifted it over her head with an effort. But it could be done. She positioned the chair behind the door and sat down on the bed to await her next visitor.

Her ears, straining into the silence, caught the sound of footsteps as they ascended the stairs at the end of the corridor. She darted behind the door and lifted the chair. The blood thudded in her ears and her heart pounded against her rib cage as if it would burst from her body. The key grated in the lock. The door swung open.

In the same instant, she sprang out and slammed the chair down on Crispin's head as he stepped inside. He yelled and fell to his knees. Chloe leapt behind him and out of the door . . . and straight into the arms of her brother.

Jasper said nothing, simply lifted her off the ground and thrust her back into the room. Crispin was rubbing his head, blinking in bemusement. But he rose to his feet immediately as Jasper hauled Chloe to the foot of the bed.

"Give me your cravat!" Jasper commanded crisply as he yanked his prisoner's arms high above her head. Crispin handed him the strip of linen. "Hold her arms." His stepson obeyed as Jasper twisted the material into a thin, strong rope and tied Chloe's wrists to the frame of the tester.

The next second she screamed as he brought his riding whip down once across her shoulders. Catching her hair, he pulled her head back and spoke softly against her ear. "I warned you, little sister." And then they were gone and the key turned in the lock.

She didn't know how long she hung there, her arms at full stretch, her toes supporting her weight. The pain of the whip cut faded to a dull ache and was soon canceled by the strain in her extended arms. The light faded from the room as dusk fell and she retreated from her body's pain, her mind taking refuge in some dark corner of her self.

It was full darkness when footsteps pierced her trance and the door opened. Jasper entered carrying a candle and a tray. He set them on the dresser and bent to pick up the fallen chair. Then he approached the still figure.

"I assume you've had sufficient time to reflect," he observed, slicing through her bonds with a knife. Chloe toppled forward onto the bed as her arms fell to her sides and her aching toes gave way. "You'll receive no more visitors until tomorrow," Jasper continued, going to the door, adding with faint mockery, "Sleep well."

Chloe rolled over onto her back as the door closed. The soft glow of the candle was comforting, and she lay for a long time, returning to a full sense of herself and the room around her. Her body ached in every limb, every muscle as sore as if she'd been in a prizefight. She wasn't seriously hurt. But she was most seriously warned.

After a while she got up and examined the tray. There was half a loaf of bread and a mug of milk—cold, punitive fare, but it was better than nothing. She ate a little dry bread and finished the milk, then crept fully clothed under the covers. Undressing seemed dangerous for some reason, as if in her nightgown she'd be even more vulnerable.

Hugo would come to find her. He wouldn't abandon her to Jasper. He didn't love her, but he wouldn't desert her. Pride, if nothing else, would bring him. And he'd walk into Jasper's trap. Hugo didn't love her and so her own future was immaterial now. But she loved him and could not bear his death.

Seven miles away, in Denholm Manor, Hugo sat with Samuel over the fire in the kitchen, explaining his plan and Samuel's role in it. But every now and again his voice faded and a haunted expression flashed across his eyes. Several times he got up and strode to the door, opened it, and stared out into the darkness, listening.

"What is it?"

"I don't know, Samuel. I just feel Chloe. I can feel her fear," he said. "But I can't do anything about it at the moment . . . I miss that damned dog," he added, slamming the door. "In fact, the whole godforsaken menagerie."

"I know what you mean," Samuel said. "It's kind of quiet wi'out 'em." He stood up. "Can you sleep?"

"No." Hugo shook his head. "I'm going to play. It won't disturb you?"

"Never 'as done before," Samuel said, going to the door. "I'm fer me bed, then." Only once had it disturbed him, he remembered as he climbed the stairs. During that dreadful time when Hugo had wrestled with his demons and his addiction and those terrifying discordant notes had filled the long night hours. He lay in bed, listening intently to the sounds of the piano—the sounds that would give him an insight into Hugo's state of mind.

Hugo played the lullaby he'd once played for Chloe, on the night of the stable fire. He played it as if she could hear it and be soothed and comforted by it. Did she know how close he was? He tried with his music to tell her, as if the sounds would carry on the crisp, clear night air the seven miles across the valley. Was she sleeping? He prayed she was.

> . . . *The innocent sleep,*
> *Sleep that knits up the ravell'd sleeve of*
> *care,*
> *The death of each day's life, sore labour's*
> *bath,*

*Balm of hurt minds, great nature's second
    course,
Chief nourisher in life's feast.*

He remembered how she'd completed his quote that day when she'd only just come into his life—a life ruled by the painted devils. Tomorrow night he would lay them finally to rest.

He played on throughout the night.

Chapter 26

CHLOE AWOKE STIFF and cold despite her clothes. There was no fire in the attic room and sleet had begun to fall, coating the grimy window and filling the cheerless room with a cold gray light.

She got up and went to wash her face. The water in the ewer was frozen solid. The remains of the loaf on the tray were dry and stale. Hungry and thirsty, with no way of alleviating either condition, she returned to bed, huddling beneath the covers in an effort to keep warm.

It was many hours later before she heard footsteps on the stairs and the key turned in the lock. Jasper and Crispin came in. Neither of them spoke to her as they approached the bed and stood looking down at her white face on the pillow, all that was visible of her body. She stared up at them, reading cold indifference in Jasper's face, hungry anticipation in Crispin's, and for the life of her she couldn't decide which was the most frightening.

"Sit up and drink this," Jasper finally said, holding out the cup he held.

"What is it?" She made no move to obey.

"That is not something you need to know. Sit up."

"I'm hungry and cold," she said.

"Soon you won't be," he returned. "Sit up. I won't tell you again."

Slowly, she struggled up on the pillows and took the cup. Its contents were thick and syrupy, giving off a strange and repulsive odor. "I don't want it," she said, turning her head away, holding the cup out to him.

Jasper said nothing. He took the cup and handed it to Crispin. Then he sat on the bed and caught Chloe's head in the crook of his arm, forcing it back. She was tightly wrapped in the bedcovers and couldn't free her limbs as she struggled violently. He held her head in a vise and took the cup from Crispin.

"Open her mouth."

Crispin's fingers brutally pulled her mouth open and the evil-smelling liquid slid down her throat. With her head tipped back as it was, she had no choice but to swallow. Crispin clamped her jaws shut and she thought she was going to suffocate. And then they released her.

"You are a little fool," Jasper said. "You have nothing to gain by resistance."

They went out and left her alone again. She fell back on the pillows, numbed with shock, tears streaming unheeded down her cheeks. A foul taste was in her mouth, like bitter aloes, and she was abruptly reminded of the potion Hugo had given her. That hadn't tasted as bad, but the herbal quality had been the same.

What was this one supposed to do? It wasn't poison. They wouldn't poison her when they had such plans for her. She lay in terror, waiting for something to happen. When it did, it took her by surprise. Her body began to feel warm and relaxed, her head slightly muzzy, but it wasn't an unpleasant sensation at all. She was no longer hungry or even particularly thirsty and soon drifted into a light-headed doze filled with a sequence of soft-edged dreams.

She lost all sense of time and, when her door opened again, looked with fuzzy lack of curiosity at her visitors. Louise's anxious face hung over her like a moon in a mist, and Chloe smiled reassuringly, or thought she did.

"Come along, dear, it's time to dress," Louise said. Her voice sounded a little peculiar, but Chloe let the speculation slip from her. She tried to sit up and the maid who had accompanied Louise moved to help her.

Her head swam and the room tilted violently. A wave of nausea washed over her and she fell back again. "No, I'll stay here," she said faintly.

"You can't, dear." Louise sounded almost desperate. "Once you sit up, it'll be better." She tugged at Chloe's arm, and because she sounded so unhappy, Chloe made one more effort. This time the room stopped spinning once she opened her eyes wide.

She submitted to being undressed and her body washed in warm water from a steaming copper jug. They brushed and rebraided her hair, fastening the braids in a coronet around her head. She tried to help her attendants, but her limbs were too heavy to lift and her mind kept slipping sideways so she forgot what it was she'd intended to do. But nothing seemed to matter. The room wasn't even cold anymore.

They dressed her in a white silk shift that covered her body from neck to ankles, white silk stockings gartered above the knees, white satin pumps. Vaguely she was aware that some article of underwear was missing, but the recognition simply flitted through her untroubled brain. Finally, Louise slipped over her head a white silk gown with long sleeves and a high, ruffled collar and the maid pinned a diaphanous veil onto the golden crown of her hair.

"How lovely you are," Louise said, her voice thick with tears as she gazed at the vision . . . the sacrifice she had prepared for her son. She tried to tell herself that Crispin would make a good husband, that Chloe was making a perfectly good match, one that many girls would give their eyeteeth for. Maybe she wasn't too eager, but what young girl was? It wasn't a love match, but such connections were rare these days and they were young; they could grow together.

All brides suffered from wedding nerves. She tried to pretend she didn't know why Chloe's eyes were blank, her movements sluggish. It was just wedding nerves.

"Come downstairs, dear."

Chloe allowed herself to be led out of her prison and down the stairs into the hall. She felt as if she were moving through some kind of filmy curtain, her feet making tentative contact with the ground as if it were made of sponge. There were people in the hall, their faces moving in and out of her field of vision.

"Behold the virgin bride." Jasper stepped up to her, his voice suddenly low. "What a vision of purity, little sister. But you and I know better." The open mockery made no dent in the warm, muzzy world she was inhabiting. In truth, she hardly heard him. He took her arm, placing her hand on his own arm, and they began to walk across the hall as the carefully selected wedding guests fell back . . . guests who bore the mark of Eden on their skin. Later they would accompany the bridal couple to the crypt in the time-honored rituals of the Congregation.

Louise moved into the shadows at the rear. She knew Jasper expected her to make herself scarce, but a mother was surely entitled to witness her only son's marriage.

The Reverend Elgar Ponsonby stood before a table, his hands nervously caressing the smooth leather·binding of a Bible. His clerical linen was limp and slightly spotted. His eyes were unfocused, his breath pure alcohol, it seemed to Crispin, standing beside him as he watched the progress of his bride and his stepfather. Old Elgar was never sober, and only Sir Jasper's purse kept bread and wine on his table.

Jasper removed Chloe's hand from his arm as they reached the table and placed it on Crispin's. As she felt Crispin's hand close over hers, Chloe looked up through the gauzy material of her veil at his face hovering in the air in front of her. Unease filtered through the rosy mists of unthinking. She was being married to Crispin. Jasper had said so and that was what was supposed to happen.

But it wasn't supposed to happen. It mustn't be allowed to happen. The passionate conviction thrust through the trance and for a second she was aware of her surroundings, of the people around her. She could smell the woodsmoke from the fireplace, the hot candle wax. Her lips moved beneath the veil as if to form some shout of protest, some screaming appeal to the shapes around her. But nothing would come. And then the moment of lucidity was gone and the warm muzziness had returned. She smiled vaguely and obediently stepped up to the table beside Crispin.

Hugo stood outside the closed door to the crypt. The ghosts seemed to come out to meet him as he postponed the moment when he would take the key from its secret shelf under the lintel, open the door, and go inside, down the shallow flight of stone stairs into the labyrinth of cold, vaulted chambers smelling of earth and mold and the grave.

Samuel stood beside him, patiently waiting. It was late afternoon and a flock of rooks circled noisily overhead before settling in a black cloud onto the gaunt branches of a nearby copse. The sleet had stopped, but the darkening sky was still heavy with snow clouds and the wind raced achingly cold across the moor.

"A bit cheerless, this is," Samuel observed matter-of-factly. "We goin' to stand out 'ere till we turn to stone?"

"I'm sorry," Hugo said. He reached under the lintel and his fingers unerringly found the little slot. It was as if he'd been here yesterday. He pulled out the great brass key and fit it into the lock. The door yawned open onto the darkness and the smell came out and hit him. How was it that once that smell had excited him, had been redolent with the exultant sense of things unknown and forbidden? But only on that last occasion had he gone down into the crypt in full possession of his senses . . . in full awareness of the evil that the excitement had masked.

Samuel lit the lantern he carried, and together they went inside, Hugo pulling the door to behind them. It was unlikely there were any watchers, but it wasn't worth taking unnecessary risks. He closed his mind to the memories, concentrating only on what had to be done.

"Gawd 'elp us," Samuel muttered as they descended to the crypt. "What kind of an 'ell'ole is this?"

"You may well ask," Hugo said, welcoming Samuel's prosaic commentary. He stood in the vaulted central chamber, holding the lantern high. Everything was in readiness for the night's ceremonies; fresh altar candles planted in the holders around the bier, the torches newly filled with pitch in their sconces on the walls. The bier was spread with a white damask cloth, a thick pillow at its head. On the long, low table against the far wall stood the flagons of wine, the little pots of herbal magic, the clay pipes for the opium.

He stood very still and let it come back to him. He had to face it if he was to overcome it. He closed his eyes and the room filled with the whispering ghosts of ecstasy and laughter. Limbs twined before his internal vision and on his tongue lingered the bitter aftertaste of the little pellets that sent a man into a world of pleasure beyond imagining as he moved between the smooth white thighs of his partner.

Did Jasper intend giving Chloe the drug before she took her place on the bier? Such an enhancement of pleasure for one normally so passionate would be beyond words. . . .

"Over here." He spun on his heel and strode to a dark hole in the far wall. The lantern illuminated the smaller chamber beyond. Samuel followed him up a rough-hewn flight of steps carved into the wall. At the top they opened onto a narrow stone gallery overlooking the crypt. "I'll be up here," Hugo said quietly, looking down at the bier.

He took a pair of épées from Samuel and rested them carefully against the low rail of the gallery. On the ledge he placed a narrow box containing two dueling pistols. Silently, he checked the other pistol in his belt, ran his finger down the sharp blade of a cutlass before returning it to the sheath resting snug against his thigh.

"Quite a little armory ye've got," Samuel remarked with satisfaction. He knew Hugo's skill with both sword and pistol, just as he knew how cold and clear he was under fire. A one-man army, he would wait in ambush and spring his surprise attack with all the careful calculation of a tried campaigner.

"Take your place outside now," Hugo said, handing him the key. "You saw where to put this?"

"Aye." Samuel took the key and the lantern. "Powerful dark it'll be once I've gone."

"It doesn't matter," Hugo said. "You know what to do?"

"Aye," Samuel repeated as phlegmatically as before. "I'll be off, then."

Hugo sat on the stone floor, resting his back against the wall, watching as the flickering light of the lantern retreated. He heard the dull thud as the door closed behind Samuel and he was alone in the darkness. He closed his eyes and emptied his mind of all but the certainty of success.

· · ·

"You may kiss the bride," old Elgar mumbled, heaving an audible sigh of relief at the knowledge that he'd somehow muddled successfully through the service.

Crispin slowly lifted Chloe's veil. His face came close to hers, and suddenly she could see him clearly, every feature sharply defined, just as his mouth came down on hers. A nameless terror chased away the warm languor of indifference, and with a dreadful rush of insight she understood what had happened. She pushed against Crispin, her eyes opening wide, her clear gaze fixed on the Reverend Ponsonby behind her husband.

Crispin drew back, aware of the change in her. Her heart thudded with fear and immediately she dropped her gaze and let her arms lie still at her sides.

"It's wearing off," he whispered urgently to his stepfather over Chloe's head.

Jasper took her arm and drew her away from the makeshift altar. Chloe was now aware that what she had perceived through the mists as a crowd was in fact only a small group of men.

"We must give her some more," Crispin was whispering as they moved to the side of the hall.

Jasper caught her chin and lifted it. He gazed fixedly at her face. Chloe fought the awareness from her eyes. It was easier than it might have been since she still seemed to have only a tenuous hold on reality. She only knew that she must prevent having that liquid poured down her throat again.

"Too much will defeat the object," Jasper said quietly. "We don't want her cataleptic. She's not eaten properly for two days and the mixture is much more potent on an empty belly."

Chloe let her eyes wander and a vague smile touched her lips.

Jasper released her face. "She's all right. I'll give her something else when we begin."

Chloe drifted over to a settle beside the massive inglenook fireplace and sat down. Her head was beginning to ache and she felt nauseated, but her senses were returning so fast now, they seemed to be tumbling over themselves as full awareness flooded her. She had been married to Crispin. She was Crispin's wife. Till death.

She kept her eyes down, her hands twisting idly in her silken lap. A spark of firelight caught the sinuous golden twists of the coiled serpent ring they'd put on her finger. Nothing mattered any longer in the face of the fact embodied in the perverted wedding ring. Except Hugo . . . Hugo was to walk into a trap when they took her to the crypt. He would be forced to watch the ceremony of her initiation and then Jasper would kill him. For herself, the crypt didn't matter. She was condemned to a life as Crispin's wife . . . his prisoner . . . what else happened to her mattered not a jot. But she must try to help Hugo. If they believed her still drugged, she might have a chance.

She let her head fall back against the settle and closed her eyes. Let them think she was dozing again.

Around her the buzz of noise increased in volume and she lost all sense of time, and then she heard Jasper's voice against her ear. "Come, little sister, it's time to prepare for your wedding night."

Samuel moved his cold-numbed limbs and took a swig of brandy from his flask. Then he heard the sound of voices. A wavering light fell across the path beyond his hiding place. Boots crunched on the icy ground.

Two men appeared. At the door of the crypt, one of them reached up. Then the door swung open and the two disappeared with their lantern.

Inside, Hugo came alert at the first sound of the key in the door above. He edged farther back against the wall, although he knew he wouldn't be visible from below. He listened as the two men lit the pitch torches and the altar candles and their light threw giant shadows up onto the vaulted ceiling.

One of the men was Denis DeLacy. He poured wine into a crystal flagon and drank deeply, his eyes roaming over the bier. He opened one of the little pots and shook a small pinch of herbs onto the palm of his hand. He put his tongue to it and licked, waiting for the crackle to start in his head.

Outside, Samuel waited. Then there were more voices, more light, and a group of men came down the path. A shrouded figure walked in their midst and the lantern caught the glimmer of white beneath the cloak and the deep golden radiance of her hair.

Tension ripped through Samuel with a surge of almost unmanageable fury. He breathed long and slow until he had himself in control again. All but two men entered the crypt.

Those two, pistols in their hands, moved to either side of the entrance, each taking up a position in the thick bushes.

They were awaiting the arrival of Hugo Lattimer.

Samuel waited until the deep night silence of the countryside had reasserted itself after the flurry of arrival. Then he moved. He moved like a sylph made of air, belying his size.

The first man didn't know what had hit him when the flat edge of a hand chopped at the base of his skull. He went down into the underbrush without a murmur. The second man half turned as the dark bulk of a figure sprang at him. His finger slipped on the trigger of his pistol, a cry, strangled at birth, broke from his lips as the hand chopped at his throat and he went down like his partner.

Samuel eased open the heavy door to the crypt. He

slid through the narrowest gap he could manage and then crouched in the shadows at the top of the stairs. He held a pistol in each hand, a wicked double-bladed knife in a sheath in his boot. He could hear the voices from below clearly.

Chloe stood still in the middle of the chamber. Her eyes darted surreptitiously from side to side as she took in her surroundings. This was the place that had created Hugo's painted devils. The evil miasma of the place rose up from the tombstone slabs of the floor, seemed to writhe out of the stone walls with the serpentine flickering of the pitch torches. This was the place where Hugo had killed her father.

For some reason she wasn't frightened. The last residues of the drug she'd been given had vanished and she was as clear-headed as she'd ever been. Even her hunger had disappeared, although she was conscious of a void inside her. But it was a void that seemed to create the energy that thrummed in her veins, infusing her mind and body.

When would Hugo come? She had to save him. It was the only thought, the only purpose, and since she had no plans, she must rely on instinct and circumstance as they arose.

Someone was taking the cloak from her shoulders. A rapt silence fell as she stood in her pure white gown with her golden hair, now loosened, falling about her shoulders.

Then Hugo spoke, his voice echoing in the silence. "It seems we finally come to a meeting, Jasper."

They all looked upward. Hugo, in his shirt-sleeves, swung one leg over the narrow rail of the gallery. He held the two épées in one hand. With a twist of his wrist he sent one of them spinning down.

Automatically, Jasper reached up and caught the hilt in his gloved hand.

In stunned silence but as if under the command of one will, the group of men moved backward against the wall. Chloe was at first thunderstruck, then filled with a wild exultation. Hugo had set his own trap.

Suddenly Jasper laughed. "I wasn't expecting you to be ahead of me, Lattimer. I forgot that you're now a model of sobriety and clear-thinking. An oversight—and a pity . . . as I had your reception so well prepared. However—" He raised his épée in a fencer's salute. "As you say, we have unfinished business. Let us finish it."

Hugo swung his other leg over the gallery rail and jumped down. It was a long jump, but he landed easily on the balls of his stocking feet—a man who'd spent many years climbing the rigging of a ship of the line.

"I've pistols, if you prefer," he offered courteously, watching as Jasper also shrugged out of his coat.

"No . . . no . . ." Jasper said calmly, bending to pull off his boots. "It should be done according to ritual, as always."

"And according to ritual, the honor of the woman falls to the victor."

"Exactly so."

Chloe understood what was happening; Jasper's bedtime story had left nothing out, and she knew all the details of the rules and rituals of the Congregation. Hugo was fighting for her as he'd fought for her mother. If he won, then she would never have to take her place in the crypt again. If he lost . . . but then nothing would matter. If he lost, he would be dead. The duels of the Congregation were always mortal combat.

Crispin was hissing through his teeth, his body very close to Chloe's. Hugo suddenly turned to look at Chloe for the first time. "Go and stand on the stairs, lass," he instructed in even tones.

"But I—"

"Do it!"

For once she obeyed immediately, and as she reached the stairs understood the reason for the order. Samuel was standing in the darkness behind her. Hugo was not going to play by the rules. Even if he lost, she would not be abandoned to the Congregation.

The two men saluted each other. Then Hugo said softly, "En garde." He lunged in a straight thrust and Jasper parried in quarte. The blades met and disengaged.

Chloe watched with a numb and dreadful fascination as the two men danced over the tombstone slabs, their blades glimmering, flashing with an almost impossible speed, moving from one position to another in a rapid series of attacks and counterattacks as they probed for an opening in their opponent's guard. It seemed to her that neither man held the attack for more than one engagement, as each attack was parried, the defender became the attacker.

Ten . . . fifteen . . . twenty minutes it went on, and it seemed impossible that any man could maintain such speed and accuracy for another second.

Finish it . . . please God, finish it. The prayer went around and around in Chloe's head. She could feel their growing fatigue amid the desperate clashing of invincible wills . . . the desperate purpose that fueled them both . . . the terrifying knowledge of imminent death.

Then came a moment when Hugo seemed to fall back on one knee, his free hand grazing the floor, then he sprang upright as Jasper's blade thrust beneath his arm, twisting sideways so the deadly attack met only air. His own blade caught his opponent's and the ring of steel echoed in the hushed vault. Hugo offered a feint to his opponent's forearm, and as Jasper jumped back to gather for a reprise, Hugo's blade came down and under.

Jasper fell to his knees, his blade clattering to the ground. Blood welled from his side.

Crispin with a frenzied hiss leapt forward, grabbing up his stepfather's weapon. His salute was perfunctory. "En garde."

Hugo didn't seem to draw breath. He parried his new opponent's attack smoothly, moving backward, allowing Crispin to press the attack as he assessed the skill of the younger man. He knew he was exhausted. Just as he knew that for one almost fatal second he had allowed himself to believe he'd won and it was over. Now he had to face the knowledge that it was far from over.

Chloe gasped in horror at this villainous intervention. She gazed around the room, waiting for someone to protest, to call a halt to such an infamously unfair fight. But they all remained still, watching closely. Denis was licking his lips almost convulsively in his anxiety, and once his eyes darted across to her, predatory and filled with hungry anticipation.

Hugo moved backward, invited a thrust in sixte, counterattacked to Crispin's left shoulder, lunged as his opponent feinted, and saw the épée snaking into his forearm too quickly to evade. It sliced through his shirt, nicking the skin. It was no fatal strike, but it was a deadly warning.

Chloe's heart seemed lodged somewhere in her throat, so she could hardly breathe. Her eyes raced around the crypt. Now no one seemed interested in her; their eyes were all fixed on the lethal combat. Jasper had been pulled to the side of the crypt and someone was staunching his wound. His eyes were closed and his labored breathing was an audible accompaniment to the ring of steel on steel.

She began to sidle around the wall until she stood against the strange, damask-covered, candlelit table. She licked the finger and thumb of one hand, slipped the hand behind her, and pinched out the flame of one of the candles. Then slowly she brought the heavy candlestick down to her side. All eyes were still on the two men locked in their mortal struggle.

She inched forward again. Sweat glistened on Hugo's brow; his face was drawn in a rictus of determination and exhaustion. Both men's movements were slowing perceptibly, but Crispin maintained the edge, pressing his attack.

Hugo felt now as he imagined Stephen had felt, facing his inevitable defeat at the hands of a younger, stronger man. But Crispin was not stronger . . . just younger and fresher. He tried to hang on to that, to keep at bay the destructive forces of hopelessness, but the blood was thundering in his head and his lungs screamed for air.

Chloe calmly, casually, put out her foot, catching Crispin's ankle as he lunged in full extension. He lost his balance, and as he swayed, she brought the candlestick down on his head. He fell sideways to the floor and lay still.

There was a moment of total silence, then Samuel, pistols in hand, appeared at the foot of the stairs. He leveled his weapons at the assembly in general and nodded curtly. "I shouldn't move if I were you, sirs."

Hugo doubled over, struggling for breath as the men in the crypt stared between Samuel and Chloe, still standing over the fallen Crispin.

"Have I killed him?" Chloe asked into the silence.

Hugo straightened slowly. "You don't play by the rules, do you, lass?" he gasped as his lungs expanded and he drew a deep shuddering breath.

"I wasn't going to let him kill you," Chloe said. "Of all the underhanded tricks."

"Shameful, I agree," he said dryly, bending over the

fallen Crispin, feeling for the pulse in his neck. "And I suppose one underhanded trick deserves another. At least you seem to have stopped short of murder."

"But he has to be dead," she said in a voice that now didn't seem to be her own. She lifted the candlestick again. "I'm married to him, and I would prefer to be his widow."

Hugo caught her arm. "Steady now, lass." He spoke quietly but firmly as he twisted the candlestick out of her grip.

"But you don't understand—"

"Yes, I do," he interrupted, picking up the cloak they had taken off her earlier. "Put this on." He wrapped the cloak around her shoulders and lightly kissed her brow. "Trust me, lass."

Jasper stirred and his eyes fluttered open. "Lattimer?" His voice was a thread.

Hugo crossed over to him. He stood over his fallen enemy and spoke with slow, deliberate clarity. "It's done, Jasper. Finished. The circle is completed. The girl is mine."

"And has been for quite some time, I understand." Blood trickled from the corner of Jasper's mouth as he moved his lips in the travesty of a mocking grin. "For all your self-righteous posturing, Lattimer, you debauched her. You're no better than the rest of us."

Hugo stood very still, his face white in the candle glow, but his voice was low and even. "Of course you would see it in those terms, wouldn't you, Jasper? You seek only to sully and you would see only defilement in love." His shoulders lifted in a dismissive shrug. "I've done finally with you and yours . . . and with this sewer."

His eyes ran around the crypt, lingered for an instant on the faces of the men gathered there, then he turned away from Jasper. As he did so, a harsh rattle came from the wounded man's throat and Jasper's head fell back. Hugo swung back to him. His expression was inscrutable as he watched death film the shallow eyes as they stared up at the vaulted roof of the crypt. Then he turned aside and strode back to Chloe.

He took her left hand and drew off the serpent ring. It bounced on the granite slab by Crispin's head as he threw it to the floor.

"Come along, lass. You've breathed this infected air for long enough." He swept her ahead of him toward the stairs where Samuel still stood, his pistols still aimed at the cluster of men in the crypt. But no one made a move.

Chloe was silent as they went up the steps and into the pure cold air of the moor. She could think only that Hugo had talked of love . . . that he'd told Jasper that he loved her. He'd fought for her . . . risked his life for her . . . as he had done for her mother.

But she was married to Crispin. Even if she never saw him again, she was his wife. Jasper was dead, but Crispin wasn't.

The horses were tethered in the copse, restless at the end of their ropes, quivering in the frosty night. Hugo lifted her onto his mount and swung up behind her. He was as silent as she, but he held her tightly against him as they rode back to Denholm. Samuel rode alongside, also keeping his own counsel.

"I'll see to the 'orses," Samuel said as they dismounted in the courtyard. "Ye'd better throw some kindlin' on the fire. Like as not it'll be out by now."

Hugo and Chloe went into the house. The kitchen was dark and cold, only the ashes in the range showing any light. Hugo lit the candles, stirred the embers, and threw on kindling and fresh logs.

Chloe stood wrapped in her cloak, watching him. She was beginning to feel as if she were slipping back into the drug-induced torpor. "Hugo, they married me to Crispin this afternoon," she finally said. The words sounded as if they came from somewhere outside herself. "Just taking off the ring can't make it go away."

He pulled a chair up to the blaze and beckoned her over. "No, I know that," he said, drawing her between his knees. "Let me explain. You're a minor, married against your will and without your guardian's consent. In addition, the marriage has not been consummated." His eyes were grave as they examined her face. "That is true, isn't it?"

"Yes."

He'd known it was, but still the fear had been there that he might have miscalculated . . . that Jasper would have found some way to defile her before he could reach her. The final relief seeped through his veins. He smiled. "Then the marriage will be annulled, lass. It's a mere formality. Crispin won't dare to contest it even if he could."

"So I'm not married?"

"Yes, you are, technically. But only for as long as it takes me to find a Justice of the Peace."

"Oh." Her knees began to shake and tears suddenly filled her eyes. "I'm sorry . . ." But the flood of tears was unstoppable.

"Hush, sweetheart." He pulled her down onto his lap, cradling her against his chest, rocking her gently. "Did they hurt you, love?"

She shook her head against his chest, tried to speak, but the words were lost in sobs.

Samuel entered the kitchen, glanced at the pair by the fire, and sat down in the chair opposite, stretching his feet to the fire.

When her tears had subsided somewhat, Hugo sat her upright and said, "Sweetheart, you have to tell me. Did they hurt you?"

"Only a little. But it was uncomfortable," she said frankly, wiping her eyes on the handkerchief he handed her. "I don't know why I cried like that . . . I expect it's because I'm hungry."

Hugo threw back his head and laughed in rich relief. Samuel grinned and went to the pantry. "Coddled eggs do ye, lass?"

"Yes, thank you." She smiled mistily and leaned back against Hugo's shoulder.

"Tell us exactly what happened to you," Hugo demanded, knowing he wouldn't be satisfied until he'd heard every detail. While she ate her supper, he listened as she rendered a faithful account of her captivity. She left out nothing, including what Jasper had told her of Hugo's past. Hugo's eyes were hard, his mouth a grim line, and when she concluded, he said with soft savagery, "He died too quickly."

Both father and son had died too quickly for the evil they had wrought. But he must let it pass from him now. It was over. Without a Gresham to lead it, the Congregation would disband. Crispin hadn't the authority or the maturity to take over from Jasper. It had been created by the Greshams and would die with them.

He glanced over to the table, where the last Gresham sat wiping her plate clean with a slice of barley bread. Stephen never knew what a pearl he'd sired. And the qualities he'd passed on to his daughter—the fire and the passion—were without the taint, the twist that marred them in the father.

He leaned back in his chair, his eyes closed as he allowed the peace to fill him. He was finally free. He had honored Elizabeth's charge; Chloe would never again be harmed by the Greshams; and he had confronted his painted devils and defeated them. He knew himself to be no better and no worse than the next man. And the knowledge was sweet.

He opened his eyes to see Chloe regarding him gravely. "Why didn't you tell me that you'd loved my mother? Why didn't you tell me what happened?"

He met her gaze steadily. "Cowardice, lass," he said. "I was terrified I would lose your trust if I told you. How could you trust a man who had played in the crypt . . . who had done what I had done? I couldn't bear the thought of losing your love and your trust—they were . . . are . . . the most precious gifts . . . gifts without price."

Sweet relief flowed in her veins. It wasn't lack of love but love itself that had kept him silent.

"It doesn't matter to me," she said. "What happened . . . what you did . . ."

His eyes held hers for a minute, then he said softly, "And it doesn't matter to me anymore. The past has ruled for long enough."

Samuel gave an audible sigh of relief and began gathering up dirty dishes.

Hugo stood up. "It's time for bed," he said, stretching and yawning. "Upstairs with you, lass."

"It doesn't seem as if there's any essential difference between adultery and fornication," Chloe observed with a mischievous chuckle, turning her head on Hugo's chest to look up at him with dancing eyes glowing with the residue of desire and its fulfillment.

"Certainly they both involve the participation of a fallen woman," Hugo stated blandly, catching up the thick golden mass clustering on her shoulders and twisting it around his wrist. Then he let it fall again, concealing the blue-black stripe where her brother's whip had fallen. It was over and Jasper had paid the price.

Chloe, unaware of the fleeting thought, smiled and drew her hand in a lazy caress across his stomach. "And a fallen gentleman, I would have said, since, in my experience, it takes two."

Hugo stroked her hair. "Well, perhaps we should expand your experience and see what difference the blessing of the church makes."

He spoke so softly that for a minute Chloe didn't understand what he'd said. Then she did. She sat bolt upright. "Are you going to marry me?"

"Someone has to," he said with an air of solemnity. "You're not safe in Society unmarried . . . or do I mean Society isn't safe?"

"But . . . but you said Society would think you were taking advantage of your guardianship." She frowned down at him, still unsure that he really meant what he was saying.

"Society can think what the hell it pleases," Hugo responded. "The question is: Do you wish to marry your guardian, lass?"

"But you *know* I do. I've been saying so this age. Only you wouldn't listen."

"No, a lamentable failing," he agreed, his eyes smiling. "I've had the most foolish tendency not to listen to you. However, I begin to understand that you always mean what you say, and that, in general, you know what's best for you."

"And for you," she flashed.

"Conceited minx." He caught her head and drew her face down to his. "I've known what's best for me for a long time, sweetheart, I just needed to be convinced that it was best for you too."

Chloe dropped her mouth to his, her body moving over his, fitting herself to his curves and hollows, reaching a hand down to guide him within her. Pushing backward, she sat on her heels, moving her body around him, her eyes languorous, her hair tumbling over her shoulders.

"I do know what's best for you," she said with a smug smile. "I'll prove it to you."

"Be my guest, lass." Hugo linked his hands behind his head and watched her face, enjoying his own passivity as much as Chloe was.

"I suppose," she said, running her flat palms over the ridged muscles of his abdomen, "I suppose you'll want to keep control of my fortune."

"Oh, I'm sure we can come to some satisfactory compromise," Hugo said, the green eyes sparking.

"But . . ." Her hand moved behind her, sliding between his thighs. "But I don't imagine you'll compromise over my wardrobe?" Her fingers moved wickedly, deftly.

"No . . ." He closed his eyes on an exhalation of joy. "That's one area in which you patently don't know what's best for you, so there'll be no compromises."

"Not even when I do this?" She put her head on one side, regarding him with narrowed eyes as her fingers pursued their intimate course.

"No, you crafty little fox." Gathering her against him, he rolled with her until she was lying beneath him. "I can be cozened just so far." He laughed down at her rather startled expression and kissed the tip of her nose. "But don't let that stop you from trying, lass."

"As if it would . . . as if anything could," she said softly, no longer mischievous. She touched his mouth with the tip of a finger. "I love you."

"And I you, little one. With every breath I breathe."

Holding her gaze with his own, he moved within her until it seemed her breath was his and his hers, until their blood flowed as one, and the future purged of the past was born of the transcendent glory of their fusion.

About the Author

JANE FEATHER is the bestselling, award-winning author of *The Eagle and the Dove, Brazen Whispers, Bold Destiny,* and many more historical romances. She was born in Cairo, Egypt, and grew up in the New Forest, in the south of England. She began her highly successful writing career after she and her family moved to Washington, D.C., in 1981. She now has over a million books in print.

Next from the bestselling, award-winning

Jane Feather . . .

Velvet

On sale in the summer of 1994

In Jane Feather's next historical romance,
a young French-English beauty offers her services
as a double agent to England's master spy.
Even as he falls under her spell, he begins to suspect
that she is not what she seems—and that the stakes
may be higher than either of them knows. . . .

The following is a preview of this thrilling tale.

Prologue

The gibbous moon hung low in the sky over the forest of Saint-Cloud. A fox moved sleekly through the bracken, a rabbit sat on its hind legs, eyes fixed and staring, nose twitching as it caught the scent of the predator. Then it was gone, a flash of white scut vanishing into the undergrowth. An owl's hollow hoot hung over a glade where a deer drank at a trickling stream falling over flat stones.

The rustic pavilion in the small clearing was in darkness, or so it appeared to the figure cleaving to the trunk of a copper beech at the edge of the glade. Black-clad, he merged with his surroundings, a darker shadow in the shadows of the forest. His eyes stretched into the darkness toward the single-story building humped in the center of the clearing. Long glass doors opened onto a colonnaded porch encircling the pavilion, and a wisp of white fluttered from the open door facing the watcher as the night breezes caught the muslin curtains.

He wore soft-soled leather moccasins and made no sound as he slipped from concealment and approached the portico. Black britches, black shirt, hair concealed under a black cap, pale complexion darkened with burnt cork, the only touch of color came from the gleam of the long, double-bladed knife he held at his side. He was an assassin who knew his work well.

In a book-lined room on the far side of the circular pavilion, a single candle burned low in its socket, its light so meager as to be invisible to anyone outside.

Charles-Maurice de Talleyrand-Perigord dozed beside the empty hearth, a book lying open facedown on his lap. A soft snore bubbled from the slightly open lips of a thin aristocratic mouth. His head jerked on his chest as if some sound had pierced his sleep, then the breathing deepened again.

The assassin moved on his leather soles to the open window on the other side of the pavilion. His night's work was no concern of Monsieur de Talleyrand, minister for foreign affairs to the Emperor Napoleon—or so he believed.

The bed in the room was a sumptuous affair, high and hung with filmy white curtains that rose and fell in the breeze as if the bed were a ship on the high seas. Amid rumpled white silk sheets and damask coverlets, two naked figures slept entwined, their bodies heavy with the deep relaxation of fulfillment. The woman lay sprawled on her back, one arm falling loosely around the neck of her partner, whose dark head was pillowed on her breast, one leg flung over her thighs, pressing her into the deep feather mattress with his weight. His back curved toward the French window, his neck open and vulnerable, the ribs sharply delineated beneath the taut skin.

The knife slid between the third and fourth ribs. Guillaume de Granville stirred as sharp pain invaded his sleep, his dreams of love. A small sound came from him, a sound of protest, of confusion, that faded into a tiny sigh as his body lost the tautness of living flesh, sinking into his mistress's body with a flaccid heaviness that bore no relation to the relaxation of a moment before.

Gabrielle should not have woken, the killing had been so silent, but her body was still in tune with Guillaume's after long hours of love, and as life left him she woke and sat up in the same instant. Her lover's body slid sideways and her sleep-filled eyes stared disbelieving at the crimson stain on the smooth pale flesh of his back. It was a small blemish, and yet not for one minute, even in the dumb trance of new awakening, did she think it was insignificant. The deadly stain began to spread in a slow inexorable flush.

It had been a matter of seconds since the assassin had entered, and as Gabrielle's stunned gaze lifted she met the cold, blank stare of pale eyes in a blackened countenance. Eyes without life, without emotion. She opened her mouth on a scream and the man lunged, the knife aimed to puncture her throat. She flung herself sideways, heaving the dead body of Guillaume de Granville aside with the superhuman strength of terror. Her scream ripped through the chamber, shattered the silence of the elegant pavilion.

For a second of uncharacteristic hesitation, the assassin stood poised on the balls of his feet, his knife hand raised. Gabrielle's scream continued as if she would never run out of breath. Suddenly her cry was met and matched by the clanging of a bell, the violent barking of hounds. The assassin spun on his toes toward the French door and leaped with the agility of a woodland creature through the opening.

Talleyrand had woken from his doze at the first

skirling scream, his hand going immediately to the bell rope beside his chair. At the loud summons, men trained to respond with the speed of thought were moving at a run through the pavilion toward the source of the screaming. In the kennels outside, the keeper, following standing orders, released the hounds.

The door to the bedchamber burst open. The men barely glanced at the bed, where the woman cradled the body of her lover, her eyes wild, her mouth still open on a continuing shriek. They ran for the open door to the portico, pistols in their hands.

Gabrielle's scream died as her breath finally failed. She gazed down at Guillaume's body, where the blood now pumped thickly from between his ribs. Her hand stroked his hair, feeling the curious deadness of him almost as if it were a purely intellectual sensation.

Talleyrand came into the room. With his halting limp, he crossed to the bed. Taking up the coverlet, he draped it around the woman's shoulders, covering her nakedness, before he examined the body of Guillaume de Granville, feeling for a pulse at the throat.

"Who?" Gabrielle spoke the one word on a hissing whisper. The wildness had gone from her eyes and her body was taut with a fierce energy that Talleyrand, who had known her from babyhood, recognized and understood.

"Will you avenge his death, Gabrielle?" he asked quietly.

"You know I will." The response was as direct as he had expected.

He walked over to the open French door. The baying of the hounds was fainter as they pursued their quarry deeper into the forest. But they had been on his heels within minutes and would catch him in the end, unless, like some spirit, the assassin had no scent and left no footprint.

Monsieur de Talleyrand had no truck with spirits. He dealt in the corporeal world where cunning and intrigue were the only efficient defenses and the only sure means of advancement and influence, both personal and political. And Napoleon's minister for foreign affairs was undoubtedly the preeminent exponent of those arts in Europe.

He turned back to the bed and his cool gaze held a spark of compassion as it rested on the young woman's white, set face. But compassion was not a useful emotion and Gabrielle had been in the business long enough to know that. She wanted the tool of revenge in her hands. A revenge that would, not coincidentally, benefit both France and Monsieur de Talleyrand-Perigord.

He began to speak, his well-modulated voice quiet yet crisp in the now silent chamber of death.

I

England, January 1807

"Who's the titian, Miles?" Nathaniel Praed put up his eyeglass for a closer scrutiny.

Miles Bennet followed his friend's gaze, although the description could only apply to one woman in Lady Georgiana Vanbrugh's drawing room.

"Comtesse de Beaucaire," he replied. "A distant cousin of Georgie's on her mother's side. They've known each other almost since the cradle."

Nathaniel let his glass fall, commenting dryly, "Presumably there's a Comte de Beaucaire."

"Not any more,' Miles said, somewhat surprised at his show of interest. In general, Nathaniel was indifferent to the charms of society women. "He died tragically soon after their marriage, I believe. Taken off by some fever very suddenly—all over in a couple of days, as I understand it." He shrugged. "Gabrielle's officially out of mourning now, but she still wears black much of the time."

"She knows what suits her," observed Lord Praed, putting up his glass again.

Miles had no fault to find with the observation. Gabrielle stood out in a room full of women in diaphanous pastels. Her dress of severely cut black velvet accentuated her unusual height and threw into startling relief the mass of dark red hair tumbling in an unruly cloud of ringlets around a pale face.

He was pleased when Nathaniel requested an introduction.

"But of course," Miles agreed promptly. "You can hardly spend the entire house party without meeting each other. I'm interested to see what you make of each other."

"Now just what does that mean?"

Miles chuckled. "You'll see. Come."

Nathaniel followed his friend across the drawing room to where Gabrielle de Beaucaire stood in a small group by the window.

Gabrielle watched his approach over the rim of her champagne glass. She knew perfectly well who he was. Nathaniel Praed was her reason for being here, just as she was his, although, if Simon had kept his word, he didn't know that yet. It pleased her that she should have the upper hand in this respect. It gave her the opportunity to make some assessments of the man unhindered by the role he would undoubtedly adopt once he knew exactly who and what she was.

"Gabrielle, may I introduce Lord Praed." Miles bowed, smiled, gestured to his companion.

"My lord." She gave him a silk-gloved hand as cool as her smile. "Delighted."

"Enchanté, Countess." He bowed over her hand. "I understand you're recently arrived from France."

"My parentage makes me persona grata on both sides of the Channel," she said. "An enviable position, I'm sure you'll agree."

Her eyes were the color of dark charcoal, framed in thick black lashes beneath black eyebrows. They were a startling contrast to the red hair and the very white skin.

"On the contrary," Nathaniel said, nettled by an indefinable hint of mockery in her gaze. "I would consider it uncomfortable to have a foot in both camps during wartime."

"You're surely not questioning my loyalty, Lord Praed?" The black brows lifted. "The only family I have are in England . . . in this room in fact. Both my parents and all my father's family perished in the Terror." A chilly smile touched the wide, generous mouth and she put her head on one side waiting to see how he would respond to being put on such an uncomfortable spot.

Nathaniel didn't miss a beat and not a hint of his annoyance showed on the lean, ascetic face. "I would hardly be so impertinent, madam, particularly on such a short acquaintance. May I offer my condolences on your husband's death. I'm sure he was a loyal supporter of the Bourbons even if expediency required token submission to the emperor."

Now that had taken the wind out of her sails. Satisfied,

he watched the flash of surprise at this hard-hitting return of serve.

"He was a Frenchman, sir. A man who loved his country," she replied quietly, and her eyes held his for a long moment.

Nathaniel was of middle height and the tall woman's charcoal eyes were almost on a level with his own; despite this proximity, he couldn't read the message they contained. But he had the unshakable conviction that Gabrielle de Beaucaire was toying with him in some way —that she knew something he didn't. It was an unfamiliar sensation for Lord Praed, and he didn't care for it in the least.

"Oh, I'm so glad you two have been introduced." Lady Georgiana Vanbrugh glided toward them, a beautiful woman, her daintily rounded figure delicately clad in lilac spider gauze. She slipped her arm through Gabrielle's and smiled with the genuine warmth and pleasure she always felt when she believed her friends were enjoying themselves.

"It's such a pity Simon had to go up to town so suddenly, Lord Praed. But when duty calls . . ." She smiled, lifted round white shoulders so that the graceful swell of her breasts rose from her décolletage. "He assured me he'd do everything possible to be here in time for dinner tomorrow."

"Members of the government are not their own masters, particularly in wartime," Nathaniel said easily.

"You speak as one who knows, Lord Praed," Gabrielle said. "Are you also involved in government work?"

Why did it sound as if she had some underlying point to make? He looked sharply at her and met a calm cool gaze and that crooked little smile. "No," he said brusquely. "I am not."

Her smile widened as if again she was relishing some secret knowledge before she turned to Miles, a highly entertained but so far silent observer of the exchange.

"Do you hunt tomorrow, Miles?"

"If you do," he said with a gallant bow. "Although I doubt I'll keep up with you." He gestured to Nathaniel. "Gabrielle's a bruising rider to hounds, Nathaniel. You'd do well not to let her give you a lead."

"Oh, I'm sure Lord Praed will take any fence that presents itself," Gabrielle said, still smiling.

"I've never failed a fence yet, Countess." He made a curt bow and walked away, annoyed that he'd allowed her to provoke him, yet intrigued despite himself . . . *almost like a rabbit fascinated by a cobra,* he thought irritably as he accepted a fresh glass of champagne from a hovering footman. A distinct aura of trouble clung to Gabrielle de Beaucaire.

"You don't appear to like Lord Praed, Gabby." Georgiana looked half reproachful, half anxious. "Did he upset you?"

Oh, he merely killed the man whose life was dearer to me than my own. "Of course not," Gabrielle said. "Was I rude? You know what my tongue's like when it runs away with me."

"I thought you'd find a sparring partner in Nathaniel," Miles remarked. "And I suspect you'll find him a worthy opponent." He grinned. "However, I think you won that round, so perhaps I'd better go and smooth his ruffled feathers." He went off chuckling with the slightly malicious pleasure of one who enjoys stirring up the complacent.

"Miles is wicked," Georgie declared. "Nathaniel

Praed's his closest friend, I don't know why he so relishes making mischief."

"Oh, dear," Gabrielle said. "Should I beg Lord Praed's pardon?" Her expression had changed completely. There was warmth in her eyes as she smiled at her cousin and a vibrancy in the previously bland expression. "I didn't mean to disgrace you, Georgie, by offending your guest."

"Stuff!" Georgie declared. "I don't like him myself, really, but he's a most particular friend of Simon's. They seem to have a kind of partnership." She shrugged. "I expect he's something to do with the government, whatever he might say. But he's such a cold fish. He terrifies me, if you want the truth. I always feel tongue-tied around him."

"Well, he doesn't intimidate me," Gabrielle declared. "For all that his eyes are like stones at the bottom of a pond."

The butler announced dinner at this point and Gabrielle went in on the arm of Miles Bennet. Nathaniel Praed was sitting opposite her and she was able to observe him covertly while responding to the easy social chatter of her dinner partners on either side.

In the absence of their host, the men didn't sit long over their port and soon joined the ladies in the drawing room. To his irritation, Nathaniel found himself looking for the titian, but the Comtesse de Beaucaire was conspicuous by her absence. He wandered with apparent casualness through the smaller salons where various games had been set up, but there was no sign of the redhead among the exuberant players of lottery tickets or the more intense card players at the whist tables.

He examined the faces of the men at the whist tables. One of them at some point in the week would be revealed as Simon's candidate . . . once Simon decided to stop playing silly undercover games. He'd dragged him down here with the promise of a perfect candidate for the service, refusing to divulge his identity, choosing instead to play a silly game with a ridiculous form of introduction.

It was typical Simon, of course. For a grown man, he took a childish delight in games and surprises. Nathaniel took his tea and sat in a corner of the drawing room frowning at the various musical performances succeeding each other on harp and pianoforte.

"Miss Bayberry's performance doesn't seem to find favor," Miles observed, wandering over to his friend's corner. "Her voice is a trifle thin, I grant you."

"I hadn't noticed," Nathaniel said shortly. "Besides, I'm no judge, as well you know."

"No, you never have had time for life's niceties," Miles agreed with a tranquil smile. "How's young Jake?"

At this reference to his small son, Nathaniel's frown deepened. "Well enough, according to his governess."

"And according to Jake . . . ?" Miles prompted.

"For heaven's sake, Miles, the lad's six years old; I'm not about to consult him. He's far too young to have an opinion on anything." Nathaniel shrugged and said dismissively, "From all reports, he appears obedient enough, so it's to be presumed he's happy enough."

"Yes, I suppose so." Miles didn't sound too convinced, but he knew which of his friend's tender spots were better left without exacerbation. If the child didn't bear such an uncanny resemblance to his mother, maybe it would be different.

Nathaniel hadn't always been like this. It had taken Helen's death to turn him into an introspective chilly character who seemed to delight in rebuffing all friendly overtures. Most of his friends had given up by now; only Miles and Simon persevered, partly because they'd known Nathaniel since boyhood and knew what a stout and unstinting friend he was when a man needed a friend, and partly because they both knew that despite his attitude, Nathaniel needed and relied on their loyalty and friendship, that without it he would retreat from the world completely and be utterly irreclaimable.

A man couldn't grieve forever and the old Nathaniel would one day inhabit his skin again. Perhaps his earlier interest in Gabrielle de Beaucaire was a hopeful sign.

Nathaniel went up to his own room shortly after, leaving the sounds of merriment behind. He had some work to do, and reading reports struck him as an infinitely more rewarding way of spending the shank of the evening.

Around midnight the house fell silent. House parties kept early hours, particularly with a hunt on the morrow. Nathaniel yawned and put aside the report from the agent at the court of Czar Alexander.

He swung out of bed and went to open the window. Whatever the temperature, he was unable to sleep with the window closed. Several narrow escapes had given him a constitutional dislike of enclosed spaces.

It was a bright clear night, the air crisp, the stars sharp in the limitless black sky. He flung open the window, leaning his elbows on the sill, looking out over the expanse of smooth lawn where frost glittered under the starlight. It would be a beautiful morning for the hunt.

He climbed back into bed and blew out his candle.

He heard the rustling of the woodbine almost immediately. His hand slipped beneath his pillow to his constant companion, the small silver-mounted pistol. He lay very still, every muscle held in waiting, his ears straining into the darkness. The small scratching, rustling sounds continued, drawing closer to the open window. Some-one was climbing the thick ancient creeper clinging to the mellow brick walls of the Jacobean manor house.

His hand closed more firmly over the pistol and he hitched himself up on one elbow, his eyes on the square of the window, waiting.

Hands competently gripped the edge of the window-sill, followed by a dark head. The nocturnal visitor swung a leg over the sill and hitched himself upright, straddling the sill.

"Since you've only just snuffed your candle, I'm sure you're still awake," Gabrielle de Beaucaire said into the dark, still room. "And I'm sure you have a pistol, so please don't shoot, it's only me."

Nathaniel was rarely taken by surprise and was a master at concealing it on those rare occasions. On this occasion, however, his training deserted him.

"Only!" he exclaimed. "What the hell are you doing?"

"Guess," his visitor challenged cheerfully from her perch.

"You'll have to forgive me, but I don't find guessing games amusing," he declared in clipped accents. He sat up, his pistol still in his hand, and stared at the dark shape outlined against the moonlight. That aura of trouble surrounding Gabrielle de Beaucaire had not been a figment of his imagination.

"Perhaps I should be flattered," he said icily. "Am I to assume unbridled lust lies behind the honor of this visit, madam?" His eyes narrowed.

Disconcertingly, the woman appeared to be impervious to irony. She laughed. A warm merry sound that

Nathaniel found as incongruous in the circumstances as it was disturbingly attractive.

"Not at this point, Lord Praed; but there's no saying what the future might hold." It was a mischievous and outrageous statement that rendered him temporarily speechless.

She took something out of the pocket of her britches and held it on the palm of her hand. "I'm here to present my credentials."

She swung off the windowsill and approached the bed, a sinuous figure in her black britches and glimmering white shirt.

He leaned sideways, struck flint on tinder, and relit the bedside candle. The dark red hair glowed in the light as she extended her hand, palm upward, toward him and he saw what she held.

It was a small scrap of black velvet cut with a ragged edge.

"Well, well." The evening's puzzles were finally solved. Lord Praed opened a drawer in the bedside table and took out a piece of tissue paper. Unfolding it, he revealed the twin of the scrap of material.

"I should have guessed," he said pensively. "Only a woman would have come up with such a fanciful idea." He took the velvet from her extended palm and fitted the ragged edge to the other piece, making a whole square. "So you're Simon's surprise. No wonder he was so secretive. But what makes you think I would ever employ a woman?"